IRRESISTIBLE

THE PHOENIX CLUB
BOOK SIX

DARCY BURKE

Zealous Quill Press

IRRESISTIBLE

Society's most exclusive invitation...

**Welcome to the Phoenix Club, where London's most
audacious, disreputable, and intriguing ladies and
gentlemen find scandal, redemption, and second chances.**

Jessamine Goodfellow has spent six Seasons avoiding the
parson's trap, and spinsterhood is finally within her grasp. A
brilliant scholar, she longs for adventure and new experiences, things her family frowns upon. Presented with the
opportunity to use her puzzle-solving talent on a secret
mission for the Foreign Office, Jess eagerly accepts. Even
when it means posing as the wife of a scorchingly attractive
Scotsman whom she must also covertly investigate as a
possible double agent.

Lord Dougal MacNair, the new Viscount Fallin, has always
completed his assignments for the Foreign Office alone.
Now he's saddled with an overly enthusiastic *amateur* partner. She possesses a remarkable intellect, but something

about her isn't quite right, and after two failed missions, Dougal is certain someone is working against him. Battling their secret suspicions, Dougal and Jess dive deep into their cover as a married couple, which arouses temptations they find irresistible.

Don't miss the rest of *The Phoenix Club*!

Do you want to hear all the latest about me and my books? Sign up at <u>Reader Club newsletter</u> for members-only bonus content, advance notice of pre-orders, insider scoop, as well as contests and giveaways!

Care to share your love for my books with like-minded readers? Want to hang with me and see pictures of my cats (who doesn't!)? Then don't miss my exclusive Facebook groups!

Darcy's Duchesses for historical readers
Burke's Book Lovers for contemporary readers

Want more historical romance? Do you like your historical romance filled with passion and red hot chemistry? Join me and my author friends in the Facebook group, Historical Harlots, for exclusive giveaways, chat with amazing HistRom authors, and more!

PROLOGUE

Edinburgh, Scotland, August 1815

*T*he low ceiling and dark beams of the Oak and Thistle ought to have felt claustrophobic, but to Dougal MacNair, the space was a warm hug, holding him close after too much time away. Glancing across the small, worn table at his cousin, Robert Clark, who was just three years younger than Dougal's twenty-eight, he felt a surge of affection. He was only sorry it had taken the sudden death of his brother to bring him home.

"Ye're going to be the earl, then?" Robbie asked.

"Eventually." Dougal still couldn't quite believe it. He'd created a life for himself—one that he liked very much—that didn't include being an earl or even living in Scotland. Now he had to change everything. On top of losing Alistair, it was too much to contemplate. And so he preferred to avoid thinking about it too deeply. At least, not yet. The time would come, very soon, probably, when he'd have to face it.

For now, he just wanted to be with his family, both here in Edinburgh and just north near Stirling, where his father's seat, Stagfield, was located.

A tall Black man brought tankards of ale and deposited them on the table. "If we weren't busy, I'd plant myself right next to ye and hear what ye have to say."

Dougal looked up at his Uncle Rob and nodded. "I know. Just as I know Robbie will tell you everything." Well, almost everything. As cousins, they shared certain secrets.

Uncle Rob grunted. "Aye, he will. I'm glad ye made it to town." Town being the Old Town of Edinburgh, where Rob's tavern was tucked into a basement along the Lawn Market. Rob owned the building and leased out several floors. He and his family lodged on the second floor. The New Town, where Dougal's father owned a new, fashionable house in Charlotte Square, was not at all what Uncle Rob had meant. Dougal might stay there when he came to Edinburgh, but this was as much a home to him.

Leaving them alone, Uncle Rob returned to the bar on the other side of the common area. Dougal took a long drink of ale, the taste taking him back to the many summers he'd spent here before he'd gone south to Oxford. He looked over at Robbie. "When are you going to start making your own ale?"

"Och, not for a while yet. I just started the apprenticeship last winter." He sipped his ale and narrowed one eye at Dougal as he set his tankard back down. "Ye sound like my father."

"We're both enthusiastic about your future. You can hardly blame us."

Robbie stared at him a moment. "What about yer future? Ye going back to London?"

That answer fell firmly in the category Dougal preferred not to think about at the moment. "Yes, at some point." He at least wanted to meet with his superior at the Foreign Office, even if it meant he wouldn't complete another mission. The thought of that made him anxious. He had unfinished work.

"I dinna think your father will like that."

Perhaps not, but he would understand. Still, Dougal hated leaving him, and it was more than just the grief of losing Alistair. So much more that Dougal wasn't yet ready to face. "He knows I need to go back, at least for a short while."

"Yer father's a good man, and he loves ye like no other," Robbie said with a confident nod before taking another pull from his tankard.

What he said was true, and it was remarkable because Dougal's father wasn't his sire. He was white, just as Dougal's mother had been white. She'd stepped outside their marriage, which hadn't troubled her husband. Their union wasn't a love match, and after four children, they'd agreed to take comfort where they might since they would not with each other.

When Dougal's mother's affair with a Black ship captain had resulted in a child, Dougal's father hadn't hesitated to claim the babe as his own son. He'd raised Dougal with love and ensured that no one questioned Dougal's parentage—at least not to their faces. There were always whispers. It wasn't unusual for a man to raise his wife's bastard as his own, but in Dougal's case, it was rather obvious he wasn't the product of his two white parents. He was a Black man in a white household, and there was no hiding that. Nor did Dougal's father—or any of the rest of his family, which had included another brother besides Alistair and two sisters—make any attempt to do so. They loved and included Dougal as one of their own.

That hadn't meant that Dougal didn't notice he looked different from them. When he asked his mother about that, she never wanted to discuss it. So he'd asked his father, and he too had avoided answering, which Dougal had later learned had been in deference to his wife's wishes. She hadn't wanted Dougal to meet his Black relatives. Aunt Mairi said it was because she feared they would want to take him away, and that Dougal would want to go.

After his mother died when Dougal was eight, his father had brought him to this very tavern to meet his sire's family. By then, Captain John Clark had perished at sea when his ship had gone down in a storm, but the rest of the family had been thrilled to learn that John had a son. They had, in fact, asked if they could have him, but Dougal hadn't wanted to leave his father. Instead, they'd agreed that Dougal would spend time with them each year when the earl and his family came to Edinburgh.

Robbie sat back in his chair and smirked as he regarded Dougal. "Will ye still come here when ye're the earl?"

Dougal scowled at him. "Of course I will. Why would you think otherwise?"

Leaning forward, Robbie sobered. "I was only jesting. I know ye'll still come here. We'd drag ye if necessary."

"It would never be necessary." They were his family, just as his father and the white brother he'd recently lost to an accident were. "Forgive my bad humor."

"To be expected as ye're grieving." Robbie's dark eyes gleamed with sympathy. "We're all so verra sorry. We loved Alistair too. Family is family."

That was a phrase they all shared. So much that it ought to have been their family motto. In addition to the brother he'd just lost, Dougal had lost another brother along with their mother to fever. He also had two white sisters who were long married with children of their own. Here in Old Town, he had Robbie, his Uncle Rob and Aunt Mairi, several other cousins, and another aunt and uncle who was a tailor.

They'd all come to Stagfield to mourn with Dougal and his father. Family was family.

"I know you loved him," Dougal said quietly. "That has always meant a great deal to me." Just as it had always touched him that his white family loved his Black family. They'd all come together—for him.

"What will happen with your position in London?" Robbie knew the truth of Dougal's life in England, that he worked in a...special capacity for the Foreign Office. That was because Robbie had been with Dougal in the Black Watch when Dougal had been recruited for this work. He was the only person, outside of the people he worked with, who was aware. Dougal had never told his father or his brother. He shouldn't have even told Robbie, but he'd been there and discovered what was going on. Besides, Dougal supposed he'd wanted, or needed, to tell someone.

And now Dougal had to consider whether he would tell Robbie another secret. About his father. He wanted to, but the words wouldn't come. If he spoke them, they would become all too real, and he wasn't ready for that. Not yet.

"I'll have to tell them I'm leaving. But there's something I'm rather desperate to do first." Dougal spoke softly so no one could hear him.

Robbie leaned over the table. "Desperate?"

Dougal oughtn't share this either, but he would. He needed to talk it out. "Before Alistair died, there was some difficulty with two of my missions. In the first, I was given what seems to have been a sham message."

"The courier system was compromised?" Robbie asked. He'd acted as a courier before leaving the Black Watch and understood how things worked.

"I believe so, particularly since the following mission resulted in the death of the courier." Dougal thought of poor

Giraud, a Frenchman who'd come to England after the revolution and pledged his allegiance, his throat torn open.

"Bloody hell," Robbie breathed. "Do ye think there's someone working against ye in the office?"

"I don't know, but I have to be open to the possibility." Dougal pressed his lips together. "Now you see why I must return to London."

"Aye. I wish I could help ye."

"You've got your apprenticeship," Dougal said.

"But if ye needed me, ye'd ask?"

"I would," Dougal assured him. "There are few people I would trust to help me, and you are one of them." The others were close friends of his in England, namely Lord Lucien Westbrook, who also served the Foreign Office in a secret capacity.

A young Black girl dashed toward their table. It was Aila, who at nine years old was Dougal's youngest cousin. "This was just delivered fer ye, Dougie." She handed him a sealed letter. "Footman from Charlotte Square brought it."

"Thank you, Aila."

"Off with ye," Robbie said with a wave when she seemed to want to linger.

She blinked at them. "But Da wants to know what it says."

Dougal smiled to himself while Robbie laughed. "I'll tell him later. Now off with ye," he repeated.

Aila shrugged before spinning about and going back to where her father stood behind the bar.

The familiar seal told Dougal where it came from— Lucien. As Dougal scanned the short missive, the tension he'd carried since Alistair's death intensified, drawing him tighter than a bowstring.

"Doesna look like good news," Robbie said before taking another drink of ale.

Dougal refolded the paper and put it in his coat. "I need to return to London immediately."

"For how long?"

"I don't know." Lucien's note had been short, which was to be expected. He wouldn't write anything of import, just that Dougal was needed back in town at his earliest convenience. That was Foreign Office-speak for get your tail to London as quickly as possible.

"Will ye go back to Stagfield first?" Robbie asked.

"Of course." Though it meant heading north before heading south, Dougal couldn't leave without seeing his father. Whatever the Foreign Office needed would keep for one extra day.

As it was, they were going to have to get used to not having him at all.

CHAPTER 1

London

essamine Goodfellow finished the last letter of the cipher she was solving and set down her pencil with a satisfied smile. Spinsterhood was going to suit her just fine. But then, she'd long thought it would, not that her parents agreed. Surely after six Seasons, they would see that it was time to just give Jess her dowry and permit her to live her life unwed. Two of their three daughters had married well. Surely that was enough?

"Did you finish?" Kathleen Shaughnessy, Jess's relatively new but very good friend, asked from the other side of the table where she was sketching furiously on a large piece of parchment. They were both the houseguests of Lady Pickering, one of London's most respected ladies, who was acting as their temporary chaperone while their families were out of town.

Jess nodded. "I did. This one was quite challenging." Every

week, she received two to three ciphers from the mysterious Mr. Torrance, whom she'd met at the British Library. A charming older gentleman, he'd seen her solving a riddle and given her a cipher to try. She'd been instantly enthralled, solving it quickly. Torrance had been delighted to offer to send her more, if she was keen to continue. She'd leapt at the chance, and for the past few months, she'd enjoyed her new hobby very much. "Once I determined that frequently used terms were given two or three numbers, everything came together."

"Well, I am *not* finished," Kat said with considerable annoyance. She was very particular when it came to her drawings, pouring all her energy into her work, just as Jess did with her ciphers.

Jess craned her neck to see Kat's sketch. "You'll get it."

Kat scowled at the drawing. "I may have gone too far to fix it. I should probably start over." She sat back in her chair and looked over the table toward Jess's completed cipher. "Well done, you. You've been working on that for, what, three days?"

"Yes. That was the last of the latest batch from Torrance. I expected a delivery yesterday, but nothing came. It was as if he knew I was struggling to finish the last one."

"How interesting." Kat didn't appear overly interested, however, as her focus was on her drawing. She could be rather single-minded about things, and if she was unhappy with her work, she would be fixated on it until she wasn't.

"Do you want to start your drawing over?" Jess asked, knowing Kat preferred to discuss that.

"I think I must," she said with great resignation. Then she launched into a lengthy monologue at what she needed to do better and how she might accomplish that. At last, she looked toward Jess, her expression slightly sheepish. "My apologies.

You are the only person who allows me to go on and on. You're such a considerate friend."

Jess gave her a warm smile. "I'm always eager to listen."

"I can't tell you how glad I am that Lady Pickering invited us both to stay here when the Season ended. I was determined not to return to Warefield with Ruark and Cassandra." Ruark was Kat's half brother and the Earl of Wexford. He and his wife, Cassandra, were visiting his estate in Gloucestershire where Kat's mother and sisters lived. Kat had begged him to remain in London, where she'd taken up residence with Ruark during the Season after causing a scandal back in Gloucestershire. Her desire not to return had far less to do with that, however, than with her love of London.

Jess agreed with her wholeheartedly. "I am equally pleased I didn't need to return to Goodacre with my parents." She did miss seeing her grandfather, to whom she wrote often. However, she'd needed a respite from her mother.

Kat set her drawing aside. "Lady Pickering rescued us both."

"I credit my grandfather," Jess said. "He asked Lady Pickering if I could stay with her." They were old friends, and he knew Jess needed a respite. It was especially kind of him when he would have preferred to have Jess visit.

"Your grandfather didn't help me, obviously, so I have to wonder how I came to be invited. I suspect it was Lord Lucien."

Jess had heard he liked to help people. He owned one of the most popular clubs—and probably the most talked about—in London. "Why do you think that?"

Kat shrugged. "He knows everyone, and he's a close friend of Ruark's, who was trying to find a way to allow me to remain in London."

Jess wrinkled her nose. "If I could be officially recognized as a spinster, then I could have served as your chaperone."

This was the primary point of contention between her and her mother—that Jess hadn't married and didn't want to. She didn't understand that Jess wanted more than to be some man's wife. She wanted to do...things. Unfortunately, she hadn't yet determined what those things could be, other than traveling farther than Kent, which she longed to do and was nearly impossible for an unmarried young lady.

"That would be deuced convenient," Kat said. "But we didn't know each other until a few weeks ago." When Lady Pickering had introduced them. Jess had liked Kat immediately.

"Perhaps in future, I can be your chaperone," Jess suggested.

"Until I'm a spinster and no longer require one." Kat frowned. "That seems so far off. You're twenty-five, and you aren't entirely on the shelf."

"I most definitely am, even if my mother refuses to acknowledge it. I came out at nineteen. *No one* will marry me now." Though, it had seemed possible at the start of the Season when the Earl of Overton had paid her attention. Jess's mother had been positively overjoyed. But then he'd been rumored to be seen kissing a maid at the Phoenix Club, and Jess's mother had declared him irredeemable. Jess had argued that gossip ought not ruin him, to which her mother had responded—not for the first time—that Jess would never understand how Society worked.

Good, because Jess didn't care to.

"I'm hoping I can avoid Society events altogether next Season," Kat said. "Thankfully, I wasn't dragged to everything this year." Her shoulders twitched, and she stood. "I think I need a walk around the square. Perhaps up to Oxford Street and back, if you'd care to join me?"

"I would, thank you. It's a spectacular day." Jess rose from the table and followed Kat to the door of the library.

Lady Pickering appeared at the threshold. Her sharp blue-green eyes glanced toward Kat before fixing on Jess. "Jessamine, may I have a word?" She spoke with a regal imperiousness that had taken a bit of acclimation. Buried beneath her somewhat intimidating exterior was a warm and generous woman of great compassion.

"Of course." Jess moved to the side.

"I'll fetch our hats and gloves," Kat said. "And let Dove know." Dove was the ladies' maid they shared, provided by Lady Pickering. She accompanied them on all their walks and errands.

After Kat had gone, Lady Pickering closed the door. That simple act catapulted Jess's interest into rampant curiosity. She gestured for Jess to join her at one of the seating areas.

Lady Pickering sat in a chair, her posture impeccable. Her still-dark hair—she was in her middle-fifties and had scarcely a strand of gray on her head—was coiled into a sleek, elegant style, and her features were that of a younger woman, with very few lines marring her dark ivory skin. Jess wondered if it was because she smiled somewhat sparingly. It wasn't that she didn't possess good humor, she just conveyed it differently—with a subtle raise of her brow or a slight quirk of her mouth.

Curiosity burned within Jess as she perched on the wide settee. "I've a letter for you, dear." Lady Pickering held a small, sealed piece of parchment, which Jess hadn't noticed. "It's rather sensitive, and I'm afraid you can't discuss it with anyone other than me. If you can solemnly agree to that, I'll give it to you."

Jess's heart had begun to hammer. This was all so surprising—and intriguing. It didn't occur to her to decline. "I agree."

Presenting the letter to Jess, Lady Pickering didn't release it immediately. "I can't overstate the importance of keeping this secret. There could be repercussions if you don't."

Jess swallowed. "I understand, and I vow I will say nothing."

Lady Pickering placed the letter in Jess's hand. Taking a deep breath, Jess stared at the missive. It was blank on the outside. She broke the seal and glanced toward Lady Pickering.

"Do you know what it says?"

"Not specifically, but I know its purpose."

Jess tipped her head down and read.

Miss Goodfellow,

You have been identified as a cryptographer of great skill. Resultingly, the Foreign Office requires your assistance. Specifically, we ask that you undertake a mission of dire importance and secrecy. The person who delivered this note is your primary contact and will ensure you receive the preparation necessary for this endeavor.

This contact has not read the contents of this note, and you must not share them with anyone *outside the Foreign Office. In addition to potentially decoding messages on this mission, you will determine if your partner, who will be revealed to you soon, is working against us. You must use all your intellect and abilities to investigate his activities and motives. You will be expected to deliver a report upon your return. Your contact is not aware of this part of your assignment.*

Burn this missive immediately after reading.

With gratitude and expectation,

The Foreign Office

Jess's heart felt as if it would burst from her chest. Her breathing grew rapid. She swallowed, trying to calm herself.

This was monumental. The Foreign Office was asking her to be a spy.

Reading it a second time did not settle her nerves. She was simultaneously thrilled at the prospect and terrified by the expectations. How on earth was she to determine the secret activities and motivations of another spy? Someone who likely had more experience than she did, seeing as she had none.

"You're awfully quiet, dear," Lady Pickering observed.

Jess looked up from the note, folding the parchment and eyeing the cold hearth. As it was August, there was no fire. And she needed to burn this right away. Indeed, it felt as if the letter with its incendiary contents might scald Jess's hand.

"I'm rather shocked," Jess said over what seemed to be the roaring of her pulse thundering through her head. But of course, Lady Pickering couldn't hear that. Taking a steadying breath, Jess asked, "How did this happen?"

One of Lady Pickering's dark brows peaked. "Are you not an excellent cryptographer?"

"I *enjoy* solving ciphers." Jess's neck turned cold. The seemingly innocent occurrence of an unknown but kindly gentleman noting her working on a riddle at the British Library and asking if she might like to solve a cipher wasn't remotely innocent at all. "Who is Mr. Torrance?"

Lady Pickering shrugged. "I'm sure I don't know."

Jess wasn't sure she believed her, but she wouldn't press to know more. At least for now. It seemed obvious that Torrance was somehow connected to the Foreign Office. Just as Lady Pickering apparently was. That alone was extraordinary.

This was a great deal to comprehend. "This is an exceptional opportunity. Pardon me." She had to get rid of this paper.

Standing, Jess went to the fireplace and struck flint into flame. She set the parchment ablaze before dropping it into the fireplace. The paper twisted and burned before Jess's gaze. She did not return to the settee until there was nothing but ash.

"Well done," Lady Pickering said. "You will spend the next week learning how to perfect a disguise and adopt a new identity."

A week? Jess's heart rate had finally begun to calm, but now it sped again, making her feel as if she'd dashed around the room about forty-seven times. "For the mission?"

"Yes. You will be playing the part of Mrs. Smythe. Further details will come later. For now, you must learn to adopt new mannerisms and to speak differently than you normally do. You must also carry yourself as a married woman."

Every part of Jess tensed. "Married?"

"Yes," Lady Pickering confirmed. "You will have a partner on this mission—your 'husband.' You would never be asked to complete a mission on your own, at least not in the beginning."

A ball of unease formed in Jess's stomach at the thought of gaining a pretend husband whom she would be investigating. This was beyond risky. Even so, there was no way she would refuse the opportunity. This was everything she'd dreamed of. No, it was far more than anything she could have expected. It could change her life completely.

"Does this come with compensation?" she asked, thinking she could perhaps live without her dowry if her father refused to give it to her.

"Yes. However, that cannot be your only motivation for accepting this invitation." Lady Pickering eyed her expectantly. "It will not be easy. You must carry out your disguise and behave as Mrs. Smythe, as well as decipher whatever you and Mr. Smythe might find on your mission."

"I understand." It was more than a trifle overwhelming, but didn't she want that? She'd been longing to feel challenged, to be excited for something.

"Good. Tomorrow, you will see the modiste who will fit your new wardrobe. We will go on an errand without Kathleen, not that she will mind." Lady Pickering was right that Kat wouldn't care at all that she was left out of an errand. Unless they were going to a museum, library, or bookstore. "Remember, you cannot tell her anything at all."

Jess nodded. Her mind kept turning back to the fact that she was to pretend to be married. Married couples behaved in many ways. Were they to pretend to be in love? Share a chamber? A bed? "How married will Mr. Smythe and I be?"

Lady Pickering's features mellowed, and she gave Jess a slight smile. This was the expression that made her the most approachable—when she seemed to let down her commanding exterior. "I think I understand. Don't be concerned, behind closed doors, everything will be quite respectable, I assure you."

Jess could almost hear her mother shrieking in horror, screaming that Jess would be ruined. "No one will know who I am?"

"You will be disguised with a wig, and you will learn to comport yourself differently. You should not be recognized, especially given the remote location of this mission. You will be on the Dorset coast. Indeed, it is possible the only people you will encounter are those you are investigating. And their household, of course."

Jess had many concerns and reservations, but the thrill of this opportunity far outweighed any of that. Still, her parents would return to London in several weeks, and if she was still in Dorset, her absence would be noted. Furthermore, what would she tell Kat? "How will my absence be explained?"

"You are going to accompany me to my home near

Winchester for a visit. This allows me to travel with you for part of the way to your destination. Your partner will meet you at my home, and you will continue from there."

"What about Kat?" Jess asked since Lady Pickering was also her chaperone.

"Wexford will be back before then."

Jess hadn't realized her time with Kat was coming to an end so soon. "You'll remain near Winchester while I'm on this mission?" Jess wondered how long that might be.

"I'll stay for a week, but if you take longer than that, I'll return to London and simply say you are enjoying your time in Hampshire." She spoke with a confidence that demonstrated she wasn't the least concerned how this would work. It was likely she'd done this many times.

"You must work for the Foreign Office," Jess said.

Lady Pickering pressed her lips together. "I do not. I help with things from time to time." Her gaze held Jess's for a moment. "It's best if you don't think too much on me or how this assignment came about."

On the contrary, Jess would think about those things a great deal. Lady Pickering wasn't aware of the full scope of Jess's assignment. She would need to learn to question everything and everyone as she conducted her investigation.

Lady Pickering stood. "You ought to go on your walk with Kathleen."

As Jess rose, she felt suddenly taller, more substantial. She also felt light and giddy, the latter of which she tamped down. She *must* contain her enthusiasm.

That's easy—just think about pretending to be some stranger's wife. And trying to determine if he's working against the crown.

Jess wiped her brow as Lady Pickering left the library. Moving toward the doorway, Jess wished she'd asked more about Mr. Smythe. She knew nothing other than that he was an experienced spy.

That wasn't precisely true. She also knew he wasn't to be trusted. *No one* was to be trusted, not even Lady Pickering. It seemed Jess would need to maintain an extraordinary level of secrecy from absolutely everyone.

She suddenly thought of her mother. She'd be apoplectic if she found out. And her father? Jess couldn't decide how he'd react. Nor could she guess if he'd express himself at all. He typically left that to her mother.

Thankfully, they wouldn't know a thing. Lady Pickering had planned everything—or someone had, and she was merely executing the details.

Before Jess stepped from the room, Lady Pickering came back toward her, another piece of paper clasped in her hand. "There's a slight change in plans. Your partner has returned to town, and you'll meet him this evening. Be ready to depart at half six."

Lady Pickering turned, leaving Jess to stare at her back and wonder how she was going to quash her anticipation for the rest of the afternoon. She'd have to manage it since hiding things was something she needed to master—and quickly.

CHAPTER 2

$\mathcal{D}$ougal walked into Lucien's compact study at the rear of his small, terraced townhouse. He'd stopped at home earlier, which meant he was no longer covered in the grime of the Great North Road. He was, however, still cloaked in a lingering sadness and unease. Sadness due to Alistair's death and unease at having to leave their father, even though he'd understood Dougal's need to return to London.

No sooner had Dougal stepped into the study than Lucien entered behind him.

"Lord Fallin, you are returned." Lucien bowed, which was completely unnecessary.

"You don't need to call me that." Dougal's brother Alistair had been the Viscount Fallin for Dougal's entire life. Dougal was still trying to learn to answer to that name. "And don't bow."

Lucien grimaced slightly and inclined his head. "My apologies. I was trying to make light, and I shouldn't have. I should have realized you would still be grieving. Indeed, I am sorry to have summoned you back to London." He turned toward the sideboard where he kept his liquor. "Drink?"

Dougal waved his hand. "I've traveled a great distance as quickly as possible due to this urgent matter. I'd prefer we got right to it."

"How are things with your father?" Lucien asked, concern etched into his features.

That was not an easily answered question. It went beyond Alistair's sudden death. Dougal was overwhelmed and didn't want to think about it. Part of him had been relieved to be called back so he could delay the inevitable.

He responded simply. "As you would expect. He lost his son." Damn, he hadn't meant to sound angry. He wanted to blame exhaustion, but the truth was that he *was* angry. It wasn't fair that Alistair was gone. He was the heir. Dougal was the one who'd chosen a life with risk. If either of them should have died young, it ought to have been him. He swept his hat from his head and ran his hand down his face from his temple to his jaw. "I don't mean to be ill-tempered."

Lucien's dark gaze was sympathetic. "You've every right to be however you like. However you *need*."

"It was difficult to leave my father." Because he'd revealed that he was in poor health, that within the next year or two, Dougal would be the earl. Just thinking of that filled him with anguish, which was why he'd been trying not to. He loved his father more than anything.

"I shouldn't have asked you to come." Lucien swore softly. "I wouldn't have, but the Foreign Office wants you. Still, I can tell them you can't, that your grief could prevent you from executing the mission."

Dougal gave him a surly stare. "I'd rather you didn't lead them to believe I'm not up to the task." His time with the Foreign Office was now temporary, and he didn't want to leave with them thinking he was a failure. This situation wouldn't have been enough to be concerned about that, but after the two missions last spring had ended badly, there was every reason to expect his superiors might find him lacking. He'd worked too hard and was too committed to his duty to the crown to allow that to happen. He wanted to leave on his terms. Actually, he didn't want to leave at all.

"There's no shame in that," Lucien said. "Your brother died. Your father needs you. You've… Well, things are different now."

"Because I'm suddenly heir to the Earl of Stirling," Dougal said flatly. "I never imagined to be in this position, nor did I ever want to be." He'd become an integral part of the Foreign Office, operating as their chief investigator in the United Kingdom, and he loved his work.

Lucien inclined his head. "They can find another investigator for this task." In a matter of time, they would have to.

Dougal shoved that upsetting thought away. "No one does what I do. Not here, anyway. It's fine, Lucien. *I'm* fine." Besides, Dougal was actually glad for the interruption. While he felt guilty for leaving his father, the truth was that he didn't want to wallow in grief *or* anger. What's more, Alistair's death had interfered with Dougal's investigation into his two failed missions. "Tell me why I've hurried back."

"A mission to the Dorset coast. You leave in a week."

Dougal frowned. "If I don't leave for a week, why am I here now?"

Lucien hesitated the barest moment. "Because you need time to prepare with your partner."

"My *what?*"

Voices in the hall interrupted further conversation, because a moment later, Lucien's butler announced the arrival of Lady Pickering and Miss Jessamine Goodfellow. Dougal was very familiar with Lady Pickering, but the other white woman was unknown to him. Taller than most ladies,

Miss Goodfellow possessed vivid cobalt eyes that assessed him with a keen curiosity. Indeed, her unabashed attention could only mean one thing—that she was to be his partner.

Lady Pickering moved her vigilant gaze toward him. "I'm pleased you could arrive so quickly, Lord Fallin. I do apologize that you were called away at this time."

Dougal inclined his head. "I am always eager to serve."

"One of your best qualities." Lady Pickering turned slightly toward the young lady. "Jessamine, this is Lord Fallin." Lady Pickering then looked to Dougal. "Allow me to present Miss Jessamine Goodfellow. She will be your wife on this endeavor."

"My *what?*" First, he had a partner, and now he had a *wife?* "I have always worked alone."

"Not in this case." Lady Pickering shifted her attention to Lucien. "Didn't you explain?"

"He's only just arrived," Lucien said. "I hadn't yet provided the details of the mission."

"I see," Lady Pickering murmured. It was hard to discern if she was perturbed. She disliked when her expectations were not met. "Let us sit, and I shall explain."

The seating arrangement in Lucien's small study was rather compact, offering just two chairs and a settee. Lucien took his favorite chair, as to be expected, and before Dougal could take the other, Lady Pickering lowered herself to the cushion. That left Dougal to join Miss Goodfellow on the settee.

"I suggest you get used to sitting together," Lady Pickering said, as if she could read Dougal's mind.

Dougal sat beside his "wife," but not too close. Miss Goodfellow turned her head toward him. A few light brown curls grazed her temples. His gaze traveled down the high arc of her elegant cheekbones to her pink, bow-shaped mouth. Her lips were on the thinner side, her chin more prominent. She was pretty, but not a classical beauty, and that made her a good choice for espionage.

She smiled, which somehow made the entrancing blue of her eyes even more brilliant. "I'm looking forward to working with you." Her eagerness was more than evident. Dougal could see and feel her excitement as if electricity leapt from her flesh.

"Miss Goodfellow is a new recruit," Lady Pickering said, as if that weren't obvious. It wasn't that Dougal knew all the other investigators. For the sake of secrecy and the protection of others like him, he communicated with only a few people who worked for the Foreign Office. But the young woman's enthusiasm and openness revealed her as an amateur.

"I can see that," Dougal said. "How was she recruited?" He didn't really expect an answer. He still didn't know how Lady Pickering had come to be involved with the Foreign Office or why she insisted on saying she did *not* work for them.

"She's an excellent cryptographer. You will need her expertise on this mission."

No, she wasn't going to tell him. Leaving that alone, Dougal pressed to get to the heart of the matter. "What is this mission exactly?"

"You and Miss Goodfellow will travel to the Dorset coast as Mr. and Mrs. Smythe. You're on your way to Poole, and your coach will become incapacitated, necessitating you to seek help from Mr. and Mrs. Gilbert Chesmore. We received a letter from their housekeeper, Mrs. Farr, about suspicious activity."

Dougal watched Miss Goodfellow from the corner of his eye. She leaned slightly forward, her attention rapt as she hung on Lady Pickering's every word. Oh, she was very green. And they had just a *week* to prepare her.

"Mrs. Farr reports that they speak to each other in French

and take many outings where they draw pictures and write. They also shoot at targets every week. The most damning piece of evidence is a parchment she found with lines of numbers."

"A code," Dougal interjected.

Lady Pickering nodded. "It sounds like it. Unfortunately, she did not send the letter to us as she feared they would notice if it went missing."

"They may be French spies," Dougal said. He'd conducted many of these kinds of investigations. He still didn't understand why it was necessary that he have a partner, let alone a pretend wife.

"Yes."

Miss Goodfellow frowned slightly. "But we are finally at peace with France."

A subtle headache began at the back of Dougal's head. "If you think they aren't spying on us even in peacetime, you don't know a thing about international affairs."

"I am eager to learn," Miss Goodfellow said quietly, her cheeks tinging a faint pink.

"And you will, my dear." Lady Pickering gave her an encouraging nod. "Quickly too, since you leave in a week." She turned her attention back to Dougal. "I'm sure you're wondering why a partner is necessary. In this instance, you must befriend the Chesmores and become as close to them as possible. The best and most expedient way for you to do that is to be guests at their home. From what little we know of them, they are inclined to make friends with other couples, not individuals."

Dougal nodded in understanding. "After our coach suffers an accident, we'll need a place to spend the night. And they will like us so much, they'll invite us to stay." He'd executed similar schemes on many occasions.

"Precisely. Once you are ensconced in their home, you

will search for a coded letter, and Miss Goodfellow will break the code."

"Assuming we find a letter," Dougal said. "I would think they'd write the letter and deliver it to a courier. It's possible we won't find a letter at all."

"That is true." Lady Pickering fixed him with an expectant stare. "I trust you will exhaust every opportunity to obtain one, however."

"That goes without question," Dougal assured her.

"We will also determine the purpose of their suspicious activities," Miss Goodfellow added.

Lady Pickering's gaze took on a sheen of approval. "You see, Fallin, Miss Goodfellow will do very well indeed."

"Time will tell. If she can't master a disguise or the ability to act the role she's given, her cryptography skills and intellect won't matter."

"I hope you aren't being defeatist," Lady Pickering said with an edge that didn't prick Dougal in the slightest. She was tough and said exactly what she desired, particularly in these instances when they discussed their work with the Foreign Office. Not that she was officially affiliated with it. In her words, she merely helped from time to time.

"I am being circumspect, which is another thing for which I am valued," Dougal said a bit sharply. "You wouldn't want me to be any other way."

"I suppose that's true, but I do hope you'll be kind and supportive of Miss Goodfellow. I understand this is a change for you, but it is necessary. The Chesmores are known for entertaining other couples. Hence, you will undertake this mission together."

Dougal understood how these things worked. He knew how to burrow deep into a role in order to obtain the necessary information. Or to plant information. He leveled his gaze on Lady Pickering. "I will execute my responsibilities as

I always do." He just wasn't going to do it right now. He needed solitude and sleep in a bed that didn't jostle.

"Excellent," Lady Pickering said crisply. "Miss Goodfellow will have her first fitting tomorrow for her new wardrobe. We will also work on her disguise." She flicked a look toward Lucien. "All is arranged?"

"Yes. She's expecting you. And before you ask, she does not know the specifics, and she is too smart to ask."

"Who is that?" Miss Goodfellow asked.

"You'll find out tomorrow," Dougal said, turning his head toward her. "This is your first lesson—don't ask questions."

"You asked questions," the young lady said with a touch of heat.

"I have earned the right to do that through years of work and proven capability as well as trustworthiness." Dougal frowned toward Lady Pickering. "Did you not explain to her how this works? That she must demonstrate the necessary attributes required of this work at all times?"

"I did, but understand that her recruitment is not the same as yours," Lady Pickering responded coolly. "You can't expect that she already possesses those skills. She was not in a regiment as you were."

Dougal had been plucked from the Black Watch. "And you really think a week is enough time to prepare her?" He slid a glance toward Miss Goodfellow. "I mean no offense."

She did not respond other than to gently purse her lips and wrinkle her nose as if she smelled bad fish.

Lady Pickering *did* respond. "A week is all we have, so I trust you will ensure it is adequate. I suggest the two of you spend as much time together as possible, without drawing notice, of course. You must be certain your story is believable and consistent."

"I am confident we can convince everyone that we are in love." Miss Goodfellow scooted across the cushion until her thigh touched his. She curled her hands around his arm and looked longingly at him.

Dougal hadn't been prepared. He twitched, pulling his arm from her grasp. Her lips parted and she blinked, her lashes sweeping against her cheeks before her cobalt eyes fixed on him in muted surprise.

"That's not very convincing," Lady Pickering muttered.

Lucien abruptly stood. "Dougal has traveled a long way at a difficult time. Let him go home and rest. I'm sure he'll be up to snuff tomorrow." He smiled blandly at Lady Pickering and Miss Goodfellow while avoiding looking at Dougal at all.

"To be expected." Lady Pickering looked at him in sympathy, clearly thinking of his loss. She stood. "Come, Miss Goodfellow. You've a busy day tomorrow."

Miss Goodfellow rose, and Dougal stood beside her. "Good evening, my lord." She dipped a brief curtsey and trailed Lady Pickering from the study.

"You might have warned me," he griped.

Lucien held up his hand. "I did try. They unfortunately arrived before I could get it all out."

"This is a mad scheme," Dougal grumbled. How could he investigate his failed missions from the Dorset coast? The least they could have done was give him a partner who wasn't new, someone he could evaluate and subtly query for information about other missions. Someone who could aid him in his investigation. A brand-new investigator was of no help to him at all.

"You've engaged in far more dangerous endeavors."

"But with only myself at risk. This is different. I must ensure her safety while watching my own back. We've a single bloody week to get her ready. *That* is the madness."

"It will be done. We've enlisted Evie to help her learn how to disguise herself. There is no one better."

That much was true. Dougal was one of only a very few people who knew Evangeline Renshaw had completely reinvented herself nearly two years ago. "Is that where I'm to go tomorrow?" At Lucien's nod, he continued, "What did you tell Evie?" As far as Dougal understood, she was not aware of his—or Lucien's—involvement with the Foreign Office.

"I told her that a friend, Miss Goodfellow, is going on an independent, secret adventure away from London and needs to pretend to be someone else. She won't know you are part of it. You and I are simply calling tomorrow since you're back in town."

"A coincidence." In his work, Dougal tried to keep those to a minimum.

Lucien inclined his head. "Just so." He clapped Dougal on the arm. "Now go home and get some sleep."

Dougal let out an indiscriminate grunt as he pivoted toward the door. "See you tomorrow."

As he made his way out to his coach, the weight he'd been carrying in his shoulders seemed to sink through him, pushing him toward the earth. Yes, sleep was required.

He hadn't been kind to Miss Goodfellow. And that was unlike him. He attributed his ill humor to his exhaustion and the shock of discovering she was to join him, but really— probably—it was the interruption to his investigation. Or the fact that this could be his last mission. The life he'd expected and planned for was not to be. Instead, he would be the Earl of Stirling.

He couldn't think of that now. Hopefully, this assignment in Dorset would be quick, and Dougal could return to London to uncover the identity of whoever had ruined his missions in the spring.

Then he'd ensure they were brought to justice.

CHAPTER 3

*L*ady Pickering dropped Jess off at the home of Mrs. Evangeline Renshaw the following day. A friend of Lucien's and the primary patroness of the Phoenix Club, Mrs. Renshaw would oversee the selection of Jess's new wardrobe. She would also guide Jess on how to successfully execute a disguise.

Two hours after arriving, Jess was weary of trying on clothing and being pinned to within an inch of her life. She was not, however, closer to understanding why Evie—whom she'd been instructed to call Mrs. Renshaw—was performing this role.

Jess returned to Evie's elegant drawing room in the clothes she'd worn and collapsed on the settee. Evie was still in the bedchamber they'd used with the modiste. Jess was glad for the moment of solitude.

She did know that Evie was not privy to Jess's assignment, nor was she affiliated with the Foreign Office. Lady Pickering had made that clear on the way from her house. Jess had been surprised when Lady Pickering hadn't stayed. She supposed she thought the older woman would want to supervise.

Evie sailed into the drawing room with a brilliant smile. "I've settled everything with the modiste. You shall have a final fitting on Monday, and all will be ready for your departure on Wednesday."

Jess quickly adjusted herself into a more ladylike posture. Evie was so poised and beautiful. It was rather easy to feel like a gangly waterfowl beside her. Jess had often felt like a bedraggled goose over the past several Seasons as she'd tried to make her way amongst a sea of swans.

Except swans, she always thought to herself with a smile, were nasty, unfriendly creatures. That had made the comparison all the more amusing since most young ladies Jess had met had promptly dismissed her the moment she began to speak about books or travel or, God forbid, politics.

"I appreciate your help today," Jess said with genuine gratitude. "I've had several wardrobes over the course of my Seasons, but never so many things in one day."

Evie gave her an encouraging nod. "It can be exhausting. You held up very well, especially considering how quickly we went. Come and join me at the table as I've rung for refreshments. You must be ravenous."

"I am, thank you." Jess moved to the round table near the windows, where a bouquet of dahlias in pink, red, and yellow overflowed from a vase in the center.

Evie looked at her with keen interest. "Now, tell me more about your adventure."

Lady Pickering had informed Evie that Jess was taking a trip away from London without her parents' knowledge. That was why she needed to be disguised.

Jess slid into a chair opposite Evie just as the young, golden-haired butler brought a tray weighted with tea, sandwiches, and gorgeously decorated cakes that looked too good to eat. Each cake was a brightly colored flower, every bit as vivid as the actual blooms on the table.

"I'm traveling to Hampshire with Lady Pickering," Jess answered. "From there, I will go...well, I'd rather not say. The goal is to determine if I'm truly ready to live an independent life. My mother does not support my desire for spinsterhood."

Evie glanced up at the butler. "Thank you, Foster." He inclined his head and departed.

"Of course, your mother doesn't want that." Evie rolled her eyes as she poured the tea. "Daughters are for advantageous marriages and little else."

That had been made brutally clear to Jess when, at the age of eighteen prior to having a Season, she'd fallen in love with an unsuitable young man—an *American*. Her parents had refused to allow them to wed and had, Jess learned several months later, paid him to leave. From that moment forward, Jess had done everything in her power to resist her parents' machinations.

"You are a widow, are you not?" Jess asked, envying the woman's freedom.

"I am, but I didn't have parents who pushed me to wed." Evie added milk to their tea. "Sugar?" At Jess's nod, Evie stirred some into both cups. "As for your disguise on this adventure, I preferred the auburn-colored wig. I think it looks best with your ivory skin tone and is a lovely contrast for your blue eyes. Which was your favorite?"

Jess was still pondering Evie's mention of her lack of parents. It seemed, however, that Evie didn't wish to discuss that as she had moved on rather quickly.

Jess picked up a sandwich. "I liked that one too."

"Good, I'll make sure you have a few hairstyles in that shade to choose from. Two for day and one for evening. You'll need to replace ornamentation as necessary. Now, let us discuss your comportment. Can you think of ways in which you might change the way you carry yourself or the manner in which you speak? Perhaps you can lower your tone or alter your accent."

"Like this?" Jess spoke slightly higher and used the soft lilt of a Welsh accent, mimicking her long-time governess, Miss Evans.

Evie's chestnut brows shot up. "That's quite good. Are you going to be Welsh?"

"I thought I might. Just to be different." Jess assumed she should ask Lord Fallin. Perhaps their accents needed to match. She just hoped they wouldn't use his—her Scottish brogue wasn't very good.

"Your task is to use that accent as much as possible over the next several days so that it becomes second nature. Now, how can you move differently?"

Jess's mother's voice echoed in her head: *"Walk slower and take smaller steps, Jessamine!"* Before her first Season, moderating her movements had been thoroughly schooled into her brain. "I could just walk as I normally do."

Evie's brow knitted. "The point is not to look or behave like *you.*"

"Allow me to demonstrate." Jess stood and walked across the drawing room in the manner her mother had demanded. She took slow, measured steps, careful not to permit her gait to be too long. "This is how I walk in Society." Reaching the other side of the room, she pivoted and returned to the table, walking as she did outside of Society and her mother's company. "This is my normal gait."

"Ah, I see the difference. The former is more elegant, but you aren't being presented to the Queen. Can you throw your shoulders back a bit more and elevate your chin? Adopt an almost haughty demeanor, as if you dare anyone to say you aren't walking appropriately."

This made Jess laugh. "I'd love to do that in front of my mother. Perhaps she might finally be rendered speechless." Jess doubted that was possible as she plucked one of the flower cakes from the tray and popped it into her mouth. Doing that in addition to the walk *might* shock her mother into silence.

"Mothers can be so very demanding," Evie said. "Often it is born of love, however."

That wasn't the case with Jess's mother. She'd never uttered a word about love in all of Jess's life. "Perhaps you speak of your own experience. My mother isn't troubled by sentiment."

"I'm sorry for that." Evie's voice was soft. "My mother loved too much, I think." She shook her head as if dispelling unpleasant thoughts. "We've settled on a distinctive style of movement for you, then?"

"I believe so."

"Excellent. How else can I help you? Perhaps you just need to visit me a few more times and practice. Don't forget to use your accent." Evie winked at her as she picked up her teacup.

What Jess really needed help with was how to pretend to be a wife. As a widow, Evie could likely provide counsel, but how could Jess possibly ask for help with that? She'd have to concoct a story as to why.

Jess realized she ought to be able to do so, that fabricating things would be *required* in her new role. But would Evie be shocked by Jess's request?

She had to risk it. Having never been married or even properly courted, all Jess's knowledge came from romantic novels and overheard conversations between maids.

"I do have one more question that I hope you can help me with," Jess said with more confidence than she felt. Apparently, she *could* act contrary to her emotions. That was encouraging. "I hope you won't think poorly of me."

Evie met her gaze directly and spoke with a genuine care that touched Jess. "I would never judge you. We women must align ourselves with one another and do what we can to support each other. How can I help?"

Jess thought she'd truly made a friend today. "I'm so glad to hear you say that. Too many women I've met seem committed to competition or superiority. Thank you." Trying to be as vague as possible, Jess said, "It may be that I meet a gentleman on my excursion. And it may be that we pretend we are married. How do I do that…convincingly?" Now Evie would think the entire enterprise was so Jess could have an assignation.

Evie's nostrils flared, but that was her only reaction. "I see. Well, *if* this were to come to pass, I would tell you to be sure to behave with confidence. Don't be timid or give any indication of nervousness. No one will look twice at you if you behave as though you are smitten, especially if you adopt that slightly arrogant tilt to your head."

"Thank you, that helps." But it wasn't nearly enough. To act as though she were married, Jess thought she ought to hold herself a certain way, particularly as she interacted with her "husband."

Perhaps she should ask Fallin. He wasn't married, but he had far more experience in the art of deceit than she did. Then again, he didn't need to act at being haughty. That seemed part of his natural demeanor.

At least it had last night. They'd actually met four years ago when he'd danced with her at a ball, and her impression had been rather different. He clearly didn't remember the occasion, but Jess had never forgotten. That was the year her middle sister debuted, and Jess had rarely danced at all. She hadn't minded—indeed, she'd been relieved for the attention that was bestowed on Marianne instead of her. All that had changed when she'd seen Dougal MacNair enter the ballroom. She'd been instantly drawn to his arresting good looks and air of confidence, particularly given the whispers she'd heard commenting on his dark skin and how out of place he looked. She'd thought he looked perfect. When he'd come to ask her to dance, out of all the other young ladies in the ballroom, she'd felt special in a way she hadn't in a very long time.

When she'd walked into Lord Lucien's last night and seen that MacNair, or rather Fallin, was to be her partner, a giddy thrill had surged through her, far surpassing the excitement she'd already been feeling. Then he'd behaved boorishly, and she decided he must have changed over the past four years. The man she'd danced with had laughed easily and complimented her with charm and grace. He'd even discussed the war with France. Gentlemen typically ignored her when she brought up such topics.

But then she recalled Evie's reaction upon seeing him today, along with something Lady Pickering had said last night about Fallin being "called away at this time." She'd also looked at him with sympathy at some point. Perhaps there was a reason for his bluntness and general disagreeability.

Regardless, Jess would do her duty and pretend to be his wife. All while she investigated whether he was working against the Foreign Office. The enormity of her task was beginning to overwhelm her. Did she possess the skill to fool him as well as those around them? He was an experienced spy who didn't seem the least interested in having her as a partner. What was she getting herself into?

"It's my turn to ask a question that I hope won't shock you." Evie smiled gently. "Your question about comporting yourself as a wife... Do you wish to convince observers or the gentleman in question? To be more direct, are you looking for advice on how to behave with him? In the bedchamber, perhaps?"

Jess, of course, couldn't tell her that the enterprise was fake. But now that Evie had posed the question, Jess couldn't deny her curiosity. She knew the mechanics, owing to certain books and other documents and again to the maids in her father's households, but hadn't ever discussed it with a woman who possessed experience. And she certainly had no experience of her own. The awkward kisses she'd shared with Asa Robinson seven long years ago didn't signify.

Shockingly, she had no trouble imagining at least the prospect of sharing Fallin's bed, despite his obnoxious behavior. He was exceptionally attractive—tall and broad-shouldered enough so that she actually felt normal instead of overgrown, with curly black hair cropped rather close to his head and rich brown eyes flecked with gold that seemed to shimmer when he'd jerked away from her. She'd felt a jolt of...*something* in that moment and had wondered briefly if he'd sensed it too. Until she reminded herself that he was completely unenthused at having her as his partner, let alone his fake wife, and that he could very well be a villain.

Before she could answer Evie's question, the butler announced the arrival of Lord Fallin and Lord Lucien.

Evie immediately stood and went to Fallin. She took his hand and stood on her toes to kiss his cheek. "How are you, Dougal?"

It seemed Evie knew him intimately, then.

"I'm fine, thank you, Evie," he said with a faint smile. They were clearly friends, probably because of Lucien. Or perhaps they'd known each other before Lucien. Jess wanted to ask how they'd met, but Fallin had already admonished her about making queries.

"I'm surprised you're back from Scotland so soon." Evie

squeezed his hand, her gaze fixed on him with compassion and concern. Why? Another question Jess couldn't ask.

"I've business to attend, but I won't be here long—just a week." Because then they would be on their way to Dorset.

Evie nodded. "Come and meet Miss Jessamine Goodfellow. Or have you already been introduced?"

Fallin looked toward Jess, who sat stock-still, wondering how he would respond. "I'm sure we've met at some point." He made his way to the table, and Jess tried not to smirk at the accuracy of his platitude. "I'm pleased to see you, Miss Goodfellow."

Jess rose and curtsied. "Thank you, my lord. I am as well."

"Lucien, do you know Miss Goodfellow?" Evie took his arm and walked him to the table.

"Oh yes." He inclined his head with a smile. "Miss Goodfellow, how delightful it is to see you here with Evie. Is she giving you wardrobe advice?"

"Of course," Evie answered, providing an excuse for their meeting. Which Lucien had neatly given her, because he knew the real reason for Jess's visit.

"You have my favorite flower cakes," Lucien said, eyeing the tray. "Are they almond?"

"The yellow and orange are, but I believe the purple and blue are lavender."

Lucien picked up a yellow daisy and took a bite. "Definitely almond." His eyes rolled back as he ate the confection. "Divine," he murmured after he swallowed. "Evie, I've a few Phoenix Club matters to discuss, if I can trouble you?" He cast an apologetic glance toward Jess.

"Perhaps Miss Goodfellow would like to take a turn around the garden with me," Fallin suggested, his dark eyes meeting Jess's.

"That would be lovely, thank you." Jess took the arm he immediately offered, and they departed the drawing room. A sarcastic comment about how he hadn't recoiled that time rose to her lips, but she didn't think that would improve his disposition toward her.

They walked downstairs, then out through the library at the back of the house. The garden was small but glorious, with an abundance of flowers. Though she'd only met Evie today, it was precisely the type of garden Jess expected her to have. "This is so pretty," she said.

"Everything about Evie is beautiful and exquisite," he noted in a somewhat perfunctory manner. "I trust your appointment with her today has gone well?"

"Yes, thank you." She realized immediately that he seemed different from last night, less agitated. She wanted to ask about Evie's concern for him.

"I can feel you are tense," he said. "You're gripping my arm with more force than necessary, and there are two lines between your brows forming the number eleven. You'll need to learn not to do that."

Damn and blast, she thought, borrowing her grandfather's favorite curse. "I didn't even realize."

"I don't blame you. For being agitated, I mean. I wasn't very amenable last night. I was tired from the journey." He glanced toward her as they walked to a stone bench beneath a small ash tree. "I was also taken by surprise to learn of you and the specifics of our assignment."

"I take it you haven't had a fake wife before?"

He smiled, and her breath snagged. She'd thought him attractive, but that vaulted him to an entirely new level of handsome. "I have not," he responded. "In fact, I've never had a partner at all."

No wonder he'd been annoyed. "Would you prefer to be doing this alone?"

"It doesn't matter what I prefer. This is required." He guided her to sit on the bench with him, his gaze holding hers with a tender longing that almost had her believing that what he told her was true.

"You're quite good at this," she said softly. Lifting her hand, she touched his jaw. His eyes widened almost imperceptibly. She dropped her hand to her lap, thinking she'd gone too far. She also wondered what had prompted her to be so bold. "I will learn." Heat infused her neck.

"You were doing well. I wasn't expecting it—as with last night. I won't let that happen again." He shook his shoulders out and took her hand. "Try again. But something different that I'm not expecting."

Jess took a deep breath and opted not to attempt another caress. She'd done it without thinking, and honestly, it had surprised her too. But then, she had almost no experience touching a man's jaw or any other part of him. Instead, she looked into his eyes and parted her lips, staring at him for a moment as words formed in her mind. "You are the moon to my sun, the ocean lapping at my shore, the petals of my flower." She realized, too late, how ridiculous that sounded.

Fallin bit his lip. His shoulder twitched.

"Oh, just laugh already," she said, wondering if his behavior last night had been an aberration. She hoped so.

He did precisely that, chortling and then putting his hand over his mouth to stop himself. When he lowered his hand, the hint of a smile lingered. "You are not a poet."

"Do I need to be?"

"No, just an excellent cryptographer. Are you?"

"Someone thought so." Jess answered him perhaps a bit too defensively. She was eager to prove herself.

He didn't react to her tone, thankfully. "Do you know who that someone is?"

She shook her head. "Not really. I was working on a riddle in the British Library one day, and a gentleman approached me. He gave me a cipher he said he wasn't able to solve." Too late, she wondered if she ought to be discussing this with him.

"You didn't learn this man's name?"

"I don't think—" She took a deep breath. "That is, I'm not certain I should be discussing this with you."

A flash of appreciation lit his gaze. "You're smart to be wary. You'll find that sharing of information is typically discouraged by the Foreign Office. However, in this case, we are to be partners. It's important for the success of our mission as well as our safety that we are open and honest. Do you agree?"

She did, but she was also supposed to be investigating him, which she certainly could *not* disclose. He offered a persuasive argument to share at least some things. Perhaps he knew the mysterious Mr. Torrance and could provide some information.

"Yes, I agree," she said. "I did learn the man's name. It was Torrance. He offered to send me more ciphers to solve, and I accepted. However, I didn't learn anything else." Her father, who'd been reading in another room, came in to tell her it was time to go. During that exchange, the gentleman had taken his leave, preventing further discussion. "Do you know Torrance?" she asked.

"I am not familiar with that name, but those in the Foreign Office sometimes use aliases. Can you describe him?"

"He was older. Perhaps fifty? Or sixty?"

"You don't sound very confident." Was that a note of disappointment? "You're going to have to learn to recall more specific details, especially what people look like, even those you think are inconsequential. You never know when someone in the background will become vitally important to an investigation."

Definitely disappointment. Jess pushed away her frustration. Perhaps she should not have told him. "Are you saying you can describe everyone in a crowded room?"

He smiled briefly. "Not quite. But I do survey the room thoroughly—and quickly. I may not remember every detail, but I can generally recall that there was an older man in a blue coat and a stout woman with gray hair and a bonnet with a yellow ribbon That sort of thing. For instance, last night, you wore a rose-colored gown with a cream-colored fichu made of gauze. Your earrings were of pale coral."

Jess couldn't recall what he'd been wearing. She vowed to herself in that moment that she would become the most aware person in England. She would strive to record everything she saw in the recesses of her mind. Then Fallin would be impressed.

Was that her goal? To impress him? She couldn't allow herself to think of the dashing gentleman she'd met four years ago. This was the Viscount Fallin, a spy, and he was potentially working against the crown.

Her goal was to succeed at this endeavor. She *needed* to.

"I will immediately start to survey situations in the same manner," she said firmly.

"Good. So, this Torrance fellow approached you at the library and gave you a cipher. Did you find that odd?"

"Not particularly. He was very kind. I suppose the odd part was that he asked if he could send me one every week. The puzzles grew increasingly more difficult. In hindsight, it seems clear he was trying to determine if I was up to this task."

"You're certain he's with the Foreign Office, then." It wasn't a question.

Jess lifted a shoulder. "Nothing else makes sense. It would be a silly coincidence."

"Precisely. Here's a piece of advice I received early on in

my career, and it has stuck with me: take nothing for coincidence. That is crucial."

She gave him a bland stare. "Such as our carriage having trouble near the house we're hoping to infiltrate?"

Approval shone in his gaze. "You can afford one coincidence—perhaps two. This is why it's so important for our behavior to be convincing. We must overcome any doubt or suspicion with our charm and wit."

Jess hadn't realized she would need to be charming or witty. She was used to being told she was boring because of her interest in political events or her love of books and language. "I'm not sure how much charm I possess. In case it passed your notice, I am firmly on the shelf."

"It has not, and I confess I am rather intrigued by that. I've deduced that you've gone out of your way to avoid marriage. That's the only thing I can think to explain such ridiculousness."

Was he flirting with her? She stared at him, trying to discern his motives. Then she realized what was happening. He was already playing the role, treating her as a man would treat a woman he cared about. "You are too kind," she said demurely. "I have been waiting for the right gentleman." That was an outright lie, but she was following his lead.

"I see." He leaned his side into hers, looking at her from the corner of his eye. "I think you'll find that you're more engaging than you realize." Then he straightened, and the moment—the utterly false interlude of mutual appreciation —was gone. "Now, tell me about your cipher solving. How did you become so passionate about it?"

"I have always enjoyed riddles and puzzles. And words. I find it extremely satisfying to solve a cipher."

He turned his head toward her. "You must be exceptionally good at it to have garnered the notice of the Foreign Office and for them to have enlisted you."

She was surprised by his respect. Perhaps this partnership wouldn't be as troublesome as she'd thought last night. She might even like him, though she must keep herself from developing any sort of friendly attachment that might interfere with her objective. She batted her lashes at him. "Have I perchance earned the right to ask one question?"

He grimaced slightly. "I was really quite beastly last night. My deepest apologies. Yes, you may ask me a question, but if it's about the Foreign Office, I won't answer."

She had no idea if it was, but reasoned he simply wouldn't respond. "Evie seemed concerned about you and the fact you returned to town. Is aught amiss?"

"That is what you wish to ask?"

"It seems I should get to know my husband, even if he's fake."

"You're right. However, you actually needn't get to know the real me."

Her mood sank. He wasn't going to tell her why Evie had appeared worried. "I understand." She really did, even if she didn't like it.

"But you raise an excellent opportunity for us to devise our history together—how we met, when we married, where we are from, all of that. Shall we begin?"

Jess shook away her disappointment as she angled herself toward him. "Yes. Should I take notes?" If so, she'd need to go inside and fetch parchment and a quill.

He slowly shook his head, the bridge of his nose creasing the barest amount. "Never, ever write anything down."

She frowned at him. "I'm afraid I must when I'm solving a cipher."

"Other than that. And then you'll have to burn your writings after so our intelligence isn't discovered."

"You people burn everything," she muttered.

"*We* people, I think you mean. Yes, we burn everything that might leave a trail or a clue."

She couldn't argue with that even if it was troublesome. What if there wasn't a fire or flint nearby?

Jess turned her mind to their faux history. "Let's say we met at church," she suggested, using her Welsh accent. That was where her mother had tried to ensnare a husband for her last autumn. Thankfully, the gentleman had avoided the trap as he'd been far more interested in someone else.

Fallin looked at her with a blend of surprise and appreciation. "Southern Wales. Very good," he responded mimicking the accent to perfection. "We shall hail from a small village that is unpronounceable."

"That's believable, considering it's Wales."

He smiled. "Just so." He offered a timeline for their courtship, and they went on for a quarter hour mapping out details.

Jess found it most exhilarating. She doubted she'd forget a thing. Certainly, she would try hard not to.

"I think that's enough for today," he said, reverting to his Scottish brogue. "It's best not to overwhelm our minds with too much to retain." Standing, he helped her up and escorted her back to the house.

She looked over at him as they neared the doorway. "How else are we to meet over the next several days?"

"At Lucien's, more than likely. Lady Pickering will let you know when we'll meet next." He paused, turning toward her. "You're certain you're up to this? We're asking a great deal of you. Most people wouldn't want to take this kind of risk."

In that moment, she realized she'd allowed her excitement to overshadow any concern she had about danger. Perhaps it was because she wouldn't be alone. She'd be with an experienced investigator. "I think I'd like to learn to shoot," she blurted.

He blinked, appearing surprised. "I'll try to find a way to ensure that happens. You are an interesting woman, Miss Goodfellow."

"You really ought to call me Jess since we are going to be working so closely together."

"Then you must call me Dougal. When we are alone, that is."

"That is nearly all we will ever be," she said with a nervous laugh. She couldn't decide what was more harrowing: pretending to be his wife or conducting an investigation into his loyalty without getting caught. He was a professional in this work, and she was a complete novice.

"True," he responded. "And in a little more than a week, we'll be married. I hope you're ready."

Jess hoped she would be too.

CHAPTER 4

a s Dougal entered the Phoenix Club on Tuesday evening, his gaze naturally rose to the large painting that Lucien had commissioned. His eye always went to the lower left, where the artist had painted him, Lucien, and their friend Tobias, who was now the Earl of Overton. Another of their friends, Maximilian Hunt, the Viscount Warfield, rode a horse toward them. The image never failed to make Dougal smile as he climbed the stairs.

The last five days had passed in a frenzy of activity. Aside from meeting with Jess three times at Lucien's, Dougal had tried to continue his investigation to determine how two of his most recent past missions had ended so badly, but he hadn't been allowed access to any documents within the Foreign Office.

Both had transpired after Napoleon had returned to power. The first was a coded message Dougal had fetched from the Isle of Wight and brought to the Foreign Office in London. Only, the message had contained gibberish. Oliver had interrogated Dougal for many hours, asking how he'd received it and whether it was ever out of his possession, plus dozens of other questions. They'd reviewed his movements at least five times. Had it been planted, or had the real message been stolen and replaced? Whatever the reason, the mission had been a total failure.

The second was similar—a pickup from a known courier. Dougal had been dispatched to Bournemouth to meet with Giraud, whom he'd discovered dead with his throat slit.

After that, Dougal couldn't ignore that something—or someone—wasn't right.

Dougal moved into the members' den on the first floor, his gaze sweeping the room, noting it was still the busiest night of the week, particularly now that the Season was over and there were no more Friday assemblies in the ballroom on the ground floor. Tuesdays were popular because it was the one night each week when the female members of the club were allowed to enter the men's side—a benefit they exercised with great enthusiasm. The men were not ever allowed on the ladies' side, save their portion of the ballroom during the assemblies.

This construct set the Phoenix Club apart from every other membership club in town. Women were not ever permitted at other clubs—they were specifically for gentlemen only. That women held full membership here and were even welcomed into the side reserved for gentlemen had caused a stir when the club had opened more than a year and a half ago.

It wasn't just the inclusion of women that separated the Phoenix Club. Lucien had founded it with the express purpose of being a haven for those who were excluded or treated as less than others. The Phoenix Club was for people like Dougal—a Black man with dubious parentage, who, as the son of an earl, was invited everywhere, but never felt as though he were truly welcome. To Dougal and to many other members, the Phoenix Club was home.

Despite that, many in Society still turned their noses up at the club. That was fine with Lucien. In fact, he preferred to keep a certain—excessively arrogant and self-important—element out.

Dougal looked about the members' den and recognized nearly everyone. Those he didn't seemed vaguely familiar, and he committed them to memory so he could later determine who they were. This was the one place where he knew just about everyone and didn't have to be concerned about unknown interlopers with nefarious agendas. Or just questionable people.

His gaze landed on a gentleman seated in a highbacked chair in the corner. Sixty years of age but often appearing younger, perhaps due to his rather thick crop of steel-gray hair, Oliver Kent possessed the sharpest, most assessing gaze of anyone Dougal knew—aside from Lady Pickering. They were birds—predatory ones—of a feather. What the devil was he doing here? He rarely used his membership.

Dougal strode to the older man, who was nursing a glass of what looked to be port. "Evening, Kent. I can count the number of times you've been here on one hand." He sat in the chair separated from Kent's by a small, low round table.

"You know I prefer the Siren's Call," Kent said with a slight smirk, his dark blue eyes gleaming. Owned and staffed completely by women, the Siren's Call was the most unique gaming hell in London. It was where gentlemen went for female companionship—but not sex.

"What brings you here this evening?" Dougal asked.

A footman delivered a glass of whisky to Dougal, for which he thanked the young man.

"Not the impeccable service," Kent murmured, answering Dougal's question. "I had to *ask* for my port."

Dougal chuckled. "Don't judge them too harshly. I am here far more than you are."

"I counted on that." Kent's eyes glittered with purpose, and Dougal had his answer. The man—his superior at the Foreign Office—had come for him. "You are leaving for Dorset tomorrow. I wanted to ensure all was well and ready."

Dougal assumed he was referring to Miss Goodfellow. He didn't for a moment think Kent wasn't aware of Jess's employment as their newest cipher solver. Mostly because Dougal would wager that the mysterious Mr. Torrance who'd given her the cipher at the British Library was, in fact, Oliver Kent.

"Things are going well," Dougal said before sipping his whisky. The familiar, musky flavor coated his tongue, reminding him of home. That made him think of his father and of course, his brother. Perhaps he should have asked for port too. "She's learned a great deal in a short amount of time. We went to Gunter's—not together—and surveyed those in attendance. I quizzed her about it afterward, and she demonstrated extraordinary observation and recollection skills." Dougal had been rather impressed. She'd said she would commit to learning how to do that, and she'd executed it to near perfection.

"That sounds most encouraging. I can't say I'm surprised. She seems exceedingly intelligent, if her cipher solving is any indication."

"How did you decide to approach her? It couldn't have been based on that one encounter at the library."

Kent's brows elevated slightly. "You know about that?"

"I asked how she was recruited, without saying exactly that, of course. She mentioned a gentleman called Torrance, who I deduced must be you."

"Of course you did." Kent chuckled softly. "It *was* just that one occasion. She was solving riddles faster than I'd ever seen anyone solve them, so I gave her a cipher—a relatively easy one. She unraveled it in a matter of minutes."

Dougal could hear the man's admiration. "So you decided to send her more to test her ability."

Kent nodded. "Lucien also managed to have her stay with Lady Pickering so she could be observed. Both her puzzle-solving abilities and her composure recommended her for this assignment. I trust you've done your part to ensure she's successful? She'll play the necessary role?"

Fairly certain Kent was referring to her pretending to be Mrs. Smythe, Dougal nodded.

"Good. That was a risk since she has never been married."

"Don't you worry she may be ruined?" Dougal asked.

"No, because she won't be identified." He looked sharply at Dougal. "You just assured me she was up to the task. Furthermore, I expect you will behave like a gentleman."

Dougal shook his head. "Forget I asked." He supposed he had a few reservations about corrupting a young lady, not that anything untoward would happen. Mostly. Dougal had to expect there would at least be hand-holding or even a kiss on the cheek. They hadn't really practiced those things, however. She'd caressed him at Evie's last week, and that had been the only time they'd touched.

He should have made sure they did. Why hadn't he?

He didn't have an answer. Only that something about her intrigued him, and he shouldn't allow that.

"Am I going to lose you now that you're the heir?" Kent asked, interrupting Dougal's thoughts.

Dougal gripped his glass more tightly, his forearm resting on the arm of the chair. He didn't want this to be his last mission. "Not now." Soon, however. His father could live another few years. Or not. Dougal couldn't see the future. "I can't be sure of the timing." Would he walk away once he'd solved the mysteries surrounding those two missions? He should.

"You will be missed." Kent held up his glass in a toast.

Dougal lifted his glass and took a drink, surprised to find his throat felt tight.

Kent sipped his port. "Will you wed?"

"Eventually." An earl needed a countess, and Dougal would do his duty.

"I do hope you'll invite me to the wedding." Kent finished his port and set his glass on the table between their chairs. "Safe travels to you as always, Mac—" He shook his head. "Fallin." Standing, he inclined his head toward Dougal before taking his leave.

Dougal surveyed the room once more, looking to see if anyone had arrived or if Lucien had come in. There were a few new faces, including one he definitely didn't know, but then he could only view her profile. A peacock feather graced her auburn hair, and large pearl drops hung from her ears. He made a mental note to ask Lucien about the woman. Continuing his perusal, he made eye contact with an acquaintance and rose to go speak with him.

From the corner of his eye, he saw deep blue skirts moving and turned his head. The unknown woman was coming toward him. Now he could see her. There was something vaguely familiar about her. It wasn't her thick auburn brows or dark red lips, nor was it the arrogant tilt of her head. Damn, but she was attractive. Dougal typically didn't allow himself to entertain the fairer sex when he was in the middle of or about to start a mission. He needed to remain focused on his work. This woman, however, might actually possess the ability to distract him.

He needed to move away before he became ensnared.

"Good evening, my lord," she drawled in a lovely southern Welsh accent.

"I'll be damned," he breathed as recognition finally settled into his brain. "Jess?"

"You didn't know it was me." It wasn't a question, and it held just as much humility as her stature, which was to say none.

"I'm not too proud to say I did not. Until you spoke. Then I knew."

She smiled. No, it was more of a grin. "Then I shall congratulate myself."

"You shouldn't." He frowned. "Have I taught you nothing? Composure at all times."

Pursing her lips, she made a rather unladylike sound of annoyance. "Am I not allowed a moment of fun? We aren't in Dorset yet."

"No, but at the moment, you are entirely Mrs. Smythe. Anyone here can look at you, describe you, talk to you, interrogate you—"

"All right, I take your point," she said crossly. "No fun ever."

"Not in public." He deposited his glass on the table next to Kent's and took her elbow. "Allow me to escort you to the library, my dear."

"How lovely," she purred, pulling her elbow from his grasp and curling her hand around his forearm.

"How did you gain access tonight?"

"Lady Pickering arranged for me to arrive earlier as Evie's guest. I donned my costume upstairs. It's rather exciting to be on the gentlemen's side of the club."

"Have you been on the ladies'?"

"No, but I am hopeful that once I'm a spinster, I might receive an invitation of membership."

Dougal could almost guarantee it. The membership committee especially liked to invite spinsters and widows, though convincing the patronesses of the ladies' side that spinsters should be included had taken some effort, and so far, that roster was too lean. Dougal wished they didn't need the patronesses at all, but Lucien had determined they were necessary to lend a modicum of respectability. They were nowhere near as stringent—or fearsome—as the patronesses of Almack's, but Dougal still preferred they weren't required. At least Evie was one of them. Indeed, she kept them—somewhat—in line.

They left the members' den and went to the library at the front of the first floor. This smaller room was generally quieter with fewer people. But since it was Tuesday, it wasn't as much of an escape as on other evenings.

Dougal guided her toward the large fireplace, which was quite cozy in the winter when a semicircle of highbacked chairs was arranged before it. "That's your goal, to become a spinster?" he asked.

The mirror over the mantel reflected the glimmer of the setting sun filtering through the windows. The light splashed across Jess's face, and he now wondered how he hadn't recognized her, even with the transformative cosmetics.

"It is, and indeed, I'm already there. I just need my mother to acknowledge it. I think my father is ready to do so, and hopefully, he will convince her. She can be remarkably stubborn."

"Your mother sounds difficult." Dougal had been fortunate to have two loving parents, even if their own relationship was rather odd. They'd been close—like friends—but their story wasn't a romantic one.

"I think she's just an unhappy person. My younger sisters and I always tried to make her smile and laugh, but it was nearly impossible. We eventually gave up." She sounded rather unaffected by the experience, but he suspected that was because she'd learned to be.

"What do you hope to achieve with spinsterhood?" Dougal asked.

"Freedom. Independence." She let out a faint laugh. "I suppose those are the same things."

"Marriage never appealed to you?"

"Perhaps once," she said softly. Then she shook her head briskly. "No." That made him bloody curious, but he didn't ask. Her striking blue eyes settled on him. "What about you?"

"Too busy." He hadn't felt the necessity to do so, not when his brother was to inherit the title.

"What a marvelous life you lead." She looked at him with a touch of envy. "I'd love to hear about some of your past escapades, but I fear you can't tell me."

He couldn't, at least not the particulars. "I can't divulge specific details, but let me think about how I might find a way to impart some of the more exciting moments of my adventures."

Surprise mixed with anticipation in her gaze. "I can hardly wait."

He fixed on her face. "Now, tell me how you achieved this remarkable affect so that I didn't recognize you."

"You must ask Evie. She devised how to add cosmetics to somehow change the shape of my face. She also made me look, dare I say, beautiful?"

He didn't like that she sounded shocked, as if she'd never been beautiful. "She made you look different. I would argue you were always beautiful."

"Oh, stop," she said with a laugh that sounded a trifle nervous.

"I mean it."

She blinked, but he caught the raw emotion in her gaze before she quickly hid it. He'd surprised her. And something else—as if she'd been genuinely flattered and thrilled by the compliment. "I thought you were playing a part," she said softly. "Isn't that what we've been doing?"

Of course it was. He shouldn't confuse things by allowing a real...friendship to bloom between them. At least not now, when they should be focusing on their mission. "Yes, that is what we've been doing."

He couldn't shake the sensation that no one had ever called her beautiful before. How was that possible? Fighting the urge to hunt down her family and rail at them for treating her so poorly, he focused on the matter at hand. "I trust Evie taught you how to accomplish this application?"

"Indeed. This is my effort—after *much* training by Evie and her ladies' maid." She leaned closer. "I'm still working on the eyes. Her maid was able to make them look as though they turned up at the corners."

"I'd say you achieved that very well, actually." It gave her a sensual appearance.

"You flatter me," she said with the faintest blush, and now he wondered if she was playing a part. He had to assume so. "But I will find a way to manage that." She lowered her voice to just above a whisper. "Let us review tomorrow's plan."

Dougal ensured they wouldn't be overheard. No one was standing within ten feet of them. "Tomorrow is easy. You and Lady Pickering will travel to her home in Hampshire. I will fetch you the day after in the afternoon. The journey to the coast will take about four hours, and we want to be sure to arrive after dark."

"And you're driving, not a coachman?"

"A gig, yes. I don't involve anyone else in my missions." The corner of his mouth turned up. "Until now, that is."

"I can imagine it would complicate matters to have to bring another person into the necessary secrecy of the endeavor. Or, if you didn't, a coachman might realize you'd sabotaged the equipage."

"I find it's better to work alone for that very reason."

"You've *never* worked with anyone else until me?" She sounded as though she wasn't sure she believed him. "I'm flattered again."

He laughed. "If you recall, I would not have sought to work with anyone now."

She smiled at him coyly and put her other hand over his forearm so that she was holding him rather securely—or possessively. "Let me be flattered, Dougal. It supports our performance." Definitely playing her part. To perfection.

"I'd say you're ready for this endeavor. Your transformation to Mrs. Smythe seems complete."

"I'm glad—and relieved—you approve." Her attention moved to the doorway. Dougal followed her gaze and saw Lucien striding toward them, his brow furrowed.

"Evening, Lucien," Dougal said in greeting.

Lucien inclined his head, but he was staring at Jess. "Dougal, you must introduce me to your guest." He leaned toward Dougal and muttered, "Whose invitation I wasn't aware of."

Occasionally, members requested to bring guests on Tuesday evenings. They were approved by Lucien.

Quashing his smile, Dougal kept a bland expression. "This is Miss Goodfellow. She is a guest of Evie's."

Watching Lucien's eyes widen as he perused Jess from head to toe was incredibly satisfying. Dougal was now beyond certain that their scheme would work. Or at least, that there was very little chance someone would recognize his partner. But it was more than that. Her accent, which she'd maintained all evening, was impeccable, she'd learned to control her reactions, and she exuded confidence. She'd absolutely surpassed expectation.

So much so that Dougal suddenly wondered if she was a new recruit at all.

"I'll be damned," Lucien remarked with a grin. "Well done,

Miss Goodfellow. You are a veritable goddess. I thought Dougal had been keeping his new love from me."

Jess's artificially auburn brows shot up. "New love?" She looked to Dougal. "Was there an old one?"

"No." He'd not only been too busy to wed, he hadn't spared time for entanglements of any kind. He satisfied himself with short liaisons or spontaneous trysts.

"Dougal is incredibly dedicated to his work," Lucien said.

"As are you," Dougal noted. "You are rarely away from this club."

"And look at how successful it's become!" Lucien laughed. Again, he looked to Jess. "Truly, you've completely transformed yourself. I had no idea of your identity. However, you may want to leave soon lest you draw too much attention. You're too alluring to ignore as you are presently. Everyone will be asking me about the stunning woman on Dougal's arm."

"I hadn't considered that. I'll just go, then."

"You do present a lovely couple," Lucien added. "I would believe you are wed."

Jess squeezed Dougal's arm before letting him go. "Because we are so in love, aren't we, dear?"

"More with each passing moment." Dougal took her hand and brought her gloved knuckles to his lips.

Her eyes flared slightly—the barest reaction, but he caught it. He didn't comment because it was a believable response between two lovers who anticipated being alone. She was more accomplished than he realized. A surprising—and very real—flash of heat raced through him.

What if she was more in control than he was? What if she was not the amateur he'd thought her to be? Except Kent had recruited her based on her cipher-solving skills, which would mean she'd completely duped him into believing she had no experience. Dougal found that impossible to comprehend. Furthermore, she would not even have been involved with the Foreign Office last spring when his missions had gone sour.

Releasing her hand, he mentally chastised himself for being overly suspicious due to what had happened on his missions. Those failures could have been flukes. Not everything went according to plan. He'd just never had two things go so spectacularly badly, particularly in close proximity.

He was simply fixed on those occurrences and trying to determine what had gone wrong. Dougal felt in his gut that the two failures were related. He just needed to discover how.

Unfortunately, he wasn't going to do it on this bloody mission.

"I'll bid you good evening," Jess said before elevating her chin and striding from the library as if she owned the damned place.

"That is quite a metamorphosis," Lucien murmured.

Dougal tore his gaze from Jess to look at Lucien, who was watching her departure. "You seem enchanted."

"Anyone would be. She's striking."

"Wasn't she before?" Dougal asked, feeling a trifle defensive on her behalf, which was perhaps silly.

Lucien pivoted toward him. "Not really, and I suggest she would agree. I think her intent has always been to fade into the background."

To avoid marriage. That made perfect sense given what Dougal knew of her.

Or was there some other, more nefarious purpose for her wanting to go unnoticed?

Now he *was* being silly. He was looking for answers at every turn instead of where it made sense. His brother's death had set him out of kilter, and he wasn't as focused as he needed to be. He couldn't be distracted by his engaging partner or by his need to solve the mystery surrounding his failed missions.

The latter he would delay until he returned to London, and the former... Well, he simply wouldn't allow himself to find her attractive. He'd always been a man of control and discipline. This would be no different.

CHAPTER 5

*J*ess surveyed her appearance one last time in the large mirror in the entry hall of Lady Pickering's Hampshire home. She still wasn't used to seeing Mrs. Smythe's reflection, which she supposed was a good thing. It meant her disguise looked nothing like her.

"Splendid." Lady Pickering moved behind her, beaming. It was the most effusive Jess had ever seen the woman. "You look magnificent. How I wish I could see your success at the Chesmores'. Alas, I shall have to settle for your verbal report upon your return." She'd informed Jess that she could and indeed would be expected to share the outcome of the mission with her.

Turning from the mirror, Jess pulled on her gloves. "I do appreciate your confidence in me."

"I see the barest flicker of doubt, but I'll repeat what I told you at dinner last night: you're ready for this," Lady Pickering assured her.

They'd arrived yesterday afternoon and enjoyed a pleasant dinner, after which Lady Pickering had given her a tour of the house. She'd also shared a few pieces of information about Dougal, much to Jess's surprise.

Apparently, he'd been a bit of a rake in his youth, racing about London in the company of Lord Lucien and Maximillian Hunt, who was now the Viscount Warfield. Jess would love to hear stories of their adventures. Dougal's father had then directed him to either farm on the family estate in Scotland or pursue a military career. Dougal had joined the Black Watch and served in the war in Spain and Portugal.

Lady Pickering started toward the door. "Come, Fallin's waiting in the drive. Don't forget the food hamper."

Jess picked up the basket that sat near the door and followed Lady Pickering from the house. A two-person gig stood in the drive. However, the gentleman waiting to hand her into the equipage was not whom she'd expected.

"Dougal?" she whispered. He possessed the same dark almond skin, strong jaw, and supple mouth, but his brown eyes were obscured behind spectacles and his black curls were covered in an umber-colored wig. His costume was fussier than what he typically wore—the waistcoat was a bright pattern, and a large ruby glinted in the folds of his cravat. He looked wholly different, even though she could recognize him.

He bowed. "Dougal Smythe, at your service." His Welsh accent slipped over her like a warm cloak on a late autumn day—familiar and welcome.

"You look quite different," Jess said, staring at his hairline.

"You've about four hours to become used to it," he said with a smile as he handed her into the gig. "I've already put your trunk on the back."

"Thank you." Jess set the food hamper next to her feet and looked to Lady Pickering, who stood watching them with her hands clasped. "And thank you. We'll see you soon."

"Good luck to you both," Lady Pickering said. "Do be careful."

Dougal climbed into the gig and picked up the reins. He nodded toward Lady Pickering and started them on their way. "I trust you spent a pleasant night with Lady Pickering?"

"I did, thank you. What about you? Where did you stay?"

"A small inn outside Winchester. It was comfortable." He tipped his head up briefly to look at the sky. "It may rain, which will only support our cause. I would just prefer it held off until we are at or near to our destination."

The gig had a cover, but it wouldn't keep them completely dry. "If we are rain-soaked, the Chesmores will be even more likely to take pity."

"Exactly so," he said with a nod.

She looked over at him, trying to accustom herself to his disguise. "Are the spectacles plain glass?"

"They are, so we must take care not to let anyone else handle them."

Jess nodded. "The wig is the most jarring thing. I prefer your natural hair."

"I do too, but this changes my appearance more than just the spectacles. The color of my skin usually sets me apart. It's not the best trait for a man whose profession typically requires him to disappear into the background."

"How did you come to be in this profession? Lady Pickering told me you were in the Black Watch. I confess I have no problem imagining you in a kilt with a scarlet coat." In that moment, she realized she also preferred his Scottish accent to the Welsh one. But they would both be using the Welsh, even when they were alone. They wouldn't chance slipping.

"Is that so?" he asked with a low laugh. "I rarely wear a kilt."

"That's a shame." She glanced at his legs, wondering how

they would look in his traditional garb. "Are you going to answer my question?"

"It's not an exciting tale, I'm afraid. I was serving in the Black Watch, and I was given an assignment to deliver information. I did so with little difficulty and apparently great speed compared to others. After that, I was removed from the regiment and sent to work for the Foreign Office." He drove the gig onto the road from Lady Pickering's drive. "You must realize you can't share that with anyone."

"Since no one can know that you—and I—work for the Foreign Office, that goes without saying. Thank you for sharing your story with me. It's good to know things about you. I know you said we didn't need to get to know each other, but I contend that if we are well-acquainted, that can only help our partnership."

"You may be right, actually. If we know each other at least a little, our scheme will be that much more credible."

He'd changed his opinion? "I'm glad you think so." She wanted to ask a dozen questions, but she still wasn't sure he'd answer them. Perhaps she ought to give him an open invitation to just...talk. "You seem guarded. Is there anything else you'd care to share with me? About your family, perchance? Or where you grew up?"

"I grew up near Stirling."

"Is that the Highlands?"

"It's about where the Highlands start," he said.

"I've always wanted to visit Scotland, especially the Highlands. It sounds beautiful."

"When you're an independent spinster, you can do whatever you like, including take a trip north."

"I suppose I can." She hoped he might say more, but began to doubt that he would. She'd prod once more and then leave him alone. "Your father is the earl?"

"Yes."

"Any other family?" Twice more, apparently.

He exhaled. "Two sisters, same as you." Jess had mentioned her two younger sisters at some point during their acquaintance. "I also had two older brothers. One died twenty years ago along with my mother, and we lost the other in July. I also have aunts and uncles and a great many cousins."

Jess turned her head to see his expression, but it hadn't altered. His gaze was fixed on the road, and his features were relaxed. He was either unaffected by the loss of his brother or he was exceptionally good at masking his feelings. She suspected it was the latter. "As in two months ago?" Now she understood both Lady Pickering's and Evie's reception of him when he'd returned to London last week. She also comprehended why he may have been agitated that first evening at Lucien's.

"Yes. He suffered an accident. He was supposed to marry this month."

"His poor betrothed," Jess whispered. "And poor you. Were you close?"

"I think so, yes." He was quiet a moment. "Yes, we were. Anyway, I am now the heir to the earldom, so I don't know how much longer I'll be doing this, unfortunately."

She heard the regret in his voice. "You'll miss it."

He glanced toward her, and she wished he wasn't wearing the spectacles so that she could see his naked gaze. "I wasn't supposed to be the earl. I was happy to find something I loved, something that made me feel valuable."

"Being the earl may be the same." She touched his arm briefly. "Different, but still fulfilling, I mean."

"I suppose. In any case, it doesn't matter how I feel about it. It's my duty."

They fell quiet for a few moments. The breeze picked up,

and Jess noted there was a blanket peeking from beneath the seat.

"Such a heavy word, isn't it?" she reflected. "Duty. I have long felt an oppressive responsibility to wed. And why?"

"I would argue that particular duty isn't the same as mine. I was born to it." His shoulder twitched the barest amount, but she caught it. "Actually, maybe they are the same. Women are born as women, and their value is often in who they wed."

She was astonished that he understood. "You wish you weren't? Born to it, I mean."

"The truth is that my father isn't my sire. He raised me as his son, but I am not his."

Goodness, she'd never expected this sort of revelation. "That was rather wonderful of him." She assumed that was the case, but what if Dougal and his father didn't get along? Perhaps that was part of why Dougal didn't want to be the earl. "Was it? Wonderful, I mean."

"It was, particularly when you know that neither he nor my mother were Black." He cast her a wry look.

What he said sank into her brain. Everyone would have known he was not his father's son. It wasn't uncommon for a man to claim his wife's child as his own. There may be speculation as to the paternity, but no one would really know. In this case, it would have been quite clear that Dougal wasn't his father's son.

"That sounds especially wonderful, then," she said softly.

"It was. It *is*. My father is a singular person. He made sure no one questioned my birth. I've had looks, and I'm aware people talk, particularly in London, but as I'm the acknowledged son of the Earl of Stirling, no one debates it. At least not publicly. I'm confident some have discussed it at length."

"That's precisely the sort of thing the worst gossips feast upon."

"It doesn't bother me," he said.

"Are you concerned your becoming the heir will provoke renewed interest?"

"Not terribly, but I can't say I have no worry at all. What I do know is that my father won't stand for any of it. He'll tell everyone—and has—that he is my father, and there is nothing more to be said on the matter."

She stared at him, hearing the pride and love in his voice. And envying him more than a little. "Thank you. I'm so glad you shared this with me. I confess it makes me feel rather close to you."

"Like a wife?" He looked her way for a moment. Before she could respond, he returned his attention to the road. "That only aids our cause."

Feeling slightly unnerved, she reminded herself that she wasn't his wife, that she was only pretending to be. As he'd mentioned earlier, this was a *scheme*. "I'll stop pestering you now."

"I'm afraid it's your turn anyway," he said. "I know your mother is controlling and cold and that your father is usually busy reading. What else should I know?"

"That my grandfather is as wonderful as your father sounds. He's Lord Goodfellow."

"I don't think I've met him."

"He rarely comes to London. My parents are at his estate now. I would normally have accompanied them, but I need a respite from my mother. I'll see him at Christmas."

"And does he support your spinsterhood?"

"I haven't spoken to him about it." She ought to have by now. "I suppose I've been nervous. What if he doesn't support me?" She wasn't sure she could deal with that disappointment.

"If he's as wonderful as you say, he must," Dougal said as

if it were obvious. "You can't be wrong about him. Trust him to be the man you know him to be."

"Aren't you just full of wisdom," she said with a laugh. "You make a compelling argument. I will speak with him about it. Thank you."

"One last question. For now," he added with the flash of a smile. "Have you tried to fade into the background? I just can't see how you haven't had at least one proposal. Or have you, and you declined?"

Jess considered whether to tell him about Asa. She hadn't mentioned him to anyone in years. But in the interest of deepening their association for the sake of the mission, she decided there was no reason to withhold the tale. "I have had exactly one, actually."

He turned his head. "Indeed? Why did you refuse him?"

"I didn't. He changed his mind. I later discovered that my parents had paid him to do so."

He muttered something under his breath, and while she couldn't discern what he'd said, she would wager he'd disparaged her parents. She liked him even more. "I begin to understand why your parents vex you so."

"I confess I refused to consider any potential husbands out of spite." She shrugged. "I suppose it became an ingrained habit after the first few Seasons."

"Is it then fair to say your resistance to marriage is due to a habit you could break for the right person?"

She laughed at that. "I don't think so. As I said, it's rather ingrained now. Furthermore, I've yet to meet another man who provoked even a hint of marriage to enter my mind."

"Not one has caught your fancy in any way?"

"No. I've no desire to be leg-shackled to a man, particularly after watching my sisters submit to their insufferable husbands."

"Not all men are insufferable. I can't imagine you'd choose one who was," he added wryly.

"I would hope not, but their insufferability didn't present itself until after they were wed." Jess cocked her head in contemplation. "Actually, my middle sister doesn't see it, but that's because she's a bit insufferable too."

Dougal laughed. "Excellent. Now please tell me there's food in that basket you set between our feet."

"Yes, it's a dinner of ham, cheese, fruit, and bread. There's ale too. Are you hungry now?"

"Not yet, but I shall look forward to it. I think we must review our stories one last time."

One last time. Very soon, she would *be* Mrs. Smythe. The nervousness she'd kept at bay stole over her quickly and settled into her bones. She slid a look at Mr. Smythe and wondered how they would get on when they were alone. More than that, she wondered what she would do if her investigation into his activities revealed something nefarious.

She rather liked him and would hate if that were true. Hopefully, it wasn't. After all, he had an earldom to inherit and a delightful father to make proud.

"Something amiss?" he asked. "You're watching me with a singular interest."

Jess shook her head. "Not at all, just thinking of the work before us. Let us start at the beginning. We met at church three years ago."

And on they went as they'd done many times before. Except in this instance, her unease remained.

CHAPTER 6

*T*he rain Dougal had predicted a few hours earlier began to fall. Because of the heavy clouds, sunset came faster than he'd anticipated. Still, he was able to get them where they needed to be—just outside the gatehouse at the end of the drive leading to the dully named Seaview House, which the Chesmores had purchased earlier in the year.

He pulled the gig to the side of the road and turned to Jess. "Stay here while I exchange the breeching straps and take care of the horse. Try to stay dry."

"I thought it would be better if we are rain soaked."

"Yes, but I have every expectation that will happen when we walk up the drive to the house." He glanced up at the sky and got a raindrop in his eye. "Blast," he muttered, blinking furiously.

"Are you sure I can't help you?" Jess offered. "I can manage the horse."

"I have no doubt, but these things can't be done at the same time. If I conduct the sabotage with the horse still in the harness, he may react poorly or at least be stressed. I don't want to do that to him." He climbed out of the gig so that he was fully in the rain, which seemed to be falling more steadily than even a moment ago.

"That makes sense. You're very kindhearted."

"Usually." He went to unhitch the horse and tied him to a nearby tree that afforded him a modicum of shelter. "You won't be out here long, my boy," he said soothingly, stroking the animal's neck.

Hurrying back to the coach, he removed the breeching strap and replaced it with one that was worn through. He tossed the good strap a fair distance into the shrubbery off the side of the road. Then he turned to Jess and offered his hand. "Time to go."

At that moment, lightning flashed overhead. A moment later, thunder roared. Jess practically leapt into his arms as she stepped from the gig.

He caught her waist and held her steady, looking into her upturned face. "All right?"

"I've never liked thunderstorms. Let's hurry."

The raindrops grew fatter. They would be soaked through in no time.

Dougal took her hand. They walked quickly to the gatehouse, then started up the drive. The house rose before them, a charming structure of stone and wooden gables constructed within the past fifty years. It wasn't terribly large, but neither was it small. He estimated thirty rooms.

"Almost there," he said encouragingly.

She quickened her pace, and he had to do the same since her legs were nearly as long as his. At last, they reached the threshold.

"Here we go," he whispered.

He rapped loudly with his fist. They waited a moment, during which the rain seemed to come down even harder. At last, the door opened to reveal an elderly butler with a stooped frame. He perused them with a discerning eye and pursed his lips. "Mr. Chesmore is not expecting you."

"No, we were passing by, and our gig has been rendered undriveable," Dougal responded. "Then it began to rain. May we come inside?"

The butler sniffed. "You will get the floor wet."

"If I promise to clean it, will you please let us in?" Jess asked, her teeth chattering.

Dougal hoped she was doing that on purpose as an effect, and that she wasn't really that cold.

His mouth dipping into a full frown, the butler opened the door wider and allowed them inside. "Wait here. Do try not to drip."

"We'll do our best," Dougal said with a bright smile instead of the sarcasm he was feeling.

The butler slowly turned and walked from the hall. He moved at a snail's pace, much to Dougal's annoyance.

"Can't he go any faster?" Jess muttered.

Dougal suppressed a smile. "You can't say things like that, even under your breath," he muttered back.

"Sorry. I'm cold."

"Are your teeth really chattering?"

"If I let them. I thought it might help."

"It did seem to convince him." Dougal noted that her face was pale and that her disguise was coming apart. "Your cosmetics are not faring well from the rain. I should have thought of that."

"I was hoping my bonnet would shield me well enough, but toward the end, the rain was coming at a bit of an angle."

He moved them so they were in a more shadowed area of the hall. "That's the best I can do."

"I'm sure it will be fine. Goodness, I am *very* cold."

Footsteps sounded from nearby—faster ones than the

butler had made—and a moment later, a man and woman, arm in arm, stepped into the entry hall. He was on the shorter side, with thick dark brows and a wide nose. She was nearly his height, with bright blonde hair and a fairly thin nose.

"Heavens, you are soaking wet!" Mrs. Chesmore declared, her blue eyes widening. "Ogelby said you had trouble with your gig. What a horrid time for that to happen. Thank goodness you found our house. Did you come far? It looks as though you've been out for hours."

"I think the rain is just that hard, my dove," Chesmore said, patting her forearm. He turned his dark assessing gaze on Dougal and Jess. "Are you far from your destination?"

"Our next stop was to be Poole," Dougal said, aware that Jess was shaking beside him. "We are the Smythes. I'm afraid my wife is terribly chilled. Might we impose on you to warm up? I'll need to go back out and fetch our things—the gig is not too far from your gatehouse, thankfully."

Mrs. Chesmore took her arm from her husband's. "Nonsense. You'll both go warm up and stay the night. My knight will send grooms for your things and to take care of your gig and livestock."

Dougal gave her a grateful smile. "One horse. Thank you. I tied him beneath a tree for some shelter, but I daresay he's quite wet by now."

Their hostess turned her head to her husband. "Sir Lancelot, if you would be so kind?"

Sir Lancelot? Dougal knew the man's name to be Gilbert, and hers was Mary.

"I'll see to it." Chesmore took his wife's hand and pressed a kiss to her wrist before departing the hall.

He passed the butler, who seemed to have finally found his way back. Did he truly walk that slowly?

"There you are, Ogelby," Mrs. Chesmore said. "I am

taking our guests, the Smythes, up to the Wordsworth Room."

The Wordsworth Room? She called her husband a knight of the Round Table, and their bedchambers were named after poets? At least theirs would be. Dougal was fast gaining the impression their hosts possessed a fascinating eccentricity.

"Please have a bath prepared with due haste," Mrs. Chesmore directed the butler. "We need to get the Smythes warmed up. I daresay Mrs. Smythe's lips are turning blue."

Dougal snapped his gaze to Jess's mouth, but thankfully, they were no such thing, just slightly pale where the cosmetic had washed away. He put his arm around her. "We'll get you cozy in no time, my love." He brushed a light kiss against her temple. She smelled of roses and rain, a surprisingly delicious combination.

"Thank you, darling," she murmured, laying her head against his shoulder.

Mrs. Chesmore smiled affectionately. "I'm so glad you happened upon us. How fortunate. Come, let's get you upstairs."

She led them into a staircase hall in the center of the house. The stairs climbed the left wall and turned at a landing on the back wall. At the top, they entered a wide gallery. "Wordsworth is just this way."

"Are all the rooms named after poets?" Jess asked, her teeth clacking with cold.

Dougal was growing concerned. He wanted to get her warm, but he also couldn't risk divesting her of the entire disguise in front of the servants. Hopefully, the bath and their trunks would arrive quickly.

"Not just poets, writers," Mrs. Chesmore said with a warm smile that seemed to be her natural state.

Jess responded:

"For oft, when on my couch I lie

In vacant or in pensive mood,
They flash upon that inward eye
Which is the bliss of solitude;
And then my heart with pleasure fills,
And dances with the daffodils."

Dougal looked at her in open admiration that wasn't remotely artificial.

Mrs. Chesmore laughed softly. "That is one of my favorite passages. How appropriate that you will be in Wordsworth. It is our loveliest chamber aside from the one I share with my knight—that is the Blake Room. It is in the opposite corner facing the sea, so similarly situated to yours."

She led them to the right of the stairs and followed the gallery to a door on the left. "It's dark now, but in the morning, you will have the most glorious view of the sea."

Mrs. Chesmore opened the door and went directly to the mantel, where she found flint and lit a lantern. Light spilled across the large corner chamber with windows on the far and right-hand walls. The hearth sat between two of those windows on the right wall, opposite the wide, four-poster bed that looked as though it could easily hold four adults. That was rather helpful since he and Jess needed to share a bed. They hadn't discussed any specifics, and he wondered if she, like he, had thought of how it would work. This bed was large enough for them to probably not even realize the other was in the same room.

"Pardon me," a high, feminine voice said from behind them.

Dougal escorted Jess farther into the room, making way for the maid to hurry inside. She went to the hearth and quickly laid a fire.

"Thank you, Polly," Mrs. Chesmore said. "Is the bath coming?"

"On its way, ma'am," the young maid said as she worked to get the fire going.

Once there were flames, Jess moved as close as possible to the hearth. Seashells were carved into the stone and a cockle shell sat on one side of the mantel.

"You poor dear," Mrs. Chesmore said to her. "What a terrible ordeal you've suffered. Are you hungry? I'll have refreshment sent up as well." She glanced toward a table situated in front of the window that faced the sea.

Two footmen entered, carrying a tub.

"Put it near the fire instead of in the dressing room." Mrs. Chesmore gestured in front of the hearth. "Make sure the water is nice and hot."

Jess stepped to the side so the footmen could set the tub down. They then bustled from the room.

"Polly can help you disrobe," Mrs. Chesmore offered. "I take it you have no maid or valet?" She looked toward Dougal.

"Not even a groom," Dougal replied, removing his hat and gloves and placing them on a small table near the door. "We are taking a second honeymoon and wished for privacy." He sent a loving look to Jess, who gave him a coy smile in return.

Mrs. Chesmore's features glowed. "How positively romantic. Well then, you must accept Polly as your maid while you're here."

"Actually, I prefer to allow my love to attend me," Jess said, her gaze settling on him as if he were a sweetmeat and she was famished.

Dougal put his palm against his breast, which he immediately regretted since his coat was quite wet. "That is my preference as well, my sweet."

"You are the most charming couple," Mrs. Chesmore said, clasping her hands in front of her chest.

Dougal was relieved their plan was working as expected.

There'd been no knowing how much sentiment would be too much. However, it seemed with the Chesmores, no sentiment would be too great.

Jess tried to remove her bonnet, but Dougal could see she was having trouble because the ribbon was soggy, and her hands were shaking. She was still wearing gloves, which were also soaked. He moved to remove her gloves first.

"Just leave your wet clothes in the dressing room. It's there." Mrs. Chesmore pointed to a door on the same wall as the bed. "I'll have Polly tend to them."

"That would be much appreciated," Jess said with a relieved smile as Dougal peeled one glove away. Her hand was pink and puckered. He removed the other glove, then hesitated as he tried to think of where to deposit them while he untied her bonnet.

Understanding his dilemma, Jess took the gloves from him so he could remove the bonnet.

"We make an excellent team," he murmured. It wouldn't matter if Mrs. Chesmore heard that. She'd likely find it just another adorable attribute of their marriage.

"We do indeed," Jess said just as quietly.

He carefully removed the bonnet so that he didn't dishevel her wig. Thankfully, it was dry due to the bonnet's protection. He took the gloves from her and went to deposit them and the hat on the dresser. Then he thought better of it and tossed them into the dressing room. At a quick glance, he noted it was a decent size, with an armoire and a dressing table.

The footmen returned with the first buckets and began to fill the tub with steaming water. Because the servants would be in and out of the room even after the bath, they needed to keep their wigs on, and he'd continue to wear his spectacles.

He went back to her side, noting, "Your hair is surprisingly dry." He hoped she understood what he was trying to convey—that she could wait to remove that until later.

Jess touched her head as her gaze met his. Yes, she understood. "I suppose I shall leave it for now."

"And now I shall remove myself," Mrs. Chesmore said brightly. "I'm sure you're anxious to get out of those wet clothes. Please ask for whatever you require from Polly. She'll be glad to help. Then get a good night's sleep, and we'll talk in the morning." She went to Jess and took her hand briefly. "I feel this was a most fortuitous event, that we shall be great friends. That you immediately quoted Wordsworth…" Shaking her head, she clucked her tongue. "Marvelous. We break our fast in our room every morning, so I suggest you do the same. Just ring when you are ready for it." Sailing to the door, she called, "Sleep well!" Then she was gone.

Dougal would have relaxed, but the footmen would return at any moment. "We're almost there," he said softly. "Do you want to get undressed?"

She cocked her head slightly, giving him a look that seemed to ask if he was serious.

"You need to get warm," he said. "And those wet clothes are doing more harm than good."

"I wish I had a dressing gown."

"I expect the trunks will be here shortly." And hopefully, the contents would be dry, but he didn't say that out loud. "Let me find a blanket." He went to a dresser and looked through the drawers, but there was nothing. "I'll get something from Polly when she returns."

More water arrived, and just after the footmen left again, Polly entered with a tray, which she carried to the table. "There are sandwiches, biscuits, and tea."

Jess's lips curved into an alluring smile that caused Dougal to stare at her mouth again. "Tea would be divine."

"Shall I prepare it for you, ma'am?" Polly asked. Petite and young—younger than Jess—with dark auburn hair and round brown eyes, she seemed eager to please.

Dougal smiled at the maid. "Actually, if you could find a blanket or a dressing gown—something Mrs. Smythe could don while she's awaiting the bath. She really needs to get out of those wet clothes."

"I'll see to it directly." Polly rushed from the room.

"I'll pour you some tea." Dougal went to the table, knowing she liked milk and sugar.

"Thank you—for the tea and for directing Polly." Jess came to the table, whose pair of chairs had no cushions. She sat and began to remove her boot. "I feel as though my brain is too cold to think at the moment."

"Allow me." Dougal finished preparing her cup and handed it to her. "Drink."

She cupped the vessel and brought it before her face. Her eyes closed in rapture, and for a moment, Dougal felt as though he may be enraptured right along with her. "Absolutely heavenly."

Dougal crouched down. She held her foot out, and he unlaced the boot. As he removed it, he slid his hand down her ankle. A surprising jolt of heat stole through him. "This is most domestic," he said, glancing up at her.

Her gaze was fixed on him, adding to the slow pulse of desire winding its way through him. "Quite." She wriggled her toes.

Her boots were thoroughly wet, and he could see the stocking was soaked through. He plucked gently at the cotton covering her foot. "Shall I remove this as well?"

"If you don't mind?"

He smiled up at her. "I'm here, aren't I?"

She sipped her tea, and if he had to describe her expression, he would have said it was intoxicated. Or as though she had just reached her climax.

Shit. He should not think such things about her, particularly when he was caressing her bare ankle, as he was now that he'd removed the stocking. This was a disturbing combination of the roles they were playing and the natural chemistry occurring between them. He hadn't considered the latter happening and now realized that was a glaring oversight.

He cast the stocking to the floor and moved on to her other foot. The footmen brought more water, and Polly returned with another footman. "Your trunks are here. I instructed him to bring Mrs. Smythe's first. He's taking it directly to the dressing chamber, then he'll fetch Mr. Smythe's."

"Bless you," Jess said as Dougal removed her second stocking and tried not to trace his finger along the delicate top of her foot.

Dougal rose and offered her his hand. She took a quick sip of tea and set the cup on the table before placing her fingers in his. This contact sent another wave of awareness through him.

This was not good. He was a gentleman, and they were working together. There was no place for arousal or any similar sensation or sentiment.

As soon as she stood, he released her. "Do you require any assistance?"

Jess shook her head. "I can manage. You should remove your coat and waistcoat at least." She looked to Polly. "Thank you for your help. You may be excused."

Polly dipped a curtsey and left the room.

Dougal looked down at himself. He should remove his outer garments. He'd been focused on her. As a caring husband should be. The intriguing thing was that he hadn't consciously thought to do it. He'd simply acted. The line between role and reality was most definitely blurred.

Jess disappeared into the dressing chamber. He peeled away his coat and waistcoat, laying them over the back of one of the chairs at the table for now. The tub was perhaps half full. Dougal was amazed at their efficiency. They must have already had water heating for a bath. Had they stolen it from the Chesmores? He would thank them in the morning.

Dougal sat and removed his boots and stockings. Unlike Jess, his feet had remained dry. Still, he was cold, so he went to the fireplace and warmed himself. More water arrived, and Jess finally emerged from the dressing chamber garbed in a dark red dressing gown that hugged her breasts. He forced his attention to the fire. "The bath will be ready shortly."

She came to stand beside him and whispered, "And then what?"

He turned his head toward her. "Are you asking what I will do?"

"Well, yes. Normally, I would bathe in the dressing chamber in privacy."

"Certainly. I'll remove myself to the dressing room until you're finished. I need to put on dry clothes anyway."

"I don't want you to have to stay in there. You should be by the fire."

"I'll take a cup of tea."

She rolled her eyes. "That won't warm you enough."

"I'm not as cold as you were. Ah, here's the rest of the water."

The footmen dumped their buckets into the tub, and Dougal informed them that would be sufficient. "Should we ring for you when we're finished?"

"Yes, sir," one of them responded. They took their leave, closing the door behind them.

"Well, that was quite a fuss," Jess said, crossing to the tub.

Dougal strode toward the dressing chamber. "I'll leave you to it."

"Thank you for everything. You make an excellent husband." She began to unfasten her dressing gown.

He tore his gaze away lest he forget what he was doing or even his own name. This reaction to her was completely unacceptable, and he had to find a way to banish it. "You make it easy," he said. "Take your time."

"I won't be long. I assumed you'd get in after me?"

The thought of sliding into the tub her nude body had only recently vacated was enough to send his cock to full attention. "I think I can skip it. You need to be warm. I'll bundle up by the fire when you're finished." He gave her an encouraging smile to underscore his words, then closed himself in the dressing chamber.

Where he tried desperately not to think of her or frig himself in frustration. He did, however, contemplate how the hell he was going to only pretend to be her husband.

CHAPTER 7

*A*fter her bath, Jess had dried, then bundled herself into her dressing gown once more. Hunger drove her to the tray of food, where she'd devoured a sandwich and a biscuit with embarrassing speed.

After taking one more biscuit, she'd nervously approached the dressing room door, feeling completely self-conscious about her barely dressed state. She had to become accustomed to it. This was how it would be for the next several days. Perhaps even a fortnight.

She'd knocked and taken an instinctive step back before Dougal had opened the door. He wore a green dressing gown and still had his wig and spectacles on. Of course he would—they were not finished being troubled by footmen yet, as the bath needed to be taken away.

Dougal kept his gaze on her face. "Did you ring for them to fetch the tub?"

"I did. You're sure you don't want to use it?"

"While you were bathing, I went to ask Polly to bring hot water to the dressing chamber. I should have thought of that sooner. But all is well." He stepped out of the dressing chamber. "I'll just let you complete your toilet."

Jess squeezed past him and firmly closed the door. Nibbling the biscuit, she looked about for her trunk, planning to finish unpacking it. When she'd removed her wet clothing and donned the dressing gown earlier, she'd taken care to remove her other wigs before anyone saw them. She'd put them in a drawer and covered them with under-clothing.

Her trunk sat in the corner beneath Dougal's smaller one, which was not where she'd left it. Lifting his trunk, she deduced it was empty. She opened the lid to verify her assumption, then set it aside. Polly must have unpacked his things. Had she done the same with Jess's?

A review of her trunk also revealed it to be empty. Jess was now quite proud of herself for hiding the wigs. If she hadn't, Polly would know about them.

As Jess stacked the trunks in the corner once more, she frowned at Dougal's. She might have searched it for clues, but it was empty. Should she look through his things? What, exactly, would she be looking for, and would she even know if she'd found it? It wasn't as if he would document his crimes in a journal and bring it to Dorset while on a mission with his very first partner.

Honestly, she just couldn't believe he was working against the Foreign Office. He seemed a man who cared deeply about his post and for his country.

Did that mean she wasn't going to do what the Foreign Office had asked?

As if she even knew *what* to do. She supposed she'd just pay close attention, but she'd do that anyway.

Noises from the bedchamber told her the footmen had come to remove the water and the tub.

Turning from the trunks, she went to the dresser, where

she'd stowed her pair of night rails. When she was once again clothed, she set to removing her wig, plucking out the many pins holding it in place. Then she moved on to loosening her plaited hair, which had been viciously coiled and pinned around her head. Sighing with pleasure, she let it down and ran her fingers through the locks, rubbing her scalp.

Finally, after the bedchamber had been quiet for some time, she cracked the door and peered one eye through the opening. "They've gone?"

Dougal stood near the fireplace. "Yes, we're alone until morning—and we won't be disturbed. I hope you weren't still hungry, as they also removed the tray." He massaged the bridge of his nose.

Alone until morning. She couldn't dwell on that. "I was just doing that to my head," she said as he moved his ministrations to behind his ears. "Do the spectacles bother you?"

"They take a little getting used to." He eyed her long plait. "Brown-haired and cosmetic-free once more, I see."

She touched the end of her hair. "Do you find it dull?"

"Not at all. You look like you." He dropped his hand to his side.

She didn't quite feel like herself, however. Though she'd prepared for this, the reality of being alone with him in this bedchamber, pretending as if they were truly married, brought forth a range of emotions: uncertainty, anxiety, and perhaps an inexplicable dash of anticipation.

"And now *you* look like you—without the spectacles." Her gaze dipped to his bare feet and calves, dark and muscular. She jerked her attention back to his face.

"Did I look terribly intellectual with them on?" he asked with a smile.

She laughed. "How does one 'look' intellectual?"

"I was only hoping. You're the one who is *actually* intellectual, tossing off poetry as if you'd rehearsed it."

"I believe I told you I read a great deal."

"Reading and possessing the ability to recite stanzas at any given moment are not the same skills. You continue to astonish me."

His compliment flooded her with warmth. Indeed, she could scarcely recall being cold earlier. From the moment she'd slipped off her dressing gown and stepped into the tub, she'd been all too aware of her "husband" in the dressing chamber. That had been enough to raise her body temperature. She reminded herself that he was playing a role, that none of this was real.

Jess moved to the side of the bed. "Where shall we sleep?"

"I was thinking the bed, since it's quite large enough."

Rolling her eyes with a half smile, Jess clarified. "Which *side* would you prefer?"

"Since you're over there, I'll take nearer the windows. Let me just put my wig and spectacles in the dressing chamber." He picked up his spectacles from the mantel and the wig from a chair near the hearth and walked past her.

When he emerged from the dressing chamber once more, he stopped short. "I thought you might already be in bed."

Well, of course she should have done. Instead, she'd just stood there like a halfwit. "Perhaps my brain is still affected from the cold." That was utter nonsense.

His gaze held hers. "This is rather awkward, in spite of our planning. The sleeping in the same bed, I mean."

"All of it, really." The memory of his hands on her calves and feet a short while ago hadn't made her feel awkward, however. She'd felt slightly dizzy and wholly wonderful. But it *was* awkward because she shouldn't feel that way. She couldn't. "Thankfully the bed can easily support the entire household."

Dougal laughed, showing his even, white teeth. "Just the same, I'd rather not invite them."

"A wise decision." Jess nervously chewed her lip. "I'd thought we would have to roll up a blanket to put between us."

He walked around to his side of the bed. "We still can, if you like."

She lifted a shoulder. "It isn't necessary. I'm a tidy sleeper. I expect you won't even realize I'm in the bed."

His brow creased, but his gaze flickered with amusement. "What does it mean to be a 'tidy sleeper'?"

"That was how my sisters described me when we shared the nursery. Their beds were always messy in the morning—pillows askew and coverlets twisted about. Half the time, Marianne had a foot or arm sticking out of the bed."

"I see. Well, I am neither messy nor tidy, I suppose. I am known to throw the coverlet about or deliver a well-placed kick. If my older brother was to be believed."

"Then I shall be glad there will be a wide berth between us."

They both stood there, looking at the bed, hesitating. Finally, he pivoted and extinguished the lamp on the bedside table.

Jess turned, putting her back to him, and put out her lamp. When she heard the bed creak slightly with his weight, she slipped off her dressing gown and laid it over the end of the bed. Then she slid between the bedclothes.

"What did you make of the Chesmores?" Dougal asked.

"I don't think I had time to form an opinion of Mr. Chesmore. I found their pet names…" She tried to think of a sufficient word.

"Amusing?" he suggested.

She smiled into the darkness. "Yes. 'My knight,'" she mimicked, dropping her Welsh accent as she tried to emulate the high pitch of Mrs. Chesmore's voice.

Dougal's laughter shook the bed. "Well done. You're quite

good at this. Have you thought of a career on the stage? You're able to memorize lines, and you have demonstrated a remarkable ability to act. I'd say you could make a go of it."

She wanted to ask what he thought of her acting specifically, but didn't dare. He was also very adept. Everything felt far more real than she'd imagined it would. She kept things light, which seemed the safest response. "I shall consider that if my spinsterhood proves tedious. Unless I'm fortunate enough to continue working for the Foreign Office."

"I'd recommend you wait and see if you like this. We've barely begun."

"True." She paused, thinking of the mission ahead. "I do think Mrs. Chesmore may be inclined to invite us to stay. She was most attentive."

"I would agree. Our primary goal tomorrow is to obtain that invitation and to have a tour of the house. That will allow us to know our battleground, so to speak. We should also try to learn how many servants are in the household— they are part of the field."

Jess nodded, even though he couldn't see her. That all made good sense. "We already know where their bedchamber is. And we can count two footmen, plus Polly and Ogelby."

"There is also Mrs. Farr, who I am keen to meet. We must ascertain if she is trustworthy. It won't do to just blurt to her that we are from the Foreign Office."

"What if we can't determine if she's to be trusted?" Jess asked.

"We'll conduct our investigation without revealing ourselves." Dougal exhaled. "Learning the location of the Chesmores' bedchamber was a stroke of good fortune. It gives me hope that Mrs. Chesmore's lips are rather loose with information."

"That's the impression I have as well," Jess said. "Naming the rooms also helps us keep track."

"It does. I am curious who the other writers are."

Jess was too. "I have to expect Shakespeare at the very least."

Dougal chuckled. "I suspect you're right."

"I suppose we should sleep." Jess yawned.

"We should," he agreed. "Good night, my pigeon." He barely finished the word before a laugh eclipsed it.

"Pigeon?" Jess giggled. "I think you must call me that tomorrow."

"And what will you call me?"

"In keeping with the animal theme, how about my stag?"

"Oh, that's majestic. I like it. Pigeon seems rather inadequate now." He fell quiet a moment. "How about my swan?"

Jess recoiled. "Swans are mean. I confess that's how I always thought of the other young ladies of the ton."

"Not that, then," he said. "I shall come up with something appropriate."

"I can hardly wait to hear it. Good night, Dougal."

"Sleep well, Jess."

~

*J*ess had been surprised that she'd fallen asleep quickly after climbing into the bed with Dougal. She hadn't even realized she'd been sleeping with another person. Thankfully, he hadn't snored.

Upon awakening, they'd donned their wigs, and he'd put on his spectacles. Then they'd rung for breakfast, dining at the table and enjoying the view of the sea.

They were mostly able to dress themselves, but Dougal had accepted her help tying his cravat, and she'd enlisted him to fasten her necklace. The word that came to her mind was one he'd used last night: domestic.

Pretending to be married was shockingly pleasant. They'd talked of writers over breakfast, speculating who else might be represented here in the naming of the rooms. Dougal was intelligent and charming, and she was gladder than ever that he hadn't turned out to be a boor, which she'd feared after their meeting at Lucien's.

They made their way downstairs. Ogelby stood in the staircase hall as if he were awaiting them.

"Good morning, Ogelby," Dougal said cheerily. "Have you been waiting for us?" His tone was teasing.

"Yes." The butler's short answer drew Jess and Dougal to exchange looks. "I'm to show you to the drawing room."

Ogelby turned and led them—glacially—through a sitting room with a pianoforte and some other instruments and then into a large drawing room. Windows faced the sea, along with two sets of doors that opened onto a patio.

Their hosts were seated close together on a settee. "Come and join us!" Mrs. Chesmore said.

Their settee faced the windows, which left a pair of chairs or a smaller settee for Jess and Dougal. She knew he would choose the smaller settee, for then they could also sit close together and demonstrate their affection.

They moved in concert to the second settee and sat down as one. Dougal put his arm across the back behind her shoulders. The bare flesh of her nape prickled, and she hoped he didn't notice.

"We can't thank you enough for rescuing us last night," Dougal said.

Mrs. Chesmore looked at them earnestly. "It is the least anyone would have done, isn't it, my knight?" She turned her head toward her husband.

"Without question, my minx." He pulled his gaze from his

wife and fixed it on Jess and Dougal. "My head groom is repairing the breeching strap on your gig, and your horse is well cared for. I trust you slept well?"

"Exceedingly, thank you," Jess responded.

"Your generosity is too much," Dougal said, placing his hand on his chest. "With the gig being fixed, we'll be able to continue on to Poole."

"Is that your final destination?" Chesmore asked. "My beloved said you were on a second honeymoon. What a splendid enterprise."

"We wished to spend time at the sea," Jess explained. "After we wed, we journeyed to the Lake District."

"How long have you been married?" Mrs. Chesmore asked.

"Two years," Dougal replied.

"Lancelot and I have been wed nearly five. We wanted to visit Paris, but the timing was rather poor." Mrs. Chesmore pouted.

"*Mais oui*," Chesmore said with a frown. "*La guerre stupide.*"

"Thankfully that is over now," Jess responded.

"*Parlez-vous français?*" Mrs. Chesmore asked excitedly.

Jess realized her error. She and Dougal were supposed to act as though they didn't speak French in the hope that the Chesmores might speak freely in French without realizing they were understood. "*Un plus*," she said, purposely using the wrong word.

"I think you mean *peu*," Chesmore corrected.

"Oh yes." Jess shook her head. "I wasn't very good at my French lessons, I'm afraid. What little I do remember, I am almost always getting wrong." She waved her hand with a self-deprecating laugh while mentally chastising herself.

A woman with dark blonde hair topped with a white cap entered. Her sharp brown gaze swung to Jess and Dougal.

"This is Mrs. Farr, our housekeeper," Chesmore said. He looked to her. "Some cake would not come amiss. And coffee, of course."

Jess exchanged a brief glance with Dougal. Now that they knew who she was, they would devise a plan to search her room and perhaps make inquiries with the other servants. Jess had no idea how they would accomplish all this under the noses of their hosts.

Mrs. Farr nodded at Chesmore, then returned her attention to Jess and Dougal. She dipped a brief curtsey before departing.

Chesmore took his wife's hand in her lap, his thumb caressing her flesh. It was somewhat distracting. Nearly everything they did was distracting. Jess had never met a couple like them before.

"My lamb and I were discussing your sudden arrival and agree the timing is too perfect to ignore." He exchanged a hopeful look with Mrs. Chesmore. "And now that we know your intent is to enjoy the sea, we would love to invite you to stay."

Jess turned her head to Dougal, who did the same. Giving an infinitesimal nod, Jess hoped Dougal would speak. She felt as though she'd already bungled things with the French and feared she might misspeak again. She was quite irritated with herself.

"We don't wish to be an imposition," Dougal said, swinging his focus to their hosts. "You've already helped us so much."

"This is the perfect place to enjoy the sea," Chesmore explained. "There's a path right down to the beach, in fact."

"That does sound tempting," Dougal murmured. He looked to Jess once more, "Darling?"

Before Jess could respond, Mrs. Chesmore interjected, "You must stay. We adore having guests. In fact, we're hosting a dinner party in a few days, and you simply must remain for that at least."

"You'll enjoy a much better aspect of the sea here than in Poole," Chesmore added.

"I think we should stay," Dougal whispered. He was so very good at this.

"All right." Jess smiled at him.

Dougal clapped his palm against his thigh. "It's settled. We shall be delighted to accept your kind invitation. We are overcome by your generosity." His eyes met Jess's. "Aren't we, my hummingbird?"

Jess had to bite the inside of her cheek to keep from laughing. She supposed it was better than pigeon. That he would think of her as something so dainty and elegant made her feel surprisingly giddy. "Most definitely."

"Brilliant!" Mrs. Chesmore laughed gaily.

"I wanted to ask you about the house," Dougal said, looking about the room with its predominantly pale blue décor. There was a wide fireplace with stone mermaids carved on each side. They held up the mantel on their hands, their hair flowing as if the wind was actually gusting toward them. "What little I've seen of it is stunning. There are so many details pertaining to the sea."

"You must have a tour," Chesmore said. "After we have our cake and coffee, we'll take you through it."

"That sounds lovely." Jess suppressed a shiver as Dougal's fingertips grazed the back of her arm.

Dougal settled his hand on her shoulder. "We're looking forward to hearing what writers you've named the rooms for."

Mrs. Chesmore laughed lightly. "It's silly perhaps, but we enjoy literature. And naming things. We still need a better name for the house, however. Seaview House is so uninspiring."

"Something from *The Tempest*, perhaps," Dougal suggested.

"Oh!" Mrs. Chesmore's blue eyes lit, and she snapped her head toward her husband. "Why didn't we think of that?"

"Prospero's Retreat," Chesmore said definitively, squeezing his wife's hand and lifting it slightly from her lap.

Mrs. Chesmore reached across herself with her other hand and clasped his upper arm. "It's perfect. Let's commission a sign for the gatehouse right away."

"Indeed." Chesmore bussed her cheek and nuzzled his nose against her temple. She leaned her head into him, welcoming his affection. They appeared as cats about to groom each other.

Mrs. Farr reentered with a tray, which she set on a table near their seating arrangement. She served up cake and started toward Mrs. Chesmore with a plate.

"Let's move over there." Mrs. Chesmore stood—and Chesmore quickly rose with her—and gestured across the drawing room, where a table was situated near another set of windows, much like the table in the Wordsworth Room.

Chesmore put his arm around his wife and escorted her. Dougal leapt up and helped Jess to her feet.

Jess resisted the urge to thank him profusely and throw her arms around his neck in abject adoration. "Thank you," she murmured.

"You need to regain your confidence," he whispered so softly she had to strain to hear. "I'm doing all the work here."

"I made a mistake." She clenched her teeth.

Barely moving his lips, he muttered, "Yes, and you need to get past it." He swept her toward the Chesmores, spreading his lips in a wide smile and clasping her waist.

Perhaps her failure of confidence was also due to his masculine attention. She'd never experienced anything like it before, and it was damnably disturbing. She couldn't afford to be unfocused.

Why did he have to be so handsome and so likeable? Why couldn't he be arrogant and rude as he had that first night at Lucien's? That would have made it so much easier to keep him at arm's length and to investigate him as she must.

But he *was* charming and attractive, and so far, she was enjoying the mission. Perhaps so much so that she'd forgotten she was on a mission, and she'd slipped up. She needed to pull herself together if she wanted to succeed, let alone a chance to do this again.

Now that she'd had a taste of a life on her own, she didn't want to go back to the way things had been before. She'd do anything to ensure that didn't happen.

CHAPTER 8

*D*ougal held the door to their bedchamber as Jess preceded him inside. "I confess I was torn between wanting to join the Chesmores for their walk on the beach and remaining here to search Mrs. Farr's room." The Chesmores had invited them while they'd been on their tour of the house.

She went to sit at the table by the windows. "Should I have gone with them?"

"I might have suggested it if I didn't need you to keep Mrs. Farr occupied." He joined her at the table. "Can you manage that?"

Jess grimaced. "Are you asking because of my earlier blunder with understanding them speaking French?"

Dougal had been surprised and annoyed, but only for a moment. She was new to this and had thus far performed with extraordinary calm and grace. He could see how much the error had bothered her. After that, she'd barely said anything, which was why he'd told her to regain her confidence. "Everyone makes a mistake now and again, including me." He couldn't help thinking of his failed missions last spring. Those hadn't been his mistakes, however. "The important thing is not to let it affect you. We must continue with our responsibilities. As to the matter at hand, I should have phrased my question differently. Do you have any reservations about detaining Mrs. Farr while I search her room?"

"I do not, thank you. What do you need me to do?"

"Find Mrs. Farr and keep her occupied for at least a quarter hour. You'll be doing more than just distracting her. Learn all you can so we can determine if she's trustworthy. We wouldn't want this to be a trap of some kind."

Frowning, Jess cocked her head to the side. "What do you mean?"

He lifted a shoulder. "There's a slim possibility that the Chesmores used Mrs. Farr to orchestrate this investigation."

"What would be the point of doing that?"

"Interrogating us for information. Planting bad information that we would then report to the Foreign Office. Other things I'm not thinking of at the moment." He looked up at the ceiling, pondering. "Ask her about the dinner party and the neighbors who will attend. Ask about visitors to Seaview Hou—" He caught himself, leveling his gaze on her. "Prospero's Retreat." He couldn't help rolling his eyes.

Jess laughed. "The look on Mrs. Chesmore's face when her husband tossed that name out... I've never seen anything like it."

"It was quite something," Dougal agreed. "Also, ask Mrs. Farr how long she's worked here and how many servants there are. After I search her room, I will go to the stable to see how many grooms there are. I'll also check on the horse and gig."

"I didn't realize you would count those who work in the stables. It's that important to know the number of servants?"

"Always. Think of what we do as a game of chess. You

must always pay attention to the pieces on the board. We've no idea how many servants there are—or how they are aligned."

"Simply counting them won't tell us the latter," she said.

"No, so we must assume they are not friendly. That is the always the safest path."

She nodded, her brow furrowing gently as it did when he imparted information such as this. It always appeared as if she were deeply pondering what he said.

"You listen in a way that is unparalleled," he remarked.

Her gaze snapped to his. "What do you mean?"

"You pay close attention, as though you really want to learn." He was surprised to find he was enjoying teaching her. If this was to be his last mission, it would certainly be memorable. For so many reasons. "I suppose I'm used to people thinking they already know things."

"You must talk to more men than women," she said wryly.

He couldn't help but laugh. "Probably." Definitely when it came to his work.

"Anything else I should know about talking to Mrs. Farr?" she asked.

He leaned forward in the chair, catching her gaze. "Don't act suspicious, meaning you can't just barrage her with questions. Make it conversational and easy."

"I can do that."

"You could even tell her we are thinking of purchasing our own coastal paradise, and you'd like to understand what it takes to run such a place."

She narrowed one eye at him. "You've done this before."

A bark of laughter escaped him. "Once or twice."

They fell silent a moment, both looking out at the sea. At length, she said, "Do you suppose they're actually writing poetry on the beach?" That's what the Chesmores had said they liked to do. Most days, they took an outing, either on foot or in their gig, and wrote their own poetry or sketched what they saw—whatever captured their fancy that day.

"What else would they be doing?" He knew what came to his mind given their excessive affection for one another, but wasn't sure that was what she'd be thinking too. He was fairly certain she was inexperienced. That didn't, however, mean she was ignorant.

"Gathering information to pass to the French? Drafting coded messages with that information? Thinking of new and more nauseating pet names for each other?"

Dougal snorted. Either she hadn't thought what he had— that the Chesmores were shagging each other silly—or she didn't want to say it aloud. Either was fine by him. Avoiding conversations about sex seemed a very good idea given how attractive he found her. And the fact that they were sharing a bed. Though it was as wide as the Thames, he was more than aware of her presence.

"Speaking of that, you almost provoked me to laugh when you called me hummingbird."

"I thought it was better than pigeon. Was I wrong?"

"Not at all. It's still funny. Can we stop with the names? Or just pick one and stick with it so I'm not thrown off?"

"My apologies. I am not used to having a partner." He supposed he was an amateur in that respect, just as she was. "I will endeavor not to cause you to break character. Hummingbird you shall be from now on."

She shook her head with a faint smile. "I suppose I shall continue to call you my stag."

"The Chesmores seem to like it when we are as affectionate and intimate as they are. Do you see how Mrs. Chesmore in particular seems to shine with delight?"

"I do," Jess said with a resigned sigh. "I find it strange, but we must do what is required."

Dougal decided it was the perfect moment to further

discuss that expectation. "It may very well be necessary for me to do more than put my hand on your shoulder or stroke your arm."

She looked out the window once more. "So I gather. Last night, you kissed my temple."

He had, and she hadn't flinched. "Yes, that sort of thing. It seems you are well prepared for that, then."

"I'm trying to be."

What if he had to kiss her? On the mouth? She'd been betrothed, however briefly, but that didn't necessarily mean they'd kissed. "Jess, have you been kissed before?"

"Yes. I've also done the kissing." She glanced toward him with a slightly perturbed expression. "Women are not just recipients of men's desire."

That made Dougal flinch. "I didn't mean to imply that. Since you're no stranger to kissing, perhaps you might even feel comfortable bestowing affection on me if it's appropriate."

"I can do that."

He kept thinking of what she'd said—about women being on the receiving end of something in which they weren't an equal partner. "I'd like to think of kissing as a meeting of two desires, the manifestation of a sensual, mutual attraction." Now he was looking at her mouth again, thinking of sharing such a kiss with her.

She stared at him a moment, her eyes taking on a hazy glow. "That's lovely." She blinked, adding, "You should repeat that to Chesmore. Perhaps he'd write it into a poem."

Dougal grinned, grateful for the humor to push aside his swelling feelings of lust toward her. They had no place on this mission. Too bad because pretending to be intimate with her was proving quite easy. Imagining it was even easier.

He stood. "Time to determine if we can trust Mrs. Farr." He

held out his hand and helped Jess to her feet. "I'll follow covertly as you go in search of her. Once you find her, I'll make my way to her chamber in the servants' area on the lower floor. I expect the housekeeper's suite to be located there."

"This work is quite fraught with risk," she said.

"I will admit that luck is often necessary. After you do it for a while, you'll learn to make it."

She strode past him on her way to the door. "I can't wait to learn how to do *that*."

~

*L*uck, as it happened, was watching over them, for Jess encountered Mrs. Farr in the sitting room with the pianoforte. She was arranging fresh flowers as Jess entered.

"Those are lovely, Mrs. Farr," Jess said loudly so that Dougal could hear and know she'd found their quarry. "The gardens here are stunning. How many gardeners are necessary to keep everything up?"

Mrs. Farr looked up from the vase as she finished her arranging. "Just Mr. Timmons. I'll pass along your compliments." The housekeeper was close in age to Jess. That made her seem easier to talk to, which consequently calmed Jess's nerves.

"You must also give my compliments to Polly. She was so helpful last night. I haven't seen her yet today and wanted to thank her again."

"She spent the day with one of the other maids and a footman gathering supplies for the party. When she returns, I will pass along your kind words." Mrs. Farr pivoted away from the table where she'd set the flowers.

"About the party, will it be very large?" Jess asked. "I hope you don't mind my asking. Sometimes I find crowds intimidating." She smiled sheepishly.

"No, not large at all. Perhaps ten people. Twelve, now that you're here. It will be quite manageable."

"That sounds lovely. I did wonder how many servants are employed here." Jess moved closer to the housekeeper. "You see, Mr. Smythe and I are quite taken with Prospero's Retreat and are now thinking we might like our own house on the coast."

Mrs. Farr's brow creased. "Prospero's Retreat?"

Jess realized the woman likely didn't know about the name change since it had just happened earlier in the day. "It seems the Chesmores have been trying to think of a new name for the house. It's rather fanciful, isn't it?"

"Yes. Which is completely fitting for Mr. and Mrs. Chesmore," the housekeeper said. She glanced away as a bit of color dotted her cheeks. She likely realized she perhaps should not have said that.

"I find the Chesmores to be *quite* fanciful," Jess said, hoping to put the woman at ease. "And rather, ah, affectionate." This wasn't what she'd planned to say at all, but Jess was learning to take cues from those around her and go where the moment led, if that made any sense at all, and she wasn't sure it did.

"Yes." Mrs. Farr looked as if she might say more but didn't.

Jess didn't blame her. Still, Jess needed to know if she and Dougal could trust the woman. "Have you worked for them long?"

"No, I was hired shortly after they purchased the house."

"Is that true of most of the servants here, or did they come with the house? I ask because I wonder if that's what I should expect as we look for property."

"I suppose it's different for every house, but yes, most of

the servants here worked for the previous owner, Monsieur Dumont."

The previous owner had been French! It could mean nothing, or it could be important. Jess could hardly wait to tell Dougal. "Why did Monsieur Dumont sell?"

"What have we here?" Mrs. Chesmore's birdsong voice carried through the sitting room.

Jess managed to keep herself from jumping in surprise. Mrs. Farr's eyes rounded, however.

"Mrs. Farr was just telling me about the house." Jess clasped her hands and smiled broadly. "I'm afraid I was interrogating her because Mr. Smythe and I are smitten with your lovely home. We think we may want one of our own here in Dorset."

"How splendid!" Mrs. Chesmore moved swiftly to Jess's side and swept her to a settee. She looked to Mrs. Farr. "Tea, if you please, Mrs. Farr. It was intolerably windy on the beach, so we cut our jaunt short. I could do with something to warm me."

The housekeeper nodded and left. Jess hoped she'd given Dougal enough time. If not, at least the housekeeper wouldn't be going to her chamber.

It seemed Mrs. Chesmore hadn't overheard anything, or if she had, she wasn't perturbed by it. Still, Jess felt compelled to compliment the housekeeper. "Mrs. Farr seems very capable."

"She is, in spite of her young age. The former housekeeper that worked here when we purchased the house disappeared not long after we arrived."

Jess's interest piqued. "What do you mean she disappeared?"

"Just that. One day, she simply left. No one knows precisely when she departed or where she went. She was there at breakfast and then gone before luncheon."

"I presume her things had gone too?"

Mrs. Chesmore nodded. "Yes, it was very strange. I wonder if she just didn't like us." She sniffed. "That happens sometimes," she whispered.

Jess had the sense there was more to that story, but wasn't sure this was the right moment to pry. She'd store the information away for another time, after she'd gotten to know Mrs. Chesmore a little better.

"Well, *I* like you," Jess said, perhaps because of the forlorn expression that had passed across the woman's features. Truthfully, she could like the woman. But that would be difficult if she turned out to be a French spy. "I wondered if we might take a picnic to the beach tomorrow if the weather is fair."

"A spectacular idea and one I should have suggested. However, tomorrow is typically the day my knight and I shoot on the beach. We do it weekly when the weather permits."

"Shoot what?" Jess kept her voice innocent and inquisitive despite being aware that they went shooting.

"At a target, of course. My knight possesses a number of firearms—rifles, pistols."

"Does he like to hunt?" Jess asked.

Mrs. Chesmore smiled brightly. "No."

That wasn't at all odd. "He simply likes to shoot at targets?"

"He's quite good. He taught me, and now I'm accomplished too—so my knight tells me." She reached over and patted Jess's arm. "You and Mr. Smythe are welcome to join us. Does he shoot?"

"Yes." They hadn't discussed it, but since he'd served in the Black Watch, Jess felt comfortable saying he did. She just hoped Mrs. Chesmore wouldn't ask if he was any good, because that she couldn't answer. She supposed she could say he was terrible and just tell him to shoot badly. Yes, that was what she would do if necessary. "We'd love to accompany you."

"Wonderful! We'll bring a picnic too. Why not? We shall pray for a nice day."

Mrs. Farr returned with tea and biscuits, and Jess transferred the remainder of the questions she'd planned to ask the housekeeper to her hostess. And instead of praying for good weather, she hoped Dougal achieved what he needed.

⁓

*J*ess had just donned her dinner wig when she heard Dougal enter the bedchamber. Hurrying from the dressing room, she stuck the final pin into her hair as she made her way to greet him.

"Is everything all right?" she asked.

He'd removed his spectacles and was once again massaging the bridge of his nose. "Yes, and you?"

"Fine. I didn't expect you to take this long."

Setting the spectacles on the mantel, he sat to remove his boots. "I didn't either. I confess I spent more time in the stables than I needed to. The two grooms liked to talk."

"Isn't that a good thing?"

"Typically, but most of what they discussed wasn't anything I needed to know," he said wryly. "Hopefully, you had better luck with Mrs. Farr."

"I think so, but Mary interrupted us. For a moment, I was distressed that I hadn't given you enough time to search her room. Then Mary requested tea, and I knew Mrs. Farr wouldn't be going there."

"'Mary'?" he asked.

"Over tea, she asked me to use her Christian name. I felt I had to ask her to do the same."

"Definitely. At dinner, I'll make sure Chesmore and I follow suit." He stood from the chair. "You look as if you're dressed for dinner. Do you mind if I use the dressing room to change?"

"Not at all. I do need to touch up my cosmetics."

He moved toward the dressing room. "I'll be quick, and then you can come back in."

"Before you go, would you mind fastening the back of my gown?" She went to him and presented her back. Anticipation rippled along her flesh.

Wordlessly, his fingers went to work, closing the garment, but also lightly stroking her with his movements. She felt as if she could easily fall into a trance.

"I'll leave the door cracked so you can tell me about your conversation with Mrs. Farr. All finished."

She felt him step back and turned to thank him, but he was already walking into the dressing room. He left the door ajar, presumably so they could continue their conversation without speaking too loudly. Accordingly, she moved to stand near the doorway.

Taking a breath, she worked to banish the lingering sense of heated expectation. "Where was I?"

"You said you were concerned I wouldn't have time to finish my search of Mrs. Farr's chamber. As it happened, I didn't require much time because it's surprisingly spartan. I didn't find anything out of the ordinary."

"That's good, isn't it?" She tried not to think of him removing clothing even though that was precisely what he was doing.

"I think so. I took the opportunity to search everything I could below stairs. Again, there was nothing out of the ordinary, just the usual preparations for a social event. Then I went to the stables. My horse seemed glad to see me. As I mentioned, there are two grooms. I also met the gardener."

Jess heard him pour water and was now actively trying to ignore the fact that he was washing. Was he nude? She clasped her hands together, wishing she could move away from the door. Since she still needed to hear him, she was unfortunately unable to do so. "I was going to tell you I'd learned there was a gardener."

"Well done," he said with a warmth that fueled her confidence. "What else did you learn from Mrs. Farr?"

"Most of the household was employed by the prior owner and stayed on after the Chesmores purchased the house. However, Mrs. Farr was hired when the housekeeper left shortly after the Chesmores arrived."

"Did Mrs. Farr know why she left?" Dougal asked.

"I learned that from Mary, not Mrs. Farr. She said the housekeeper's departure was odd, that she simply packed her things and left one day without notice. Mary assumed it was because she didn't like them." Jess still felt bad about the tinge of sadness when Mary had said that.

"Perhaps because of their eccentricity," he said.

"Probably, but I didn't ask." She should have, she realized. "Anyway, what I thought was most interesting was what Mrs. Farr revealed about the prior owner. He was *French*."

A moment later, Dougal peeked his head around the doorframe. She saw his bare shoulder and knew that he was at least shirtless. "Indeed? Did you get his name?"

Jess swallowed and averted her gaze from him. "Monsieur Dumont. Unfortunately, I didn't learn anything else. That's when Mary interrupted our conversation."

"Good work." He disappeared into the dressing chamber once more.

Pacing to the window, Jess pressed a hand to her flushed face. This would not do! They were partners working in concert, not actually husband and wife. And yet it felt so very intimate as they spent so much time in each other's company and did all these...*intimate* things together. She needed to gather her wits and stop being distracted by her attraction to him. *He* wasn't having this problem, and neither should she.

His voice carrying from the dressing room startled her. "I should love to know why Monsieur Dumont sold the house and where he is now. Perhaps he simply hired the former housekeeper away."

She strolled back toward the dressing chamber, but still kept her distance from the door. "I suppose that's possible, but why would she leave without notice, without saying a word at all?"

"I wonder if Ogelby might know anything."

"It seems Ogelby is somewhat of a titular head of the household," Jess said. "I got Mary talking about the servants, and she confided that they don't have the heart to send him into retirement. He's very slow, but he's apparently worked here his entire life."

"I shall definitely speak with him then," Dougal said. "What was your general sense of Mrs. Farr? Or did you not have enough time to speak with her?"

"She seems as baffled as we are by the Chesmores' behavior. I mentioned the new name of the house, and she hadn't heard it. I suggested it was fanciful, and she agreed. It seemed to me that the Chesmores may make her uncomfortable."

He emerged from the dressing chamber dressed entirely except for his cravat, which hung loose about his neck and his coat. "Would mind tying my cravat again? I am woefully inadequate when it comes to fancier styles."

"I don't think I'm much better," she said with a laugh. But she also wouldn't turn down the opportunity to touch and be close to him. Keeping her attention entirely on the cravat, she moved as quickly as she dared.

"Do you think we can trust the housekeeper?" he asked.

She lifted her gaze to his. "You're asking *me*?"

"Just trying to get your impression. It's probably too soon to say yet."

Moving her focus back to his cravat, she quickly finished and stepped back. "What should we do, then?"

"We can try to find a coded letter without her assistance." Dougal went back into the dressing chamber, and she followed him to reapply her cosmetics for dinner. "It would be far more efficient to just get it from her, but I suspect I'll need to search the William Blake Room. Probably sooner rather than later. I'd like to get you started on breaking the code." He fastened a jeweled pin into the cravat.

Jess sat down at the dressing table and started with her brows, ensuring the auburn was evenly applied. "I'm anxious to get started too."

He stood and watched her for a moment, making her feel self-conscious. She turned her head. "What?"

"Nothing, just watching you work. You've become rather accomplished in a short time."

"I had to, didn't I?" she said with a smile.

"Yes, but you absolutely rose to the occasion. Not everyone would have been able to do that."

She went back to her application. "I'm still learning, but I appreciate your confidence in me. There is more from my tea with Mary. If the weather is fine, we are to take a picnic to the beach tomorrow and practice shooting. They shoot at targets every week."

"They both shoot?"

"Yes, Mary said her husband taught her. I thought it would be a good time for you to teach me as well. She said they have plenty of guns."

"I have my own gun with me, but I won't reveal that to the Chesmores."

She paused in applying the color to her lips and turned to face him. "You do? You haven't mentioned it before."

He shrugged. "I always carry one on a mission. It didn't occur to me to tell you. My apologies."

Was that suspicious? Jess had no idea. She didn't like him keeping things from her, but was that because she was supposed to be learning everything about him in order to investigate whether he was working against the Foreign Office? Or was it because she felt a connection with him that invited full disclosure and sharing? It was an entirely artificial connection, and she needed to remember that. "Should I have a gun?" she asked.

"Not until you can shoot," he replied with a laugh.

"Where do you keep yours?"

"I carry it with me unless I'm sleeping, and then it's in the bedside dresser. It's currently tucked beneath my waistcoat." He touched his hand to his left side close to his arm. "I brought a small pistol for this assignment."

"Have you ever had to use one on a mission?"

"Do you really want to know the answer?"

She turned back to the mirror to finish her lips. "Probably not. For then I shall want to hear the details, and you'll refuse to tell me. It's best if my curiosity is only partially piqued."

He didn't respond, and when she glanced toward the door, she saw that he'd left the dressing room. She set down the lip color and stared at her reflection. They were barely one day into this performance, and she was already having a hard time separating the fabricated from the reality.

She was going to need to find a way to keep her thoughts from wandering in inappropriate directions. How was she to do that when she suspected they were only going to grow closer?

CHAPTER 9

*L*ater that night, Dougal poured two glasses of brandy in anticipation of Jess finishing her toilet. He'd already prepared for bed. They took the dressing chamber in turns, and she'd insisted he go first tonight.

Before she'd gone into the dressing room, he'd unfastened her gown, which had been even more taxing than when he'd fastened it earlier. Temptation had overwhelmed him as he'd closed up the gown, but tonight as he'd exposed her flesh instead of covered it, his body had flushed completely—and hotly—with desire.

He'd spent the many, many minutes she'd been closeted in the dressing room imagining that he'd finished the act of disrobing her. In his mind, he'd stripped her bare, one garment at a time. And that was how he'd come to pour brandy. He needed something to do besides lust inappropriately after his partner. He also needed his erection to go away before she finished.

Jess emerged from the dressing chamber with a freshly scrubbed face and without her wig, her natural brown hair neatly plaited and hanging over her shoulder so the end caressed her breast. Just as he'd regained control of his body, he lost it again. He was grateful he was sitting at the table near the windows.

Averting his eyes, he sipped his brandy to distract himself. As she approached, he nodded toward the glass he'd poured for her on the opposite side of the table. "Their French brandy is excellent."

"Another piece of evidence against them?" Jess asked, sliding onto the chair.

"Hardly. Many people have French brandy."

"Yes, but do they speak more and more French as they fall deeper into their cups?" she quipped, referencing Gil's behavior tonight.

They'd had an excellent madeira at dinner, and he'd drunk several glasses. Then there'd been port followed by the same French brandy he and Jess were sipping now.

"I don't. Do you?"

Jess picked up the brandy and inhaled its scent. "I haven't tried. I only had two glasses of wine at dinner, and I didn't finish the port."

"I think it's safe to say most would not lapse into French unless it was their native language." Dougal sipped his brandy.

"Gil demonstrated that for him it is *not*. Honestly, it was difficult not to correct him." She tasted the brandy and set the glass back on the table.

Dougal chuckled. The man's French had become more and more inaccurate as his alcohol intake had increased. "I don't disagree. Sometimes in this profession, it can be almost painful to suppress certain skills or knowledge. On one assignment, I had to act as if I knew nothing about swords and knives. I had to spend hours listening to a blatherskite tell me about his varied collection of rapiers, cutlasses, and on and on. It was positively grating. I can tell you I drank a fair amount after that. After the mission concluded, I mean."

Her brows rose. "Blatherskite?"

"Have ye not heard o' that?" Dougal allowed himself to revert into a full Highland brogue before shifting back to the Welsh accent. "It's from a song. 'Jog on your gait, ye blatherskite, my name is Maggie Lauder!'" he sang, laughing at the end before taking a drink.

Jess smiled. "I am not familiar with that. You've a nice singing voice. Is a blatherskite someone who talks too much?"

"Yes, and like me, Maggie Lauder would prefer him to move along than waste her time. But I suppose we must be grateful for blatherskites in this profession."

"Would you describe Mary as that?" Jess asked.

"She does like to talk. Especially to you," he added, recalling how often the two women had bent their heads together over dinner. "It seems you are beginning to like Mary."

"I'm afraid I am," she answered sheepishly. "I know I shouldn't."

He remembered what Jess had told him about her conversation earlier in the day with Mary—when Mary had said their former housekeeper might have left because she didn't like them. "It's fine to like her. Just know that if she *is* a French spy, any affection you hold for her will not matter."

"I understand." She studied him a moment, her expression contemplative. "How do you manage all this subterfuge without becoming attached to people?"

"It's never been an issue. I suppose I've been lucky that my missions aren't terribly long. I concede this one is quite different from any other. The Chesmores are exceedingly friendly and…likeable." Then there was her and their pretend marriage that even after one bloody day felt far too real. "I might even allow myself to like Gil."

"It's hard not to. He's so gregarious." She gave him a slight smile. "I'm glad I'm not the only one who's fallen prey to their charm. But I will remain on my guard. If I were a spy, I'd employ an excess of charm to lull those around me into a sense of comfort and trust."

Dougal was impressed at how far she'd come in barely over a week. "You've proven rather adept at this position," he said. "I'm impressed with how you recovered yourself after the mishap with the French, and you did well gathering information this afternoon."

"Thank you. I only want to be of use and ensure this assignment is successful. I daresay I will feel more helpful when I have something to decipher."

That was also occupying his mind. "Yes, hopefully I will have a chance to search for a coded letter. I only hope there's one to find."

"Perhaps you should leave the picnic early. Say you're unwell."

"I don't want to miss the shooting." He wanted to observe Gil to determine the man's skill. "I need to teach you to shoot."

"That's true." Her lips curled into an alluring smile as she picked up her brandy and took another drink. He focused much too hard on the press of her lips against the glass. Then he imagined the slide of the brandy across her tongue, the taste of it in her mouth.

Dammit.

This entire exchange—sitting together, drinking brandy, conversing—felt incredibly normal, as if they did it every night. As if it were perfectly fine that he anticipated taking her to bed.

For the first time in his life, he could imagine a domestic

tranquility such as this. That didn't mean he wanted it, just that he could envision it. He could also see how it would appeal to some, provided they had the right mate. His aunt and uncle came to mind. They worked together, raised their children together, and provided warmth and love to the entire extended family, including Dougal. On the contrary, his parents had never been like this, and Dougal now wondered if his father had missed it. He'd never seemed unhappy, but Dougal knew how much joy his children gave him. Perhaps it had been enough to fill the romantic void of his loveless marriage.

Dougal shook the thoughts away. If he allowed himself to think of home and family, the grief over Alistair would come at him along with anguish over what was to come with his father, and Dougal had no time for that. He'd have to face it all soon enough when he left this life behind to settle into familial duty and—probably—domestic tranquility. No, not tranquility, but chaos. As Earl of Stirling, there were too many responsibilities and too many people. He took a long pull of brandy.

"I'm looking forward to tomorrow," Jess said, interrupting his thoughts, for which he was grateful.

"The picnic or the shooting?"

"The shooting, but both, really." She finished her brandy.

As she set the glass down, he reached for it, saying, "I'll take that."

Their fingers collided around the vessel. Her gaze lifted to his. She didn't withdraw her hand. Neither did he. A long moment stretched in which time seemed to float between them and stand still.

Finally taking her hand from the glass, she said, "I'm going to bed."

Dougal blinked, feeling, ludicrously, as if he'd tumbled back to earth. "Good night."

He busied himself with putting the glasses on the tray with the brandy bottle, which he'd moved to the table earlier. He didn't want to return it to the cabinet near the fireplace from whence he'd fetched it. That would take him closer to her side of the bed, and he would be too tempted to look at her as she removed her dressing gown.

This was a bloody mess. He couldn't spend the entirety of their partnership lusting after her. It was not only unprofessional, it was distracting. This was not how he wanted his last mission to be.

Did he really think this was the last one? Probably. That filled him with disappointment, which coupled with the grief he was holding at bay, threatened to send him into a state of anguish. He refused to let that happen. He did not allow emotion to rule him. Ever.

And he wouldn't let his sexual urges do it either. He could stop fantasticating about Jess, and he bloody well would. Immediately.

She'd already extinguished her candle and was curled on her side beneath the coverlet. After seeing her barely disturbed bedclothes this morning, he now understood what her sisters had meant by a tidy sleeper. He had a sudden desire to show her how best to thrash the covers.

So much for ceasing his lustful imaginings.

He quickly put his candle out and shrugged out of his dressing gown, laying it on the foot of the bed. He slid into the bedclothes, steadfastly ignoring the awareness that Jess was within reach. In a bed. Wearing very little.

He was fast becoming a beast.

Rolling to his side so that his back would be to her, he closed his eyes. He needed to sleep. He ought to be tired. There was much to do tomorrow. He was supposed to be conducting this investigation with haste so that he could return to London to get back to his other investigation.

Yes, think of that instead of Jess. He needed to look through reports at the Foreign Office, preferably without anyone realizing what he was doing. Luck, as he'd mentioned to Jess, would be required.

Oliver Kent had been dismayed at the failures of those two assignments, but he hadn't blamed Dougal—not for the worthless message he'd delivered or the death of Giraud. Dougal hadn't talked to Kent about his suspicions regarding someone working against the Foreign Office. There hadn't been time before he'd had to go to Scotland because of Alistair.

When he returned to London, he should speak to Kent as well as enlist Lucien's help. He'd wanted to do that before this mission but had decided to wait. He'd needed to put his focus on this assignment, particularly since he had a partner for the first time. A partner who was new to espionage.

Turning to his side so that he faced Jess, he made out her form on the other edge of the bed. She might as well have been across the channel. He stuck his leg out as he'd done the night before, as if he could possibly come into contact with her. By mistake, of course.

But she was too far away. As she should be. With each passing day, she became more of a temptation. He had to do everything in his power to resist.

❧

Jess clutched the thick thatch of his hair as he put his mouth on her breast, his lips and tongue teasing her flesh with a relentless hunger. She writhed beneath him, desperate for more. Opening her legs, she wrapped them around him and lifted her hips. He pressed down, his rigid cock gliding against her sex. "Yes, more," she moaned.

His hand slipped between her thighs and stroked her folds. She thrust up again and again, her release coiling within her. She could see the light, and beyond that, the stygian darkness that would envelop her in sensation.

She needed him now. Reaching between them, she found his shaft and guided it to her sheath, eager to join their bodies. He lifted his head and looked down at her, the gold flecks in his eyes shimmering with desire.

"Please, Dougal."

His hand covered hers, and together they slid him into her. The simple act of him moving inside her was enough to propel her to the light. It was right there—she need only step into it fully.

Suddenly, everything went dark.

Jess's eyes opened, and she stared up at the bed hangings. Then she realized her hand was between her legs, and her body pulsed with need. Oh God, what was she doing?

She'd been dreaming. She realized that now. Turning her head sharply toward Dougal's side of the bed, she held her breath. What had he heard or seen? Had she said his name aloud? Humiliation raced over her, changing the kind of heat in her body from sensual to humiliating.

Was he not there? She couldn't make out his shape, but there was barely any light in the room—just whatever the dying coals in the hearth provided. After blinking several times, she looked again. His side of the bed was empty.

Jess snatched her hand away from her sex, despite the fact that she hadn't found her climax. She couldn't bother with that now. Dougal was likely in the dressing chamber.

She sat up and perused his side of the bed. The coverlet was folded back, and his dressing gown was gone.

Frowning, she slid out of the bed and grabbed her dressing gown, throwing it around herself before going to the dressing chamber door. It was ajar, and there was no light coming from inside. Still, she looked. He wasn't there either.

Agitation curled in her gut, driving her to pace to the windows, where she pulled back the edge of the curtain and looked toward the beach. Did she think he'd gone outside?

She moved away from the window and went to his side of the bed, noting that his slippers were also missing. Her gaze strayed to the bedside table. Looking toward the door, she carefully eased the drawer open.

Why am I trying to be quiet? And why would I care if Dougal came in and found me looking to see if his gun is also missing? He's the one who left without saying anything.

Blowing out a breath, she pulled the drawer all the way open. There was no pistol. Where the devil had he gone with a gun?

Jess closed the drawer. Should she go look for him? Had something happened?

Just then, the door opened, startling her. Her body flinched, and she walked around the bed as Dougal stepped inside and closed the door.

"You're awake," he said, his gaze moving over her before jerking back to her face in surprise.

"As are you. Where did you go?"

"I heard a noise in the gallery, so I went to check. It was Mrs. Farr. She'd dropped a tray. It was quite fortuitous because as I helped her tidy the mess, our conversation led to her disclosure that she wasn't sure how much longer she'd remain in the Chesmores' employ. I asked why, and she said she wasn't sure she suited them. I pressed further, and she revealed what you had already astutely determined, that they make her uncomfortable. I asked her some questions that would encourage her to reveal more about herself and found her very credible. I decided in that moment to tell her we are from the Foreign Office."

"How could you be sure she is trustworthy?"

He shrugged. "I've been doing this long enough to get a sense of when someone is lying or being evasive and when they are telling their truth. I could see her discomfort in addition to hearing her say it. It did not appear artificial to me."

Jess was disappointed she hadn't been there. She wanted to learn all she could, and that included how and when to reveal yourself to someone whose help you wanted. "What was her reaction?"

"She was quite surprised, as you can imagine. Mostly, she was relieved. She is going to look for the coded letter and deliver it to us. The one she found that prompted her to write to the Foreign Office was in Mrs. Chesmore's bedside dresser." His gaze met hers. "What awakened you?"

"A noise, like you," she fibbed. She certainly wasn't going to tell him the truth. "I was exceedingly concerned when I realized you weren't here. Why didn't you wake me?"

"I didn't think it was necessary. It was just a noise."

Jess couldn't ignore the niggling sensation at the back of her mind that he wasn't telling her something. Was that because of her bias, which she owed to the Foreign Office for asking her to investigate him? Or was she discomfited because she wasn't telling *him* something? Namely, the fact that she'd been about to pleasure herself while thinking of him.

She refused to think it was the latter. Revealing her growing—she had to accede that's where things seemed to be —desire for him had nothing to do with their mission. Whatever he might be keeping from her did. It wasn't as if he was harboring the same passionate thoughts toward her. He was far too professional for that.

"We should get back to bed." Dougal moved toward her,

and for the briefest moment, she wondered if he was going to embrace her.

He is not, you flibbertigibbet! He simply wants to get to his side of the bloody bed.

She turned sideways, so he could pass her more easily, and his arm grazed her breast. He moved quickly past. Did he know where he'd touched?

The heat and need that had faded since she'd awakened came rushing back, reminding Jess that she hadn't ever found her release. Turning her back to him, she scowled briefly as she returned to her side of the bed.

"Next time, I'd like if you could wake me," she said as she climbed into the bed and drew the bedclothes up to her chin. "It was rather unsettling to find you—and your pistol—gone."

"I'm sorry to have concerned you. I'm not used to informing anyone of my activities, but I'll do better."

It was a convenient excuse. He could have gotten up to do any number of things. What if he was working with the Chesmores? What if he hadn't spoken to Mrs. Farr at all? What if she was part of this?

Clenching her teeth, Jess stared up at the bed hangings as she'd done when she'd awakened a short while ago. Only now, her body wasn't nearing a blissful climax; her mind was traveling a terrible path on which suspicion and distrust were the guideposts.

She didn't like those feelings *at all*. She wanted to trust Dougal. She wanted to be his partner.

Actually, she was beginning to think she wanted to be his lover.

CHAPTER 10

*T*he sun was bright overhead as they finished their beach picnic. Dougal tossed back the last of his ale and watched his "wife" talk animatedly to Mary. If she hadn't mentioned last night that she was beginning to like their hostess, he would have found her act utterly convincing.

Dougal couldn't blame her. Mary was most amiable—eager to please, cheerful, and eminently positive. They were odd traits for a spy, probably because she appeared as a person without secrets. What she showed you was entirely who she was. Or so it seemed. Perhaps *she* was the consummate actress.

Jess turned her head, and her eyes met his. One of her brows rose infinitesimally, as if she were asking why he was watching her.

Because I find you incredibly attractive. Because I can't not watch you. Because this pretend marriage is far more enticing than I could ever have imagined.

He looked to Gil, who was reaching for more ale. "Time to shoot?"

"Definitely!" Gil refilled his tankard, then got to his feet and strode toward the shooting area that two of the footmen had set up. Dougal set his empty tankard down and followed him.

There was a table with an impressive selection of firearms—two rifles and four pistols. Thirty yards or so distant, the footmen had set up three posts with a rope joining them—perhaps twenty feet between the two outer posts, with the third in the center. Targets hung at intervals —pieces of wood or clay. Some were as large as ten inches across, while others were no bigger than four. It appeared as though Gil took his shooting very seriously. In any other situation, Dougal would have enjoyed this activity immensely—both the discussion of the weapons and the art of the sport. However, that was not the purpose of this endeavor.

Gil set his tankard on the table. "What do you like to shoot?"

"Anything, really." Most of Dougal's experience, of course, was shooting military weapons, which weren't widely available. The army didn't let you keep your gun.

"Did your father teach you?" Gil asked.

"He did, in fact." Dougal typically relied on details from his own life rather than fabricate everything. It was easier to remember things that way. He thought of his father teaching him and Alistair to shoot. "I shot my first stag when I was eight."

Gil's shoulder twitched. "My father used to take me pheasant hunting. I'm afraid I never took to shooting animals, though I was quite good at it. I do enjoy the sport of hitting a target."

The ladies joined them. Mary went to her husband and clasped his arm while pressing against him as she was wont to do. "Is my knight boring you with the details of his weaponry?" She smiled up at Gil, who quickly pressed his finger to her nose as if she were a kitten or a puppy.

"Not at all," Dougal answered, sliding his arm around Jess's waist as she came to his side. It was such a natural movement and felt so right that he could actually believe they were wed. He looked to Gil. "You've a nice collection here." Dougal's attention went immediately to what looked to be a French double-barreled flintlock. "Where did you get that?"

"Spectacular, isn't it?" Gil said with obvious pride. "It is a copy of one in Napoleon's private collection."

"Do you suppose he was allowed to keep that?" Jess asked with a laugh.

Dougal tamped down his admiration for her question and waited to hear how their host would answer.

"I can't imagine he was," Gil responded. "Though I have to think he did try!" He laughed at this, and Mary joined him.

Smiling to go along with them, Dougal couldn't make out Gil's personal opinion, which would perhaps tell them where his affinity lay. Not that he expected the man to openly admit he was working for the French. "Are you a supporter of Napoleon?" Dougal asked.

"Goodness no," Gil answered quickly, his expression horrified, as it should be as an Englishman. But was his reaction genuine? "I am passionate about many French things, however, including that gun in particular. I saw a sketch of it a couple of years ago, and it swept me off my feet." He laughed and looked to his wife. "Not in the same way my mermaid did, however."

Jess had joined in with their amusement, but now wrinkled her nose. "I'm glad Napoleon is back in exile."

Mary nodded in agreement. "It is for the best."

Dougal couldn't tell if she believed that, but there had been no glances between her and Gil. They didn't seem at all uneasy or anxious about the topic at hand. Later, he would compliment Jess on the question. It was innocuous and yet about a subject upon which it was beneficial to see their hosts' reactions.

"How did you get it?" Dougal gave him a pleasant smile. "If you don't mind my asking. It's stunning."

For the first time during their visit, Gil shifted his gaze and appeared uncomfortable. "It was a special favor. I'd rather not say as I don't wish to cause trouble for the gentleman who procured it for me."

Probably a smuggler. Now Dougal was doubly curious. "What if I want one of my own after shooting it?" he asked jovially.

"Well, in that case, I could try to broker something for you," Gil said affably. "Is that what you want to shoot?"

"Yes." Dougal turned his head to Jess. In the glistening sunlight, the blue of her eyes made the sea pale in comparison. "I think you should shoot the simple flintlock since it's your first time."

"Whatever you think is best, my stag." She beamed up at him and pressed into his side.

God, she could completely distract him. The feel of her against him was a heady temptation. He could think of many things he'd much rather do on this fine afternoon than shoot.

"Do you mind showing us your skill?" Dougal asked. He was curious as to the man's abilities. One would think they would be excellent given his collection of firearms.

"Not at all. Allow me to demonstrate with the rifle first." Gil plucked up the gun on the far edge of the table. "I loaded it before you arrived," he explained, moving a few feet in front of the table, where he took careful aim.

"Which target do you mean to hit?"

Gil glanced toward him, a smile lifting his mouth. "Would you care to wager?"

"Not at all." Dougal wanted to know how good the man was—hitting one of those targets wasn't as difficult as saying which one he meant to hit.

"Third from the left," Gil said, indicating one of the smaller targets. A moment later, he squeezed the trigger. The wood splintered apart.

Mary clapped her hands. "Bravo, my knight!"

Gil turned and gave them a sweeping bow. "One more barrel, my pigeon. Your turn."

At the word pigeon, Jess gripped Dougal's arm and pressed her lips together. He watched her jaw quiver, and knew she was fighting back a laugh just as he was.

Taking the rifle from her husband, Mary offered up her cheek, which he kissed soundly. And lingeringly. Then he whispered something in her ear, and her lips turned up.

She took a similar position to her husband and stated, "Second from the right." This was larger than the one her husband had taken out. After a moment's concentration, she destroyed the target.

"*Bien fait!*" Gil called out. He rushed forward to take the rifle from her and handed it to one of the footmen. Then he swept Mary around in a circle before setting her down and dropping a kiss on her lips. Their casual display of affection would have turned every head in London.

"My goodness, that was excellent," Jess said. "Do you always shoot that accurately?"

"How can we answer that without appearing immodest?" Mary asked with a laugh.

"Yes, we always shoot that accurately," Gil affirmed. He grinned at his wife. "*Mon coeur* worked very hard to improve her skill. It does pay to practice every week." They exchanged adoring looks.

While both shots could have been flukes, Dougal was inclined to believe them, that they were both that good. Was it really just a pastime, however, or had they been trained to shoot like that? The fact that Gil had a gun fashioned after one in Napoleon's private collection lodged in Dougal's mind.

"Your turn," Mary said to Jess.

She laughed nervously, and Dougal wondered if that was real or improvised. "Oh no, I shall let my accomplished husband go first. I don't even know how to hold a pistol."

Gil picked up the double-barreled French pistol and handed it to Dougal. "It's already loaded."

Dougal took his hand from Jess's waist and transferred the pistol to it. He could shoot from either hand but preferred his right. Moving to where the Chesmores had fired from, he held up the pistol to test its weight. Should he choose a larger, easier target? That depended on whether he wanted to display his true skill or if he preferred Gil to think he wasn't as accomplished as he was.

"First on the right of the center post," he said. Taking aim, he fired and shot the clay disc apart.

"Well done!" Mary said, applauding once more.

"*C'est magnifique!*" Gil exclaimed.

"I think I would like one of these," Dougal said in appreciation. "If you could procure one for me, I'd be delighted."

Gil flashed a brief and perhaps slightly insincere smile. "Of course." He quickly turned to Jess. "And now your turn, madame."

Dougal had to wonder if the man realized how he might appear to others with his French speaking, French brandy, and French pistol procured under secretive circumstances. These things might be seen as unremarkable, but Dougal also knew they wrote coded letters and crept onto the beach late at night. While their investigation was by no means concluded, Dougal was inclined to believe they were, in fact, spies. But did they have a specific goal? Or were they biding their time until the next conflict inevitably broke out?

Jess went to the table and looked at the guns before raising her gaze to Dougal, who moved to her side. "Which one?" she asked.

He picked up the simplest. "This, I think." Like the others, it had been loaded already. "I shall have to teach you to load another time. Or after this first round." He placed his hand against the small of her back and guided her to the shooting area.

"The most important thing is to aim with your eye and not your hand. Move your hand to match your line of sight so you're pointing the pistol where you want to shoot." Dougal put the pistol into her hand and moved behind her, fitting his body to hers. Her floral scent filled his senses, and he had to keep himself from closing his eyes in sensual appreciation. He clasped the outside of her hand and raised her arm. "Lift it like this and point it at the target."

"Which one?" she asked, keeping her face directed toward the targets. "Please say that large one to the left of the post."

He smiled next to her ear. "Yes, that one. And don't be disappointed if you don't hit it."

She took a deep breath. "All right. I just pull the trigger with my finger?"

"When you're ready, yes. Do you have your eye on the target?"

"Yes." She adjusted the gun a bit to the right and raised it slightly. "I'm ready."

"Fire at your leisure, my hummingbird." He wished he hadn't said it. A slight tremor passed across her shoulders as she pulled the trigger. The ball didn't come close to her target.

Jess pressed her lips together and lowered her arm. "That was terrible."

"Might I offer some advice?" Gil stepped forward.

Jess turned toward him and handed him the fired weapon. "Yes, please."

Gil took the gun with a nod and returned it to the table. A footman immediately picked it up and began to reload it. Selecting another pistol, Gil came back, hesitating as he looked to Dougal. "Do you mind stepping aside?"

"Not at all." Dougal moved back toward the table.

Gil took up the same position as Dougal behind Jess. She was actually slightly taller than him, but he fit himself against her just the same. Indeed, he looked as if he were pressing more firmly than Dougal had done. He spoke softly into her ear, so that Dougal couldn't make out what he was saying.

Irritated, Dougal stalked to the blanket to refill his tankard. As he picked up the ale and cup, he watched Jess laugh at something Gil said. They looked annoyingly intimate, and jealousy spiked through Dougal, making him slosh ale over his hand as he poured.

He was being ridiculous. Gil was devoted to his wife. He was simply trying to help Jess.

Gil held her hand, his arm extended alongside hers. Then everything happened in a blur. She moved suddenly. The pistol fired. Dougal felt the ball whiz past his head.

What the absolute hell?

Dropping both the tankard and bottle without a care, Dougal strode toward Jess, who was staring at him, her eyes wide and her chest heaving. The pistol dangled from her fingertips.

"Are you all right?" She looked pale and terrified.

"I'm fine." Dougal took the gun and handed it to a footman. As Jess began to shake, Dougal gathered her in his arms and held her close, stroking her spine from the nape to the midpoint and back again. She looked more troubled than the night they'd arrived. "I'm fine. You'll be fine."

She trembled against him, her hands clutching his lapel. "I don't know what happened. Gil said something, and I startled. Why did the ball fire that way?" She looked up at him, stricken.

"Because you moved—your arm had to have moved," he said calmly, though he wasn't as completely fine as he let on. He'd faced danger before and accepted it as part of this job. However, things were different now. He was his father's sole heir, and he couldn't allow him to outlive another son, let alone his last remaining one. "It was an accident, and there was no harm done."

"But there could have been," she whispered, blinking back the tears that had gathered in her brilliant blue eyes.

"Shhh," he soothed her, despite the chill permeating his spine. "All is well." He kissed her temple and cupped the back of her neck, cradling her while he kept his other arm anchored around her waist.

She closed her eyes, and he felt a bit of the tension seep from her frame.

Dougal looked over her shoulder toward the table where the Chesmores stood together—she clung to his arm, and one of his hands covered one of hers. Gil appeared nearly as upset as Jess. Only nearly, because Dougal was certain no one could be as distraught as she was currently.

Jess slid her hands up to his neck, then cupped his jaw. "You're sure you're fine?" She searched his face, her features a mask of concern.

He stared into her eyes, and for that moment, the world fell away. It was just him and her, and the emotion churning between them.

Emotion?

"These things happen, my hummingbird," he said, reining himself back under control. Missions were no place for emotion of any kind, even in the midst of an accident. *Espe-*

cially in that instance. Steady nerves and common sense *must* prevail.

He brought his hands from her back and clasped her hands. Giving her a reassuring smile, he released her and stepped away, moving toward Gil.

"What happened when she fired?" Dougal cursed himself for his distraction with the ale. Because he'd been jealous. Proof that emotion could not be tolerated.

"I'm not certain. I said she was ready to fire at any moment. She pulled the trigger, and her arm went to the left —toward you." Gil cast a worried look toward Jess. "Is Jessamine all right?"

"A bit shaken up, but she'll be fine." Dougal didn't like Gil's explanation. Jess had said he'd spoken, and she'd startled. Why would she have done that based on what he said? There was more to this. And he'd be lying if he said he wasn't considering the notion that Gil had directed her to shoot in Dougal's direction. What if he suspected Dougal was here to investigate him? What if Dougal had been wrong about Mrs. Farr? What if she was working with them and had sent the letter to the Foreign Office in order to get investigators here so Gil could assassinate them?

Dougal's blood went cold. He'd never felt his mortality more keenly than in that moment. This *had* to be his last mission. For his father's sake.

He looked to Jess, saw her pallid expression, and wondered if it would be her last mission too. He needed to get her away from there. "If you'll excuse us, I think I'd better escort my wife to our chamber."

"Of course," Mary said, her brow deeply furrowed. She let go of her husband and hurried to Jess. "I'm so sorry. You mustn't blame yourself. Accidents can happen. When I was first learning, I shot a tree by mistake." She gave Jess a brief but substantial hug. "Please let me know if you need anything."

Jess nodded. "Thank you."

Dougal offered her his arm, which she took quickly and firmly—with both hands. They made their way up the path toward the house.

"What did he say to you that made you startle?" Dougal asked.

"I—I'm not sure. I'm having a hard time remembering." She paused, then turned her head toward his. "It wasn't what he said. It was his breath. I was so upset about nearly shooting you." She squeezed his arm. "I forgot. He breathed on my neck, and it startled me. Plus, it smelled very strongly of onions and ale."

"Should I call him out?" Dougal had an urge to laugh and an even stronger one to hit Gil.

"He didn't do anything wrong, just annoying. I was too nervous." Her shoulders drooped. "I feel like an utter failure."

"Stop that. I won't allow you to berate yourself." He pulled her with him along the path, eager to get inside, lest someone come upon them. "I am *fine*." He was getting there anyway. He wasn't sure what had rattled him more, the near miss or the realization that he *couldn't* do this anymore. "I won't tolerate indulging scenarios that didn't happen. It's a useless endeavor. You learned something, yes?"

"Not to ever fire a gun again."

They'd reached the garden and would be at the house in a few moments. "Nonsense, you must fire a gun again."

She shook her head vigorously. "Absolutely not. I'm a menace."

"Only if Gil is at your side. I will stand with you as I did the first time. You must regain your confidence, just as you did after that French business yesterday." Dougal opened the door to the drawing room.

She released him and walked inside. Joining her, he grazed the small of her back with his hand and guided her toward the staircase hall. "This is hardly the same thing," she protested.

"It is. You mustn't discount yourself. I was incredibly impressed with your question on the beach about Napoleon. Very well done, getting Gil to comment so we could see what he thinks of the man." He kept his hand at her back as they climbed the stairs.

When they reached the top, she paused. "You don't have to keep doing that."

"What?"

"Behave as if we're married when there's no one watching."

"What am I doing?"

"Touching me."

So he was. "I would do that for any woman I was climbing the stairs with." Except that wasn't true. He could think of times he'd ascended the Phoenix Club stairs with women he knew, and he hadn't touched them in any way.

They continued toward their chamber. He sought to get back to their conversation about Gil. "I confess that after today, I'm inclined to think they are working for the French."

"Because of the French gun?" she asked.

"Yes. The timing is suspicious since I revealed myself to Mrs. Farr last night." He'd learned not to doubt himself over the years, but his confidence had taken a hit—however slight —with the failed missions several months earlier.

Jess stopped and stared at him, her expression concerned. "Do you think Mrs. Farr alerted the Chesmores that we're from the Foreign Office?"

He ushered her toward the room. "Probably not, but we do need to consider every possibility."

Jess reached the door, and he hastened to opened it for

her. "How does he even know what guns are in Napoleon's private collection?" she asked, removing her hat and gloves.

"Exactly." Dougal closed the door firmly, and the tension he hadn't realized had built up in his neck released. Tearing off his own hat and gloves, he sailed them toward the bed. He massaged his nape and went directly to the bottle of brandy.

"I'll have one of those too," Jess said as she sat in one of the chairs by the hearth. "And don't be stingy." She'd unlaced her boots and kicked them off by the time he returned with the drinks. Accepting the glass from him, she smiled gratefully. "Thank you. You really think I should shoot again?"

He sat down opposite her near the hearth. "Perhaps not here, but yes. When we're back in London, I can even ensure you have lessons—in a safe environment."

"I'm not sure there is such a thing if I'm wielding a gun," she murmured.

He heard the humor in her voice and smiled. "You'll get back to it. You aren't the sort of person to quit something so easily."

"You think so?"

"Have you ever given up on a cipher?"

"No."

"And I imagine some of them weren't easy."

She exhaled. "No, they were not."

"I assumed as much. I know you, Jess, and you're tenacious."

"We haven't even known each other a fortnight," she scoffed. "Not officially anyway."

"What does that mean, 'officially'?"

She took a generous drink of brandy. "We *have* met before. Four years ago. I remember it distinctly."

"Four years ago?" Damn, now he felt terrible. "How can you be sure?"

She gave him a haughty look of certainty that quite

frankly pricked his desire. "Because I am. You asked me to dance at the Edgemont Ball."

He'd danced with her. Four years ago. And never again. Worse, he didn't remember it. He was an absolute cad. "I should have remembered you. I can't imagine why I didn't," he said softly.

Sentiment, which he preferred to indulge in small, manageable doses, threatened to send him to her chair, to take her hand and beg her forgiveness. A husband would do that. A lover. He was neither, and since they were alone, there was no reason to continue the pretense. Only, he was fairly certain he was no longer pretending. He was simply behaving as he ought. As he *wanted*.

He was saved from further reflection by something he saw out of the corner of his eye. "What's that on your bedside table?"

Jess stood, her features creasing as she made her way to the table. She set her brandy down and picked up the folded parchment, pivoting toward him. Opening it, her eyes scanned the paper. Slowly, her lips spread into a wide, satisfied smile.

"It's a coded letter."

CHAPTER 11

"Mrs. Farr must have brought it," Dougal said.

Jess stared at the numbers as her pulse quickened. A puzzle stretched before her, and she could hardly wait to solve it. Dougal joined her, perusing the letter over her shoulder. He was close, nearly as close as when he'd helped her to shoot. The memory of his body pressed against hers combined with his scent—sandalwood and the sea. If she inched back, she'd feel him again…

"I should get started. I'll copy it first so you can return this to Mrs. Farr. That way she can replace it, hopefully before the Chesmores realize it's missing." She left his intoxicating presence for the small desk in the corner. Perching on the small chair, she laid the letter flat on the desktop.

"How will you decipher it?" Dougal asked, moving to the table by the windows, which was behind her.

"I'll look for repetitive numbers, which are typically common letters such as a or e or s." Plucking a piece of parchment from the corner of the desk, she set it next to the letter. Then she grasped the quill and began studying the letter for repetitive numbers—both individual and groupings that could indicate entire words.

"I don't suppose you'd describe your methodology," Dougal said, interrupting her thoughts. "I'm quite keen to know how you work."

Jess turned her head to look at him. "I am flattered; however, now is not the time if you want me to work this out as quickly as possible. I shall be happy to share my process once I have broken it."

"Of course."

She nodded at him, then turned back to her work, copying the letter meticulously. The sound of his fingers drumming against the table interrupted her once more. Stretching her neck, she redoubled her efforts to remain focused.

A few minutes later, he stood and paced to the hearth, where he tapped his fingertips on the mantel. She slid a look at him. He'd braced his hands on the mantel, his body stretched so that he formed a triangle with the floor and fireplace. He seemed to brood into the hearth, as if something of grave consternation was located within.

At last, she finished her copy. "Here, you can take this to Mrs. Farr." She held up the original letter. "Then perhaps you should go for a walk," she suggested. If he didn't leave her alone, he was going to continue to distract her.

He pushed away from the fireplace and came to retrieve the letter from her. "Am I bothering you?"

"A little. I'm not used to interruption when I work on my puzzles." She also wasn't used to deciphering something of actual value. This wasn't an amusement; it was a vital piece of national safety.

"Of course, my apologies. I'm feeling unsettled after the shooting—and not because of what happened when you fired. I have questions about our hosts."

Jess understood, and yet she wasn't sure she believed him about her near miss. How could he not be upset by it? If he'd been standing just a little more to the left, she would have hit him. The thought made her stomach turn.

He'd said she should give it another try, but after that, she wasn't sure she could ever touch a gun again. She was also beginning to doubt whether this kind of work was right for her. What sort of spy was afraid of guns?

"I'll leave you to it, then," Dougal said, going to the door.

"What will you do after you return the letter?" she asked.

He lifted a shoulder. "Talk to the servants. Poke around in whatever rooms I can access. That sort of thing. Good luck."

"You too," she called after him as he closed the door.

She returned to the code for a few minutes, but her mind wandered back to Dougal. Perhaps he was the reason she was doubting herself. The more time she spent with him, the more she liked him, and the less interested she was in investigating him as she was required to do. She just couldn't see him working against the crown.

But what did she really know? He was an accomplished spy. Presumably, he could fool her with little effort. Honestly, it probably wouldn't be difficult since she was already completely dazzled by him.

Perhaps she ought to give him a fake version of the deciphered letter—one that would supposedly threaten the execution of a French plan. If he never turned it into the Foreign Office, that would prove he was working in contradiction. But how on earth would she come up with something like that? Furthermore, doing that would jeopardize their primary objective with the Chesmores. If she gave him something that incriminated them, and he wasn't working for the French, she would have damned the Chesmores.

She put her forehead in her palm. This was utterly overwhelming. Had Dougal ever felt this way? He'd been new to espionage once. She had to think he'd had misgivings.

Only, Jess worried her uncertainty came from a different place. She'd been positively thrilled to take this adventure. To serve her country in this way was the opportunity—and dream—of a lifetime. Why then was she more interested in the pretend part of the assignment? She'd begun to think marriage was not the trap she'd long envisioned. With the right person, perhaps it was even...attractive.

Bother, Mary and Gil's loving and companionable union was clearly having an effect upon her. It was much more acceptable to blame that instead of the comfort and ease of her fake marriage with Dougal.

She needed to put her job at the forefront, and that included investigating Dougal, not fixating on how she felt about him. Better to recall his suspicious activity, particularly the stealing off into the night with his pistol and hiding the fact that he'd brought it until he'd had to tell her.

Except he had perfectly acceptable reasons for everything he did. It wasn't as if he was the one who'd tried to shoot her. That would certainly have added to her doubt.

Letting out a groan of frustration, she redirected her attention to the letter. *This* was her primary purpose for being here—not investigating Dougal, not learning to shoot, and not anticipating the next time she'd have an excuse to touch Dougal or for him to touch her.

Definitely not that.

Jess put her quill to parchment and pushed him from her mind.

≈

*T*he house was quiet as Dougal prowled the library late that evening. The Chesmores had retired earlier than usual, and Jess had pleaded exhaustion after dinner so she could work on the letter. Dougal had avoided returning to their room so she could work in peace.

Or was he avoiding being alone with her in a small space that included a bed?

It was becoming increasingly more difficult to ignore his desire for her. He was also growing increasingly irritated with himself for his inability to separate his base urges from what should be a professional arrangement.

But he couldn't spend the night in the library. Sooner or later, he had to go to their chamber and fight temptation once more.

"Dougal?"

He whipped around at the sound of Jess's Welsh accent. She'd changed into her dressing gown and carried a candle. She hesitated just inside the library.

Moving toward her, he stopped in the middle of the room, worry coursing through him. "Did something happen?"

"No, I came to look for a book." She stepped farther into the library, her gaze fixed on him.

"What book? I'll help you." Anything to keep from thinking of her. From looking at her.

Her mouth twisted. "I'm not sure." She glanced toward the open doorways—the one she'd come through and another that led to a separate room.

Dougal quickly moved to close both doors. One of them creaked, and he winced, hating when houses made noise. It was incredibly unhelpful in his endeavors. He went to join Jess, speaking in a low tone. "Why do you think you need a book?"

"There's a key for this code. There are repetitive words that I think mean 'the' or 'and' or 'or'—those kinds of words that appear more frequently. If I could isolate those, that might help me determine letters, which I can then use to decipher the rest."

He nodded, admiring her intellect. "You think the key is a book." He stroked his chin. "They do like writers."

"Or a poem—any sort of writing. I believe they would use a key from something they love. Something by one of the writers the rooms are named after."

"An excellent notion," he said. "Shall we look?"

"Yes." She set her candle on a table. There were sconces on the walls and two chandeliers offering illumination, plus the fire. "Do you know where they might be located?"

"As it happens, I spent some time in here this afternoon while you remained in our chamber." Dougal went to a case where he'd seen Shakespeare and Wordsworth.

Jess looked at the shelf and groaned softly. "I am overwhelmed by the prospect of having to look through Shakespeare. All the plays *and* the sonnets."

"I would think they would choose one of the most romantic of the sonnets."

"That would make sense."

Dougal pivoted toward her. "Rather than randomly try things, perhaps we should ask the Chesmores what their favorite poems or books are. We'll need them to be specific."

She nodded with enthusiasm. "Brilliant."

The creak of the door signaled that someone was arriving —that was the only good reason for noisy houses. It wouldn't be strange for him and Jess to be caught here at this time of night, but the fact that he'd closed the doors would appear odd.

Instinctively, Dougal snaked his arm around Jess's waist

and drew her against him. "Just go along with me," he whispered. "Arch your neck."

Her eyes widened slightly and briefly before she did precisely as he asked, exposing the slender, delectable column of her neck. He could see her heartbeat in the vein just beneath her ivory skin, like a beacon. Dougal lowered his head and kissed her just there. She gasped softly, her hand clutching his nape. His body thrummed with want. It would be so easy to lose himself…

"Oh!" The feminine exclamation forced Dougal to—begrudgingly—lift his head.

Jess didn't immediately release his neck, which only stoked his desire.

The Chesmores, garbed in their dressing gowns, moved into the library. Mary's blonde hair was gathered into a queue with the long waves pulled over her left shoulder, making her look rather young.

"Goodness, didn't mean to interrupt," Gil said with a hearty chuckle. "I see we're not the only ones who find the library stimulating."

Mary cast a longing glance toward her husband. "We often come here to read and…snuggle."

Dougal was willing to wager a large sum they did more than snuggle. Shag was far more like it.

Jess released him and faced their hosts. Dougal also turned, but he kept his hand around Jess's waist.

"You're welcome to stay," Gil suggested.

"We really just came to find a book or two." Dougal exchanged a hooded look with Jess, assuming she had the same incredulous reaction as he had. What on earth was Gil expecting, inviting them to remain with them? It occurred to Dougal that the Chesmores might like to experiment sexually. Perhaps they regularly invited others to join them.

Dougal hoped the dinner party was just a gathering for *dinner* and nothing else.

"It didn't look like that was *all* you came for," Gil joked. He and his wife laughed, and Dougal resisted the urge to roll his eyes.

Jess straightened against Dougal's side. "If you could recommend one book, or poem—your *very* favorite—what would you have me read?"

"That's easy," Gil said. "Voltaire. The poem *From Love to Friendship*, to be exact." He put his hand to his chest. "Utterly sublime. I'm afraid I can't offer it to you at the moment as I keep it in my chamber."

Jess clasped her hands together and spoke eagerly, "If I could borrow it at some point, I'd love to read it."

"Well, that copy is in French, so I don't think it would help you," he said with a sympathetic moue. "There's a translated version around here somewhere. Voltaire is particularly dear to me because my great-grandmother met him in France." He said the last with more than a bit of pride.

His family was from France? "Is that why you're so fond of all things French?" Dougal asked. "Because your family hails from there?"

"I do realize we have not been on the best of terms with them, but that is my heritage," he said with a slight shrug.

Dougal stored his information, then looked to Mary. "What would you recommend?"

She tapped her finger against her lips.

"You are most distracting, my gosling," Gil teased before pulling her against him. "It's Wordsworth, of course."

Mary giggled. "Of course. Let me just fetch it. I was reading it earlier." She had to disengage herself from her husband, who pretended to hold her against him. He let her go with a jovial laugh, and she skipped away from him.

Dougal stared at their antics, marveling at the joy they shared.

After plucking up a thin volume from a table near a chaise situated by the windows looking out to the sea, Mary brought it to Jess. "Here you are. Some of my favorites. It has Coleridge too."

"Thank you." Jess took the book with both hands and held it to her chest. "I look forward to reading it."

Dougal looked to Jess. "Shall we, my hummingbird?"

She nodded and said good night to their hosts as Dougal escorted her from the library.

They didn't say a word until they were in their chamber and Dougal had closed the door firmly. He leaned back against the wood as Jess went to the middle of the room, between the end of the bed and the seating area before the hearth.

Swinging around, she stared at him a moment, her expression one of disbelief. Then she promptly burst into laughter. Dougal wondered if she'd lost her wits. But only for a moment, because he then laughed with her. Deep, belly-aching guffaws that made his eyes water.

Jess collapsed into one of the chairs by the fire, still holding the book. Dougal took the other chair and struggled to draw in a breath.

When they'd finally recovered, she wiped her hand over her eyes. "What was so funny?"

"I'm not sure," he said, regaining his composure. "I suppose it was Gil inviting us to stay and snuggle with them?"

"Do you think they meant for us to snuggle all together or that we should watch them snuggle? Or that we should snuggle separately?" She shook her head, still smiling. "They are the most interesting couple I've ever encountered. I can't fault them, for they are undeniably happy."

"I know, and I agree. However, it's...odd. They seem to have no care for propriety."

"Perhaps because they are in the privacy of their home?" Jess suggested. "I wonder how they behave in public."

"I would say we'll see at the dinner party, but that is also in their house, and they don't seem to mind what their guests think." Dougal couldn't find fault with that. To know oneself and be comfortable in one's skin was an enviable existence. Dougal hoped he knew himself, but after years of disguises and secrecy, he wasn't sure that was true.

Jess's eyes rounded, and she fixed a horrified stare on him. "What if the other guests are like them?"

Dougal snorted. "I wondered the same thing. Or something like it, anyway. I suppose we shall find out." He kept wanting to look at her neck, to the spot he'd kissed.

"Why did you kiss my neck?" she asked, startling him.

"I, ah, because I'd closed the doors. It might have seemed peculiar—not that we were there, but that the doors were closed."

She nodded. "That makes sense. But why not kiss me on the mouth?"

Oh God. Now he looked at her mouth, a focal point that often drew his attention. Her lips were always so pink and soft. Not that he knew if they were actually soft or not. They just appeared that way. And that was how he imagined them against his.

"I, well, it just seemed less...forward."

"None of it is forward," she said matter-of-factly, setting the book on a small table next to the fireplace. "You've said we may need to do things that married people do."

"Would you have preferred I kiss you on the mouth?" Dougal wished he could take the question back. What good could come of it?

She shrugged, standing. "You know I've been kissed before."

Yes, he knew that. Why hadn't he kissed her? It would have been the perfect opportunity to finally see what she tasted like. Perhaps then he could stop thinking about it. About her.

Except, if he kissed her, he wasn't sure he'd be able to stop with her mouth.

So you started with her neck? That makes no sense.

She'd walked into the dressing chamber while he'd been woolgathering. Now, she poked her head into the doorway, a hairpin in her hand. "I was just curious."

He got up and walked to the dressing chamber, leaning against the doorframe, watching as she removed her wig. "Next time, I'll kiss you on the mouth. Is that better?"

"It's not better or worse. As I said, I was just curious." She set the wig aside and uncoiled the braid from the back of her head. Then she unplaited the thick, light brown curls and shook the mass over her shoulders. Dougal stared, utterly captivated by her movements and her hair. His fingers itched to brush through it, and he longed to bury his face in the silken strands to inhale the sweet scent of her.

She'd tied it into a queue with a ribbon while he'd been fantasticating and now brushed past him to return to the bedchamber. Her arm had met his, and though layers of clothing separated them, he felt the connection deep into his bones. His body simmered with need as his cock started to rise.

This was *bad*. He braced his hand against the wall and tipped his head down, blowing out a pent-up breath.

She popped back into the doorway, making him jump back from the wall. "I am quite angry with myself. I should have asked Mary which of the Wordsworth poems was her favorite. And now I can't go back down because I've already taken my wig off." She frowned. "I suppose I could put it back on." She touched her head. "I just don't think I can, not after liberating my scalp. You could go?"

He shook his head without even pondering the suggestion. "Absolutely not. You couldn't bribe me to interrupt their 'snuggle.'"

She grimaced. "You make a good point. I'll ask her tomorrow. Still, I think I'll take a look at the book now. Are you going to bed directly?"

"I need to change for bed and wash up." Actually, what he really needed was for her to leave. His cock was not diminishing, and he feared he was going to have to satisfy his primal urges.

"Good, I can take some time to work on the letter without disturbing you."

"Stay up as long as you like. You won't bother me." That was a bald-faced lie. Whether she slept, sat at the desk, or danced around the room, he would be bothered.

"Thank you." She smiled at him, and that only increased his discomfort. When would she leave him alone? Apparently not soon, because she leaned against the doorframe as he'd done a few minutes before. "Are you still inclined to think they're spies?"

Dougal exhaled. "Gil clearly has an affinity for all things French. He speaks French often and possesses a French-made gun designed upon one in Napoleon's private collection. Then there is the coded letter. I'd say they look suspicious, but that's all it is so far—suspicion. Until that letter is deciphered, I don't think we can know for certain. I should also mention that we are trusting Mrs. Farr completely. She says she obtained that letter from the Chesmores' private things, but what if she's lying? Tomorrow, I must search the Chesmores' suite."

"You make excellent points," she said. "It's almost as if

you've done this before." The corner of her mouth lifted in a teasing smirk.

Why did she have to be so damned likeable? In addition to everything else: capable, adaptable...desirable.

"Do you need any assistance searching their rooms?" Jess asked.

"No, but I appreciate the offer. It will be better if you can keep them occupied."

"That makes far more sense. I'll leave you to it." She flicked a glance over him and abruptly spun about, leaving the dressing chamber rather quickly.

Dougal leaned around the doorframe and saw her pick up the book of poems on the way to the desk. Sitting, she opened it and began to read.

Dougal withdrew into the dressing chamber and closed the door. There was a lock, but he hadn't used it and didn't think she had either. What was the point when they knew the other was in here and wouldn't intrude? Even so, he locked it, setting the mechanism as quietly as possible.

He needed absolute privacy.

CHAPTER 12

*A*fter reading all of *Lyrical Ballads* last night, Jess had crawled into bed long after Dougal had fallen asleep. She'd watched him for a few minutes, his lashes dark and lush against his almond skin. Just looking at him had given her an ache, as if something was unfinished. Perhaps it was because he'd barely kissed her neck before they'd been interrupted. From the moment his lips had touched her flesh, a passion had ignited within her—and it still flamed this morning.

Why hadn't he kissed her on the mouth instead? She'd asked him and found his answer lacking. It was possible that contributed to her feeling unsettled. He'd said he would kiss her mouth next time. She only hoped there would be a next time.

Except it wouldn't be real. No matter how badly you want it to be.

He'd been gone when she awakened, which had been later than usual for her given when she'd finally gone to sleep. There had been a note, however, written in his strong, efficient hand, saying he went for a ride.

Glowering at the completely unhelpful book atop the desk, Jess had pulled herself from the bed, eaten breakfast, completed her toilet, and was now prowling the rooms at the back of the house, her mind churning with how to decipher the bloody letter. She needed to find Mary to ask which of the poems was her favorite. Without that, she would have to start imagining a key for the cipher, which was sometimes required. She'd have better luck finding treasure washed up on the beach.

From the sitting room, she looked out toward the sea. Dougal! He was coming up the path from the beach. The stables were quite removed from there. Had he gone riding and then gone to the beach? Or had he lied to her about riding and done something else entirely? She wished the Foreign Office had never asked her to investigate him. She didn't know how, nor did she want to.

Blowing out a disgruntled breath, she squeezed her hands into fists, then shook them out again. This suspicion coupled with desire was creating a cacophony of frustration in her brain. She didn't want either of those things. She wanted to be successful at this assignment. So far, she had absolutely nothing to show for her efforts, either with deciphering or her investigation of Dougal.

He was nearing the house. She moved away from the window quickly, not wanting him to see her.

"Jessamine!" Mary swept into the sitting room with a bright smile. "I hope I'm not disturbing you."

"Not at all." Jess was definitely grumpy, because her first reaction was to remind the woman that it was her house and she could do whatever she liked, particularly walk into a room. Instead, she kept her mouth clamped shut.

"I'm so pleased to have found you," Mary said. "Will you sit with me for a minute?" She went to a pale yellow and peach floral-patterned settee and sat, patting the cushion beside her.

Jess needed to tame her mind and focus on the objective at hand. She'd been looking for Mary, after all. "I'd be delighted." Summoning a smile, she sat next to Mary.

With her blonde hair artfully styled and a light gloss of cosmetic adorning her pretty face, Mary could very well hold her own in London. Jess idly wondered how she would be received there, particularly if she and Gil couldn't keep their hands off each other in public.

"I wanted to apologize about last night." Mary gave her a wan smile that barely signified as one. "I do hope we didn't make you and Dougal uncomfortable. We try to be very welcoming, and I realize we can be a tad enthusiastic. I'm also aware that our enthusiasm can be objectionable to some."

Jess felt trite for laughing about their…enthusiasm. It was awkward at times, but there was no harm in it. "You aren't to us. Truly." She patted Mary's hand to assert the sentiment.

Mary's features brightened. "That's lovely to hear. I must also apologize for interrupting the two of you. The doors were closed for a reason, and we should have respected that. I'm afraid Gil and I weren't thinking beyond ourselves." She waved her hand with a laugh. "I can only imagine what we intruded upon—it looked quite diverting." She waggled her brows at Jess.

It seemed as though Mary expected a response, so Jess said, "Ah, we finished what we started upstairs." She was suddenly quite jealous of Mary and Gil and their…enthusiasm. It was difficult to see them together and not envy their intimacy.

"I'll wager that was a delightful trip upstairs," Mary said with a knowing look. "There's nothing better than the anticipation between lovers just before you know you'll find release. The excitement is in the surprise of the act. What will it be to tease out each other's climax? A fast coupling or a lingering seduction? Gil was in the mood for fondling and mouth play. What was it for the two of you?"

Mary spoke candidly, as if this were a normal conversation between married women. Jess couldn't say as this had *not* come up in her tutelage with Evie. Perhaps it might have if their conversation about bedchamber behavior hadn't been interrupted.

Jess's brain fixed on the words fondling and mouth play. The only "mouth play" she'd experienced beyond kissing was what Dougal had done to her neck last night. However, she knew what else could happen, that men put their mouths on women's breasts—she'd dreamed of Dougal doing that—and on their sex. This time, there was no stopping the heat that rushed to her face.

"Oh dear, I've embarrassed you." Mary wrinkled her face up and closed one eye. Then she blew out a breath and relaxed her features. "Again, my apologies. I'm accustomed to sharing those sorts of intimacies with my married friends, but perhaps you are not."

"Ah, no." Jess wished she could lie, because she desperately wanted to hear more. "I'm afraid my married friends are more conservative than you and Gil. Is your marriage what you imagined? What I mean is, you must have had examples of close, loving relationships."

Mary glanced toward the doorway, then lowered her voice. "I'll tell you a secret: I'd vowed never to wed because my mother was so dreadfully unhappy in marriage."

"What changed your mind?"

"Gil," she said simply. "I know it sounds terribly fanciful, but he charmed me completely and—despite my resistance—I fell unexpectedly and wholly in love with him."

"He completely changed your mind about marriage?"

"Yes. I think if you find the right person, anything is possible. For instance, I used to be afraid of guns, and now I possess an exceptional skill. I never would have guessed! Life is such an adventure, Jessamine, especially with a partner who can make even the most mundane exciting. That seems to be how it is between you and Dougal."

"Does it?" Jess asked softly as she pondered Mary's words. Ordinary things such as dressing and bathing had taken on new meaning with Dougal. Good heavens, she shouldn't be talking to Mary about such things when she needed to focus on the mission. "It's nice that you see us in that light," she said before turning the conversation where she should have long before now. She pretended to stifle a yawn. "I confess I stayed up rather late reading *Lyrical Ballads*. They are all so lovely. Which is your favorite Wordsworth?"

"Well, my favorite is the one you quoted after you first arrived, but that's not from *Lyrical Ballads*. Let me see... What is my favorite from that collection?"

Jess recalled what Mary had said that first night when she'd recited the lines. She'd said it was one of her *favorites*. Jess wanted to groan with annoyance. It seemed she was not a very good spy.

Mary went on for a moment about one of the poems from *Lyrical Ballads*—the one about Tintern Abbey—while Jess thought about the other poem about the daffodils. She could recall a few other lines beyond what she'd recited the other night, but not the entire thing. When Mary finished, Jess asked if she had a copy of the daffodil poem.

"I'm sure I do, but I don't know where. I have it memorized, so I don't read it!" Mary laughed gaily, and Jess joined in even though she preferred to cry.

"Good afternoon, ladies!" Gil strode into the sitting room, his gaze settling on his wife with unadulterated love. It was really quite beautiful, and it was no wonder Mary had fallen for him. Jess had never seen such emotion before meeting the Chesmores, and for the first time thought it might be nice if someone looked at her that way. Alas, she had absolutely no expectation that would ever happen.

He smiled brightly at Jess as he squeezed down next to Mary on the end of the settee. "Ogelby found the English Voltaire. He's taking it to your chamber."

"I hope he's quick about it," Mary said. "We're meeting with him and Mrs. Farr in an hour to review the final arrangements for the dinner party tonight."

Gil snorted a laugh. "Poor Ogelby. We really ought to retire him, you know."

Mary's face creased with sympathy. "Yes, but he's so fond of Prospero's Retreat."

"He did not like that we chose a new name," Gil said with a great amount of drama. "He may decide that's a sign of changing times."

"He's been here that long?" Jess asked, hoping she might collect more information about the Frenchman who'd owned the house before.

"Nearly all his adult life," Gil replied. "He came here as a novice footman."

"That's a long time to be in one place. He survived new ownership in the recent past, so perhaps he'll come around on the name," Jess suggested.

Mary exchanged a look with Gil. "He does miss Monsieur Dumont, but it wasn't as if he could follow him to the hospital."

"Hospital?" Jess asked.

"A sad tale," Gil said, clucking his tongue. "Poor Monsieur Dumont grew quite frail, especially in his mind. That is why he sold the property. He had no family to care for him either. I confess I felt rather bad for him when he left for Bath."

"That is where he is?" Jess was eager to relay that information to Dougal.

"Last we heard." Mary put her hand to her cheek. "What a maudlin topic! Let us focus on happier things. Jessamine, we are so pleased you and Dougal will be here for the party."

"We're delighted to be included. I wouldn't have chosen to suffer an accident with the gig, but I'm glad we did." Jess winked at them as she rose. "I'll leave you to it."

After departing the sitting room at a sedate pace, she hurried to the stairs and practically sprinted to their chamber. She encountered Ogelby closing the door.

He inclined his head at Jess. "Mrs. Smythe. Is there anything you require?"

"No, thank you. I understand you delivered a book."

"I did, at Mr. Chesmore's request."

"I appreciate that." She gave him a warm smile before entering the room and closing the door behind her. Her gaze went to the desk, where there were now two books—the useless Wordsworth and the Voltaire.

"Jess?"

She turned her head to see Dougal peeking from the dressing room. Only his face was visible. "Dougal. I just encountered Ogelby."

"Yes, he delivered the Voltaire. I took the opportunity to query him about Monsieur Dumont."

"Oh?" Jess pivoted toward the dressing chamber. "I was speaking to the Chesmores about him downstairs."

"Let us compare notes," he said with a smile. "Ogelby was fond of the man. He owned the house for a little more than twenty years. Before that, the family who built it were the owners—they also hired Ogelby."

"As a novice footman, the Chesmores indicated," Jess said.

"Yes. Did they tell you Dumont is in a hospital in Bath?"

"They did. His situation sounds very sad."

"Ogelby corresponds with him," Dougal noted. "Rather, he writes to a nurse who responds on Dumont's behalf."

"That's lovely. It's also more than I learned. I had no way of knowing if Dumont was simply a Frenchman or if he had any ties to his homeland."

"Ogelby said he fled after the revolution. It sounds as if Dumont was quite happy to leave France and had a great love for his new home here."

"Does that mean we don't need to investigate him any further?" Jess asked, thinking investigations were bloody complicated.

"I don't think so. I'm satisfied that the prior owner being from France is merely a coincidence."

Jess arched her brows. "That's one."

Dougal laughed. "So it is. I should get to my bath before the water cools too much."

His bath. All this time, only his head was visible, and it was because he was likely nude. She shouldn't think about that, especially after what was already swirling in her mind due to Mary's rather provocative conversation. Unfortunately, it was impossible not to envision what he might look like without his clothing. She'd seen his neck and far upper chest and his calves and feet. It was enough to feed her imagination.

She pulled herself back to reality. "Ah, before you go, I've determined which poem is Mary's favorite—the one about the daffodils, which she *said* was one of her favorites right after we arrived. I am angry with myself for not recalling that." It could have saved her a night of reading.

His eyes widened briefly, then he gave her a warm, gentle smile. "You are too hard on yourself."

Probably, but she couldn't change how she felt. "The Chesmores will be meeting with Ogelby and Mrs. Farr in about an hour if you wanted to search their room."

"Then I'll have to hurry my bath. I'd best get to it." He withdrew and closed the door.

Jess had already arranged for a bath later this afternoon prior to the party. She looked forward to the solitude to hopefully quiet her mind. Or at least exorcise lurid thoughts of Dougal from it. Perhaps she ought to finish what she'd started in bed the other night. That might settle her.

Somehow, however, she suspected it might take more than self-gratification to banish the ache inside her.

~

*F*irst, Dougal made sure the Chesmores, Ogelby, and Mrs. Farr were gathered in the dining room. Then he quickly made his way to the William Blake Room. It was quite similar, at least in arrangement, to his and Jess's Wordsworth Room, except it was larger. The dressing room was also configured a bit differently, its door on the same wall as the door to the bedchamber.

He closed himself inside and started with the bedchamber, going first to Mary's bedside dresser where he quietly opened drawers and carefully searched the contents. Finding nothing of interest, he moved on throughout the room, working rapidly and efficiently, having done this countless times.

When he reached the desk, he found several drawings spread across the top. They were of Mary in the garden and on the beach. And they weren't particularly good. These must be the sketches Gil made on their outings.

Dougal searched the drawers next and found more of his drawings as well as some writings. They were in French and English and seemed to be poetry. Extremely flowery, romantic poetry. He also found other sketches made in a different, lighter hand. These were better. They depicted landscapes. Several were clearly the prospect of beach and ocean from the house. These must be Mary's.

Finding nothing of import, Dougal closed up the desk and turned to consider where to go next. The door to the dressing room was ajar. Dougal slid inside and executed the same methodical approach. Until he reached the jewelry cabinet. It was locked.

Removing one of the pins holding his wig in place, Dougal inserted it into the lock and searched for the release. It took a bit of angling, but he found the mechanism and the lock clicked.

Dougal thrust the pin back into his hairpiece and opened the top. There was a tray with rings, bracelets, and earrings, which he picked up and set aside. The next tray was actually a drawer accessed by the front. He pulled it open, ignoring the contents of necklaces. Looking back into the open lid, he saw straight to the bottom now. There sat a stack of letters tied with a pink ribbon. His pulse quickened, hoping one of them might be coded.

Picking them up, he flipped through the stack. They were all numbers. All of them were coded.

Had they not sent these to France? Perhaps they wrote many before they met with a courier for transport and stored them here. Or mayhap they made copies, which would be exceptionally foolish. And if they'd arrived from France and hadn't been burned? Well, that would be the height of idiocy.

He couldn't take them all, but he could slip a few from the center. He did just that, taking two more beyond the one he'd already removed, and quickly dropped the stack into the box. Then he replaced the drawer. As he pulled down the lid, the door to the bedchamber opened. There was no mistaking the sound.

Holding his breath, Dougal made sure everything was as it should be and crept behind the door. He peeked through the tiny opening between the hinges and saw that it was Gil. Hopefully, he wouldn't come into the dressing chamber.

He moved toward the windows so that Dougal couldn't see him any longer. However, he could hear the man, and he was talking to himself in French. Dougal couldn't make out every word, but he spoke of love and comfort and excitement and...birds. It reminded Dougal of the "poetry" he'd found in the desk. It was hard not to be charmed by their host.

Gil left the room, and Dougal waited several minutes before following. He tucked the letters into his coat and stole from the room as carefully as he'd entered. He made his way to the library with haste, intent on searching for the daffodil poem Jess was trying to recall.

Her frustration bothered him. He wanted to help her, and not just for the sake of the mission. He wanted her to be successful—for her.

In the library, he started in one corner and worked methodically, just as he'd done in the William Blake Room. He pulled each book from the shelf and reviewed its contents. After a half hour, he realized this would take him the rest of the day. Which he didn't have.

He began to share Jess's frustration.

He was also eager to take the letters to her. Perhaps having those would be helpful to her cause. Then he could come back and look for the Wordsworth.

"Can I help you, Mr. Smythe?"

Dougal turned from the shelves to see Mrs. Farr standing just inside. Her meeting with the Chesmores must be finished. "I was just looking for a book of poetry. I find myself wanting to read Wordsworth since we are in his room." He gave her his most disarming smile, which typically helped smooth the way with ladies in particular.

"There are a few of those," she said, her brow pleating. "I

think they're over here." She strode across the room to a case near the fireplace.

Dougal followed her, watching as she took one book from the shelf and quickly replaced it, then tried another.

"Ah, here's one." She handed him the small book.

He opened it and read *Poems in Two Volumes*. Flipping the pages, he scanned for the words that were familiar to him—there it was: *dances with the daffodils*. He had it!

Snapping the book closed, he bestowed another smile on the helpful Mrs. Farr. "Thank you. Truly."

She glanced toward the doorway and lowered her voice to a whisper. "Does this have anything to do with why you've come?"

Dougal preferred not to say. The less she knew, the better. "As I said, I had a penchant for some Wordsworth. I appreciate your help." He turned and departed the library before she could query him further.

He took the stairs two at a time and rushed into the chamber. Jess was not at the desk. Her cipher notes and the letter were nowhere in sight. The door to the dressing room was closed.

Striding to the dressing chamber, he lifted his hand to knock. At that moment, he heard the slosh of water. She was in the tub. His cock went instantly and irritatingly hard. He couldn't recall the last time a woman had jumbled him so thoroughly. The mere thought of her nude in the next room was sending him into a fit of lust.

He let his head fall gently forward against the door. There was no bloody satisfaction in *that*.

Satisfaction would be Jess in his arms, her sandy-brown hair cascading over her shoulders, her breasts cloaked by the silken locks.

This was torture. He had to stop.

He lifted his head. "Jess, I found the Wordsworth poem."

Another slosh. "You did? I'll be right out."

It was several long minutes, of course. She'd have to get out of the tub and dry herself off. He almost offered to help.

Almost.

Instead, he strode from the windows to the door and back again. He lost count of how many times when she finally emerged. Her wig was slightly askew, and one of the buttons on her red dressing gown was unfastened.

He glanced toward the latter, just below her breasts. "You're undone," he murmured.

She looked down and hastily tucked the button through the hole. "Thank you. I was in a hurry. You have the book?" She seemed blissfully unaware of the effect she had on him. It was just as well.

While pacing, he'd continued to hold it. Now he placed it into her hands. "I also have three more letters." He pulled them from his coat and set them atop the book.

She tipped her head up to look at him, her eyes wide. "*Three* more letters?"

"There were actually several more than that. I counted eight in total. I didn't want to take them all and risk their absence being immediately noted."

"So you took a few instead. Brilliant." She narrowed her eyes. "Why are there so many? Shouldn't they have sent these to France?"

He was pleased she'd gotten there so quickly. "I had the same question, and I would think so. They either haven't had an opportunity to send them, or they're making duplicates."

She scoffed. "That wouldn't be very smart."

"Precisely."

Sweeping past him, she went to the desk and laid them out. "These are in different hands."

Dougal joined her, standing shoulder to shoulder as he looked down at the parchment. "You're right." It reminded him of the difference in the drawing styles he'd found in the desk—clearly two different people putting pencil to parchment.

"This one looks feminine and matches the one I've been trying to decipher." She hurried back to the dressing chamber and returned with the letter. "I keep it with me when I'm not working on it, and I'm ashamed to say I left it behind in my excitement for the book. You must think me an abysmal disappointment."

"Not at all. This *is* exciting, and there was no harm done."

Her teeth snagged her lower lip briefly. "You keep saying that, but I fear I will make a mistake that will cause trouble."

"You won't." He put his hands on her shoulders. "On the contrary, I think you're brilliant. You're going to decipher these letters, and we'll determine what the Chesmores are up to."

Her gaze met his and held. It would be so easy to run his hands along her collarbones and cup her face. Lower his head. Kiss her. She'd said he should aim for her mouth next time.

But this wasn't next time. There was no reason to kiss her save his rampant desire.

He took his hands from her and looked toward the desk. "Are you sure there are just two writers of the letters?"

She went to the desk and laid the other letter down with the rest so they formed a two-by-two square. Then she exchanged it with another in placement. Gesturing to the top row, she said, "These are the feminine hand. This one is the one Mrs. Farr gave us." She pointed to the one on the left. "These on the bottom seem to be a masculine hand, if I had to guess. They are also longer than the others."

"I think you're right about feminine and masculine. Definitely two authors, and just those two. I found a number of sketches in their room. They were clearly done by two different people. There were drawings of Mary, which I assumed Gil made. The stroke of his pencil seems similar to the letters here that you saw are more masculine. The other letters seem more like the landscapes I found, which I assume were drawn by Mary."

"How helpful that you found those," Jess said. "Were they any good?"

"Mary's showed promise. Gil should probably stick to writing poetry. On second thought, that effort wasn't much better," he added with a grimace.

"You found poetry too?"

"I did. Quite effusive and overwrought."

"That sounds about right," she murmured with humor. Her gaze went back to the letters laid out on the desk. "I wish we didn't have this dinner party, because I should like to sit down and work until I've found the key." She pulled a face. "Can you tell them I'm ill?"

"I suppose I could, but you know Mary will be terribly disappointed."

Jess exhaled, frowning. "You're right, of course. But I can't promise not to come down with a headache."

Dougal grinned. "I won't quarrel with that. I suppose we should get ready."

"In a moment. I just want to look at these two poems together." She sat at the desk. "The key has to be in these. If it's not, I don't know where else to turn."

He touched her shoulder. "You'll get it. I know you will." She tipped her head up to look at him, her expression grateful. He reluctantly removed his hand. "I'm eager to understand why the Chesmores have so many letters in their possession. It just doesn't make much sense to me."

"The sooner I can decipher these, the better." Jess slid into the chair and opened the Wordsworth, turning pages until she found the poem she needed.

"I'll leave you to it, then." Dougal retreated to the dressing chamber and closed the door so he could change for dinner.

He hadn't wanted a partner, but he couldn't deny that he enjoyed working with Jess. While he was looking forward to finishing this mission and getting back to his investigation, he would miss her.

Perhaps he ought to make the most of the time they had left.

CHAPTER 13

The dinner party seemed a smashing success, particularly due to the surprise arrival of Gilbert's older brother, Sylvester Chesmore. Taller and more reserved —which perhaps wasn't saying much—than his younger sibling, Sylvester was charming and droll, and Dougal was glad to be seated next to him at dinner. The other guests were neighbors, some from along the coast and others from neighboring towns, including Bournemouth and Poole. Oddly, none of them were spending the night, save Sylvester, who'd come from Bristol.

The men lingered over port in the dining room while the ladies moved to the drawing room. Dougal could tell that Jess was nearly crawling out of her skin with the need to return to her deciphering. She'd been somewhat quiet at dinner, and he imagined she was working out possible solutions in her head.

"How long have you been visiting?" Sylvester asked Dougal.

"Just three days."

"Long enough to get to know my brother and his wife fairly well, then. I daresay you could do that after one night," he added with a chuckle before lighting a cheroot.

Dougal smiled before sipping his wine. "He's quite forth-coming. He seems to be somewhat enamored of French language and French things."

Sylvester rolled his brown eyes. He leaned toward Dougal. "He's rather obsessed, if you must know. Our great-grandmother was French. She eloped with a young student to England, and Gil likes to say she met Voltaire on several occasions before that."

"He mentioned that," Dougal said. "It's not true?"

"It's as true as me having met the Prince Regent." He took a puff on his cheroot. "I have not."

"I see. Well, there's no harm in a little embellishment, is there?" Dougal asked with a smile. "I did wonder how he managed to obtain a gun fashioned after one in Napoleon's private collection."

Sylvester smirked. "Another fantastical imagining. The gun was manufactured here, and it's supposedly similar to one Napoleon owns, but how on earth would my brother know that for certain?"

He might if he were a spy.

But what if he was only a French-obsessed gentleman with a penchant for exaggeration? Except, why the myste-rious behavior around the procurement of the pistol? Or was that because he was trying to disguise the gun's true prove-nance? He wanted Dougal to think it was French and not just an English-made copy.

"Do you visit often?" Dougal asked.

"This is my second trip since Gil purchased the property. He spent every last shilling he had on securing it, insisting it was vital to the health and welfare of his marriage. Appar-

ently, he and Mary require privacy and the brisk sea air. And
to be closer to France, but not actually *in* it," he added the last
in a low, wry tone.

"It is a lovely home. My wife and I are considering
looking for property nearby."

"And where is it you call home?"

"Llanedeyrn, near Cardiff," Dougal responded smoothly.

"You've got the sea over there too. Why not look on the
Gower Peninsula? That's a beautiful location."

Dougal nodded. "It is." Or so he'd heard. He'd never been.

"Unless you'd prefer to be closer to France too?" Sylvester
seemed to ask sincerely, but then he erupted into laughter.
"Only jesting."

It wasn't clear to Dougal whether Sylvester making fun at
Gil's expense or simply making light of an eccentric brother.
Either way, Dougal decided he liked Gil better, despite
quirks, potential treason, and even the way he'd behaved
with Jess while shooting. Dougal recognized he'd been jeal-
ous, which was silly given how devoted Gil was to his wife.
In fact, it was the man's demonstrativeness that prompted
Dougal's appreciation. In some ways, it reminded him of his
father. He'd always been open with his love of his children.
Dougal wondered if he could be like that. Or if he wanted to.

Returning his thoughts to the current situation, Dougal
was grateful for the opportunity to glean information from
Gil's brother. To that end, it was time to see who else would
share what they knew of the Chesmores.

Dougal finished his port and rose. "I think I'm ready to
join the ladies." That way, he could also relieve Jess. He knew
she was desperate to get upstairs, and he wouldn't delay her
work any longer.

"Capital idea," Gil said, smacking his palm on the arm of
his chair at the head of the table. He tossed back the

remainder of his port and stood, then he led them all to the drawing room.

The ladies were mostly seated. Only Jess and one of the neighbors—Dougal believed it was Mrs. Woolford from Bournemouth—were standing. Dougal suspected Jess couldn't bear to sit when she was ready to flee, and Mrs. Woolford was probably just being kind and keeping her company.

Dougal moved to join them, arriving just before Mr. Woolford. A tall, angular gentleman with a receding hairline, he inclined his head at Dougal before standing next to his wife.

Sidling next to Jess, Dougal asked about her headache. She gave him such a grateful look that he nearly kissed her forehead.

"My goodness, you've a headache?" Mrs. Woolford, who was perhaps a few years older than Dougal, asked.

"It was slight, but it's increased throughout the evening. I'm afraid I must retire. I'm so sorry to miss the rest of the party." She put her hand on Dougal's arm. "You must stay and enjoy yourself."

"I'll just walk you upstairs and return." He nodded toward the Woolfords, then escorted Jess from the drawing room.

"I can't thank you enough," she said with an almost amusing level of relief.

"I could tell you were rather, ah, eager to return to your work."

Her brow creased. "I hope it wasn't obvious to everyone."

"They would have no way of knowing that you were anxious," he assured her as they started up the stairs. "If they detected anything, it will be easily explained by your headache."

"I'm glad. You should speak with the Woolfords, or at

least Mr. Woolford, when you go back down. He has shot targets with Gil on several occasions."

"I'll do that, thank you. I had an enlightening conversation over port with Sylvester."

"Oh?" She turned her head toward him as they reached the gallery.

"He describes Gil as a man who likes to embellish things and is obsessed with the French. Specifically, the gun modeled after Napoleon's was made here in England and may or may not be a true copy."

"I see. Are you beginning to doubt the Chesmores are spies?"

Dougal opened the door to their chamber for her. "Not yet, but until you decipher those letters, or we catch them in the act of delivering information to a French courier, we don't really have any solid evidence. It's still just suspicion."

She went directly to the desk. "I'm not sleeping until I work this out."

He didn't doubt she meant that. "Shall I have tea sent up?"

"Not yet." She took the letters from the pocket of her dress and sat down, her features settling into deep concentration.

"You should have been a scholar. Teaching at Oxford, perhaps."

Looking toward him, she blinked. "What?"

"You've a brilliant mind, and your dedication is admirable."

"That hardly makes me a scholar," she said, blushing slightly. Damn, she was attractive when she did that. And every other moment.

"You wouldn't like that?" he asked, leaning against the doorframe.

"No. I'd much rather be out in the world, doing some-

thing like this. Being a scholar doesn't sound very adventurous. I love to read, but if given the choice, I'd rather *do*." She
waved her hand at him. "Now leave me be so I can focus."

He didn't want to leave her at all. He wanted to offer his
help and support. More importantly, he wanted to be here
when she triumphed over that bloody code. "Good luck."

Closing the door, he started back toward the stairs, his
thoughts fixed completely on Jess. Her commitment was an
excellent trait, but if she couldn't decipher those letters,
they'd be no farther along than when they arrived. Dougal
began to worry they would be here longer than anticipated.

It's only been three days!

Three days plus the day it took to get here and the day it
would take to return to London—all valuable time during
which he wasn't investigating the failures of his previous
missions. A troublesome thought rose in his mind—what if
this mission failed too? If they couldn't find evidence that the
Chesmores were spies and it turned out they were, in fact,
working for France, he would have failed again.

Dougal couldn't let that happen.

~

*T*he letters Jess had written began to dance across
the parchment. Perhaps she did need some tea. Or
brandy. Or tea with brandy.

How many hours had she been working on this? At least
two. Probably three. She actually had no idea what time
it was.

The door opened, and Dougal came inside. He immediately loosened his cravat and swept his gaze over her. "You
look comfortable."

She glanced down at herself. "Because I'm in my dressing
gown? I still have my wig on."

"So you do." He removed his spectacles and set them on the table by the door. "Any progress?"

Leaning back in the chair, she huffed out a frustrated breath. "Not really. I'm beginning to think this is impossible. Is the party over?"

He nodded. "I thought it would never end."

"What time is it?"

"Nearly three."

Good heavens, much more than three hours even. "Did you learn any more useful information?"

"Not particularly, just that the Chesmores appear equally eccentric to everyone, which isn't surprising. That is just who they are. They've gone out of their way to make friends here—paying calls and having monthly dinner parties like this one tonight. They seem to be very well liked, in spite of their behavior." He lifted a shoulder. "Or perhaps because of it."

Jess put her elbow on the desk and rested the side of her head against her hand. "You really think that?"

"I think they are driven by joy and love for one another, and for some, that is a most admirable trait."

"For some. But not for you?"

"I was speaking as to why the guests might like our hosts. I was not offering my opinion about them."

"So I gather," she said with a slight smile. Dougal seemed to avoid sentiment, which she could understand given his job.

He nodded toward the parchment sprawled atop the desk. "Can I help you at all?"

Jess had enjoyed the brief respite from thinking about the code. "I don't know how. I'm looking at the Wordsworth."

"Her favorite," Dougal said, removing his cravat completely.

The triangle of almond flesh peeking from his neckline

drew her gaze. It wasn't as if she hadn't seen that, or at least part of that before. Still, it never failed to quicken her pulse and arouse her desire.

"It is a nice poem," he went on. "I recognized it when you recited it after we arrived."

Jess froze for a moment, the letters of the final stanza swimming before her eyes. There were forty-two letters in the French alphabet, if one included the diacritics. The first two lines were forty-five letters, slightly more. What if they somehow corresponded?

She wrote the first two lines of the final stanza on fresh parchment. Beneath each letter, she wrote a number.

"Bloody hell," Dougal said, startling her.

Lifting her head, she saw him standing near the table staring out the window. "What is it?"

"There's a light moving on the path to the beach."

"What?" She bolted from the chair and joined him in looking out the window. Light bobbed in the darkness. "Who is it?"

"I can't tell. I need to find out." He was already moving toward the door. "Glad I didn't remove my shoes or wig."

Torn between her work on the cipher and whatever was happening outside, Jess hesitated. Her gaze flicked to the desk—she was close to solving this. She could feel it.

"Wait," she said, hurrying toward him. "I want to go with you."

"You don't need to," he said. "You should work on breaking that code."

"I will just as soon as we get back." She didn't want to miss any part of the mission. Returning to the desk, she gathered all the papers. The stack was more than she could fit in her dressing gown, unfortunately. She frowned. Perhaps she should stay. Disappointment washed through her.

Dougal took the papers from her. "I've got them." He folded the stack and slid them into his waistcoat. "We must hurry." Picking up the spectacles from the table, he set them on his face.

Jess didn't bother exchanging her slippers for boots. "Let's go."

They hurried from the room, moving as stealthily as possible. Downstairs, they made their way to a seldom-used sitting room with a door to the garden.

Once they were outside, Dougal picked up the pace, his long legs devouring the earth as they moved toward the path. Jess hastened to keep up with him, glad she possessed long legs too.

Dougal took her hand at the top of the path. "Stay close to me," he whispered.

They crept along the path and eventually saw the light. It was no longer moving. Dougal pulled her behind a rock that they were able to peer over.

It was the Chesmores. They'd laid a blanket on the sand and were just sitting down.

"What are they doing?" Jess asked.

"I don't know. They could be meeting someone to deliver information. I would guess someone in a boat rowing to shore."

Jess grabbed his arm. "What about the letters you took? Won't they have missed them if they are meeting with someone to give them the letters?"

His mouth pressed into a grim line. "I'm sure they will have noticed. However, they would likely still need to show up for the meeting. Presumably, they will report the missing letters and will be charged with finding out what happened."

"Should we replace them? I could go back inside."

He shook his head. "That's pointless now. They likely

know they are missing. But they won't necessarily suspect us —they had a house full of people tonight."

"That's rather helpful," she murmured, watching the Chesmores together on their blanket. Wait, were they kissing?

"Is that how they pass the time waiting for the courier to arrive?" Dougal laughed softly. "It's hard not to like them. I was truly beginning to hope they weren't spies."

"Has this ever happened to you before? Liking people you were supposed to investigate?" Because Jess definitely liked him and couldn't imagine how he could be working against the Crown. The thought made her ill.

"Not quite like this," he said. "Good Chr—" He cut himself off.

Jess stared in disbelief as the Chesmores' embrace grew more...intimate. They lay back, their bodies entwined. Then Mary lifted her skirt as Gil put his hand between her legs.

In response, Jess's sex began to pulse. Heat and desire spread through her body, making her breasts ache and her limbs quiver. Mary's cries floated to them on the breeze as Gil appeared to unbutton his fall.

She ought to look away. And she absolutely shouldn't be aroused. She couldn't do the former, and she simply couldn't help the latter. Gil and Mary moved as one, their bodies rolling together like the waves rising and falling nearby—a melodic, natural movement as primal as the sea licking relentlessly at the shore.

Dougal's fingertips brushed against hers. Had he done that on purpose? She looked toward him, but he was watching the Chesmores, so perhaps not. Was he as affected as she was?

Mary let out a keening cry. It sounded as though she were in great pain. Then Gil shouted several times.

Jess was utterly confused. The scene had been so beautiful, so enchanting. "What just happened?"

Dougal looked at her, his lips parted. "They, ah, finished."

"Oh." Jess understood what that meant. She'd found her own release on many occasions, but it had never sounded like *that*. "Well, I think perhaps I am missing something, then. Would you mind explaining it to me?"

CHAPTER 14

*W*hat had she just asked him?

Dougal stared at her while also glancing from the side of his eye to keep watching the Chesmores. "I'm sorry, what don't you understand?"

As soon as the question left his mouth, he regretted saying it. He'd just invited her to ask him about everything they'd just witnessed. Not only would he probably be very bad at describing it—he'd much rather demonstrate—he shouldn't be the one to tell her such things. It ought to be her lover or her…mother. Although, given what he knew of her mother, he expected the latter wouldn't happen.

"I, ah, never mind." She looked back toward the Chesmores. "Forget I asked."

He watched her jaw clench and unclench and noted that her hands were flexing and unflexing. He could practically feel the energy coming from her body. She seemed quite…agitated.

Perhaps she was aroused. He certainly was. Hell, he'd been fighting his desire for her for days, and now they were standing in the moonlight watching two people have breath-takingly glorious sex.

"We shouldn't have watched," she whispered.

He redirected his attention to the Chesmores, who were now lying on the blanket and appeared to be looking at the stars. "We had to—we're on a mission. Do not admonish yourself for that."

"It seems so intrusive. I wouldn't want people watching me do...that."

"I can't say I disagree," Dougal said, suddenly overcome with visions of her doing...that. With him. He nearly groaned with a mix of lust and frustration. How he needed this mission to conclude before he did something extremely fool-ish. "Still, it was necessary. We must see what they are doing here. It's the entire reason we were dispatched to Dorset."

"I suppose that means we can't leave?"

"You can if you want. Can you make it back to the house on your own?" He glanced toward her.

"No, I'll stay. I'm not going to lose my nerve over a sexual display." She stuck her chin out.

"You're no shy wallflower."

"No, not a shy one. But I've been a wallflower for six years, which was precisely who I wanted to be."

He wasn't sure he believed her, not knowing that she'd once planned to marry. Until her parents had intervened. "That's really all you wanted? To be left alone?"

Her gaze met his. "I don't expect you to understand. You have always been in command of your own life with the ability to do as you please."

"Not entirely," he said drily, looking back to the Ches-mores. "Now I'm the heir—my future is suddenly laid out before me. And it is not at all what I planned." The familiar foreboding twisted his gut.

Gil stood and helped Mary up. He plucked the blanket from the sand, and she folded it while he grabbed the lantern. They soon made their way back to the path, hand in hand.

Dougal crouched down, pulling Jess with him. He put his finger to his lips.

Her eyes were wide and alert, narrowing slightly when they heard the Chesmores walking nearby. Mary's laughter floated on the night air. Dougal peered around Jess and the rock and watched them ascend the path. He kept his sight on them until the light from the lantern disappeared.

"They're gone," he said quietly, rising and pulling Jess with him. "This wasn't a clandestine delivery of information."

The number eleven was once again etched between her brows. She'd been very good at not doing that. "They came to the beach in the middle of the night to do…that? They're absolutely brazen."

"Unlike anyone I've ever met." Dougal exhaled. "Shall we return to the house?"

"Is there something else we should do?" She looked up at him expectantly for a moment, then her nostrils flared, and her eyes rounded the barest amount. "I didn't mean to imply —" She snapped her mouth closed. "Yes, let us return to the house."

He was going to offer her his arm, but she'd already turned and was stalking toward the path. Hurrying to catch up, he said, "I didn't think you were implying that."

She didn't respond.

He had to imagine this excursion tonight had left an impact on her. It was one thing to witness others' passion and another thing entirely to do so in the presence of someone else. Particularly someone to whom you were attracted.

Did he think she was as drawn to him as he was to her?

He doubted he'd ever find out. If what he suspected was true, their mission was soon to come to a rather unsatisfying end.

"You don't have to go so fast," he called after her, careful not to raise his voice too loud.

"I'm eager to get back to the code. I was on the verge of something. I should have just stayed to work on it."

He heard the edge to her tone. Was it disappointment or some other emotion?

Dammit, why did he care? If he was content to hide and ignore his own feelings, why should he be curious about anyone else's?

They were quiet until they reached the chamber. Jess turned to him and held out her hand.

He suffered a moment's confusion before he realized why —her work was in his waistcoat. Removing the parchment, he acknowledged that the trip to the beach, rather what they'd viewed on the beach, had upset his equilibrium. And possibly hers. He'd witnessed a great many things in his work for the Foreign Office, but watching two people copulate was a new experience.

She took the papers to the desk and laid them out once more. Sitting, she immediately began writing.

Dougal went to look over her shoulder. "What are you doing?"

"Thinking. Shh." She kept her focus on the work in front of her.

Going back to the poem, she wrote two more lines from the third stanza. She underlined the letters she'd been missing. That left a few letters that were not in any of the lines she wrote down.

Dougal thought he was fairly intelligent, but she began to move very quickly, and he was already lost. She rewrote the four lines from the poem and numbered each letter, her hand gliding the quill across the parchment. Pulling one of the letters toward her, she bit her lip. On a fresh piece of parchment, she began to write single letters, looking from the four lines to the coded missive and recording a letter. She did this over and over until words began to take shape. She had it.

Triumph flowed through him, along with anticipation for what she would find. He went to pour two glasses of brandy and brought them to the table where he sat down to wait.

After a while, when he was on his second glass of brandy, she finally looked up, the lines between her brows in place once more. "This can't be right."

Before he could get up to look at it, she moved from the desk to the table. She slid the paper with her deciphered message across the top, then picked up the brandy for a long drink. He started to read.

My darling, I can't wait for your touch. I burn for the pleasure only you can give me. My breasts are heavy and tingling, desperate for your mouth. Deliver me into rapture as only you can.

Dougal looked up at her weary face. "It's a...love letter?"

"That one is. So I tried one written in the other hand—Gil's. Turn the paper over."

He slowly flipped it, apprehensive as to what he might find.

My beloved minx, I can hardly wait to plunge deep into your wet sex, to feel you tighten around me, strangling my flesh until we both reach our climax. Then I will spill my seed upon your thighs

Dougal stopped reading because that was all there was and looked over at her. "Does the letter just stop?"

Her cheeks were an alluring shade of pale pink. "No, but I'm familiar enough with the key now that I can see what these letters are, and they are *not* secrets or intelligence for the French."

"I realize these are...private." What he really meant was titillating, but saying that word seemed as though it might be throwing fuel on the fire. "You need to fully decipher them."

"But I know what they say!" she argued.

"Still, we need to be certain. Give me the key, and I'll help."

Grunting in frustration, she fetched the key and a second quill along with fresh parchment. They worked together at the table for some time until all four letters were completely written out.

"These are nothing more than love letters," he said, staring in disbelief at their work. Jess's work—she deserved all the credit. "Sex letters, really."

"Rather graphic ones at that." She sat back in the chair and sipped her brandy. "I don't even know what some of these things mean." Her face turned an even brighter shade of pink, and Dougal wondered if that had happened on the beach when she'd asked him to explain about the climax.

"They are the most sexually obsessed couple," she said, not meeting his eyes.

"It seems to work well for them," he quipped. "They appear quite happy."

"Indeed. I'm just surprised they don't have a dozen children by now."

Dougal picked up his brandy. "There are things that can be done in order to prevent having children."

Now her gaze shot to his. "There are?"

"Er, yes." Dougal realized he could give her an entire education, and he had to admit he was sorely tempted to do so.

She scooted forward in the chair and set her glass back on the table. "What does this mean now that we know the letters aren't about anything nefarious? Unless there is some code based entirely upon sexual acts."

Dougal laughed. "I doubt that. It means we have no real evidence to prove the Chesmores are French spies. We can confirm the letters aren't secrets, and we can explain Gil's obsession with French and his penchant for exaggeration and embellishment. I am now, shockingly, inclined to believe they are not spies. Do you disagree?"

She shook her head. "They aren't remotely secretive. They'd be terrible spies."

He chuckled again. "Yes."

She sagged back against the chair. "The entire mission was pointless. It feels like such a waste of time."

"Not at all. I've conducted many of these types of investigations, and I've concluded several suspected people were not, in fact, spies. This is not terribly unusual."

"Have you ever been wrong?" she asked. "Did any of the people you found not to be spies turn out to be spies after all?"

"No." He sincerely hoped that wouldn't be the case here either. But he doubted that very much. "We were charged with investigating the Chesmores, and we have completed our duty. It wasn't time wasted at all. If nothing else, I got to know you and show you what it means to work for the Foreign Office. Do you really think it was without benefit?"

"Not entirely. I have enjoyed working with and learning from you. I do have one regret, however."

"What's that?"

"That you never had occasion to kiss me on the mouth." Her eyes met his, and the blue had never looked more vivid or intoxicating.

Dougal sucked in a breath, every nerve ending in his body instantly becoming completely and wonderfully aware. Setting his glass down, he slowly stood and moved to her chair. "Would you like me to do that right now?"

"No. I mean, there's no reason to." She dropped her gaze to the floor. "I shouldn't have said that."

For the first time, he suspected she might reciprocate his feelings of attraction, that she may be open to an...overture.

"I would kiss you," he offered, hoping she would say yes. If she refused him, he would be crushed, and not because his body was raging with lust. It was more than that. She had questions, and he wanted to give her answers. He wanted to be the one to show her that sometimes it was good not to be left alone. Sometimes, it was vital to make a connection and fulfill desires—even if she wasn't sure what they were. Yet.

Her lips parted as she lifted her gaze to his once more. "Even without the purpose of our charade?"

"Yes. Indeed, I've wanted to for some time, but as you said, there was no reason to. Aside from my persistent and overwhelming desire for you."

She stared at him. "All this time, I thought we were playing our roles, that everything that passed between us was pretend." She shook her head gently. "No, that isn't true. I've found it far too easy to pretend to be your wife. Sometimes, it didn't feel fabricated at all," she added in a tentative whisper.

"Then we are the same, because it's been a long while since I could separate my act from reality. Since before we came to Dorset, even." He held out his hand. "May I kiss you now?"

She took his hand, and he pulled her gently to stand. Her eyes glittered with heat and anticipation. "I should like that very much."

$\sim$

*H*e hadn't been pretending. At least not entirely. The attraction she felt for him was returned. "Have you really struggled?" she asked, not believing this could be true.

"More than I would care to admit. I am supposed to be a professional."

And she was supposed to be a confirmed spinster. His words made her giddy, and the knowledge that he wanted her as much as she wanted him filled her with joy as well as an unexpected sense of power and purpose.

She'd never imagined feeling this kind of attraction for someone, this incessant, undeniable pull. Seven years ago, she thought she'd been in love with Asa, but now she realized that had been a silly infatuation. He'd been handsome, charming, and from a faraway land. He'd represented excitement and the unknown. Her parents had also disliked him from the start, and perhaps that had made him all the more enticing.

What she felt toward Dougal was entirely different. They shared a familiarity with each other, an intimacy, that made it feel as if something were missing. It was as if they were married without one of the best parts of being married.

Dougal kept hold of her hand as he curled his other arm around her waist, drawing her close. His gaze fixed on hers, dark and seductive, eliciting a wonder of sensations within her. Inexplicably, she felt both heavy and light, eager and tentative.

Releasing her hand, he brought his hand up to her chin, his thumb tracing over her flesh, then moving to her lower lip. "If you only knew how many times I looked at your mouth and wondered how it would feel against mine," he whispered.

He skimmed the pad of his thumb over her lip, and her breaths began to grow more rapid.

"I wondered that too," she managed. Her hands were trapped between them. She turned her palms flat against his coat.

Tipping his head to the side, he kissed her temple, his lips soft and lingering against her. Jess closed her eyes and pressed her fingertips into him. He kissed her check next.

Her heart fluttered faster, as if they were the wings of a hummingbird, as the world shrank to just the two of them and this moment.

Without lifting his lips, he kissed over her flesh, his nose gently nuzzling hers just before his mouth finally reached its destination. The moment his lips met hers, she felt a surge of passion. It was like climbing a hill and finally seeing the spectacular view. *This* was what she'd been anticipating. What she'd longed for.

Jess slid her hands up to his neck and held him, her fingers splaying against his nape. The kiss, soft and sweet at first, began to change. He angled his head, pressing his mouth against hers. She opened for him, inviting his tongue to mate with hers.

He moved with expert precision, his hand cupping her head as he deepened the kiss so they could taste one another. His arm clasped her firmly, his palm against her lower back, holding her against him. She felt his body in the most delicious places—pressed to her breast, her thighs, and of course the joining of their mouths in an increasingly arousing kiss.

The hand on her face moved back slightly and began to pull pins from her head, loosening the wig. She tried to keep count to know when he was finished, but failed utterly. The pins fell to the floor, one grazing her shoulder, and a moment later, he eased the wig from her head, all while continuing to kiss her, his lips and tongue learning every aspect of hers.

Next came the pins from her tightly coiled hair. This would be more difficult. She gasped softly as one scratched her scalp.

Dougal pulled back. "Did I hurt you?"

"No. Just…I can do it more quickly."

He lowered his hand, caressing her nape. "Do you want to? I've kissed you on the mouth, and we didn't discuss anything further." He didn't give her an explicit question, but it was there—or so she thought—dangling between them like an overripe fruit. The scent was intoxicating, and she couldn't deny she wanted to taste it entirely.

She curled her hands around the collar of his coat, ready to push it off him. "I do. If you are inclined."

A slow smile spread his lips, causing a spasm of lust low in her belly. "Inclined is an insufficient word. I am…inspired. Driven. Positively *desperate*, if I dare say so." With each word, his voice lowered and intensified. She imagined she felt each syllable deep in her being.

"I want you to dare everything," she breathed. This *was* madness, but she didn't care. When in her life would she have this chance again? She knew Dougal. She wanted him. Whatever happened, she would always have this night.

His eyes narrowed as he released her. "I don't want to damage your head, so you take down your hair while I remove my wig."

In response, she began to take the pins from her head. Their gazes were locked as heat built between them. The removal of their hairstyles felt like some sort of mating ritual. As each pin fell to the floor, her body grew more taut, her blood ran hotter.

He tossed his wig aside as she ran her fingers through her loosened plait, freeing the locks so they fell about her shoulders. "Yes, this," he murmured, reaching for her hair with both hands. Lifting a curl, he inhaled, then dragged it across his lips. "Roses and silk."

He thrust his fingers into her hair, his hands gripping her scalp, just before his mouth descended on hers with a hungry abandon. She clutched his coat once more and tried, awkwardly, to push it from his shoulders.

Letting her go, he tossed the coat away and set to work on the buttons of his waistcoat. She knew, because her fingers were already there. Together, they opened it, and again, he pulled the garment off and cast it aside.

He wrapped his arms around her, and she reveled in the newfound sensation of his chest pressed to hers with far less clothing. Still, there was too much separating them. She wanted to see and feel him. This was an adventure she'd never planned to take, but now that it was here before her, she would indulge in every part of it.

Perhaps he read her mind, for he brought one hand between them and unfastened her dressing gown. Jess kicked her slippers away and shrugged out of the gown, letting it pool to the floor.

Dougal kissed her neck, starting with the spot he'd found the other night. Shivers danced up and down her body. She clutched at him, holding him fiercely as she basked in his attention. He gripped her waist, his hand massaging her through the linen of her night rail before it crept upward. His thumb moved across her breast, making her gasp.

He lifted his head, and she looked up at him, momentarily confused. Why had he stopped?

"Are you certain this is what you want? I realize things have seemed very…intimate between us. But we aren't truly married."

Jess let out a short laugh. "I know that. And I don't care. Yes, this is what I want, but if you are having second thoughts—"

He claimed her mouth for a fast, searing kiss. "Not second or third thoughts, even. Indeed, my first thought every morning is how I must avoid touching you."

"Avoid?"

"The more I touch you, the more I want you. Avoidance gives me some semblance of control. Or at least the illusion of it."

She blinked at him, astonished by these confessions. "I thought I was alone in my yearning." Until tonight.

Another sensual smile lifted his lips. "I had no inkling you felt anything for me beyond a passing friendship."

She put her hand over his and moved it fully to her breast. "Feel me. I want you. Completely. You said there was a way to prevent a child. I trust you to do whatever that means."

"It means I won't finish inside you. Without my seed, there is no child."

Of course. Heat flamed her cheeks. "I'm afraid my lack of knowledge is most embarrassing."

He rubbed his thumb over her nipple, making her eyes narrow as sensation rocked through her. She snagged her lip with her teeth as he pinched her gently.

"You must tell me if you don't like anything. And if you do," he added with a slight smile, his brow arching provocatively.

He turned her and backed her legs against the bed. "I should like to see you without this night rail. Is that acceptable to you?"

"Heavens yes. Please. I want to see you too."

Nodding slightly, he released her so he could remove his stockings. Straightening, he lifted his shirt over his head, his muscles flexing with his movements.

Jess stared, enchanted, at his chest. She put her hand on him, in much the same way he touched her. Brushing her thumb across his nipple, she smiled as he shivered in response. "Breeches?" She let her fingers skim down his abdomen to where a path of dark hair led to his waistband and beyond.

He unbuttoned the fall and pushed them down his hips slowly, inviting her expectant gaze as he revealed himself inch by tantalizing inch. She held her breath until his sex emerged. Long and dark, with a thatch of black curls, it was as beautiful as he was.

He stepped out of the breeches. "That is all of me."

"Turn." She'd said it without thinking, but she absolutely wanted him to.

Without hesitation, he rotated, unhurried, allowing her to take in every part of him. From his broad shoulders to his rippled abdomen to his rounded backside, he was absolutely perfect. No statue in any museum or grand house came close to the allure of a real masculine form. *His* masculine form.

When he faced her once more, he narrowed his eyes slightly. "Your turn."

Jess grasped the night rail and drew it over her head. A tremor passed over her from exposing her flesh to the cool night air, but she wasn't cold.

"You are lovely," he whispered. "Remember, tell me at any moment to stop if that's what you want."

In response, she took his hand. "Please touch me."

"Gladly." He cupped her face and kissed her fiercely. His other hand returned to her breast, cupping her.

She grasped his waist and pulled him against her. His sex, hard and warm, collided with hers. Mostly—he was taller than her. She longed to feel him just where she wanted, so she stood on her toes. *There.*

Desire swept through her, and he seemed to feel it too. With a groan, he picked her up and put her on the bed. He climbed on beside her, but didn't renew their kiss. Instead, he found her neck again. Once there, he made his way down to her breast, holding it in his palm as he closed his mouth over her nipple.

Jess clutched his head, just as she had in her dream. How had she envisioned this when it hadn't happened? Had she somehow brought it to be? Thought abandoned her as need pulsed lower and lower, driving straight to her sex.

Then his hand was there, his fingers drifting across her hip and thigh until they reached the folds nestled between her legs. He kissed her breast, teasing the passion curling inside her to new heights. This was an arousal she'd never known, a need so desperate, she could only imagine how it might be satisfied.

Stroking her flesh far better than she'd ever touched herself, he found the most sensitive spot. She arched up as his thumb pressed and swirled over her.

She grasped his waist again, her fingers digging into him. Her hips began to move with his hand, seeking more as her need intensified. "More," she rasped, not entirely sure what she was asking for.

He moved from her breast, kissing back up to her neck, to her ear. "You are ready for me. Here, anyway." He nudged his finger into her sex.

"I'm ready. I want more. I need more. Don't stop. Please." She lifted her hips, wanting more of him inside her.

"This?" He slid his finger into her, moving slowly until he buried the entire digit into her sheath. "My cock will be much larger."

God, yes, she wanted that. She parted her legs, opening herself to him completely. "Please," she begged, her hips moving in a circle.

He pumped his finger into her, withdrawing and thrusting. This was what she wanted, what would bring her relief. He moved his hand faster, giving equal attention to her clitoris and her sheath, stroking and filling her with a measured, insistent pace. She rose from the bed, clutching him wildly as she spiraled toward the end. Or would it be a beginning?

He licked her ear. "Come for me, Jess. Surrender to the rapture." His teeth tugged her earlobe, and he slid two fingers into her, finding a spot inside she never knew existed.

The world crashed and split asunder, surrounding her in light followed by a liberating darkness. Jess wasn't sure if she was still a part of herself or if he'd actually set something within her free.

He continued to touch her sex as she settled from her climax. Her body thrummed with pleasure and bliss. She couldn't help but smile. "That was so much better than I've ever done."

Laughter caressed her neck just before he kissed her there. "I know what you mean."

"Do you?" What an asinine question. Of course he did. Unlike her, he had experience with this. An odd, irritated sensation crept over her as she briefly considered how much experience he might have.

That was absurd to think about. Whatever had happened before and whatever would happen, he was hers right now. This moment was for them, and she wouldn't let silly thoughts intrude.

Wriggling beneath him as she came fully back to herself, she moved her hand forward on his hip until she met his rigid shaft. He moaned softly, and she was encouraged to encircle him with her fingers.

"Tell me what I should do," she whispered, moving her hand along his length. He felt marvelous—hard, but also velvety soft.

"Just that. Start at the base and slide up to the tip." He sucked in a breath as she did what he said. "Yes. That. Again."

She complied. Eagerly. And while doing so found she apparently hadn't been completely satisfied. The same hunger began to build inside her once more, coiling in her belly and blooming into her sex, her breasts, every corner of her trembling body.

Dougal moved between her legs. Instinctively, she lifted them, opening her thighs so he could settle against her. She continued to stroke him. When she reached the top, she pulled back the hood and stroked her thumb over the tip. Moisture coated her flesh.

Her hand stilled. "Are you finished?"

"What?" He sounded confused. "No. God, no."

"But you feel…wet."

"That happens. There's a bit of wetness at the start usually. When I finish, there will be much more." He kissed her. "I'll tell you when I'm there. More like, I'll warn you that I need to pull out."

She nodded, feeling foolish for misunderstanding. Her gaze met his, and he seemed to understand.

"I'm glad you asked. I hope you will ask me anything. It's better to know what's happening, what you like, what you don't like, and what you'd like to try."

She couldn't even think of the latter, but the notion was intriguing. She'd ask him later since he was being so accommodating. For now, she wanted to know what it meant for him to finish. And to feel what it was like when he was inside her.

Before she could ask what would come next, his hand covered hers. "Help guide me inside you." Together, they put him at her sex and slid him into her sheath.

He was right. This was much larger than his fingers. There was discomfort as she stretched around him, but he went slowly. Then his mouth was on her breast again, tonguing and sucking her flesh, and she all but forgot about anything but the pleasure winding through her.

When he was seated within her, he paused, lifting his head. She opened her eyes to see him looking at her.

"All right?" he murmured.

She nodded, utterly aware of how this was a moment she would treasure forever. "Thank you."

He grinned. "Thank me later. Now, I want you to wrap

your legs around me and hold tightly. I'm going to do my best to keep myself in check, but you feel so damned good, Jess." He closed his eyes as he began to move.

She watched him for a moment, clinging to him as he made shallow thrusts. Then he drove deeper, and something inside her shifted. The desire she'd so recently overcome roared back, claiming her once more as she dug her heels into his backside.

He began to move faster, driving into her with relentless, delicious strokes. The friction was almost maddening, pushing her to the edge of tolerance, where it was somehow both excessive and insufficient. She began to blather, eliciting words and sounds, just incoherent nonsense as their bodies strained together.

She could feel her climax coming, this climb longer than the last. The apex seemed just out of reach. He stroked between them, finding her clitoris. His touch delivered her to the stars. Digging her hands into his slick back, she cried out his name, reveling in the blissful completion he gave her.

"I have to—" He finished on a grunt as he left her body, falling to his back. She missed him already, rolling to face him.

Her gaze fixed on his hand, stroking his cock as his seed pulsed from the tip. Without thinking, she put her hand over his and lent her assistance.

"God, Jess." He moaned, his hips rising as they finished him together.

An unknown but welcome feminine power stole over her. She felt glorious.

He let his hand fall to his side, so she released him. Sated —she thought—she rolled to her back, breathing deeply as her pulse slowed.

"That was astonishing," she said after several minutes. "Thank you."

"That's the second time you've thanked me."

"You're right. That's nowhere near enough. Thank you. Thank you. Thank you."

He laughed, and she turned her head to find him looking at her. "I'm glad you enjoyed it. I must thank you too. It's been a long time since I—" He shook his head. "Never mind."

"Since you pleasured a woman?"

"Yes."

"I'd ask you what constitutes a long time, but I don't think I want to know. Just the thought of you doing this with someone else fills me with a rather improper sense of possession." She couldn't believe she'd told him that.

Pushing himself up on an elbow, he leaned over and kissed her. "I'm flattered." His gaze roved over her body, and he trailed his fingertip around one of her nipples. "You are irresistible. Though, I did try."

Her breath caught, and she feared her body was once again rousing to his touch. Was that normal, or was she insatiable? "To resist?"

"Mmm." He kissed her breast, gathering the mound in his hand so the nipple stood taller. He licked across the tip, hardening her flesh.

"It's late," she said, thinking they should sleep but not at all wanting to.

He exhaled, and the rush of his breath over her damp nipple was an intoxication of its own. "It is. We should sleep. Tomorrow will be busy as we determine our next steps."

"What will we do?"

He flopped back, releasing her, and she decided instantly that she wasn't really tired.

"We'll confront Mary and Gil."

She sat up in surprise, looking down at him. "We will?"

He nodded. "I'll explain in the morning. Well, in a few hours."

"So we'll be taking a nap?" She moved over him, throwing her leg across his hips.

He arched a brow. "I thought you said it was late."

"It is, but I didn't say that was a problem. It will just be a short nap. Unless you'd rather sleep."

"I don't wish to overtire you after your first foray." He stroked her clitoris, and need thundered through her once more. "But I'm sure we can come up with something…satisfying."

He cupped her neck and brought her down for a thoroughly torrid kiss.

Jess was beyond satisfied.

CHAPTER 15

*S*itting at the table, clothed and bewigged, Dougal poured tea for Jess while she finished her toilet in the dressing chamber. They'd barely spoken this morning. Was it because they were likely exhausted after their rather short nap? Or did she regret what had happened?

He did not. Indeed, he was an absolute scoundrel because he was eager to do it again. Even when he knew they must not.

Hell, they shouldn't have done it last night. They were partners on a mission for the Foreign Office. They were *pretending* to be married, for heaven's sake, not actually doing so. Only it turned out they'd both been unable to ignore a very real and persistent attraction.

The gentleman he'd been raised to be said he should marry her now, that she deserved nothing less after he'd ruined her. Didn't he need a countess? Hadn't he revealed himself to her in ways he never had with another woman?

Except she didn't want marriage. She'd been clear about her objective: spinsterhood with a dash of adventure. Perhaps more than a dash.

Jess emerged from the dressing chamber, her natural hair covered with the auburn wig and her face made into that of Mrs. Smythe. She wore a simple day gown of pale yellow with tiny blue flowers. She'd don a blue overdress before they went downstairs, and she'd transform from charming young miss to experienced wife in a matter of seconds.

He winced inwardly as he realized he could have been describing last night's activities.

"The tea is here, thank goodness." She hastened to the table and picked up her teacup for a quick sip. Her smiling gaze settled on him. "Perfection. Thank you."

He knew precisely how to make her tea. And how much jam she liked on her bread. He also knew a bit of jam would inevitably get on her finger, and she'd lick it off. Every day she did that, he grew increasingly aroused watching her. What would happen today? Would he be more or less impassioned?

He couldn't imagine being less, not after experiencing her passion firsthand. He wanted more, even as he knew he couldn't have it. What they'd shared had been a one-time occurrence. Anything more, and he would insist on marriage.

"What is our plan today, then?" she asked as she spread jam on her bread. She took a bite and as expected, there was a smear of jam on her thumb. She inserted it between her lips and sucked away the fruit. He nearly groaned.

As it was, his cock began to lengthen. He shifted in his seat and sipped his tea in an effort to redirect his thoughts. Setting the cup back in the saucer, he picked up a piece of cheese. "We need to speak with Mrs. Farr before we confront the Chesmores."

"I'm surprised we'll confront them." She took another bite of her bread.

"First, we'll tell Mrs. Farr what we've concluded, that the

evidence she shared is circumstantial, that everything is explained, and the answer is not that they are spies."

Jess swallowed, then picked up her napkin to dab at her lips. "So it's all just a series of coincidences. I thought you said only one was allowed."

"I did say that. And I suppose these are coincidences, of a sort. However, people can look to be one thing while in actuality being another. As I've mentioned, this is not the first time I've investigated a potential spy only to learn they are not." He popped the cheese into his mouth.

"Would you say the Chesmores seemed more or less likely than those instances?"

"I don't think it matters, particularly since we've deduced they aren't spies. Have you changed your opinion?"

"I don't know that I'd fully formed it. I'm still considering all that's happened. Perhaps my hesitation to exonerate them is due to my inexperience. Or my eagerness. Somehow, I feel as though I've failed to deliver what was expected."

"Not at all. We've done our duty."

"Yes, you said that last night."

He could tell she wasn't convinced. "I suspect you're right. This is your first assignment, and it didn't turn out the way you anticipated. You fully expected the Chesmores to be spies."

"I suppose I did. Even after I liked them," she added, shaking her head. "I don't enjoy admitting that."

He chuckled. "You are really too hard on yourself. Take your time to consider everything if that will make you feel better."

She narrowed one eye at him. "Will it matter? It seems you've already decided they aren't spies. I don't expect I'd be able to convince you otherwise."

"Not true. I'm open to new evidence. Which is why I want

to speak with Mrs. Farr. We'll lay everything out and give her the opportunity to add anything she may have forgotten or missed. Her reaction will be important. It may be that she acknowledges she was being overly cautious—which the Foreign Office appreciates. It's always better to be too careful than not careful enough."

"I'm sure you're right," Jess said, lifting her teacup. "I do think I'm just having to adjust my expectations. In the end, I am relieved the Chesmores aren't traitors. And I honestly don't think they'd be able to do it. They just can't be that secretive." She sipped her tea and set the cup back in the saucer. "All right, I'm convinced. Forgive my amateur uncertainty."

He laughed again, then reached across the table to take her hand. "No more disparagement. You are learning, and from what I can see, you've the makings of an excellent spy." How he'd love to watch her blossom. Instead, he'd be in Scotland, learning to be an earl.

Her features softened, and underneath Mrs. Smythe's cosmetics, he saw the woman who'd brought him immeasurable pleasure. More than once. "Why, thank you," she said softly. "That means a great deal to me, coming from you."

Reluctantly, he let her go and sat back in his chair. "Even though we will tell them we are from the Foreign Office, we must continue to be the Smythes. It's best if they know as little about us as possible."

"That means we maintain the Welsh accents?"

"Yes."

Jess's forehead creased. "And why would we tell them we are from the Foreign Office?"

"In some cases, I do not. However, I rather like the Chesmores, and I think they should be aware of how their behavior looks."

"You don't think they'll tell anyone we are from the Foreign Office?"

"Do you?" he asked wryly.

Jess shook her head with a slight smile. "Not if you tell them not to."

"Agreed. Now, let us finish our breakfast and go in search of Mrs. Farr." Dougal could have dwelled in here all day. Indeed, he could have gleefully told the Chesmores that both he and Jess were suffering from headaches and would need to spend the day abed.

He couldn't think of a place he'd rather be.

Alas, there was work to be done. For the last time.

❧

A short while later, they found Mrs. Farr in the dining room setting things to rights after last night's party. She was clearing the table of candelabras and flower arrangements.

"Good morning, Mrs. Farr," Jess said warmly.

The young housekeeper, whose back was to them as she set a candelabra on the sideboard, jumped, dropping the piece to the floor. The candles clattered out of the silver, and she hurriedly knelt to clean up the mess.

Jess rushed to help her. "I didn't mean to startle you."

Dougal moved to pick up the remains of a candle that had rolled off the carpet onto the wood floor. He set the stub on the sideboard as Jess and Mrs. Farr did the same with what they'd collected.

"I didn't hear you come in," Mrs. Farr said. "Is all well?" She looked to Jess. "I do hope you're feeling better this morning, Mrs. Smythe."

"I am, thank you. We are both quite well. We were, in fact, hoping to find you."

The housekeeper clasped her hands. "How may I be of service?"

Dougal stepped toward her. "I wanted to report back to you regarding the conversation we had the other night."

Her brown eyes widened briefly, and her brows shot up. "Oh! Did you break the code in the letter I gave you?"

"We did." Dougal glanced toward Jess. "Rather, Mrs. Smythe did. We also found others. They are love letters between the Chesmores."

Mrs. Farr gaped at them. "Why would they code them?"

Dougal shrugged. "They enjoy literature, and they like to have fun together. It seems most likely this was merely an amusement they devised."

"That's so...odd." Mrs. Farr blinked. "But then nearly everything they do is odd."

Dougal didn't disagree, but he also found their activities somehow charming. "We can't find any evidence to indicate they are spies. Mr. Chesmore is a trifle French-obsessed, but overall, their behavior is best categorized as eccentric rather than suspicious. I do see how you might think it was the latter, however, and the Foreign Office appreciates you drawing our attention to the matter. You can never be too careful."

"I feel rather foolish for writing now."

Jess gave her a sympathetic smile. "You mustn't. I should think finding a coded letter would be reason enough to notify someone. You've done very well."

Mrs. Farr exhaled. "Thank you for saying so."

"Is there anything else you might have forgotten?" Dougal asked. "We want to be sure we've been thorough in our investigation."

After thinking a moment, Mrs. Farr shook her head. "I don't believe so. The letter was the most concerning thing. Honestly, I'm ashamed to admit I was uncomfortable working for them. I let my imagination run amok and should have realized there was nothing untoward happening."

"What made you uncomfortable?" Jess asked gently, noting she spoke in the past tense and hoping that was no longer the case.

"Their eccentric behavior. They're kind enough—truly. I just...sometimes it's awkward to be around them, but now I'm wondering if it's because I was all but certain they were spies. I'd considered leaving, but I think I'll stay."

"Well, you must do what's best for you, but I do think the Chesmores are not only safe employers, but kind ones too," Jess said with an encouraging smile. Dougal had never appreciated having a partner more. She comforted the housekeeper in a way he never could.

Dougal was about to tell her not to follow her employers onto the beach at night, but Gil sauntered into the dining room.

"Morning, Smythes!" Gil called. "I thought I heard voices in here. Come and join me and Mary in the drawing room." He looked to Mrs. Farr. "Coffee, if you please."

"Certainly, Mr. Chesmore." Mrs. Farr departed without sparing so much as a glance for Dougal or Jess.

"Lead the way," Dougal said to their host, anticipating the coming conversation. There was something diverting about informing someone who wasn't a spy that they'd been suspected of being one. Reactions varied from horrified to amused to angry. He wasn't quite sure how the Chesmores would respond, or whether they would both share the same sentiment.

Dougal offered his arm to Jess. Their eyes met, and he saw the same hunger he felt reflected in her. How on earth were they going to keep their hands off each other?

They must. He'd already overstepped and behaved very

poorly. He needed to tell her so. If their expectations were not the same, they needed to set that straight.

Gil preceded them into the drawing room, where Mary was seated on their favorite settee. She looked tired, or at least not quite her usual buoyant self. Still, she smiled brightly upon seeing them.

Mary's smile turned into a concerned frown as she regarded Jess. "Jessamine, please tell me you're feeling better this morning. I was so disappointed that you retired early. We played cards quite late. You would have had such a wonderful time."

Jess perched on the smaller settee, which had become "theirs" during their visit, and Dougal sat close beside her. "I am much better, thank you. Dougal regaled me with tales of the party over breakfast. I am so glad he had a wonderful time." She clasped his hand and brought it to her lap.

Damn, he was going to miss this. What had started as a performance had become second nature. And he didn't mind at all. It was rather shocking for a man who hadn't spent even a moment contemplating marriage or domesticity.

Yet now he must.

"We kept him entertained," Gil said with a laugh as he put his arm around Mary's shoulders.

"I think you must return for next month's party," Mary said with a firmness that indicated she felt strongly. "Or stay until then!" She glanced at Gil, who nodded enthusiastically.

"That will give us time to train Jessamine into a proper shooter. Isn't that right, Dougal?"

Dougal squeezed Jess's hand. "I don't know that Jessamine wants to shoot again. Let's not press the issue, if you don't mind. On that note, I've decided I'm not interested in the French pistol."

Gil's brows pitched together. "Why not?"

Now was the moment. "Because it's not French." Dougal

didn't relish the look of unease that passed over Gil's features. "I do hope you didn't pay too dearly for it."

"No." Gil's voice squeaked on the word. He tried again. "No." That time, he spoke evenly, but he was clearly shaken. "At least, I don't think I did. The man who procures my French brandy sold it to me. I didn't want to give you his name. He made me promise not to reveal his identity."

"Of course not," Dougal said affably. "I'm not angry. I'm more curious why you would want anything that was a replica of something belonging to Napoleon."

"I—" Gil snapped his mouth closed as pink flooded his neck and face.

"He likes French things," Mary said softly, patting her husband's leg and looking at him with the purest love Dougal had ever seen. "And he likes to feel important." She transferred her gaze to Dougal. "Don't we all?"

He contemplated that for a long moment, but it was Jess who answered. "Yes, we do."

Dougal supposed that was why he did what he did for the Foreign Office, so that he could do something that mattered. And if that wasn't a kind of importance, what was it?

"Let me speak bluntly, Gil," Dougal began. "Your French obsession is suspicious. Your eccentric behavior—shooting targets weekly with a supposed copy of a gun owned by Napoleon, your speaking French, writing coded love letters —all of it is more than odd. It begs the question if you are up to something."

Mary had gone pale, her eyes rounding in mortification. "How did you know..." She slowly lifted her hand to her mouth. Then she dropped it again, her eyes narrowing. "*You* stole our letters!" She turned her head to Gil. "I told you I didn't misplace them."

Feeling Jess tense beside him, Dougal quickly revealed the

truth. "Yes, I took the letters. We came here to determine whether you are French spies."

Gil pulled his arm from Mary's shoulders and nearly vaulted from the settee. "*What?*"

Mary grabbed his wrist. "Gil, control yourself."

"But this is *marvelous*." Turning his head to Mary, Gil grinned, his expression rapturous. "Can you imagine, Mary. Us as French spies?" He laughed with delight.

Forehead creasing into ever deeper lines, Mary stared at him. "You can't *want* to be a French spy?"

"Goodness no," he said with a wave of his hand and a hearty laugh. "But isn't it exciting to think that someone believed we might be?"

Mary stuck out her chin, her face still scrunched up with confusion. "I'm not sure I find that exciting, but if you do—"

Gil snapped his attention back to Dougal. "Who was it? Did someone turn us in?"

"It wasn't anyone specific. Your…odd behavior has not gone unnoticed. The Foreign Office monitors suspicious activities, particularly along the coastline."

Mary folded her arms over her chest. She'd gone from horrified to annoyed. "I don't understand how you read the letters."

"I deciphered them," Jess answered evenly. "I was, ah, curious as to why you encoded them."

Dougal was surprised she asked that, but glad, since he wanted to know too.

Gil shrugged. "Just a fun diversion to liven things up a bit."

Did they really need to do that? Dougal found them plenty lively.

Mary cast her gaze toward her floor. "I can't believe you read them."

Jess reached to touch Mary's arm. "I'm sorry. Please don't

feel embarrassed. They were very…sweet." Jess's expression flashed with a brief grimace as if she realized sweet was perhaps not the best description.

Dougal could understand how Mary would feel violated to have their private things read. "I offer my deepest apologies, Mrs. Chesmore. We were conducting our duty to the Crown. I do hope you'll understand, even if you can't forgive."

"You don't have to stop calling me Mary." She sniffed, then straightened, her gaze moving to Jess. "How did you break our code?"

Jess gave her a sheepish smile. "It wasn't easy. Your key was most difficult. Though we were here to conduct an investigation, I want you to know that my affection for you and our friendship is absolutely real."

Mary softened completely then, uncrossing her arms and clasping her hands in her lap. "I'm so pleased to hear that." She put her hand to her cheek. "Heavens, I can only imagine what you thought of our letters!" She laughed finally, turning her head toward Gil, who joined with her.

Dougal couldn't help smiling.

Jess leaned close to him and whispered, "Is this typical? Never mind. This is the Chesmores. Of course it's not."

"Actually, it's not far off the mark," he murmured.

Gil composed himself and settled back against the settee. He put his arm around Mary once more. "I suppose your breeching strap wasn't really damaged?"

"No." Dougal needed to put an end to the conversation. He didn't want to get into all the specifics, nor should he. "Again, our apologies, but I do hope you understand. Now, we must be on our way." He looked to Jess, who started to rise. Dougal stood and helped her up.

"Must you?" Mary leapt up as well, and Gil came with her.

"Stay," Gil implored. "We were having such fun."

"I'm afraid we must return to London," Jess said, and Dougal kept himself from reacting. She should not have said that, and she knew it, for she instantly stiffened. "We have thoroughly enjoyed ourselves here," she hastily added. "We greatly appreciate your hospitality."

"Well, we shall hope you'll visit again." Gil turned to Mary. "Spies! What a titillating thought. Not for the French, of course." He looked back to Dougal, his expression arresting in wonder. "Would the Foreign Office want our help? We would be excellent spies, keeping everyone abreast of the activities along the Dorset coast."

Jess nudged Dougal's hand.

He summoned a benign smile for their hosts. "We can certainly, ah, put in a recommendation. If you'll excuse us, we need to pack, as we plan to depart this afternoon."

Surprise and disappointment washed across Mary's expressive face. She really would be an awful spy. "So soon? Can't you stay until tomorrow at least?"

"I'm afraid not." Jess reached out and took Mary's hand briefly. "Thank you again. We'll see you before we go."

Dougal nodded at Gil as he ushered Jess from the room. They were quiet until they reached the upper floor, at which point Jess let out a sound that was suspiciously like the start of a laugh. She pressed her hand to her mouth.

Biting his lip, Dougal kept his humor in check until they reached their chamber. Once inside, they let loose until Jess suddenly sobered.

Dougal composed himself. "What is it?"

She put her hand to her forehead. "I bungled things *again*. I'm afraid you're going to tell the Foreign Office that I'm an abject failure, and you'd be right to do so."

He moved toward her and gently clasped her upper arms. "You are not a failure. You are new to this."

Her eyes held a flicker of unease. "I've made many mistakes. You can't deny that."

"I wouldn't characterize it that way. Yes, you've made a few errors. That happens to everyone."

"Did you do anything wrong on this mission?" She arched a brow at him.

He released her arms and resisted the urge to turn away from her. He'd absolutely done something wrong. He'd breached the trust between them when he'd surrendered to passion with her last night. He needed to apologize, but reasoned there would be time on the journey to Lady Pickering's. They ought to start packing.

"I'm sure I did," he said lamely. "We should get on." He turned toward the dressing chamber, but allowed her to go before him.

She strode to the door. "I do think Gil will be disappointed when the Foreign Office does not enlist his assistance."

"You may be right. I hope he doesn't send word to them."

Pausing, she looked back at him over her shoulder. "I have to think it would look suspicious. Here's a couple who were suspected of spying for the French, and now they want to spy for the English?" She walked into the dressing chamber.

Dougal stared after her. Had he ruined another mission? No, that would mean he'd ruined other missions, and he absolutely had not. He hadn't killed Giraud, and he hadn't known the message he delivered was full of nonsense. He'd done his job as he'd always done it.

Still, those things had happened.

He'd done his job here too, and he'd found the Chesmores innocent of espionage. There was simply no convincing evidence.

But what if he was wrong? What if they were spies and had managed to outmaneuver him?

That was preposterous.

If the Chesmores were spies, then Dougal had no business working for the Foreign Office, because he just couldn't see it. And after four years, he trusted his instincts.

Unfortunately, none of that even mattered. Very soon, he *wouldn't* be working for them. He just hoped he could determine what had gone wrong before he had to walk away.

In the meantime, he had a matter of hours until he had to walk away from Jess.

~

The drive from Prospero's Retreat had gone much more quickly than the trip there. Or so it seemed to Jess. She could feel the time with Dougal slipping away as if she were desperately holding onto a branch of a tree and was down to her last fingertip. They would arrive at Lady Pickering's soon.

And then what?

Instead of asking, Jess kept the conversation easy. "This weather is much better than when we traveled the other direction."

"I should say so," Dougal responded. He'd been quiet, pensive, even. She'd asked what he was thinking about earlier, and he'd only said that his mind was on many things. He hadn't indicated a desire to talk about any of them.

They were nearly out of time. Jess would be thoroughly angry with herself if she didn't ask about the future. Or discuss last night. They hadn't exactly acted as if it hadn't happened, but neither had they addressed it. "What will happen when we're both back in London?"

"I don't know what you mean."

Jess pressed her lips together in a slight frown. Was he being purposely obtuse? "I mean, is our work finished? Will we deliver a report to the Foreign Office?"

"I will deliver a report. I don't know what will be required of you. Presumably, you will be directed as to what to do."

She took that to mean that Lady Pickering would instruct her on what happened next. But that wasn't what Jess wanted to know. That was, however, what she'd asked. In a cowardly fashion, she'd talked about the mission instead of what she really wanted to discuss—what had happened between them.

"What about last night?" she asked, stealing a glance at him to see his reaction.

He didn't reveal a thing. His attention remained on the road ahead, and his features were bloody impassive. At least he'd given up the damned spectacles.

"Yes, about that," he said. "I owe you an apology."

An *apology*? "For what?"

Now, he slid a look her way—but only very briefly. "I should think it would be obvious. I overstepped the boundaries of our partnership. I breached your trust, and I'm wholly sorry for all of it."

All of it? Anger swirled through her and gathered into a hot ball in her chest. "Well, I am *not*. I have no regrets whatsoever. In fact, I'd harbored hope that we might share such an evening at some point in the future. If you were amenable. Apparently, you are not." She felt like such a fool.

"You sound angry."

"I am. I thought we mutually desired each other and decided to act upon that. Yet here you are, prattling on about overstepping boundaries and breaching trust. Did we not both agree to do what we did?" Multiple times, in fact!

"Yes, of course. But I shouldn't have allowed that to happen. You trusted me to be a gentleman, and—"

"You were a perfect gentleman. Last night. Today, I may need to revise that opinion."

He exhaled, and they drove in silence for a few minutes, during which her frustration did not lessen. "I didn't mean to give you the impression that I didn't enjoy last night. I did. Very much. I will treasure the memory always."

She believed him, but it still didn't take away the sting, both of his earlier words and the knowledge that it truly wouldn't happen again. Hadn't she known that?

He drove the gig onto Lady Pickering's estate. "I expect when we return to London, you will continue as you did before. Just as I will. We can't act as if we know each other, because in the eyes of Society, we do not. Furthermore, if we are familiar, we risk exposing how we know each other. And that, we cannot do."

She hadn't even thought of that. It would be as if this stretch of days, this wonderful time as Mr. and Mrs. Smythe had never happened.

Only she would know it had. And so would he. They just had to behave as if they didn't.

Jess had a sudden sharp and visceral dislike for the Foreign Office and its bloody missions.

"You understand, don't you?" he asked.

"I do."

"I doubt we'll see each other anyway. I will soon be embarking on my new life, and I'm afraid that will be about as far from the Foreign Office as one can get." He spoke ironically, but she heard the discontent buried far beneath that. He would act as though this change didn't bother him.

She began to think that he didn't know how else to behave. He'd pretended to be someone else for so long and in so many different ways, perhaps he was incapable of being himself, of letting himself…be.

She realized he'd done that a few minutes ago. He would

play the part of the gentleman, apologizing for taking advantage of her or some such nonsense instead of acknowledging the fact that he'd wanted her as much as she'd wanted him.

Or perhaps that was just what she'd tell herself to keep the sadness and disappointment at bay.

Whether to support that goal or because she saw no point in pursuing anything with him, she summoned a smile. "Perhaps you'll enjoy being the viscount. I'm sure it has other allures than espionage."

This earned her a laugh. "I appreciate your optimism and shall grasp it for myself."

He steered the gig to a stop in front of the door to the house. A footman immediately came outside and helped Jess down before Dougal could make his way around.

Dougal told the retainer which case to remove from the back. Then Dougal grabbed the food hamper, which Mrs. Farr had filled with more items than they'd been able to eat or drink.

"Keep that," Lady Pickering called as she strolled toward them from the house. "Are you staying in Winchester tonight or heading back toward London for as long as you have daylight?"

"The latter," he said, grinning. "You know me well."

Jess wished he'd stop looking so handsome. At least when she was within visual distance.

"I presume there's still food in the hamper," Lady Pickering said, stopping beside Jess. "If so, you'll want to have it with you for dinner."

Dougal returned the basket to the gig. "Thank you." He transferred his gaze to Jess, and she caught a flicker of warmth before a veil seemed to drop. He suddenly looked more like the man she'd become acquainted with last week instead of the one who'd been her faux husband.

"It has been a pleasure working with you, Jessamine."

Dougal took her hand and pressed a light kiss to the back. So light, she could barely feel it through her glove.

And then he released her. She wondered when she would see him again.

"Thank you, Dougal. I've learned a great deal." She could muster only a weak smile as she clasped her hands.

He climbed into the gig, touched his hat, and drove away.

"That seemed stilted," Lady Pickering said as she pivoted toward the house.

"I'm exhausted. We were up quite late last night." Jess immediately realized how that sounded and quickly added, "I refused to sleep until I broke the code."

"Oh, splendid! You found a letter, then?" Lady Pickering preceded her into the house. "Come have some tea with me —just for a bit. I want to hear about the mission." She instructed the butler to bring a tray to the library.

Though Jess would have preferred to collapse into bed— and to be alone—she followed her into the library where she'd encountered Lady Pickering several days ago. "We actually found several letters."

Lady Pickering took a chair at a small table and gestured for Jess to take the other one. "Several? That's odd."

"We thought so too. The key to break the code was challenging. The Chesmores are lovers of literature and used a favorite poem as the key."

Lady Pickering stared at her a moment. "I'm surprised this only took you four days. You have proven yourself to be a valuable asset, Jessamine. But what happened? Since Dougal drove you back here, I must presume the Chesmores were not taken into custody?"

"No, Dougal, rather Fallin, determined they aren't spies."

"*Dougal* determined that?" Lady Pickering watched her intently. "What was your opinion?"

"We didn't find any evidence that proved them to be

spies. On the contrary, everything that looked suspicious was explained away by their eccentricities. For instance, the coded letters didn't contain secret information. They were love letters between them. That's why there were so many."

"Love letters? I can scarcely credit that. You're sure?" She waved her hand. "Of course you are. And their other behavior?"

"Mr. Chesmore is merely obsessed with French things. His great-grandmother was French, and for some reason, he likes to embellish, particularly as it pertains to all things French-related."

"Fascinating. You'll need to draft a written report while everything is fresh in your mind."

"Why, so someone can read it and burn it?" Jess *was* tired. She hadn't meant to be sarcastic, but was she really meant to write something down after being told she must never do so?

Lady Pickering's eyes crinkled at the corners, the only hint she was amused by Jess's question. "Mission reports are kept under lock and key at the Foreign Office. These are important for historical purposes and to have a record. When you have it finished, let me know, and we'll have it handled appropriately. Do be careful not to let anyone see what you are doing. I suggest writing it in one sitting, without interruption, and never letting it leave your sight until it is delivered to the assigned person."

"Who would that be?" Jess asked.

"I don't know yet. It may be me. Be as detailed as possible. That is crucial."

"And my compensation?"

"Will be delivered to you as soon as we return to London." Lady Pickering pressed her lips together firmly as her gaze shot to the door.

The butler entered with the tray and brought it to the table.

"Thank you, Daniels. I will pour."

Inclining his head, the butler turned and left.

When he was gone, Lady Pickering poured the tea. "Now, tell me how things went between you and Fallin. I notice you call him Dougal, but I suppose that's to be expected given the roles you were playing." She handed Jess her cup and tipped her head to the side. "I can't tell if you got on well or not. Did you?"

"Yes. It was most...enlightening. He did well, introducing me to this type of work. He's very good at it. The Chesmores liked him and trusted him, as did the servants with whom I saw him interact." In her mind, Jess was also drafting a report about him since that would likely be required. Presumably, someone would contact her about that, but how could she know? She couldn't mention that to Lady Pickering, of course. "It's a shame he won't be doing this anymore."

Lady Pickering had picked up a biscuit and now froze while lifting it toward her mouth. "What's that?"

Damn and blast. Jess hadn't thought that Lady Pickering wouldn't be aware of his plans. It wasn't a secret that his brother had died and he was now the heir. "You know his circumstances have changed," Jess said smoothly, hoping she hadn't spoken out of turn, but also not seeing how she could have.

"Yes. I just didn't realize he would be leaving so soon." She frowned at the biscuit before taking a bite. A moment later, she murmured, "Such a pity."

Jess sipped her tea, nervous about what came next. She'd been so excited for this mission, but now that it was finished, she wasn't entirely certain how she felt about working for the Foreign Office. Her favorite parts were all to do with the scheme of pretending to be Dougal's wife, not the investigating and not even the cryptography. Furthermore, she wasn't sure she could be as secretive and guarded as necessary or if she wanted to be. She'd watched as Dougal had closed up during their trip to Lady Pickering's. Then, upon arrival, her "husband," Dougal Smythe, had just disappeared. She was honestly curious how he would react to her when they met in the future.

Except they likely never would.

CHAPTER 16

*A*fter spending the night at a small inn near Frimley, Dougal continued on to London, arriving at his house on Grosvenor Street by late morning. He went directly to bed and slept until dinner.

Bathed and refreshed, he read his correspondence, including a letter from his father. He asked when Dougal was coming home and hoped it would be soon. The ache Dougal had buried since Alistair's death rose to the surface. As if losing Alistair hadn't been awful enough, now he must prepare to lose his father too.

And give up the thing he loved and that defined him. God, he sounded so bloody selfish.

Dougal left for the Phoenix Club, intent on seeing Lucien and informing him about his mission. Tomorrow, he'd document his report and take it to the Foreign Office. He also planned to read whatever reports he could find about his failed missions. He hoped he wasn't the only person who'd documented the assignments.

As it was Tuesday, it was difficult not to recall that it had been only a week ago that Dougal had been at the club.

When he'd met "Mrs. Smythe" for the first time. How had that only been a week? It seemed as if they'd spent much longer together. Certainly, her impact felt greater.

He'd never imagined he'd experience the sense of comfort and domesticity that he had with Jess. He would greatly miss their breakfasts, their chats before going to sleep at night, and just the simple act of *living* with someone. He'd always expected to be alone. What's more, he'd not once thought that was anything but fine.

Now, however, he was having different thoughts. Was that because of his time with Jess or because he knew that as earl, he needed to find a wife, that being alone was no longer an option? He couldn't deny that Jess had evoked something in him, that he'd shared things with her that he hadn't with any other woman.

Dougal entered the Phoenix Club and found it typically busy for a Tuesday night. He nodded to people he knew, but didn't pause to talk. Going straight to the stairs, he went up to Lucien's office on the first floor, hoping he'd find him there. Instead, he met him at the landing.

"Dougal, you're back already," Lucien said. "I hope that means you had a productive trip?"

"I'll tell you about it." Dougal inclined his head toward Lucien's office to the right.

Lucien gestured for him to precede him. "Lead the way."

Once inside, Dougal went to where Lucien kept his liquor and poured himself a glass of Scottish whisky. He heard the door snick closed and asked Lucien what he wanted to drink.

"What you're having is fine," Lucien said.

Dougal filled a second glass, then turned to hand one to Lucien. "To easy missions." He lifted his whisky, and Lucien tapped his glass to Dougal's.

"Easy?" Lucien's brows rose as he moved to take one of the chairs arranged by the fireplace, which was not currently lit. It had been rather warm today as summer made it known that it wasn't yet finished.

Sitting opposite his friend, Dougal sipped his drink. "Somewhat. The code Miss Goodfellow had to break was challenging, but she worked it out."

"Rather quickly too, it seems. What was the result?"

"Can you believe the letters were sexual in nature? They may have made even you blush."

Lucien gave him a look that clearly indicated that was impossible. "Not state secrets, then?"

Dougal shook his head. "Not even close. There was a stack of them, which was curious. Why wouldn't they be sending them to France?"

"Because the French are quite capable of shagging without instruction?" Lucien asked.

Dougal couldn't suppress his laugh. "Here I concluded it was because they weren't actually spies. Just an exceedingly eccentric couple with an overenthusiasm for sex. They are, in fact, very nice people, if a bit odd. He possesses a weird obsession for French things, but not Napoleon. There was simply no evidence to support them working for France."

Lucien leaned back in his chair and stretched out his legs. "That's that, I suppose. How was Miss Goodfellow, beyond the code breaking?"

Dozens of words rose in Dougal's mind and not one of them had a thing to do with her espionage skills. "She acquitted herself well. She did nearly shoot me one day."

Having just taken a drink of whisky, Lucien sputtered. "What was that?"

"The Chesmores practice shooting every week. They're breathtakingly accomplished."

"Oh yes, why would we ever think they were spies?" Lucien murmured ironically.

Dougal shook his head with a faint smile. "Miss Goodfellow wanted to learn to shoot. She is as bad as our hosts were good. After missing the target by a wide margin with my assistance, Chesmore helped her. She startled, and her arm went wild."

Lucien's mouth dipped into a deep frown. "This sounds very suspicious to me. The man who was thought to be a spy nearly helped your partner shoot you?"

"I did think that at first, but you must admit that's a ridiculous way to try to kill someone. Why not poison me? Or take me out on the ocean and throw me overboard? Or shoot me himself by accident?"

"Did you ponder this at length?"

"I often ponder how I might meet my demise, particularly when I am on a mission." Though he'd never done so and felt a visceral reaction that he could *not* die as had happened in Dorset. Risk was part of the assignment, and Dougal could no longer accept it, for his life—and death—was no longer just about him. Perhaps it never had been, and that made him feel rather selfish.

Lucien adopted a more serious tone. "What happens now? Will you return to Scotland?"

Dougal hadn't told him about his father's illness. "Why would you think that?"

Lucien shrugged. "Since you were called away so soon after Alistair's death, I thought you might want to go back."

"I should." Dougal hadn't meant to say so, but the burden was weighing on him. And he was thinking about mortality again, due to their discussion. "I'm afraid I must accept that my time with the Foreign Office is extremely limited. Indeed, I haven't said so, but I've completed my final mission." But not the last investigation. That was still before him, and until he found answers, he wouldn't go home. Unless, of course, he had to.

Hell, he *should* go now. What good would it do to delve into what had happened on his other missions?

Because regardless of his future, he still wanted to uncover the truth behind those failures. If someone was causing havoc for a nefarious purpose, he needed to root them out.

Lucien brought up his legs and sat forward in his chair, his dark eyes narrowed with concern. "The last one, truly? I didn't realize you would leave so soon. Has something happened?"

Dougal exhaled as he glanced toward the cold hearth. "I neglected to tell you that my father is ill. I must prepare to become the earl sooner rather than later."

"Good Lord, Dougal, why didn't you say anything? You shouldn't have come."

Gripping his glass more tightly, Dougal shot Lucien an irritated look. "It is not for you to say."

"Well, no, but we're friends, aren't we? As your friend, I say you should have perhaps stayed with your father. I would have understood, and so would the Foreign Office."

"Would you have turned down the chance to complete one last mission?" Dougal stared at him, daring him to lie. The sense of self-indulgence rose within him again.

"No."

Dougal rolled his shoulders back. "Especially not on behalf of your father, ill or not."

"He wouldn't want me to," Lucien said grimly. "That would be Con's responsibility. And he'd expect Cass to tend him." Lucien's father made no secret of feeling a closer kinship with his eldest and youngest. To say his relationship with Lucien was fraught was perhaps an understatement. Watching them spar and seeing Lucien's pain—which he buried quite deeply—over the years had made Dougal appreciate his father and their closeness even more. The thought of losing him was almost unbearable.

"What is your plan, then?" Lucien asked. "File your report and head north?"

It was time to confide in Lucien about his investigation. "I need to do something first, and I'm hoping you can help me. You knew something went wrong on one of my assignments last spring." At Lucien's nod, Dougal continued, "There were actually two failures."

Lucien sat back and took a sip of whisky. "What happened?"

"The first one was puzzling—the message I received was filled with nonsense and completely useless. The second was disastrous. I went to meet a courier, and he was dead."

"Shit." Lucien winced. "At the meeting point?"

Dougal nodded. "Whoever killed him either followed him or knew about the meeting."

"I take it there was no message on the courier?"

"No, and I searched him thoroughly." Dougal woke sometimes thinking of Giraud, his throat cut and his clothing stained red as his eyes stared into nothing. He massaged the back of his neck as if that would dispel the image from his mind.

"What does Kent have to say about all this?"

"He was upset, of course, but it's not unheard of for things to go badly. I just hadn't experienced it before." Dougal hadn't been given another assignment for some weeks after that. He'd wondered then if his career might be over. Then he'd been called to Scotland because his brother had died.

"Upset with you?" Lucien asked.

"Not entirely, but it didn't look good having missions go wrong only a matter of weeks apart."

"This was last spring? Before Waterloo and Napoleon's abdication."

"Yes." Dougal gave Lucien a stern stare. "You know I don't like coincidences."

"Nor do I. I'm surprised you didn't tell me about this sooner."

"I would have, but then Alistair died, and it didn't matter at the time. It does matter, however, and I don't like leaving the Foreign Office without conducting an investigation."

Lucien tossed back the rest of his whisky and sat up straight. "Then let's get to it. Where should we begin?"

"I want to read through the reports pertaining to both missions."

"That may be difficult," Lucien said with a grimace. He looked past Dougal for a moment, clearly immersed in thought. "I might be able to get inside."

"I hoped that would be the case. You seem to enjoy privileges I do not."

Lucien rolled his eyes. "I don't know about that. You're the one who gets to gallivant about the kingdom and do actual things that matter."

"You've a point," Dougal said, cocking his head. "What *do* you do?"

Laughing, Lucien stood. "Sometimes, I'm not sure. Mostly, I provide support, such as maneuvering things so that Miss Goodfellow could stay with Lady Pickering. Or getting Evie to help Miss Goodfellow with her disguise." He went to deposit his empty glass on the cabinet.

Helping people and managing such things were what Lucien did best. It was why he'd established this club—to help those in need and to provide a haven for all who might need one. He was a singular person.

"And you'll help me access the reports I need."

"I'll try. It may be that I can look through them and tell you what I see. I'll do my best." At Dougal's skeptical expression, Lucien held up his hands. "You trust me, don't you?" He was joking, but there was something to his question, because there was likely someone Dougal shouldn't trust.

"Of course, but it does seem someone interfered in our operations. Whether I was targeted, or it was just a...*coincidence* that those two missions went badly, I am inclined to think there is someone working against us."

"Or someones," Lucien said. "It certainly bears investigation. What if we don't find anything?"

"Then I shall have to accept that coincidences happen." Dougal thought of the Chesmores and how they'd looked like spies based on circumstantial evidence. What had seemed suspicious was merely eccentricity. Dougal doubted that would be the case here, not when a trusted courier had been murdered.

Dougal finished his whisky and went to set the empty tumbler atop the cabinet. "Shall we?"

Lucien stared at him with the hint of a smile. "You really don't have anything to say about Miss Goodfellow beyond her code breaking and nearly shooting you?"

"What *should* I say?" What could he say that wouldn't completely reveal the way she'd affected him?

"Will she make a good addition to the Foreign Office?"

"I would recommend her, certainly."

"I'm glad to hear it. I like her immensely. I take it you came to like her?"

Dougal was suddenly assaulted with images of her in bed: arching beneath him with sultry moans, stroking him while her lips spread in a wicked smile, crying out his name as she came apart in his arms. Dammit. He'd done such a thorough job of banishing that from his mind.

For one bloody day. Congratulations are not *in order.*

"Yes. The entire mission was very enjoyable, which is satisfying since it was the last."

Lucien clapped him on the shoulder. "I can't imagine what you're feeling about that."

The anguish and grief Dougal struggled to keep buried tried to surface, but he tamped it down. "It hardly signifies since my path is clear. There is no choice to be made. I am the heir, and my father needs me."

"I know how much your father—your entire family— means to you," Lucien said, squeezing Dougal's biceps before dropping his hand to his side. "I'll let you know when I have something to share about the reports."

"Please do." Dougal followed Lucien from the office, then made his way to the library. For the first time, he felt out of place. Not as though he didn't belong here, but that he ought to be somewhere else. Scotland.

He passed a friend leaving the library. The gentleman inclined his head. "Fallin."

The name still jolted him. He wasn't Dougal MacNair, spy, anymore. Nor was he Mr. Smythe or any other role he'd played. He was the Viscount Fallin.

Wasn't it just another role to play? Surely he could manage this just as he'd donned countless other disguises.

Only this wasn't temporary. This was the life he would lead instead of the one he'd planned.

He kept coming back to the fact that the time he'd spent as Jess's pretend husband was the closest he'd come to what the future would hold for him. If he could find someone like her to be his countess, perhaps this sudden change wouldn't feel so overwhelming.

He was taken back to a week ago, to when he met the alluring Mrs. Smythe in this very room. Looking to the door, he wished she'd materialize. When she did not, he took himself to the bottle of whisky and tried to focus on the mystery of his future instead of the bliss of his recent past.

～

*T*he words on the page blurred before Jess's eyes. She gave up trying to read the page for the—she'd lost count—time and snapped the book closed. Tossing it atop the table, she leaned back in her chair and stared up at ceiling in Lady Pickering's drawing room.

Since arriving in London three days ago, Jess had felt incredibly out of sorts. Kat had returned to her brother's home on George Street during the mission to Dorset, which meant Jess's primary source of companionship and entertainment was gone. They had caught up yesterday over tea and a walk around the square. Jess had told her all about how she'd spent several lovely days at Lady Pickering's Hampshire estate. How she hated lying to her friend. And she desperately wanted someone to talk to about all that had happened.

Lady Pickering had taken Jess's written report about the mission, but there had been no communication from anyone regarding Jess's investigation of Dougal. She'd received her payment—a tidy sum that she very much appreciated—but no communication about Dougal whatsoever. Had they forgotten? Were they expecting her to make some sort of contact? With whom? She couldn't ask Lady Pickering, because she apparently didn't know anything about it. She certainly hadn't indicated that she did. The whole thing was bloody frustrating.

In any case, what would Jess even say about Dougal? She hadn't found any evidence of misbehavior, nor had she witnessed anything questionable. He'd acquitted himself admirably and had taught her well. How the devil was she, a novice, supposed to adequately investigate someone like him? She couldn't even remember not to speak French in front of the Chesmores, and she'd slipped up and mentioned their return to London when they were supposed to be from Wales.

No, she wasn't out of sorts, Jess acknowledged as she set her book aside. She was lonely and bored. While she may not have made the best spy, she had enjoyed the challenge of deciphering the Chesmores' letters. More than that, she'd enjoyed Dougal's tutelage and company. She'd never imagined that being someone's wife might prove satisfying. Or even thrilling.

Her only regret was that they'd waited until the very last night to indulge in the physical aspects of a real marriage. If they'd only started that on the first night...

It would have been even harder to part from him. As it was, she missed him. She missed waking up to him in the morning, sharing breakfast, and working close together toward a common goal. She'd never done that with anyone before. Was she beginning to change her opinion about marriage as Mary had?

"Miss Goodfellow?" The butler came into the drawing room. "Your—"

Before he could say whatever he'd planned to say, Jess's parents walked into the drawing room. It was as if the mere thought of spinsterhood had roused her mother to appear.

"Jessamine, sit up straight," her mother admonished as she perched on a chair near Jess's.

"It's a pleasure to see you too," Jess murmured. She glanced toward her father. Tall and thin with a nearly bald pate, he had round, kind eyes. "Good afternoon, Papa." She rose and gave him a kiss on the cheek.

"You look well, my girl," he said with a fond smile. "How was your visit to Hampshire with Lady Pickering?"

"It was lovely, thank you. I found Hampshire quite beautiful."

"You begged us to allow you to remain in London while

we went to Goodacre to visit your poor grandfather, and then you traipse off to Hampshire." Her mother sniffed.

"It's good for her to experience new things," Jess's father said calmly. He took another chair as Jess sat back down.

"Thank you, Papa. And thank you, Mama, for allowing me to remain in London with Lady Pickering." Jess knew it was better to soothe her mother before she became too agitated. Particularly when Jess wanted to win her over. "She has been an excellent chaperone and guide."

"I do hope she made a positive impression on you."

"I think she has." Jess gathered her courage and prayed for luck. "I've had plenty of time to think over the past several weeks, and I am more than ready to embrace spinsterhood. Won't it be wonderful to no longer concern ourselves with chaperones or expenses for the Season?" She gave them a broad, serene smile.

Her mother responded with a tight...no, it wasn't quite a smile. At best, it was an expression of tolerance. "I will be quite delighted to no longer spend my Season trying to see you wed. Indeed, I think we may have, at last, found the perfect husband for you."

Jess gritted her teeth while maintaining her smile. "That isn't necessary. I'm quite enthused about becoming a spinster." Which they already knew. Just as they knew Jess didn't want to marry. Particularly someone her mother selected.

"Just hear us out," Papa said gently, surprising Jess. Had he turned on her? "I believe this may actually be a good match. Lord Gregory Blakemore is intellectual. I think you will have much in common."

Jess had met Lord Gregory several times. She'd even danced with him. He was intelligent and charming, not at all annoying, but he was also a religious scholar and intended to take a living as a vicar. Since he was the son of a marquess, he might even aspire to become a bishop one day. Jess had no interest in becoming a wife, *especially* that of a vicar. They'd be tied to his church. She'd never go anywhere. She suppressed a shudder.

"All we ask is that you give him a chance," Papa said. "Will you do that?"

Sliding a glance toward her mother, she addressed her father. "Does Lord Gregory know you are trying to orchestrate this match?"

Despite Jess trying to converse with her more reasonable father, her mother answered. "No. He has been in mourning. Perhaps you forgot that his father died last spring."

Jess *had* forgotten. But it wasn't as if they were close friends with their family. Why should she have remembered?

"There is to be a ball in a few days where you can reestablish your acquaintance with him." Before Jess could ask why he was expected to be there when he was in mourning, her mother went on. "The ball is being given by Lord and Lady Ringshall in honor of their daughter's engagement to the Marquess of Witney—Lord Gregory's brother. Lord Gregory will be there."

Jess's father looked at her earnestly. "I promise, Jessamine, that if you try with Lord Gregory and it doesn't progress to courtship, we will let you alone."

They'd never said anything like that before. Jess flicked a look toward her mother. Her hands were clasped tightly in her lap and her expression was stoic. She did not return Jess's attention.

"No more Seasons?" Jess asked.

Her mother's tongue clicked the roof of her mouth before she spoke. "It is our hope that you and Lord Gregory will suit and become engaged this autumn. I don't expect there will be any need for another Season."

"Papa just said that if a courtship with Lord Gregory doesn't occur, you'll let me be. So either way, there will be no

Season. Correct?" She asked the question of her mother, but glanced toward her father in happy anticipation.

He was the one who answered. "Yes. But you must respect our promise to you by making your own, Jessamine." Her father's surprisingly stern tone broke into her jubilation. "You must try. That means you can't dismiss Lord Gregory out of hand."

"But what if I spend time with him at the ball and I know immediately that we won't suit?"

"You can't know that so quickly," her mother answered sharply. "I've always told you that everyone has bad days or nights. You certainly do. You will meet him a minimum of six times in a variety of settings for different lengths of time." She pinned Jess with a humorless stare. "I know you think refusing to wed hurts us, but it really only hurts you. The life of a spinster is not what you anticipate. You will no longer be invited many places. Some people will no longer associate with you. It will not be the same for you."

Biting her lip, Jess nodded solemnly. She wanted to say she'd be invited to the Phoenix Club and that would be enough for her, but she didn't.

"I really do think you'll like Lord Gregory when you spend time with him," her father said with a hopeful smile. "You promise to give him a chance?"

"I promise to try." Jess couldn't help it if he didn't do the same. She'd make sure he wanted nothing to do with her by the time the ball was finished.

"Excellent!" Her father stood.

"How long will it take you to pack your things?" her mother asked.

Jess should have immediately realized upon seeing them that they would expect her to return home with them. Why would she stay with Lady Pickering?

Because she was more comfortable here. She'd started an

entirely new life here, not that her parents would know that. What would they say if they learned their daughter had worked in service to the Crown? They likely wouldn't believe it. Indeed, who would?

Lady Pickering strolled into the drawing room. "Good afternoon, Mr. and Mrs. Goodfellow. I was told you'd arrived. I suppose this means I'm to lose my lovely house-guest." She gave Jess a sympathetic look. "I'll have Dove pack your things, and I'll send them to your father's house. Come, dear, let us fetch your hat and gloves." She held her arm out to Jess as she looked toward her parents. "I really did love having her here. She has such a brilliant mind and a wonder-fully kind demeanor."

"Don't forget her independent streak," Jess's mother said.

"One of her very best qualities," Lady Pickering said. "It's a shame she hasn't found the right husband, but I'm sure you know how special she is. It will take someone equally excep-tional to match her. We'll meet you downstairs."

Jess linked her arm with Lady Pickering's, and they left the drawing room together. "You are my new favorite person."

Lady Pickering let out a short, rich laugh. "Your parents mean well, but they'd do better to try to understand you. Sometime you'll have to tell me why you so vociferously avoid marriage."

Asa came to Jess's mind. "There was a man once. My parents wouldn't let us wed."

"You made a choice, and they didn't honor that. Pity. Was he inappropriate?" She cast a glance toward Jess as they neared her chamber.

"He was American."

Lady Pickering twitched. "Good heavens. I might have forbidden it too, dear."

"I was rather young. Perhaps if they'd managed things

differently…" There was no point in reimagining history. Her mother had become apoplectic, and her father had been displeased, which was probably the strongest negative emotion she'd ever seen him display. Jess had naïvely thought they would be happy for her.

Jess shook the thoughts away. The past didn't matter. She was on the precipice of a new future. "Thank you, Lady Pickering, for inviting me to stay. This time with you has quite changed my life."

"It has been my pleasure. If there is ever anything you need, anything at all, I hope you'll come to me." She met Jess's gaze intently, her predatory eyes sharper than ever. "You can trust me to take care of you."

Jess nearly gave her a hug, but wasn't sure the woman would appreciate that. Instead, she gave her arm a gentle squeeze. "I appreciate that more than you can know."

After saying farewell to Dove, Jess fetched her hat and gloves and made her way downstairs to her parents. She moved slowly, her mind turning over the possibilities before her.

Dispatching Lord Gregory as a potential husband would be easy, but would her parents hold to their end of the bargain? A tiny voice in her head said she wouldn't be upholding hers, but they hadn't given her a choice. She was absolutely on the shelf, and pretending she would attract Lord Gregory was absurd. He'd want someone young and probably malleable. Didn't they all want a wife they could control?

No, actually. She thought of the Chesmores. Their relationship was egalitarian and rooted in mutual adoration and respect. She also couldn't help thinking of Dougal. He hadn't sought to manage her, but then their marriage had been fake. Still, she had a hard time imagining him as that sort of husband. And he would be *someone's* husband. That realization made her stomach tighten.

She couldn't keep thinking of him or their time together. It was a distraction from what she needed to focus on—her future. Whether it included the Foreign Office or not, she was soon to embark on a new life. Alone.

Wasn't that what she'd always wanted?

CHAPTER 17

*H*at and gloves in hand, Dougal hurried down the staircase and into the entry hall where Lucien awaited him. "Sorry to keep you waiting. I lost track of the time."

Lucien stood in the center of the hall. "Not a problem. I was a trifle early, and we've plenty of time to walk to the Wexfords'."

After setting his hat atop his head, Dougal pulled on his gloves. The footman opened the door, and Lucien preceded Dougal outside into the early evening.

"There's a touch of autumn in the air, I think," Lucien said, inhaling.

The day had been cooler than the last several with a gray sky, but it was still pleasant. The sun would be setting soon, and the temperature would dip.

They walked toward Grosvenor Square, which they would cut through on their way to George Street, where the Wexfords' house was located.

"Is there a specific occasion for this dinner?" Dougal asked. He'd received the invitation just yesterday.

"Just that Wex and Cass are back from Gloucestershire and wanted to see people. I don't know how many people will be there. Perhaps it will be just family." Lucien shrugged.

"Since when does that include me?" Dougal asked with a laugh.

Lucien blinked at him. "You're one of my closest friends. And you're a good friend of Wexford's. I'd say that makes you family, wouldn't you?"

Dougal hadn't really thought of that. He'd been so removed from his family in Scotland, despite still feeling close to them. He hadn't considered that he had a sort of family here in London. It was surprisingly comforting.

It wouldn't take long to reach the Wexfords', and Dougal wanted to discuss the investigation before they arrived. "I was hoping you might have something to report by now." He looked over at Lucien expectantly.

"I do, in fact. Just today, I was able to glean an interesting piece of information."

"You could have led the conversation with that instead of the bloody scent of the air."

Lucien chuckled. "I knew we'd get to it. It's not much, particularly when I've been denied access to the reports, but it's something. When I specifically asked for these two missions, they were recognized as Giraud's last two."

"How did you learn that?" Dougal doubted Lucien would say. He wouldn't want to get anyone in trouble.

"From someone I trust."

"Giraud was the courier I found with his throat cut. He was not the courier who gave me the nonsense missive."

"He must have been somewhere in that chain," Lucien said. "Is it possible he was behind the bad message?"

"You think he was killed because of that? Giraud was a Frenchman who changed allegiances and began working for the British before I started at the Foreign Office. If he was still working for France all that time, he hid it well. I'd been told he was closely watched for years."

Lucien's features remained pensive. "The French are crafty scoundrels. It could be that he bided his time or that he was exceptionally skilled at hiding his treachery."

"You think he was discovered and assassinated? I would have been told about that."

"Perhaps. Perhaps not. One never knows with Castlereagh."

The foreign secretary, Lord Castlereagh, could be difficult. "It doesn't make sense for them not to at least question me. I interacted with Giraud on several occasions."

"I agree that doesn't make sense. Regardless, that could explain both of your failed missions."

"It was all Giraud." Dougal frowned. It was a reasonable explanation, but it seemed odd. If it was a planned assassination, he supposed he just felt excluded from whatever had happened.

"Seems that way. I'll still poke around, but this may be all we learn."

"I'm considering asking Kent about it again."

Lucien looked at him in surprise as they turned onto George Street. "You haven't already?"

"He told me to let it go, that everyone had things go wrong from time to time."

"That isn't bad advice."

No, it wasn't. But Dougal was still bothered by it all. Or perhaps he was just looking for a reason to stay attached to the Foreign Office when he needed to leave it entirely and return to his father.

A coach stopped in front of the Wexfords'. The coachman jumped down to open the door for the occupants. Dougal nearly tripped upon seeing who stepped out.

Jess, her lovely brown hair elegantly styled with pearls and a small blue feather, straightened as she reached the pavement. Dougal fought to take a breath. He felt as though he hadn't seen her in months, not days—and that the absence had been terrible.

Because it was. He didn't realize until that moment how keenly he'd missed her, how desperate he was to breathe the same air as she did.

Dougal quickened his pace. Lucien worked to keep up with him. "Who's that? Miss Goodfellow?"

She turned just as Dougal was nearing her. The look of surprise on her face was quickly replaced with detachment. He could almost imagine her admonishing herself for allowing anything to show when others were around, even if it was just Lucien who was aware of their acquaintance.

"Good evening, Miss Goodfellow." Dougal bowed and took her hand. He hesitated, but ultimately brushed a kiss across her knuckles. "What a pleasure to see you here."

"Good evening, Lord Fallin."

He released her hand, wondering if he'd held it too long. Hell, he felt like a young buck with his first infatuation.

Jess turned her attention to Lucien. "Lord Lucien."

Lucien bowed. "Miss Goodfellow, always a delight."

Dougal looked into the coach, but it was empty. "Are you alone?" Had she successfully assumed the title of spinster? He would toast her later if that was the case.

"Yes, my parents allowed me to come under the chaperonage of Lady Wexford. It helped that they weren't invited," she added.

"Wex's sister's doing, no doubt?" Lucien asked. "I understand you and she formed a close friendship while you were under Lady Pickering's care."

"We did. I like Kat—Kathleen—very much. She was kind enough to invite me to the dinner party tonight." She glanced toward Dougal. "I wasn't sure what to expect. It certainly wasn't you."

"We were just as uninformed," Dougal said. "May I escort you inside?" He offered her his arm.

"I suppose." She moved close and curled her hand around his sleeve. Her scent had haunted him for days, and now he could bask in it. Again, he had to keep himself from behaving like a besotted fool.

He realized her grip was tense. And her answer, *I suppose*, gave him pause. Perhaps the change in her demeanor outside the coach wasn't due to her masking her reaction upon seeing him—at least not for the reasons he thought. She'd been angry with him when they'd parted at Lady Pickering's.

Lucien trailed behind them as they made their way to the door, so Dougal seized the moment to say something. "Are you still upset with me?" he asked softly.

"Not at all." Her voice was just above a whisper. "I'm only surprised to see you, especially since you said we would not encounter each other again."

"I didn't expect to. But I'm incredibly glad we have."

"Are you?" She turned her head, and their gazes locked as they stepped into the entry hall.

Dougal couldn't bring himself to look away. It was as if he'd walked through a desert and had finally found water. He was enraptured. Despite the fact that she still seemed annoyed with him.

"Welcome!" Lady Wexford's voice greeted them. She also fairly destroyed the lovely moment.

Not completely. Dougal was now looking forward to the evening in a way he hadn't before.

Cassandra moved toward Jess. "I'm so glad you could come, Miss Goodfellow. Kat is looking forward to having a friend here. Come, let's go to the library, where we've gathered before dinner is served."

Jess met his eyes once more as she took her hand from his arm. Then she joined Cassandra and walked with her toward the library at the back of the house.

"That was quite a reunion," Lucien murmured close to Dougal's side.

Dougal rolled his shoulders. "We became good friends. Wouldn't you be if you'd done what we had?" He looked toward Lucien and immediately regretted doing so.

Lucien's brows shot up. "What was that, pray?"

Letting out an exasperated sigh, Dougal started toward the library. "Don't make insinuations. Miss Goodfellow doesn't deserve your adolescent humor."

"Humor you typically share," Lucien mused.

They reached the drawing room and saw that it was to be a small party. Aside from their hosts, Wexford's sister Miss Shaughnessy, and Jess, there was Lucien's brother Constantine, the Earl of Aldington, and his wife, Sabrina. Dougal noted it was a neatly organized gathering with equal numbers of men and women.

Dougal made the rounds greeting people. As he finished, his friend Tobias, the Earl of Overton, and his wife, Fiona, arrived.

"Everyone is here," Cassandra declared before going to greet the latest arrivals.

A few minutes later, dinner was announced. Before Dougal could get to Jess, Lucien had offered to escort her into the dining room. That left Dougal to offer his arm to Wexford's sister, Miss Shaughnessy. At the table, Dougal was seated between her and Jess.

"I don't suppose you'd swap seats with me?" Miss Shaughnessy asked him. "I'd like to sit next to Jess."

Dougal didn't know how to respond. Aside from not wanting to ignore their hostess's seating arrangement, *he* wanted to sit next to Jess.

Cassandra must have overheard her sister-in-law's question. "Kat, are you trying to upset my table arrangement?" She was smiling. "I gather you want to sit next to Miss Goodfellow, but I've situated everyone so that we are male-female. You can talk with her after dinner."

"Or I can talk around Lord Fallin," Miss Shaughnessy muttered.

"It's fine," Cassandra said with a patient smile. "You may swap seats with Lord Fallin."

Dougal clamped his jaws together to keep from protesting. Instead, he took his new seat between Miss Shaughnessy and Lucien. He shot a look over Miss Shaughnessy's head at Jess, who happened to be looking in his direction. She arched a brow at him and gave an infinitesimal shrug.

She was definitely still upset with him, regardless of what she said.

Dougal thought back to that last day of their mission. He'd told her he shouldn't have allowed their tryst to happen. What was wrong with that? Was he not allowed to regret his ungentlemanly behavior? He'd also made a point of saying he'd enjoyed their night together. Hell, he'd been practically spellbound by it ever since. He went to sleep thinking of her, he dreamed of her, and he woke aching for her.

Wine was poured and the soup course was served. Dougal contemplated how he might converse with Jess around Miss Shaughnessy. In the meantime, he listened to their conversation.

"I'm sorry you had to go back to your parents' house," Miss Shaughnessy was saying. "I'm just glad they let you come tonight. I feared they would insist on coming with you."

"My mother did try, but my father dissuaded her, thankfully. But then they think I'm being an obedient daughter." Dougal heard the sarcasm in her tone and wished he was part of the conversation. He had to listen more intently as Jess went on because she lowered her voice. "They want me to wed Lord Gregory Blakemore. He's in the market for a wife, and they think we would suit. Even my father supports the match. He made me promise I'd give him a fair chance. I'm to meet him at the Ringshall ball, which they are holding in honor of their daughter's engagement to Lord Gregory's brother, the Marquess of Witney."

Dougal knew Lord Gregory and liked him. But the idea of him spending time with Jess, potentially courting her, made him cross. No, it made him jealous.

Miss Shaughnessy shook her head. "Terrible. What will you do?"

"The deal I made ensures they will allow me my spinsterhood if this match doesn't come to fruition, which it won't."

"What if Lord Gregory is perfectly acceptable?" He was, and therein lay Dougal's apprehension.

They were silent a moment, then both laughed. Dougal had to stifle his own smile.

"My goal is to ensure I am not," Jess said.

"Brilliant plan. Make it his decision that you don't suit." Miss Shaughnessy smirked. "Then your parents can't find fault with you."

"Precisely."

Dougal gave her credit for a clever plan. If anyone could pull that off, it was Jess. He knew how well she could act. If she wanted Lord Gregory to find her wanting, she would. She just couldn't be herself, for he would be utterly captivated by her intellect and wit. On second thought, he wasn't entirely certain she could suppress that. She'd been acting with Dougal, and he'd become entranced.

"Are you eavesdropping on them?" Lucien whispered, startling Dougal.

"Perhaps. I'm afraid I'm nearly always tempted to do so when people speak quietly."

"Comes with the job, I suppose," Lucien said with a light laugh.

A job Dougal would soon no longer have. That thought kept taking up space in his mind. He didn't want to entertain it tonight. Feeling grumpy again, he focused on his soup. And his wine. Mostly the wine.

Dougal diverted his attention from Jess to the other end of the table. Lucien's sister was at the end of the table next to him, and their brother was on the other side. Lady Aldington was directly across from Dougal. She was expecting a child in the coming weeks, and the expectant joy emanating from her and Aldington was almost palpable.

The rest of dinner passed with amiable conversation, and when it was finished, the gentlemen were not inclined to remain in the dining room for port. Everyone would withdraw to the drawing room.

This time, Dougal was certain to reach Jess first. He offered her his arm. She hesitated, but only briefly.

He also made sure they were the last to depart. "Shall we take a turn outside?" He glanced toward the staircase hall where everyone else had gone, but steered Jess back through the library to the door that led out to a small patio.

"Won't we be missed?"

"We'll explain we wanted to view the garden," he said smoothly as he guided her outside. "How many more pleasant nights will there be? Summer is nearly at an end."

"I suppose that's believable." She still sounded reluctant. Or annoyed. Both, he realized.

"You *are* still angry with me. Don't deny it again."

She took her hand from his arm and turned to face him. "You really don't understand why, do you?"

"Not entirely." He clasped the underside of her elbow and

ushered her to a bench beside a bed of late-blooming flowers. "Please explain it to me. I gather I said something wrong before we reached Lady Pickering's." He pulled her down to sit beside him.

She folded her arms over her chest. "You were very cavalier that day. You behaved as if you were the sole person responsible for what had transpired between us. You also made it seem as though you regretted it."

He frowned. "I said I enjoyed it."

She blew out a breath. "I despair for your future wife if you are this blockheaded. You said you shouldn't have allowed it to happen, as if I had no say. Did you not once describe kissing as the meeting of *two* desires?"

"I did." He inwardly flinched as he recalled saying that.

A righteous anger shone in her eyes. "You asked me if I wanted you to kiss me on the mouth. I did, along with everything that came after. I even told you I would be keen to do it again, which you promptly disdained."

Now he understood. "I *am* a blockhead."

She uncrossed her arms and angled herself toward him. "Yes!"

"Will you accept my apology? I have no experience in these matters." Because he'd never felt this way about anyone, owing to the fact that he'd never allowed himself to. "I appreciate you telling me what I did wrong."

"That's…good. And surprising."

"I misspoke that day. About many things." Particularly the part where he'd declined to repeat their intimacy. Sitting here with her now, he wanted nothing more than to take her in his arms, to lower his guard and bring her close.

She watched him warily. "Such as what?"

"Actually, it's what I failed to say—that I would indeed be…amenable to another night like the one we shared."

"Did you change your mind?"

"Not really. I was trying very hard to be a gentleman that day. Contrary to what you might think, it's not terribly acceptable for a man to take a woman to his bed and not marry her."

"But I didn't expect that, nor do I want that."

"I know. It's just...I've never met anyone like you before. I've never met a woman who provoked such a visceral attraction in me. You are utterly irresistible, Jess." He couldn't stand another moment not touching her. Lifting his hand, he brushed at the soft brown curls cascading along her temple.

Her breath had grown rapid. "Shouldn't we go up to the drawing room?"

"Soon." He trailed his fingertip down her cheek to her jaw. "No one will care. It's not as if your parents are here."

"I'm not sure they would care. You're an eligible bachelor *and* you're titled," she said drily. "My mother would have probably shoved me out the door on your arm."

Dougal laughed softly as he caressed the skin beneath her ear. "I am quite looking forward to meeting her." As soon as the words left his mouth, he realized he likely wouldn't have cause to. He lowered his hand to his lap as disappointment curled through him. "I overheard your plan regarding Lord Gregory Blakemore. I know him, and he may not be as easily manipulated as you think. However, your acting abilities are such that I do believe you'll be successful. I almost feel bad for him—he's a good sort."

The light from the lanterns on the patio danced across her features. "I've met him, and yes, he is. I'm confident he'll find an eager and appreciative wife. I confess he was one of the least annoying gentlemen I've met over the years."

"I shudder to think of how you might describe me."

She cocked her head. "You're rather changeable. At first, I would have said haughty. Then helpful and capable." Her eyes narrowed briefly. "Then wrongheaded. I haven't decided what you are tonight."

"What can I do to ensure your charitable opinion?"

"You could kiss me again, but I daresay you won't." She was staring at his mouth with her lips parted, and he nearly surrendered.

He studied the planes of her face—the soft angle of her nose, the arch of her cheekbone, the plump sweep of her lower lip. The memory of her mouth and body were imprinted upon him.

"It isn't that I don't want to," he said, his voice low as desire pulsed through him. "I fear I wouldn't be able to stop with just a kiss."

She inhaled, her gaze bonded with his. "That would be inconvenient given our location."

"My thoughts exactly."

"Then we shall have to find another location. And another time."

Dougal looked up toward the upper floors of the house. The drawing room was on the front of the house, so no one would be looking down on them. Just the same, he jumped up. Taking her hand, he pulled her from the bench toward the house. Instead of going back inside, he tucked them between the door and the window, positioning her against the brick.

Before she could react, he kissed her. He pressed his body into hers, one hand clasping her hip while the other cupped her head. She responded in kind, putting her hands on his waist and shoulder.

Heat and wonder overtook him as he lost himself in their embrace. Her hand moved to the back of his head, holding him fiercely as she kissed him with a passion he'd never known.

He slid his hand up her rib cage until he found her breast. She pushed into him with a soft moan deep in her throat.

Dougal pulled back, breaking the kiss. Their frantic breaths filled the night air. "We need to go inside," he rasped.

"What about this?" She brought her hand from his waist and stroked the front of his breeches along his rigid cock.

"Temptress," he growled, unable to resist kissing her again.

She gasped as he stroked her flesh above the bodice of her gown. He forced himself to stop again.

"We must go inside. In a moment. But no more kissing." He stepped back and took deep breaths.

She leaned against the house, her eyes slitted with lust as she perused him with a lazy sensuality that did nothing to calm his erection.

"You need to stop looking at me like that." He turned from her. "Speak of something…unarousing." He latched onto a topic about which he was interested but would hopefully not provoke him to touch her again. "Did you write a report about our mission?"

"I did. Did you?"

"Yes." A cool breeze stirred around them, and he hoped it would chill his ardor. "It was bittersweet since it may be the last time I do so." That was an excellent way to quash his desire. Think about how his life was about to change and that he didn't want it to. He turned back to face her. "I imagine it will be the first of many reports for you."

"Actually, I don't know if that's true." She pushed away from the house, straightening. "I'm not sure I make a good spy. If I'm honest, it was stressful, despite your calm and expert tutelage."

While he was thrilled to hear that she valued and appreciated him, he didn't believe she wouldn't be an asset to the

Crown. "You're the most capable, intelligent woman I've ever met. The Foreign Office would be fortunate to have you."

"Perhaps if I had another partner as good as you," she said with a smile.

On second thought, he didn't want to contemplate her working with someone else. The thought of her pretending to be another man's wife made him want to pound the other —as yet nonexistent—man into the ground.

"Jess?" Miss Shaughnessy's voice carried out to the patio.

Jess sucked in a breath and pivoted toward the door. "I'll go inside."

"I'll go with you. I'm fine now. Wouldn't want you to face everyone alone."

She took his arm, her eyes meeting his. "We aren't finished."

No, he didn't think they were. And he was beginning to think they never would be.

Most shocking of all: he didn't want to be.

CHAPTER 18

$\mathcal{T}$he following afternoon, Jess walked in the park with Kat. Her brother and sister-in-law had escorted them, picking Jess up at her parents' house on Cumberland Street, which was just across from Cumberland Gate. The Wexfords were talking with another couple near the Ring, leaving Kat and Jess to promenade.

Kat slid Jess a suspicious look. "You still owe me an explanation about Lord Fallin."

After Kat had called her name last night, Jess and Dougal had gone inside and encountered her in the library. She'd asked, with her typical lack of pretense, what they were doing. Dougal had responded that they'd enjoyed a walk around the garden. Later, Kat had pulled Jess aside and demanded to know why a walk around the garden had taken so long. Jess had jokingly told her they'd circuited it more than once, but Kat had not been amused. So Jess had promised to explain later.

Apparently, now was later.

"There isn't really anything to explain. He escorted me for

a walk around the garden, and we got caught up talking. He's, ah, charming."

Kat stared at her a moment. "A gentleman has turned your head."

This would be so much easier—and better—if Jess could tell her everything. But she was, of course, forbidden from discussing anything to do with the Foreign Office.

"He's interesting."

"He's also a new viscount who is probably in search of wife," Kat said heavily. "Be careful. Dark gardens are perfect locations for compromise."

Jess laughed. "That didn't concern you when you met what's-his-name in the garden at the assembly in Gloucestershire so you could examine the activity of kissing." This was how Kat had become the center of a scandal. As if being caught in a kiss wasn't bad enough, the gentleman was already betrothed.

Kat lifted a shoulder. "I knew I wasn't in danger of having to wed him. He was already promised to another."

"It was still a risk. There was every possibility the other young woman would have cried off, and then you may have had to marry him."

"Bah. That was never going to happen. The alignment of their families had been planned for some time. I plotted my course with great care. Is that what you're doing?" she asked. "Or are you dazzled by him and making foolish choices?"

"There is nothing between Lord Fallin and me." That was the best Jess could do. "You know full well I am destined for spinsterhood."

"As am I, but that doesn't mean we can't enjoy the forbidden—so long as we are discreet. I don't plan to stop my mating research with just a few kisses." Kat wrinkled her pert nose. "They weren't very good, in my opinion."

"What do you have to compare them to?" Jess was under the impression they were her first and only kisses.

"Given the way people seem to almost universally enjoy and seek sexual acts and the fact that I did *not* particularly enjoy his kisses, I can deduce there are better kisses to be found."

"An excellent conclusion, actually. I've kissed more than one gentleman, and their skills are not all equal." Indeed, after kissing Dougal, she could barely remember what Asa kissed like. She was confident in assuming it wasn't as good as Dougal.

"I am not surprised to hear that. Did you kiss Fallin?" While Jess contemplated how to answer, Kat waved her hand. "I assumed you must have. You were too flushed."

Damn, she'd been worried about that. She'd thought enough time had passed between their kissing and when they'd entered the house. But in truth, the heat in her body had remained. It was still there—a low thrum reminding her of how last night had only stoked her desire. She'd told him they weren't finished, and she'd meant it.

"Have you continued your investigation?" Jess asked.

"Do you mean have I kissed anyone else? Not yet. I did consider Lord Fallin after he arrived last night. He's very attractive. Is he a good kisser?"

Jess saw no point in prevaricating. Kat would only persist. "Yes." She also didn't want Kat trying to kiss him. Which wasn't fair of her. He didn't belong to her, nor did she want him to.

Or did she?

Shoving that thought away, she said, "You make a compelling argument about discreet…indulgence."

"Spinsters can't be expected to remain celibate. Unless they want to." Kat cocked her head and adopted the expression that meant an idea had rooted in her brain. "I think this requires investigation too. I confess I did wonder if perhaps I wasn't meant to enjoy kissing. I felt no anticipation, no thrill. You felt those things with Fallin?"

Most definitely. Indeed, the current anticipation was tying her in knots. "Yes."

Kat looked over at her. "Are you going to kiss him again?"

"I don't know when we'll have occasion to meet." And that was a problem. How could she convince him to conduct an illicit liaison if she didn't see him? She needed advice. Or help. Or both. Lord Lucien immediately came to mind.

She doubted he'd help her execute an assignation with Dougal. Evie helped people too. She'd helped Jess, *and* she was aware that Jess may have spent time pretending to be married to someone.

"Then perhaps we should put our focus to that," Kat said with great enthusiasm. "I'll think on it."

They made their way back to the Wexfords, and a short while later, Jess parted from them near Cumberland Gate, saying she could walk the rest of the way by herself. She wanted a few moments of solitude.

As she passed through the gate, she heard her name. Turning to the left, she saw a familiar face smiling at her from farther down the pavement.

Mr. Torrance waved. "Good afternoon, Miss Goodfellow!"

Jess was surprised to see him, but she supposed she shouldn't have been. She'd been wondering when—or if—the Foreign Office would make contact with her, particularly since she hadn't delivered a report about Dougal despite the expectation that she would.

She walked slowly to where he stood. "Good afternoon, Mr. Torrance. I began to think I wouldn't hear from the Foreign Office."

"You put that together, then," he said with a smile.

"It wasn't difficult."

"Definitely not for someone of your intellect. Why would you think you wouldn't hear from us? It hasn't even been a week since you returned from Dorset. You'll find that time is relative, especially in the Foreign Office. You may hear from us quite often, or it may be months until you are called upon to serve."

"I see." She wasn't sure she liked that sort of uncertainty. She made a mental note to ask Dougal when she saw him next. Hopefully, she *would* see him.

"I take it this means you are ready to be of assistance in the future?"

"I don't know." She'd liked the financial benefit of working for the Foreign Office, but if the work wasn't reliable, how could she depend on it to support her? It seemed she would need to secure her unspent dowry after all.

His expression drooped. "Did you not enjoy your mission?"

"I'm just not certain I'm right for that sort of work. I found it…stressful."

"Ah. I can see we asked too much when we tasked you with investigating your partner."

Jess riveted her gaze to him. "You knew about that?" Clearly, he did. "I still can't understand why you would think that *I*—a novice in this work—could possibly investigate anyone without assistance, especially someone as experienced as my partner."

"It was all for naught since it seems he is as loyal as ever."

"How would you know that? I didn't include anything in my report because I wasn't sure if I should. Honestly, one of the primary reasons I'm not interested in this work is because it's bloody confusing."

Torrance chuckled. "That's fair. We thought you were the right person to note anything odd about MacNair because you *were* inexperienced and acting as his partner. He's never had to deal with that before, and if there was ever a time for his guard to be shaky, we supposed that would be it."

"Well, he is a consummate professional and an asset to the Foreign Office. He would never act against the Crown." She spoke with absolute confidence.

"I believe so too," he said. "I have a way you can prove that. If you wouldn't mind solving another cipher?" He smiled hopefully.

"I do enjoy deciphering, and I'd do anything to ensure Dougal is held blameless."

"Brilliant." Torrance slipped a piece of folded parchment from his coat and handed it to her. "Tuck that into your pocket, if you wouldn't mind." He glanced toward Oxford Street.

Was someone watching them, or was he merely being cautious? She slid the paper into the pocket of her gown as her body thrummed with anticipation. She'd hated having to investigate Dougal and relished the chance to prove he was loyal. "What should I do when I break it? Besides burn the parchment, I mean."

"In this case, you must keep the document as it is. I'll need to have it along with your deciphering. Put a candle in your window when you've finished."

"Is someone watching our house?" A bead of unease worked its way down her suddenly chilled spine.

"Don't concern yourself. It's all quite safe and above reproach. Your country needs your expertise, my dear. Don't let us down!" He turned abruptly and walked swiftly away from her.

Jess stared after him. She wanted to yell for him to stop, to explain how this cipher would prove Dougal's loyalty. But then she supposed she'd find out when she deciphered it.

She could hardly wait to get started—and hoped it would go quickly.

∼

*D*ougal sat brooding in the corner of the library at the Phoenix Club. Sunday nights were the quietest of the week, and he typically enjoyed the silence. However, his thoughts were rather loud this evening. Between his father's letter asking when he would return to Scotland and his impending departure from the Foreign Office, as well as the slightly unfinished business of the missions that had gone badly, he felt overwhelmed.

And that didn't take into account his obsession with Jess. Perhaps obsession was too strong a word. He closed his eyes and saw her—the stirring blue of her eyes, the sleek column of her neck, the lush curve of her breast.

Actually, obsession felt just about right.

He glanced toward the liquor, thinking he should have poured some whisky. Except he needed to think, painful as that was.

The man he was waiting for strolled into the library and straight to the liquor. The library was the only room where one could serve oneself. Everywhere else, a footman delivered the libations.

Glass of port in hand, Oliver Kent made his way to a chair next to Dougal. "Evening, Fallin." He eyed Dougal's empty hands resting on the arms of his chair. "Nothing to drink?"

"Not yet. I'm woolgathering."

"Plenty of wool to gather in Scotland," Kent said with a low chuckle before he sipped his wine. Holding the glass up as he swallowed, he narrowed his eyes at the port. "Lucien always has the very best. How does he manage that?"

"Mrs. Renshaw and Lady Warfield are excellent

procuresses." Dougal shouldn't know that, but since he was on the membership committee, he was privy to the workings of the club. Mrs. Renshaw managed things such as what liquor was served and the menus offered in the dining rooms, and Lady Warfield, the bookkeeper, ensured they obtained the finest quality of goods. Occasionally, Lucien lent assistance, particularly with the wine.

"Indeed? They are to be congratulated." Kent took another taste, then set the glass down on a small table between their chairs. "Are you anticipating your next assignment?"

Normally, Dougal would have answered yes. "There aren't going to be any more assignments for me," he said resignedly. Saying it out loud to Kent, making it real, he was surprised to find it didn't carve a hole in him. Finishing his career with Jess somehow felt...right.

"I knew this was coming, but I'd hoped it wouldn't be so soon."

Dougal didn't tell him why, that his father was ill. He supposed he'd spent too long keeping secrets that he didn't see a point in sharing such things. There was one thing he did want to mention, however.

"I'd hoped to settle something before I left," Dougal said. "Those missions last spring—"

Kent held up his hand. "No need to continue. I know you were upset, particularly after Giraud was murdered, but I'm fairly confident he was working against the office."

Dougal angled himself toward Kent. "Do you think he was assassinated?"

"I'm almost entirely convinced."

"Why only almost?"

"As it happens, I'm awaiting a final piece of information that will confirm it." Kent plucked up his glass with a bit of a flourish.

"Why would this have been kept from us?" Dougal asked. "You questioned me extensively about both missions. We should have known." Dougal should have at least been made aware. They'd been his bloody assignments.

Kent swallowed a drink of port. "You know how secretive everything is. Don't waste time going over it in your mind. What would be the point in tormenting yourself when you are about to embark on a new endeavor?"

He had a point, but Dougal didn't like unsettled business. "You'll let me know when you've confirmed this was what happened?" How many times had Dougal recollected both events trying to determine when they'd gone awry and how? If he'd known Giraud had been involved with the delivery chain with the bad message, Dougal might have been the one to uncover the man's murder. Except Dougal had been occupied with his family. At least someone in the office had been on the case.

"Of course," Kent said.

Dougal almost asked if Kent had withheld information from him until now. It seemed unlikely he wouldn't have known about Giraud's involvement. But Kent was right—there was no reason for Dougal to dwell on this.

"Are you truly finished with the Foreign Office?" Kent asked softly, his gaze fixed on Dougal. "Or might I be able to persuade you to come back and help from time to time?"

"I can't imagine how that would happen, but I would always like to be of service to the Crown."

"Excellent." Kent finished his port and started to get up.

Dougal pinned him with a serious stare. "Just know that my priority is now my family. It has to be."

"I understand." Kent reached over and clapped him on the shoulder. "Your father is a fortunate man to have you as a son. Your bond is forged in something far stronger than blood."

"What's that?"

"Love." Kent gave him a warm smile, then stood and departed, depositing his empty wineglass on a table near the library door.

Dougal leaned back in the chair, feeling as though he'd ridden across England. And Scotland. Had he really just terminated his affiliation with the Foreign Office? Not entirely, it seemed. Kent was clear that Dougal would always be welcome.

For the past four years, he'd worked hard and loved being in service. He'd known who he was and what was expected. Before that, he'd done the same in the Black Watch. And that had resulted from his father prompting him to decide what he would do. He couldn't live an aimless life as the younger son of an earl. Somewhere inside, Dougal had known that, but the lure of London to a young buck fresh out of Oxford with his friends had corrupted him for a while. Until his father had forced him to remake himself as a soldier. Now, he would do so again.

Dougal stood, finally intent on that whisky. Lucien intercepted him. "What did Kent want?" he asked.

"I summoned him so I could tell him I am finished with the Foreign Office."

"It's official, then?" Lucien grunted. "You need a drink. Or I do." He went and poured them both Scottish whisky.

"Kent said he may call on me sometime."

Lucien handed him one of the tumblers. "You'd be open to that?"

"I would, provided it didn't interfere with my duties. My family and the Stirling estate must take priority now."

"I really hope Con and Sabrina's child is a boy. If something happens to Con, I do *not* want that responsibility." He grimaced at Dougal, then lifted his glass. "Sorry."

"You'd excel at it, and you know it. Just look at what you've done with this club."

"Running a membership club is not managing several estates and an entire legacy." Lucien shuddered. "No, thank you."

"Thank *you* for making it sound completely overwhelming," Dougal said wryly before sipping his drink.

"You're up to the task. The question is, when do you plan to take a viscountess?"

Dougal snorted. "I have no plans."

"Really? I wondered if you might after you and Miss Goodfellow went missing last night."

"We didn't go *missing*. We took a walk around the garden on a pleasant evening. If you must know, I wanted to see how she was faring after the mission. It can be quite jolting to go from one reality to another." That was utter nonsense, but the truth was that Dougal should have done that. It seemed he owed her another apology. Another reason to see her.

But when? How?

"You could do worse than her," Lucien mused softly over the rim of his glass before taking a drink. His eyes shone with teasing mischief.

"Do not meddle," Dougal said sternly. "Have you learned nothing from your experiences with your brother and sister?"

Lucien rolled his eyes. "People keep telling me not to get involved, but this is literally what I do at the Phoenix Club. I put my nose in others' business for the greater good." He spoke passionately. "I created an environment that would be welcoming to those who most need a haven. And I help those who need it. If you need assistance finding a wife, my services are at your disposal."

"Careful, or we'll have to start calling you the Gentleman Matchmaker." Dougal shook his head. "I don't need your help. Truly. There is no chance Miss Goodfellow will become my viscountess. She is quite committed to spinsterhood."

Their conversation was interrupted by the arrival of two very dear people—Maximillian Hunt, the Viscount Warfield, who had been a close friend of Lucien's and Dougal's for many years, and his wife, Ada, now Lady Warfield, who was one of the very people Lucien had helped. He'd hired her as the club's bookkeeper two years earlier.

"You've come," Lucien said, smiling. "I feared you weren't going to make it tonight after all."

Max shook his hand, then Dougal's. "We arrived in town this afternoon."

"So you've been in the club for hours." Lucien arched a brow in silent insinuation.

Ada rolled her eyes at her employer. "I was doing work in my office." Which was on the ladies' side of the club and part of her suite where she and Max stayed when they came to town.

Lucien bussed Ada's cheek then Dougal did the same.

"It's lovely to see you, Ada," Dougal said. "I'm sorry to have missed your wedding to this bumpkin."

"We understood." She took his hand and gave him a warm squeeze. "How are you? You look well."

"I am, thank you." He didn't want to discuss Alistair's death. He realized he never did. And he never had.

"I'm so glad." Ada turned her gaze to Lucien. "Can we discuss a few things?"

"I expected to." Lucien nodded toward Max while speaking to Dougal. "Look after him, will you?"

"Yes, I need minding," Max murmured drily.

Ada's eyes shone with love as she kissed her husband's cheek. "See you in a bit."

She and Lucien departed the library.

Max glanced at Dougal's glass. "Scottish whisky, I presume?"

"Certainly not that Irish swill."

"Precisely what I'm going to pour." Max went to fill himself a glass, then they moved to stand in front of the windows. He took a sip and smiled. "Definitely not swill." He studied Dougal for a moment. "How can you be well after losing Alistair?"

"It's been two months."

"Bah. I lost Alec years ago now, and it still hurts." Max's gaze was sympathetic as he drank from his tumbler. "At least you still have your father." He couldn't have known those words would slice into Dougal like a well-sharpened blade.

"For now." Dougal felt suddenly bitter and angry. It wasn't fair. His father was still a young man. He should have years ahead of him. What the hell was Dougal still doing in London? He should be halfway to Scotland by now—to be with his father. "He's dying."

Max blanched, his face stricken. "*No.*"

"So the physician says. His heart is weakened."

"How long do you have together?" Max asked softly, anguish evident in his tone.

Dougal hated rousing Max's grief at losing his own father and brother, but couldn't deny the shared experience was most welcome as he struggled to come to terms with his own loss. "That is unclear. It could be months, but it could also be a year or more."

"I will pray for the latter," Max said.

"Thank you. I'm sorry this dredges up your grief."

The corner of Max's mouth edged up. "I don't have to dig too deeply to find it. Ada has made it more bearable, however. She reminds me every day that there is still love and happiness in the world."

Dougal knew his perspective wasn't as dark and hopeless

as Max's was—or had been. He'd suffered terribly during the war. He did seem to have found some serenity at last. Dougal briefly clasped his old friend's shoulder. "I couldn't be more thrilled for you, Max."

"It's certainly an improvement." He lifted his glass in silent toast, and they both drank.

Swallowing, Dougal decided to seek his friend's advice. "I hope you don't mind my asking, but how did you adjust to inheriting the title when you never expected to? I find I can't reconcile what I must do with what I thought I would be doing. It's…overwhelming."

"That's one word for it. You recall that Lucien sent my wife to help right my estate because my accounting and ledgers were in tatters? I drove my steward away with my beastliness, and I didn't care that the estate needed him. I sat and did nothing while my tenants struggled to manage without support. It wasn't just overwhelming, it was *impossible*. I simply couldn't do a damned thing. I daresay you aren't that bad off."

"Not in that way, but I haven't the slightest notion how to manage an estate or to be an earl."

"I didn't either, but I'm learning. You will too. At least you don't have to serve in the Lords like I do."

"Not unless the Scottish Parliament elects me to do that someday." Dougal hadn't considered that. For the first time, he thought he might be useful as the Earl of Stirling. "I don't think I'd mind that, actually."

"You wouldn't," Max said good-naturedly. "But then you've been involved in the Foreign Office for years now, haven't you?"

Max knew that Dougal had left the Black Watch to complete an assignment for them, but he hadn't known it was permanent. "Why do you think that?" Dougal asked.

"I may have had my nose buried at Stonehill these past

two years, but I'm not stupid. Lucien kept me abreast of your travels. I didn't for a moment think you were gadding about the kingdom to see the sights. I also know how bloody clever you are. There was no way the government was going to let you go after one task."

Dougal neither confirmed nor denied his friend's accurate conclusion. "I can see how that would look."

Max snorted. After taking another drink, his brow furrowed. "You can't do that work anymore. I imagine that troubles you."

"It makes me angry, actually. I enjoyed it. I'd hoped to move up in the ranks."

"Which is why you'd be an excellent addition to the Lords. Would that I could give you my seat," he said with a chuckle.

Dougal lowered his voice to an intense whisper. "Tell me how you've reconciled the change to your life. I don't know how to do it. I am torn between duty and desire."

"Then find a way to make the duty something you desire."

"Is that what you did?"

"Not on purpose, but it did work out that way. Find yourself a wife and a helpmate. Without Ada, I would still be stumbling around in the darkness. She gave me something to desire—not just her." His lips curled into a brief but wicked smile. "She inspired me to become a better man, to live up to the duty I now carry but never wanted. I am shocked to find I quite like running the estate. When you called me a bumpkin, you weren't wrong."

Dougal laughed. "Your solution, then, is for me to find a wife. Lucien was just pestering me about that."

"Oh hell. Did he offer to play matchmaker? He's so bloody meddlesome."

"He did, in fact. I refused him soundly."

"You don't need his help. You're heir to an earldom with a

vast fortune. I suppose you're also passably good looking and in possession of a meager wit."

"I thought you said I was clever." Dougal snickered.

Max waved his hand. "That too."

"I've never thought about taking a wife."

"Never?"

Dougal shook his head. "I didn't think I needed to. I've been focused on other things."

"I suppose we know what you'll be doing next Season."

Unless Dougal had already met the perfect helpmate. He and Jess had played husband and wife most successfully. He could easily envision her as his viscountess. She'd be magnificent.

Except she didn't want to wed.

"Your mind has gone off," Max observed. "If you aren't ready to wed, don't rush it. I wasn't looking for Ada at all, but there she was. When love happens—and if you're lucky enough to recognize it—every plan you've made is suddenly worthless. Nothing is more important than that other person."

Love…that was absolutely not in Dougal's plans. And Max was right. There was no rush. However, he was beginning to think he already knew his wife, that she'd actually *been* his wife. Their time in Dorset had felt so surprisingly natural and…good. The culmination of their passionate night together had seemed right and even necessary. And he'd been ridiculous telling her that he shouldn't have allowed it. He couldn't have denied it if he tried.

"I actually do know someone who would make an excellent partner. However, she is dedicated to spinsterhood."

"You can't change her mind?" Max asked.

"She reaffirmed her commitment just last night, in fact." Before they'd kissed. Before she'd told him she wasn't finished with him. God, he needed to find her tonight.

CHAPTER 19

$\mathcal{T}$he candle was low before Jess finally set her quill down atop her desk. Shaking her hand out, she reread the translated message one more time. This was the proof Torrance was looking for. A man called Giraud confirmed delivery of a worthless message he'd created while destroying the real missive that had come from France. He also commented on the fact that he'd soon receive valuable information from MacNair, and that MacNair was not suspicious of him at all.

Jess felt a surge of triumph. The most satisfying part of breaking this particular cipher was knowing with certainty that Dougal hadn't been working against the Foreign Office. This man Giraud had been the culprit.

Yawning, Jess rubbed her eyes. She'd no idea what time it was, but it had to be late. Past two at least.

The sound of the door latch clicking and the slight creak of the hinges made her jump. Quickly gathering the papers on the desk into a pile, she grabbed a nearby book and set it on top of them. She slid from the chair and crept toward the fireplace, where she reached for the poker to use as a means of defense. Perhaps she *should* have tried shooting again. That would be of no consequence unless she owned a pistol, which she did not.

A figure slipped into her chamber. She started toward him, her arm raised so she could strike him over the head. He started to turn, and she brought the weapon down.

"Shit!" Dougal stepped to the side, but she hit his shoulder with the poker.

"Dougal!" She dropped the weapon and rushed toward him. "I didn't know that was you. What are you doing here?"

He rolled his shoulder back and closed the door. Though the only light was her waning candle and the coals in the hearth, she could make out his startled features. "I came to see you."

"It's the middle of the night. How did you get in here?"

He stared at her. "You know what I do? Or did, rather."

"Well, now I feel silly. I continue to be impressed with your skills. Not only did you steal into the house without being detected, you knew where to find me."

He shrugged. "I am good at this. As are you." He bent to pick up the poker. "Not a bad weapon. I also continue to be impressed."

"I was lamenting the fact that I perhaps gave up shooting prematurely."

Laughing softly, he replaced the poker on the hearth and faced her. "I would be more than happy to begin your tutelage once more. I will be shooting many things in Scotland, probably."

"Doesn't your estate have a gamekeeper?"

"Yes, but my father always took us hunting. He says there is something satisfying about the laird providing for his clan."

She blinked at him. "Will you be laird of a clan?"

He shook his head. "No, but my father likened his role as

earl to that. The estate has many tenants. He refuses to clear any of them away to make room for sheep. Indeed, he's provided a sanctuary for many who were forced to leave their homes."

"He sounds like such a wonderful man."

"I've a great deal to live up to. I will not, however, need to steal into rooms or conduct secret searches. Nor will I be required to deliver messages in the dark of night or eavesdrop on conversations in seedy places."

"If you ever think you'll be able to share details of your exploits, I shall be thrilled to be your audience."

"Perhaps when we are old and gray." He winked at her, and she fixed on what he said. Did he think they would still be acquainted then? An image of them together—aged and grizzled—as he regaled her with tales of his daring flashed in her mind. Along with it came a curious ache. His question thankfully interrupted her wayward thoughts. "What are you doing up so late?"

The urge to tell him everything—that she'd been tasked to investigate him and why and, most importantly, that she'd just deciphered the evidence that cleared his name for certain. But the words didn't come. It wasn't just that she wasn't allowed to reveal any of it. She supposed she didn't want him to know she'd been investigating him in Dorset, even though she'd done an exceedingly poor job of it.

"I was reading." Her gaze stupidly strayed toward the book atop the desk. It was really for the best that she wouldn't be spying.

He pivoted toward the desk and took a step. "What's the book?"

Moving quickly, Jess dashed in front of him. "You steal into my chamber and ask *me* what I'm doing up so late. You shouldn't even *be* here."

"No, I should not," he said softly, his voice a caress that

stoked the longing that had lingered within her since their kiss the night before. Really, since they'd parted in Hampshire nearly a week before.

"Yet here you are," she whispered.

"I believe you said you weren't finished with me. That left me curious. I've come to allow you to finish."

Jess wasn't certain she ever could—not with him. She thought of her conversation earlier with Kat. Would he be interested in a liaison? If not, why would he be here?

"Then I suppose we should get started." Jess moved toward him, but he met her halfway, sweeping her into his arms as his lips crashed into hers.

The feel of him against her made her spirit soar. She'd feared she would never experience this again.

Tearing her mouth from his, she pinned him with a fierce stare. "You aren't going to later say we shouldn't have done this, are you?" She didn't have patience for that nonsense.

"No, I am not. I am taking you to that bed and shagging you senseless without regret. If you have any opposition to that, say so now."

She pressed her fingertips into his nape. "Hurry, please."

~

*D*ougal kissed Jess again as he carried her to the bed. After barely sleeping last night and thinking of her almost incessantly all day, he was nearly overcome with want. How had he ever thought they could share just one night in Dorset and never see each other again, let alone never share a night like this?

He hadn't been thinking. He'd been conducting his life without consideration, going about things as he had for the past several years. Connections and romantic liaisons didn't last. He didn't have time for them, nor had he been interested in fostering or maintaining any sort of ongoing relationship.

It seemed a fake marriage had changed all that. Or, more accurately, a certain captivating woman who'd captured his attention and attraction.

Suddenly, a lasting liaison and even domesticity were appealing.

Dougal set her on the bed. She was wearing the same red dressing gown she'd worn in Dorset. It looked strange—as if she shouldn't be wearing it when she wasn't Mrs. Smythe. What a thoroughly possessive notion. It made him kiss her even more deeply, his lips and tongue claiming every part of her mouth.

She clutched at his head and shoulder, her movements as frenzied as he felt. He wasn't entirely sure he wanted to wait until they were disrobed. At the very least, he needed to remove his coat as it was inhibiting his movements.

Straightening, he pulled the garment from his shoulder and let it drop to the floor. Then he tugged his cravat loose. It knotted, and he had to fuss with pulling it free.

While he was distracted, she'd unbuttoned his fall. Now her hands were on his cock, and he was glad he'd gotten the cravat off. If not, he wouldn't have been able to accomplish the feat, not while she was stroking him so wonderfully.

She sat on the edge of the bed, her head so very close to his cock. He imagined her taking him in his mouth... Then she did precisely that.

Pushing his breeches down over his hips, she held the base of his shaft and put her lips around him. One of her hands caressed his backside while the other scored her fingernails over the flesh of his balls. Sensation and pleasure crashed over him as she drew him deeper into her mouth.

"Jess," he murmured, grasping the base of her plait and threading his fingers through her hair. He closed his eyes and tipped his head back, relinquishing himself completely to her control.

He knew she'd never done this before—they'd discussed it last time after he'd pleasured her similarly. She'd asked if she could return the favor. He'd said yes but hadn't thought it would actually come to pass. Now, here she was giving him more of herself than he'd ever dreamed.

Her fingers dug into his flesh, urging him to thrust into her mouth. He tried to retain control, to not overwhelm her, but she was quickly pushing him to the edge of reason.

It would be so easy to let himself go, to completely surrender and climax into her mouth. But he wanted her to come with him.

Clutching the back of her head, he pulled away from her. His cock pulsed with the almost painful need to finish.

"What's wrong?" she asked, her voice deep and husky. The tone was incredibly erotic and did nothing to ease his torment.

"I want to finish with you." He unbuttoned her dressing gown, and while she obligingly shrugged it off, the garment remained pinned beneath her.

She stroked him again, her hand moving expertly over his shaft. "I wanted to experience what it felt like for you to finish in my mouth."

Dougal groaned. "Next time. I promise."

She looked up at him with a sensual smile, her eyes slitted. "I am thrilled there will be a next time."

"I am more concerned with this time. I'm afraid I can't wait another moment." He realized as soon as he said the words that his current situation would make shagging her rather difficult. He needed his breeches off, which meant he needed to discard his boots.

Cursing rather profanely, he worked his garments off until he wore nothing but his shirt. In the meantime, she'd removed her night rail so that she was nude. She also scooted back on the bed, her legs splayed before him while her hand rested above her sex.

"Touch yourself for me," he whispered, the pain of near-release reaching a terrible crescendo.

Her fingers slid down to her clitoris. "Like this?" She stroked herself and brought her heels up to the edge of the bed, bending her legs.

"And your nipple." He closed his hand around his cock and pumped it from head to base.

Her hand stilled over her sex. "Only if you take off your shirt."

He quickly moved to respond, whipping the garment over his head and throwing it away. "Do it."

Her fingers started again between her legs, and her other hand moved to her left breast, cupping it at first and then closing her thumb and forefinger over the nipple. She breathed heavily, her rapture an audible sensation that fed his desire.

"Harder," he said. "Pinch it like I do."

She closed her fingers over the nipple and pressed. Gasping, she held tightly, pulling at her breast as she slid one of her fingers into her sheath.

Dougal moved his hand from his cock to her sex, putting his finger with hers and thrusting them inside her. She cast her head back with a moan as her wet sheath gripped him.

Unable to stand another moment without being inside her, Dougal put his other hand around his shaft and put himself at her sex. She pulled at her folds, opening herself for him. He slid the head inside, then thrust deep.

She wrapped her legs around his waist and used every part of herself to pull him into her. Her hands gripped his hips and backside, urging him to drive hard into her. The feel of her around him was bliss. He moved onto the bed, pushing them farther onto the mattress.

Arching up, she cried out his name. He vaguely wondered if they were being too loud, but he was having a hard time with rational thought. Either way, he didn't care. He let go, thrusting into her with deep strokes as her body quivered around him. Feeling she was close, he ground down against her sex. She dug her heels into his backside and let out a keening cry.

Dougal claimed her mouth, both to own her completely and to quiet her passion. The last thing they needed was someone coming to see what ailed her.

Her muscles clenched around him as she came. Dougal's balls tightened, and he knew his orgasm was imminent. Now was the time to pull away from her to prevent a child.

But her legs clamped tighter around him, and she held him close, kissing him with a feverish need that made him senseless. His orgasm raced over him with a startling ferocity. He found her breast and squeezed, his body shuddering with its release.

Silently swearing, his wits returned, and he rolled away from her, his cock twitching as his seed poured forth, slicking his abdomen and hip. He grasped himself and worked through the finish.

"I wish you didn't have to leave," she rasped between breaths. "I wasn't quite done."

He hated that. Rolling back, he put his hand on her sex and found that she was already there. He pushed two fingers into her and pumped as her hips moved. She moaned long and deep as she contracted around him once more.

He drew her nipple into his mouth and sucked. Then he withdrew and blew over her heated flesh as her movements began to calm. "I thought you already came."

"I did. But there was another one right after."

"You are absolutely astonishing." He'd never encountered such an inquisitive and eager partner. She met him with every touch and thrust. He kissed her long and deep, moved to an almost unimaginable place by her generosity and curiosity.

She rolled toward him so that they faced each other. "Please tell me you aren't leaving right away."

"Not right away, but soon. It was just after two when I came in downstairs. What time do the maids wake?"

"Before five. We have a little time." She snuggled closer to him, putting her arm around his waist and tucking her head beneath his chin.

He kissed her forehead, his lips lingering against her flesh as he trailed down to her temple. "I missed this."

"I keep thinking we should have done this on the first night in Dorset instead of waiting until the last."

"I won't say it didn't occur to me," he said with a smile.

She tipped her head back to look at him. "Really?"

He looked into her familiar eyes. "I've been attracted to you since you touched me in Lucien's study."

Grinning, she brought her hand up to his chest and stroked her palm over him. "It's been much longer for me, I think. If I'm honest, my interest was sparked four years ago when you danced with me."

He leaned his head back against the pillow and groaned. "I hate that I can't remember that."

"It's all right. I take enough pleasure in it for the both of us."

Her words thrilled him. Four years ago. What about four years from now? The thoughts that had been swirling in his mind for days finally coalesced into something real, something *good*.

"Our partnership was very successful, wouldn't you say?"

She nodded. "I would. I don't think I could have done any of it without you."

He tipped his head down to look at her once more. "Then let's not allow it to end."

Her gaze snapped to his. "But you're leaving the Foreign Office."

"*Left*. I've told them Dorset was my last mission. I have to return home. My father and the estate need me." He took a breath. "And I need a partner. A wife." He cupped her head and caressed her cheek with his thumb. "I can give you the independence you crave. Yes, you'd be my viscountess, but if you want to work for the Foreign Office, I'll support you. I'll support you in anything you want."

She stared at him, the pleats between her eyes more pronounced than ever. "You want me to be your wife?"

"Think of the adventures we will have. You said you wanted to see Scotland."

She was quiet a moment, her hand still against his chest. "Yes, but I can do that without submitting to become your wife."

A hard knot formed in his gut.

"You weren't interested in marriage until you became the heir. How do you feel about it now?" she asked, sounding slightly distant. Or perhaps that was just the thrum of his suddenly fast pulse in his ears.

"I am optimistic for the future with you. I think we could be a formidable team."

She pressed her lips together, and he knew what she was going to say even as he feared it. "I appreciate you asking, but my outlook on marriage has not changed. I must decline your proposal."

∾

*J*ess pushed up to a sitting position and reached across the bed to grasp the edge of her night rail that had been flung across the now-rumpled coverlet. Drawing the garment over her head, she kept herself from looking toward him.

He also sat up. However, he did not attempt to clothe himself, so she either had to look at his tempting naked chest or keep her gaze averted. She chose the latter.

"I know you didn't plan to marry, but we make a good team, don't we?"

She couldn't deny that. "Working together as a productive team on an investigation doesn't mean we'd be a good husband and wife." Except she'd considered that on many occasions and seemed to have trouble separating their pretend scheme from reality.

He turned his upper body toward her, his brow furrowing. "Our mission *was* as husband and wife." His features relaxed. "I enjoyed it more than I expected to, honestly."

"That is a riveting testimonial," she murmured wryly. But she didn't disagree with him, dammit. Furthermore, if they wed, her parents would never bother her about marriage again. That alone almost made her rethink her response.

Was she really going to change her stance on marriage after all these years? If she were honest with herself, she'd already started considering it, at least when she'd spoken of marriage with Mary, if not sooner. She *had* liked being married to Dougal. So much that when he'd said he shouldn't have allowed them to become intimate, the words had hurt more than they should have.

"You didn't?" he asked. "Then I was mistaken."

She didn't answer him. It wasn't a question of how she felt about their faux marriage. They were discussing the future, making that pretend union *real*. "Enjoying our time together and wanting to make it permanent aren't the same thing." Her mind was still tumbling through her shifting thoughts.

He'd asked her to *marry* him. Actually, he hadn't. He'd blathered on about being a team and having an adventure.

"I see." He slid from the bedclothes.

She glanced toward him as he pulled his shirt over his head. Returning her attention to the coverlet, she plucked at a loose thread. She flattened her hands on her thighs as she listened to him dress in silence. From the corner of her eye, she saw him sit on the chair at her desk to put on his stockings and boots. Tension stiffened her frame. She hoped he wouldn't see the papers beneath the book. Not that he could read them without moving the novel, which he had no reason to do.

He went on, diverting her from her anxiety. "I'd hoped you might see the benefit of marrying me. Are you really going to avoid marriage to continue to spite your parents?"

She met his gaze, but only briefly before she focused somewhere to the right of him instead. "You wouldn't understand. They took away my choice. I swore I would never marry."

"That seems a shallow and immature reason to reject a perfectly sound proposal."

Asa's proposal from seven years ago rose in her mind. She hadn't thought of that day in a long time. He'd knelt before her under the pink blossoms of a cherry tree and proclaimed his love for her. He'd said he'd come to England to explore and to learn, that he'd never dreamed of finding the woman he'd want to make his wife. He'd promised her a life of love and adventure, knowing she wanted both. She'd quite forgotten about the love part.

Until now.

Dougal had taken her on an adventure and—unwittingly

—given her love. Not that he possessed it and gave it to her, but that he'd given her something that had summoned that feeling inside her. He'd cared for her, laughed with her, supported her. He'd made her feel special and important. Perhaps it *was* a sound proposal...

She didn't want sound. If she was going to abandon her pledge to become a spinster, it was going to be for more than convenience. She wanted love.

"Jess?"

His Scottish brogue pulled her from her reverie. She could almost pretend that Scottish Lord Fallin and Welsh Dougal Smythe were two different people. They seemed to be. She just couldn't see her "husband" from Dorset speaking to her so callously—as he'd done on the way to Lady Pickering's and again tonight.

She turned her head to look at him. "Did you come here tonight intending to ask me to marry you?"

Surprise flickered in his eyes for a slight second. If he hadn't taught her to study people, she might have missed it. "You play a role quite well," she said softly. "Indeed, I'm not at all certain who you are tonight."

He stood, completely dressed save his cravat, which he draped around his neck. "I would be your husband."

"But who is that, Dougal? You are in the midst of a huge change. How can you even know what you want? Or who? I may seem a good solution for a problem you need to solve, but you are no longer an investigator seeking answers and resolving situations. That is definitely not how you should go about finding a wife." She straightened her spine. "You've known my position on marriage. It should come as no surprise that I would refuse you. Our liaison has not changed my mind."

"Then I bid you good evening." He bowed before leaving her chamber, closing the door with a barely audible click.

Jess picked up the pillow from behind her and punched her fist into the center. Fluffing it against the headboard, she settled back with a deep frown.

What had just happened? They'd had a perfectly wonderful encounter, which he'd ruined by bringing up marriage. That had provoked her to think about him in ways she'd been avoiding. She had no issue with being attracted to him, to wanting him, to carrying on a liaison with him. She did not, however, want to be in love with him.

Unfortunately, she feared she was.

Then why hadn't she said yes to marrying him? Because it didn't seem that he loved her in return. Years ago, she'd wanted to marry a man she'd loved, but her parents had forbidden it. So she'd refused to submit to their plans, to align herself with a man of whom they approved. She wasn't about to accept a proposal they would wholeheartedly endorse, even if she loved him. *Especially* since she loved him, because he didn't love her back. That would be the union her parents wanted, the one that had been expected all this time.

But if Dougal loved her, it would be the marriage *she* wanted.

What if in spiting her parents, she'd actually been denying herself something wonderful? They'd disappointed her, and she'd sought to disappoint them. What an absurd manner in which to live.

If this mission with Dougal had shown Jess anything, it was that she did want an intimate relationship, a companion, a husband. She wanted love. She envied Mary and Gil, and if there was any chance she could have what they shared, she'd take it. Unfortunately, the proposal Dougal had given her was not that.

The candle on her desk finally sputtered out, casting her into near darkness. The coals in the fireplace didn't put out much light. Or warmth. Suddenly, she felt quite cold.

Jess burrowed under the covers and rolled to her side, pulling her knees to her chest. Had it really just been a short while ago that she'd been in Dougal's arms, awash with incomparable passion? Apparently for the last time. She had to think they were truly finished now.

How devastating, since she'd only just realized how wonderful they might have been together.

A tear slid from her eye, and she wiped it away in frustration. She refused to cry over him. She hadn't even realized she loved him until his stupid proposal. Couldn't she go back to when she didn't know, to when spinsterhood was her goal? She'd learned to pretend quite well. Surely, she could behave as if her entire time with Dougal was nothing more than a dream.

Tomorrow was the engagement ball. She would speak with Lord Gregory and dance with him if he asked. She would ensure he never called on her and never paid her another moment's attention. Then she would be free.

She was no longer entirely sure what she'd be free from.

CHAPTER 20

*D*ougal would have left for Scotland that very morning, but after arriving home just before dawn and proceeding to drink himself into a dreamless slumber, he was in no shape to travel. Tomorrow it would have to be.

In the meantime, he went to the study and drafted a note to Lucien telling him about his departure and that he wasn't sure when he'd be back in London. That felt so odd. London had been his home the past four years. And before that, he'd been abroad with the Black Watch.

He recalled what Jess had told him upon learning he'd served in the Highland regiment. She'd wanted to see him in a kilt. Now, she never would.

Avoiding thinking of her, he let his mind return to his time in the regiment. He rarely thought of it. War was not something he wanted occupying space in his head. It was much easier—and better—to think of it as something that had happened to someone else.

Again, he thought of Jess. This time recalling what she'd told him last night:

"But who is that, Dougal? You are in the midst of a huge change.
How can you even know what you want? Or who? I may seem a
good solution for a problem you need to solve, but you are no
longer an investigator seeking answers and resolving situations.
That is definitely not how you should go about finding a wife."

She'd seen right through him to a depth he hadn't even seen himself. Looking back, he'd been many people—the eager son and brother, the young buck who'd enjoyed himself with his friends, the earnest soldier, the confident spy. Who was he supposed to be now? The heir who didn't know what the hell he was supposed to do when his father died, when he would be alone to manage the family's legacy.

Dougal leaned back in his chair and stared at the ceiling of the study. He'd thought marrying Jess was such a good plan. Not just for him, but for her too. He'd been so wrong. Apparently, she'd only wanted him for sex. It was rather fitting, since that was all he'd ever sought from women and infrequently in recent years at that.

It seemed no matter what he tried, he couldn't stop thinking of her. Perhaps he needed more liquor. Grunting in frustration, he stood and walked around the desk. Then he stopped short as a familiar figure entered the doorway.

"Da!" Dougal grinned as he rushed forward.

Malcolm MacNair, Earl of Stirling might now rely on a walking stick, but he still looked as imposing as ever to Dougal. Tall with thick white hair that had once been copper and impressively bushy eyebrows, he regarded Dougal with piercing blue-green eyes.

"Careful there, my boy," he said as he embraced Dougal. "Don't break him."

Dougal looked past his father to see Robbie smirking at him. Right away, Dougal knew his cousin had escorted his father, and he was incredibly grateful.

Patting his father's shoulder, Dougal took a step back. "You dragged Robbie with you?"

"He insisted." Da moved into the study so that Robbie could come in too. He embraced Dougal.

"Thank you," Dougal whispered to his cousin before they broke apart. Turning to his father, he asked, "Why did you come all this way? I was planning on leaving tomorrow."

Da waved his hand. "I was impatient. Besides, I haven't been to London in ages, and I wanted to come at least once more, if only to see how you've been taking care of the house." He looked around at what was really his study. "It looks good on you. And now you can show Robbie around."

Dougal couldn't deny the appeal in that. "What about your apprenticeship?"

"Och, Johnson understood. Dinna fash yerself. I'm here as long as ye need me."

Glad to have them both here, Dougal started toward the door. "I'll ask Henderson to prepare your rooms."

"I've already done that." Da ambled to what had always been his favorite chair when he'd come to London and sat down with a huff. "Pour us some whisky."

"None for me," Robbie said. "I'm going to let the two of ye talk."

Dougal poured three glasses anyway and handed one to his cousin. "Take it with you at least."

Robbie grinned. "Twist my arm. See you later." He left the study, closing the door behind him.

Dougal delivered another tumbler of whisky to his father's hand. Da gave him the walking stick in exchange, and Dougal stood it against the side of the chair.

Plucking up his own glass, and sitting opposite his father, Dougal smiled. "I rarely sit in that chair."

"Why not?" Da sipped his whisky and closed his eyes in silent appreciation.

"It's silly, but I like to sit here and imagine you're in that chair. Then we have a conversation." Dougal had never shared that with anyone. Why would he?

"What do I say?"

Dougal laughed. "Not much, unfortunately."

"Well, it's good to know you miss me as much as I miss you. Sometimes I've wondered."

"Have you?" Dougal found that surprising. He wrote often.

"There's been something different about you since you left the Black Watch. I would have thought you would spend more time at home. In Scotland, I mean."

Da, of course, didn't know that Dougal had been a spy. Dougal had only ever said that he'd departed the Black Watch to complete an assignment for the Foreign Office. He hadn't ever mentioned ongoing employment or the nature of that assignment. Thankfully, Da hadn't questioned anything. Until now.

"What do you mean by different?" Dougal asked, feeling slightly uneasy.

"I would ask where my son has been hiding." He leaned forward, his features creased with grave concern. "Did something happen during the war? Did it damage you in some way?"

"No." Dougal could think of plenty of men who had been damaged, especially Max.

"Then why didn't you come home more? And don't give me that nonsense about traveling."

Lies sprang to Dougal's tongue, but he didn't say any of them. Since he was done with the Foreign Office, there was no harm in telling his father—who wouldn't be on this earth much longer—the truth. Indeed, he suddenly regretted not telling him sooner, especially since he'd revealed his secret to Robbie. "I continued to work for the Foreign Office. I couldn't tell you." He gave his father an extremely sheepish and hopefully apologetic stare.

"Ah." Da sat back and was quiet for a moment. "I imagine you were very helpful to them. I'm proud of you, son."

Emotion clogged Dougal's throat. He worked to swallow past it. "Thank you. That means everything to me."

"I'm glad to hear it. Will you continue to do so now?"

"No. I've left my post." Dougal kept his voice even. He didn't want his father bearing any guilt for the end of his career.

Da grimaced anyway. "I would ask if that bothers you, but I'm certain it does. You have never done anything halfway." He regarded Dougal with pride and admiration. "You've always worked harder than anyone. I know you felt you had to because of how you look and your paternity, that you felt the need to prove you belonged. I hope you know that none of it was necessary to earn my love. You had that the moment you entered this world. I promised to raise you as my own, and it has been my great honor to do so."

Long-buried emotions swelled in Dougal's chest and mind. He took a moment to rein them under control. "You humble me."

"Hardly. You're one of the humblest people I've ever met," Da said with a laugh. Sobering, he added, "I truly am sorry to have cut your career short."

"You don't need to apologize. It's all right," Dougal said, recalling his conversation with Max and grateful that he'd had his friend's advice. "It isn't what I planned, but I am up for a new challenge. I've been giving it some thought, and I would be interested in serving in the Lords if that ever came up."

As he laughed, Da's eyes sparkled with joy. "That's my boy. I will make sure the right people know that. You'd be an excellent representative for Scotland."

Dougal loved how his father always championed his children. "You don't think my...parentage would be a problem? It isn't exactly a secret that I'm not yours."

"You are mine in every way that matters, particularly under the law." Da's blue eyes narrowed, glinting with a sheen of fury whenever the topic of Dougal's paternity was raised. Which, because of Da's ire, wasn't often. "That is long settled, at least at home. I thought it was here. Are you not treated well?"

"I am," Dougal assured him. There were looks and whispers, which would always happen, whether people knew of his birth or not. He was a Black man in a society where Black men, particularly of his status, stood out.

"Good. If I witness anything untoward while I am here, I will not tolerate it."

Of that Dougal was absolutely certain. "Does that mean you don't want to return to Scotland immediately?"

"Hell, no. That's a bloody long journey. You're going to take me and Robbie around and show us all your favorite places, starting with this Phoenix Club you're involved with."

Dougal was quite glad he'd come. "We will visit tomorrow, after you're rested. Tuesdays are the best night anyway."

"Right, that's when the ladies are invited into the gentlemen's side of the club?" Da smiled as he raised his glass. "How things have changed. I am glad to see it." He barely swallowed his drink before adding, "But I'm up for an outing this evening after I take a short respite. If you had plans, Robbie and I will join you."

In fact, Dougal had originally wanted to attend the engagement ball for the Marquess of Witney and his betrothed because he knew Jess would be there working to deter Lord Gregory Blakemore from courtship. But after she'd refused him last night, he no longer saw the point in going. "I don't have plans, actually."

Da's eyes narrowed, and he pointed at Dougal. "There."

Dougal blinked, wondering what in the devil his father meant. "What?"

"There's more to what you just said. I can see it behind your eyes. When I asked where you'd been hiding, it wasn't just about your physical presence and not being at home. When you did come home, you were reserved, different. You were not the boisterous, openhearted boy you'd once been." He exhaled, and there was a tinge of sadness to the sound. "I suppose you grew up."

"Yes." While the war hadn't ruined him, it had certainly changed his perspective and likely his demeanor.

"I would also assume you've spent the last several years being very secretive. Hiding was a necessity. Perhaps now that you are finished with that, you can come out from behind the wall."

He did hide himself. Jess had been partially right in saying he didn't know himself—he hadn't given himself the chance. "I hadn't realized I was doing that, but you're right," he said softly.

"Does that mean we can finally talk about Alistair?"

There it was. The clearest indication of Dougal's practice of burying emotion, of pretending it wasn't a strong, driving force—or of not allowing it to be. "We've talked about him." While that was true, Dougal knew what his father meant. Then why was he hesitating? Because he was still trying to hide behind the wall, and he couldn't. Not anymore. Not with his father. Not with Jess. And certainly not with himself.

"I miss him," Dougal said simply. "I try not to think about him."

"Why?"

"It hurts."

His father nodded. "I would hope there is also joy. The

problem with suppressing or ignoring emotion is that you keep out the good along with the bad. All of it is worthwhile. It pains me to think you don't allow yourself to experience that."

Dougal hated that he caused his father worry. He had enough to be concerned with. "How do you do it? How do you think of Alistair and not succumb to grief?"

"I did and I still do, though it's less than it was. I think about happy times, and I remind myself that Alistair wouldn't want me to be sad. He'd want me to live."

Except even that was in danger. "I will try to do that." Dougal spoke in a low, anguished tone. "But Da, I can't do all that and contemplate losing you too. Yet, I must."

Da sat forward, his eyes misting. "Don't do that. I'm here, and I plan to be here for a while, no matter what the doctor said. We've too much to do together."

Relief rushed over Dougal, and not because his father would somehow miraculously heal himself, but because this —letting his emotions in—felt good. Da was right about what Alistair would want. "I remember the first time I fell off my horse," Dougal said. "I was six, and Alistair came to help me up. It hurt and I was crying, but as soon as Alistair arrived, I tried to be brave. Alistair told me to have a good cry, that I would feel better for it, that it would give me the resolve to get back on the horse."

"Good Lord, he was eight when he told you that?" Da laughed softly. "That boy's soul was so very old."

"Except when it came to women." Dougal snickered. "He was like a tongue-tied schoolboy."

"Yes, you were the one giving *him* advice on that front."

Dougal smiled, but then a wave of sadness hit him. Alistair had finally found the right woman, and now he was gone. Stepping out from behind the wall completely, Dougal realized he'd also found the right woman.

Aside from his father, no one had understood him like Jess did. Was that because she was just that astute? Or had he somehow let down his guard with her in a way he hadn't before? Whatever the reason, she was a singular person, and he'd be a fool not to fight for her. Not because she was a good partner or would make an excellent viscountess. Because he loved her.

"Do you truly not have a plan for this evening?" Da asked, interrupting the glorious flow of emotion washing over Dougal.

"I did, but I was going to skip it. However, you've made me realize it would be a mistake to do so. There's a ball, and a woman I'd like you to meet will be there."

Da's face lit with first surprise then happiness. "I was not expecting that."

"I wasn't either. But it seems that there were many emotions just waiting for me to no longer hide them, including my love for her." He looked to his father. "Have you ever been in love?"

Da chuckled. "Oh, yes. I even loved your mother. I don't know that she truly returned the emotion, however. I think it may have been infatuation on her part."

"Did you always love her? I'd thought you did not, that your marriage was mutually beneficial, and you were friends." Dougal and Alistair had discussed this on several occasions.

"It was absolutely beneficial, and we *were* friends—after we fought for a few years. That was settled before you were born. By then, of course, we were living relatively separate lives. And quite happily." He paused, his expression resolute. "I wouldn't want that for you. Does this woman love you in return?"

"I don't know." Dougal grimaced as he recalled the debacle of his proposal the night before. "I asked her to marry me last night—poorly. The worst of it is that she asked me if I'd intended to propose. Truthfully, I hadn't. I asked spontaneously, and I completely botched it. I wouldn't blame her if she fell out of love with me right then."

"It doesn't happen that quickly," Da said with a smile.

"That's a relief. However, I'm not even sure she loved me to begin with."

"There is only one way to find out, my boy." Da finished his whisky. "I'm going upstairs to rest, and then we're going to charm this poor woman until she can't possibly refuse you. I can't imagine why she would anyway."

Reaching for his walking stick, Da got to his feet. Dougal started to rise, but Da waved him back down. "Sit and strategize. You were always good at that. I can imagine the Foreign Office appreciated that about you." He clapped Dougal on the shoulder on his way out.

"I love you, Da," Dougal called without turning his head.

"I love you, Dougal."

Smiling to himself, Dougal felt incredibly grateful for the man who'd raised him. If he hadn't been impatient and come all the way to London, Dougal might still yet be wading through the morass of his stunted emotions. Not stunted— buried. Hidden. Ignored.

No longer. He was in love with Jessamine Goodfellow, and he wanted the entire world to know.

❧

*I*f Jess could have begged off the Ringshalls' ball, she would have done, for she was so very tired after barely sleeping the night before. However, she knew her mother would never stand for it. Even if Jess had been suffering some terrible illness, her mother would have dragged her to see Lord Gregory.

On the way to the ball, her father was cheerful and talkative. It wasn't that he was never those things, but Jess couldn't remember the last time he'd displayed any sort of enthusiasm for such events. But then, she couldn't recall the last time he'd accompanied them to a ball or a rout. He seemed unaware of the tension in the coach—from Jess's desire to be anywhere else and from her mother's anxiety that tonight go well.

Then there was the underlying weight of melancholy stealing any sort of enjoyment Jess might have had. She struggled not to think of Dougal and his terrible proposal. No, she was trying not to focus on the fact that he didn't love her while she was hopelessly in love with him.

Hopeless because she'd given up hope that there was anything to be done about it. He was likely on his way to Scotland by now. As he should be.

They arrived at the Ringshalls' and Jess adopted her meekest behavior. She just wanted to get through this evening without agitation.

Once they were inside, her mother immediately located Lord Gregory. He stood near the doors to the terrace, surrounded by a group of women. He was very attractive, despite looking pale. His blond hair was trimmed shorter than the fashion, and his costume was almost entirely black.

The poor man. Jess felt an urge to rescue him, but then reminded herself that she was supposed to make herself unappealing. Perhaps that would annoy him—she couldn't assume he didn't want the attention he was garnering. Although, judging from the stoic expression he wore, she would wager he would welcome a reprieve.

"Look at them," her mother said in a brittle, cynical tone. "Carrion, the lot of them. Come along, Jessamine."

Jess bit her cheek lest she say something ironic that

would only annoy her mother. What were they if not carrion as they went to join the feast?

It took several minutes to reach the inner circle, and Jess heard everyone using the same excuse for bothering him—paying their condolences and respects over the death of his father.

She sank into a deeper than normal curtsey. While she didn't want him to pursue her, she had a great deal of sympathy for him. "Good evening, Lord Gregory. It's lovely to see you again."

"We are so sorry for the loss of your father," her mother put in, also offering a curtsey.

"Mrs. Goodfellow, Miss Goodfellow. Thank you for coming to celebrate my brother's engagement. This is a happy occasion, but I do appreciate your kindness." He spoke as if he'd repeated this dozens of times. Jess was fairly certain he had, that she'd heard those exact words as they'd waited their turn. He also failed to make eye contact with anyone. His gaze passed briefly over each person, then settled somewhere on the middle distance.

Elbowing Jess, her mother whispered, "See if you can get him alone."

Jess turned toward her mother. "No. He doesn't seem to want to be here."

"But I have it on good authority that he's in the market for a wife."

"Not tonight, he isn't." Jess could see her mother didn't want to give up. "Please, just look at his eyes. He doesn't want to be here."

Her mother sniffed. She also didn't move.

Jess tried to find their father, who'd remained back by the ballroom door they'd come in. Instead, she saw a surprising face—Dougal. He'd just walked in, and he wasn't alone. He was flanked by an attractive, older white man and a young

Black man who looked as though he could be Dougal's relative. They shared the same eyes and face shape. Was he one of the cousins Dougal had mentioned?

Her heart skipped at the sight of Dougal, and she had to stop herself from cutting a swath through everyone who stood between them. Instead, she watched as they moved into the ballroom and conversed with several people.

"He's leaving," her mother said in dark disappointment.

Of course she meant Lord Gregory. Jess tore her gaze from Dougal and turned back toward her mother's quarry. Lord Gregory was extricating himself from those clamoring around him. It took a moment, but he slipped outside through one of the doors to the terrace.

That left Jess and her mother amidst a gaggle of disappointed mothers and daughters. Jess wanted to applaud him for finding an escape. Even if he was inclined to marry, he just didn't seem up to the task this evening.

"My goodness, is that the Earl of Stirling? He hasn't been to London in years." This came from somewhere nearby, though Jess couldn't see who'd said it.

"It's rather jarring, isn't it?" Another woman said. "One wonders why Stirling claimed him."

Jess didn't know who had uttered such awfulness, which was probably for the best. She would never have been able to keep from responding.

"I knew his youngest—I suppose now he's Lord Fallin—wasn't his by blood, but seeing them side by side is shocking." This comment came from just behind Jess.

Jess turned, glaring at the woman who'd said it. She knew precisely what the woman meant and didn't bother trying to disguise her contempt. "Do tell us how that is shocking."

"I don't understand how it's been accepted, let alone tolerated. They clearly aren't father and son. And who is that other Black man with them?" She didn't realize that

Jess's disdain was directed at *her* not at Dougal and his father.

"It isn't shocking at all, you obnoxious harpy. I doubt anyone cares about your opinion on the matter. Anyone can see they share a close bond. I wonder if the same can be said of you and your children." Jess had no idea who the woman was, but assumed she at least had a daughter since they were in the swarm around Lord Gregory.

Spinning around, Jess started toward Dougal and his family.

"What was that about?" her mother demanded.

"Those horrid people were making nasty comments about Lord Stirling and Lord Fallin. Did you not hear?" Jess dearly hoped her mother didn't agree. If she did, Jess didn't know what she would say that wouldn't ruin their relationship forever.

"I thought I heard something to that effect." Her mother sent an angry look back toward where they'd just been standing. "I detest malicious gossip."

"Why should the specifics of a father-son relationship matter to anyone but them?" Jess asked, her indignance still quite hot as she continued moving.

"Where are you going?"

"I thought I would say good evening to them."

Her mother looked surprised. "You know Lord Fallin?"

Jess almost asked how her mother could forget that she'd danced with him four years ago since she seemed to catalogue every gentleman who'd paid her even a breath of interest. But she realized in that moment that she wasn't being entirely fair. Perhaps it was the situation she'd just witnessed and her need to defend the relationship between a parent and his child that gave her pause. Her mother had made mistakes and was singularly-minded, but in the end, she had

Jess's best interests at heart. At least, what she believed to be Jess's best interests.

So instead of picking at tired wounds, Jess said, "He was at the Wexfords' dinner the other night."

"Was he?" Her mother's eyes lit. "Why didn't you tell me?" She waved her hand. "Never mind. I can well imagine. You wouldn't want me to encourage anything or, God forbid, stick my nose in. What sort of impression did you make?"

Jess nearly smiled, but that would reveal too much. "A good one, I think." Right up until she'd refused his marriage proposal. She'd leave that part out.

"Then let us go speak with him." Jess's mother cut right through the now-dispersing crowd that had been around Lord Gregory with relative ease. But then she'd had years of such navigation.

As they neared Dougal, Jess's step faltered. Would he even want to see her? She'd refused him.

Wait, did this mean she wanted to change her mind? Would she accept his proposal without his love knowing, as she did now, that she loved him?

She considered walking right past him and out of the ballroom, but it was too late. His gaze met hers. The man who'd led a life of secrecy and subterfuge was in full effect. His expression was pleasant, but revealed nothing to her.

"Lord Fallin," Jess's mother said loudly, her lips curved into a beguiling smile. "We are so pleased to see you." She made sure Jess moved to stand right in front of him.

Dougal bowed to her and then to Jess. "Allow me to intro-duce my father, Lord Stirling, and my cousin, Robert Clark. Da, Robbie, may I present Mrs. Goodfellow and Miss Goodfellow."

Jess made a graceful curtsey, and her mother did the same. "I'm so pleased to make your acquaintance, my lord." She meant every word. To meet Dougal's father was a wonderful honor she'd never expected. "Lord Fallin speaks so well of you."

"Does he?" Stirling chuckled lightly as he glanced toward his son. "I might wonder why he mentioned me to you." His gaze took on an assessing quality as if he were solving a puzzle.

"This is the lady I spoke of," Dougal said.

Robbie's eyes glinted as he met Jess's gaze. "Well met, Miss Goodfellow. Ye must possess an astonishing fine character to suffer Dougal here."

Dougal rolled his eyes, and Jess could feel the close camaraderie between the two men. She had so much she wanted to ask Dougal about the family he'd barely mentioned. He'd kept a great deal from her, she realized. Was that on purpose, or was it just that he hid things from everyone? She suspected it was the latter.

Jess's mother touched her forearm. "This all sounds very promising." The excitement in her tone was palpable. Jess hoped she wouldn't combust.

At the same time, Jess couldn't help but also feel a surge of elation that Dougal had told his family about her. She opened her mouth to say that she was delighted and flattered, but she was interrupted by a most inopportune arrival.

"Could it be the Smythes?"

Jess and Dougal swung their heads at precisely the same moment. There, standing in a London ballroom were the *Chesmores.*

Gil had spoken, his blue eyes wide with shock. Mary appeared equally stunned, her mouth open as she stared at Jess and Dougal. Being Mary, she recovered quickly with a bright smile. "It *is* the Smythes! My goodness, I nearly didn't recognize you. Your hair looks so different." She turned her attention to Dougal. "And you aren't wearing your spectacles."

"Who on earth are the Smythes?" Jess's mother asked. She gaped at the Chesmores as if they were mythical monsters from the sea.

"Our very dear friends," Mary responded.

Gil had smiled too, but his ebullience faded, his brow furrowing. "Perhaps they are not the Smythes, my cygnet," he said quietly, reaching gently for his wife's arm. "We may be mistaken."

"Of course we aren't. I realize they look a bit different, but they are the people who came to investigate us."

The word investigate landed like a stone to Jess's ears. From the corner of her eye, she caught the earl murmuring something to Dougal. Did he know? Had Dougal told him about his secret life?

Jess's mother puffed out her considerable chest. "I don't know who you think my daughter is, but she is Miss Jessamine Goodfellow. And this is the Viscount Fallin and his father, the *Earl of Stirling*. You are grossly mistaken if you think they are anyone named Smythe or that you've met them before."

And there was Jess's father standing just behind Mary. He'd moved closer to hear what was going on. As had many —many—other people. They were now at the center of a crowd larger than had surrounded poor Lord Gregory.

"I don't understand," Mary said, looking quite confused. "How can these not be the Smythes? I would know my friend anywhere—and they share the same Christian name. How many Jessamines do we know? Precisely one." She looked to Dougal. "Isn't your name Dougal?"

Dougal's eyes met Jess's. He gave his head an infinitesimal shake and mouthed *I'm sorry.*

Gil pulled Mary close and whispered in her ear. She gasped and clapped her hand to her mouth.

"How does she know your name?" Jess's mother asked

with quiet urgency. "Why does she think you're married to Fallin?"

Mary reached for Jess's hand. "I'm so sorry. I didn't realize. And here you aren't even really married."

"Come, my kitten," Gil said with a forced laugh. "Let us go and find your cousin so we may give her our congratulations on her engagement." That explained why they were here.

Jess watched them go and wished she could escape with them.

"Married?" Someone said the word quite loudly, but Jess had no idea who'd done it.

The whispers were already growing and spreading out across the ballroom.

Jess's father came toward them, moving close enough so he could speak in a soft but thoroughly furious tone. "Will someone please explain what the devil is going on here? Why did those people think you were the Smythes and that you were *married*?"

Frantic that this would become the biggest scandal of the year—and it still might—Jess pivoted toward her father. "It is a long and complicated explanation, Papa. However, the important part is that Lord Fallin and I are betrothed. He was going to speak with you tonight."

Her mother was probably going to see right through this nonsense, but it was the best Jess could come up with in the moment. She only hoped Dougal would go along with it. If he'd changed his mind and didn't wish to marry her, he could cry off later, and while it would still be a scandal, it would at least happen in a far less public arena. Then Jess would go on to become a spinster and everyone would forget about her. As a viscount, he could find a woman he loved and marry her while no one would care that he'd once been at the heart of a great embarrassment.

Oh God, what had she done? Perhaps it would have been better to skulk away than to bear his rejection.

She was afraid to look at Dougal, but did so anyway. Once again, he was unreadable. He didn't, however, refute anything she said.

A gentleman stepped closer to them. "Did I hear you say you were betrothed?" he asked, either unaware of his rudeness or not caring that he was inserting himself into their conversation. His gaze moved to Robbie. "And who is this?"

Dougal turned to the man, his features hard and unreadable. "You're sticking your nose where it doesn't belong."

The earl leaned on his walking stick. "Let us find a more private location to talk, shall we?"

"Yes, let's," Jess's father said tersely. He offered her his arm, and, given that she'd never seen him so angry in her entire life, she accepted it without question.

As they made their way from the ballroom, she tried to ignore the stares and whispers, but mostly she hoped Dougal would understand.

CHAPTER 21

*a*nger roiled through Dougal as they left the ballroom. He'd heard the whispers and seen the shock on people's faces turned in their direction. Was it because of what Mary had said? Or was it because he was a Black man daring to wed a white woman? Couldn't it be both?

"Try to take a breath," Robbie whispered, moving to his side as they walked.

"I am."

"Ye look as though ye're readying to take someone's head off their shoulders. Probably not the best impression if ye want to convince Miss Goodfellow's father that he should allow ye to wed his daughter."

Dougal shook out his shoulders, but it did little to relieve his tension. Had Jess actually changed her mind about marrying him, or was she only trying to lessen the damage?

Goodfellow, with Jess on his arm, led them away from the ballroom and did not stop until they found a small sitting room a good distance away. Presumably he wanted to be as far from eager eyes and ears as possible. Dougal couldn't blame him. He couldn't imagine a more disastrous spectacle than the one that had just occurred.

Not only were he and Jess now in the center of a massive scandal, they were in danger of being exposed as some sort of secret investigators. Speculation would run rampant, and the Foreign Office would distance itself from them. As they should. If Dougal's career wasn't already over, it would be now.

What he most wanted was to take Jess far away so they could talk privately. He completely understood why she'd said they were betrothed. What else could she do in that situation? Since she'd already refused him, he reasoned that she didn't plan to actually marry him.

Da entered the sitting room in front of Dougal, and Robbie closed the door behind everyone. Moving to Good-fellow, Da offered his hand. "I'm delighted to welcome your daughter and all of you to our family."

Dougal was so damned grateful for his father's presence. He would have a calming effect, and the truth was that when an earl spoke, people just tended to listen.

"Your family," Goodfellow said, swinging his gaze from Da to Dougal to Robbie. "And who is this young man?"

"My cousin," Dougal said tightly. He realized acknowledging Robbie as a member of his family was also acknowledgment that he couldn't share his father's blood—as if that had ever been in question. However, claiming his Black family publicly wasn't something he'd ever had to do, at least not in London, and for the first time, Dougal felt exposed. The double life he'd long led crumbled, and he realized—finally—that it had little to do with his work for the Foreign Office.

No, he'd spent years living up to the ideal of a white nobleman's son. While he *was* that, he was also a Black cousin and nephew to good, working-class people. He wanted to be both and wouldn't settle for anything else.

Goodfellow faced Dougal, his dark brows pitched low over his light blue eyes. His ivory face was splotched with red. Dougal didn't have to know the man to recognize he was furious. "I am extremely disappointed in whatever has happened here. I expect a full explanation."

"I'll give it, Papa," Jess said from beside him. She'd taken her hand from his arm and now clasped her hands tightly in front of her. "It's entirely my fault. I insisted Dougal and I spend time together—alone—before I would accept his proposal. I wanted to be sure we would suit."

Mrs. Goodfellow's face was entirely red. "You did *what?*"

"I wanted to be sure after all these years of not wanting to marry," Jess explained. "Why do you think I've avoided it for so long?" Dougal knew she was feeding her mother nonsense and wholeheartedly applauded her quick thinking. She'd make an excellent spy yet. Or she would have if she hadn't been exposed.

"I thought it was just to annoy me," her mother said, getting the right of it. "Are you saying you went to Hampshire with him and not Lady Pickering? I must have a stern conversation with her for allowing this to happen!"

"You aren't going to blame anyone but me, Mother. This was entirely my doing. Dougal was kind enough to humor me."

"He will not avoid recrimination," Goodfellow said darkly, shifting his attention back to Dougal. "You absconded with my daughter without at least having a marriage contract. This is intolerable."

"I understand, and I would be angry too," Da said before Dougal could respond.

Dougal gritted his teeth. "Can I please speak?" He didn't wait for anyone's permission. "This was *our* decision. Lady

Pickering had nothing to do with anything." Moving to Jess's side, he put his arm around her and immediately felt her stiffen. He tried not to read too much into it but couldn't imagine it boded well for their actual future.

"It isn't going to help matters to belabor what is done," Da stated calmly. "I think we can all agree that our children might have handled things differently, but they did not and now we must mitigate the damage. That is why I will obtain a special license for them to wed tomorrow."

Goodfellow looked from the earl to Dougal and back again, doubt etched in the lines around his eyes. "He is truly your son?"

Dougal was sorry to hear him ask it, but couldn't say he was surprised. He was even sorrier that Da had to hear it, because he would consider calling the poor man out.

Da's eyes glittered with outrage. "Of course he is. Why would you question me?"

Goodfellow had the intelligence to look away, and the splotches faded from his face. "I didn't mean to," he mumbled. "He said Clark is his cousin, and how can that be when I know his mother was..." The man pressed his lips together until they were white—a good choice given the fury simmering in Dougal's father. "Please accept my apology," he added quietly.

"Things are rather heated," Robbie said with a tame smile. "Let us all take a moment. There is happiness to celebrate here, for certain."

"Yes." Dougal tipped his head toward Jess. "Isn't there, my hummingbird?" He felt her relax and caught the slight tick of a smile. Hope bloomed in his chest.

Robbie continued, "What they did may not have been traditional, but they got there in the end."

Mrs. Goodfellow still looked cross. "What did that woman mean about an investigation?"

"I didn't catch that," Dougal fibbed. He really didn't want to address that issue. Best to let everyone speculate and hope they eventually determined that they'd misheard what Mary had said.

Again, Jess tensed beside him, and Da sent Dougal a mildly amused look.

"Yes, let us celebrate this happy union," Da declared. "Does anyone object to me obtaining a special license? I think the sooner they are wed, the more quickly the gossip will die down. This will become an oft-repeated tale of true love and the art of romance."

Dougal wanted to hug his father—and Robbie. Later, he would do just that. "I have no objection. Indeed, I am quite eager to be wed." He meant that. He only wished he could tell Jess that he loved her—privately—and offer a second, much better proposal than what he'd done last night. "If you would all excuse us, I'd like a moment with my bride—"

"Absolutely not," Goodfellow said with a firm head shake. "You can be alone after the ceremony and not a moment before. At least not more than you've already done."

"That's probably for the best," Da agreed.

Dougal wanted to argue. He was frankly beginning to seethe at how this entire situation seemed entirely out of his control. Not that he was disappointed since the result was precisely what he wanted. He just hoped it was what Jess wanted. Right now, he had no way of knowing, and that was eating at him like nothing ever had. That included everything to do with the Foreign Office. He supposed that's how he knew he loved her—she'd become the primary focus of his life. Everything else paled next to her.

"Please don't be hard on her." Dougal didn't want Jess to go home with them for fear they would berate her.

"We won't," her mother said, surprising Dougal, and it seemed Jess as well, for she twitched against him. "Our daughter is marrying a viscount. I think that is cause for great celebration, even if the path was rather…bumpy." The creases in her forehead disappeared, and she actually smiled at Jess.

Again, Jess relaxed. "Thank you, Mother," she said quietly.

"Let's steal away," Goodfellow said. "I've no desire to return to the ballroom. Come, Jessamine." He went to the door.

"We'll call on you as soon as we have the special license," Da said.

Goodfellow inclined his head in response, then held the door for his wife and daughter. Jessamine glanced back at Dougal, but she had no idea what she was thinking. Her face held a jumble of emotions, and all he wanted to do was smooth them away.

Soon.

The door snapped closed, and Da blew out a breath. "Well, that was exciting."

"That's one word for it," Dougal grumbled. He wiped his hand over his brow.

"She's quite lovely—your…hummingbird, was it?"

Robbie snickered, and Dougal managed to laugh.

"It's a joke between us," Dougal explained. "The couple from the ballroom—the Chesmores—we were investigating them in Dorset. That is how Jess and I came to know each other. We were tasked with pretending to be married so we could determine whether the Chesmores were spies." Dougal massaged his temple. "You should both forget everything I just said."

"Some mornings, I forget who I am," Da said blandly.

Dougal stared at him in horror. Was he that bad off already? "Are you serious?"

"No." Da laughed rather too hard, and Robbie tried—and failed—to stifle his amusement. "You should have seen your face. It was a jest, Dougal." He took a moment to compose himself. "My apologies. This has been a very strained evening. Rest assured that your secrets are our secrets." Da glanced toward Robbie, who nodded in response. "I know this didn't happen the way you'd hoped, but the end result is what you want."

"It is. I just hope it's what she wants. She was very agitated. It may be that she blurted the first thing that came to mind and doesn't really want to wed."

"Why would you think that?" Robbie asked.

"Because that's long been her intent. She's spent several Seasons avoiding marriage and has been anticipating her spinsterhood. She may prefer to cry off and go quietly into the future. Alone."

"You said you pretended to be married," Da said. "Surely you have an idea of whether you suit."

"I think we do."

Da gave him an encouraging nod. "Then you'll convince her. Perhaps you should try to see her alone."

"You've read my mind, Da."

Robbie cocked his head to the side. "Dougal, why did you introduce me as your cousin?"

"Because you are. Should I not have?"

It was Da who answered. "Of course you should have."

Dougal took a deep breath. "I realized something tonight in that ballroom. I've been masquerading pretty much my whole life. I play many roles and tend to keep them separate. I don't want to do that anymore."

"Nor should you," Da said quietly. "I'm sorry you felt the need for that."

"I don't know that it was conscious," Dougal explained. "But now that I recognize it, I can't continue."

Robbie smiled. "Amen, Dougal."

Da watched him with obvious pride. "I've raised you well, my boy."

Dougal went and hugged him fiercely. "Thank you for everything you said, and mostly for your soothing presence." Then he hugged Robbie. "And thank you for being here. I hope you'll stand up with me when I wed Jess—assuming she actually wants to go through with that."

"She will," Robbie said fiercely, thumping Dougal on the back before they separated. "Ye're damn near irresistible. At least ye were when we were younger. Remember Sorcha—"

"That'll do, Robbie," Dougal said with a laugh as he sent a nervous glance toward his father, who was shaking his head with a faint smile.

Da gestured toward the door. "Let us escape before we are discovered and endlessly hounded." As they made their way out, he asked, "Did you say I was soothing?"

"He did," Robbie answered.

"I don't know if that's true, but sometimes being an earl has its advantages. Dougal, you'll find that out soon enough."

Not too soon, Dougal hoped.

~

*W*hy wasn't he here yet?

Jess paced her bedchamber and checked the clock. It was precisely five minutes since the last time she'd looked. Surely, he should be here by now. It was nearly two, and they'd been home for hours.

Thankfully, her father had gone directly to his study without a word. Jess felt bad, as if she'd let him down. Because she had. What young lady secretly left town to see if she and her potential husband might suit?

Not Jessamine. But she couldn't tell them the truth, not without revealing that which she'd pledged to never disclose.

Her mother, on the other hand, had talked nearly nonstop since they'd left the Ringshalls'. First, she'd asked why Jess had let her advocate a courtship with Lord Gregory instead of telling her about Dougal. Jess had—lamely—said she was just trying to avoid an argument, particularly when she knew her betrothal to Dougal would happen imminently.

That had been the one time her father had spoken on the way home. He'd said that was just one of many errors. Mother had rushed to settle him, saying they must focus on the future when Jess would be a viscountess! And someday, a countess! Wasn't that wonderful!

If the wedding didn't happen—and Jess wasn't certain it would—her mother was going to be inconsolable.

Perhaps he wasn't coming. At least then she could put the candle in the window for Torrance. She hadn't done it the night before. Not only had she been too exhausted when Dougal had left, she'd reasoned it was too late. She hadn't done it tonight either, not when she expected Dougal. She had no idea what would happen after she set up the signal. Would Torrance arrive at her door as Dougal had? Or would he contact her in the light of day? It irritated her that she didn't know. This was yet another reason she wasn't certain she was a good candidate for working for the Foreign Office. She didn't like not knowing what to expect.

At last, she heard a creak outside her door. She knew precisely where Dougal had stepped to make that noise.

Hurrying, she opened the door before he could. "I was afraid you weren't coming."

He moved past her, and she pressed the door closed. Turning, she saw that he was no longer dressed in his ballroom finery. Pity, for he'd looked incredibly handsome in his impressively starched cravat and embroidered emerald waistcoat.

"You changed your clothing." She hadn't meant to say that out loud. It was absolutely inconsequential.

"So did you." His gaze swept over her with a heat that penetrated every part of her. She was suddenly not remotely interested in discussing anything, least of all their clothing.

Their eyes locked, and she saw her arousal reflected in his. They came together quickly, clasping each other as their mouths connected in a desperate, rapturous kiss. This was everything she wanted—this irresistible attraction that neither of them could deny.

He shrugged out of his coat as she steered him back to the cushioned bench at the foot of her bed. Stumbling on the garment, he fell back onto the bench, breaking their kiss. Jess lifted her dressing gown and straddled him, putting her knees on either side of his hips. He clasped her waist as she lowered her mouth to claim his in another searing kiss.

Grinding down, she felt his rigid cock against her sex, separated only by his clothing. Before she could remedy the situation, he moved one of his hands to unbutton his fall. Lust arced through her like lightning across a dark night sky.

She palmed the back of his head, kissing him deeply as he guided his shaft into her. He drove hard and fast, making her gasp into his mouth. Then he was pulling at her dressing gown, unfastening the front before shoving it from her in reckless abandon. One hand returned to her waist, squeezing her through the linen of her night rail while the other cupped her breast.

Sensation overwhelmed her as she fought to retain control. She didn't want to spin into oblivion yet, but she was so very close. Breaking their kiss, he put his mouth on her breast, suckling her through her night rail. She cried out, then slapped her hand over her mouth before she woke the entire household.

Desperate for release and knowing it was so near, she

gripped his shoulders and rode him with a furious precision. He thrust his hands beneath her night rail and grasped her hips, guiding her as he rose to fill her with long, fast strokes. His fingertips dug into her backside, massaging her and manipulating her so that she felt more open to him than ever before.

The pleasure pounding through her reached a swift and shattering crescendo as she came in a torrent. "Don't leave me," she managed to say, rasping against his ear.

To punctuate her demand, she held him more tightly and pressed down harder, taking him deep inside her. He made a low, guttural sound just before he captured her mouth with his. He held her fast as his orgasm swept through him. She reveled in the feel of him shuddering beneath and around her.

He pulled back, gasping as he drew deep breaths. She did the same, moving her slick thighs against his as their bodies began to calm.

"You're still wearing your cravat," she observed, finding that somewhat humorous.

"You are fascinatingly distracted by my wardrobe this evening," he mused.

"It's easier than addressing the necessary." She looked away, feeling sheepish. Then she climbed off him, moving quickly before he could hold her.

She went to her dressing area, where there was a basin behind a screen. After tidying up, she emerged to see him buttoned up and standing with one hand on the chair that sat at her desk.

"We must address the necessary," he said. "Whatever that means. What happened at the ball tonight?"

Jess went to perch on the side of her bed. She wished she'd grabbed her dressing gown. She felt dreadfully exposed, and perhaps a bit embarrassed after the way they'd fallen on each other. "You were there."

"I mean, why did you announce our betrothal? You refused me."

"I didn't notice you offering a better solution," she said defensively. "We were rather under fire."

His shoulders drooped, which she found to be a puzzling reaction. "That's it, then? You sought to mitigate the disaster."

"Of course. What should I have done?"

He smiled faintly as admiration flickered in his gaze. "Precisely that. It was quick thinking on your part. You really would make an excellent spy."

"I was just thinking the opposite. I really dislike not knowing what will happen as well as all the secrecy. I'd much rather be open and clear about my motives."

"I'm glad to hear that. Not that you don't like working for the Foreign Office, but that you prefer honesty and straight-forwardness. I have been lacking in both for some time as I've been cloaking myself in a variety of roles." He let go of the chair and straightened. "In my quest to be secretive and to be multiple people, I've kept my emotions buried. My father has reminded me that wasn't always how I used to be. Indeed, my brother, if he were here, would smack me aside the head and tell me to be myself."

Jess stared at him, amazed at these revelations. "Who is that?"

"A man like my father and my brother. And my cousin. Someone who allows emotion along with reason and delib-eration. That is the man I want to be, the man I need to be as viscount and someday as earl. And hopefully as your husband."

He held up his hand with a slight grimace. "Forgive me, I don't want to botch this again." He dropped to his knee, took her hand, and looked up at her with a naked emotion she was afraid to name. "I humbly ask you to be my wife because I love you. There are a thousand other reasons, but that is the most vital: I love you, Jess, and the future will be ever so much more wonderful if I have the honor of sharing it with you."

A long moment stretched as she let his words settle into her mind and find their home in her soul. "That's all I wanted," she whispered. "Your love. I love you too. I refused you because I didn't think you loved me in return."

"I was, as you so aptly put it, a blockhead."

She squeezed his hand. "Yes, but I love you anyway. And you aren't always a blockhead."

He chuckled. "I hope not. I shall endeavor not to be." Uncertainty passed over his features as he hesitated. "Does this mean you accept my proposal?"

"Yes, happily. Now stand up and kiss me."

He rose, but he didn't take her into his arms. "There aren't other reasons for you to decline?" His brow furrowed. "You've been so against marriage."

Jess exhaled. "Yes, but I didn't give it any real consideration. Not until I pretended to be married and found it so incredibly wonderful. My commitment to spinsterhood was more about spiting my parents instead of fulfilling some dream I harbored for an independent future. I didn't recognize that until I began to see the benefits of marriage. Not just any marriage, but one with a partner who appreciated and encouraged me. And who showed me the potential of a union between two like-minded souls."

His gaze searched hers. "Did I do that?"

"I think *we* did that—without meaning to," she added with a gentle laugh.

"I would agree with that assessment. But will the life I'm offering, will *I* be enough?"

Jess put her hands on his cheeks and looked into his eyes.

"Oh, yes. To become your viscountess and live in Scotland—what an adventure that will be. In truth, I would go anywhere you lead." She recalled Mary's counsel. "So long as we're together, even the most mundane will be exciting."

"I like the sound of that. And I wholly concur."

"I should like you to reveal yourself to me completely," she said. When he glanced down at himself and lifted his hands to the buttons of his waistcoat, she laughed. "Not that way, though I would like that too. What I meant was that I want to know all the different people you've tried to be. Will you share them all with me?"

"Nothing would make me happier."

"I'm quite eager to hear about your cousin. Though we barely met, I sense a strong bond between the two of you. Indeed, I find it odd that you didn't mention him during our time together."

"I kept everything so separate." He shook his head. "I shall tell you all about Robbie, my other cousins, and my wonderful aunt and uncle. They own a tavern in Edinburgh's Old Town. You'll love it."

She grinned. "I can't wait to meet them."

"Now, if I may, I'd like to continue what we started when I arrived."

"Here I thought we'd finished."

"Never." He swept her into his arms and carried her to the bed. "I hope you won't mind if I take a more...disciplined approach this time." He set her on the coverlet and began to disrobe.

Jess whisked off the night rail and cast it behind her. She lay back and spread her arms. "I will try to be patient."

When he joined her, she acknowledged that would be nearly impossible. But she *would* try.

CHAPTER 22

*A*fter they regained their senses for a second time, they lay entwined amongst Jess's bedclothes perfectly content. At least that was how Dougal felt. He ought to tell her so.

"This is lovely," he murmured, kissing her temple. "I don't think I've ever been so happy."

She turned her head to look him in the eye. "That is a surprising admission. You don't normally wear your emotions on your sleeve."

He grimaced. "I'm going to change that, starting now."

"It sounds as though I shall have to thank your father."

"He could tell that I'd been hiding behind something." Dougal did more than grimace now. He winced. "I'm afraid I broke my oath to the Foreign Office. Again."

She leaned up on her elbow to look down at him. "You didn't! Forgive me, I understand why you did. I'm just surprised. And what do you mean, 'again'?"

"Robbie has known about my position since I was recruited. He was in the Black Watch with me. He'd puzzled it out on his own, really, so I only confirmed what he'd already determined to be true. I'd always kept it from my father—and my brother. I suppose I was simply tired of hiding. From my father, from myself, from you. I wasn't doing it on purpose. It had just become second nature."

She grinned. "You couldn't resist me."

"I could not. I am in complete surrender." He pulled her head down and kissed her.

When they broke apart after a long moment, she frowned, the familiar pleats forming between her brows. "I hope you won't think poorly of me, but I am also going to break my oath. Frankly, it's been torture to keep quiet. Actually, I hope you won't be angry."

Alarm spread through Dougal, icing his veins. He sat up, situating the bedclothes at his waist. "What is it?"

Jess also sat up. She pulled the coverlet up around her chest. "When the Foreign Office asked me to go on this mission, they also tasked me with investigating you."

Dougal stared at her in disbelief. "Why would they do that?"

"I had no idea, and I was terrified. What did I know about being a spy, let alone investigating another spy?"

That anyone would ask that of her made him incredibly angry—not just because they doubted his loyalty. They'd put her in an untenable position. What if he'd discovered her investigating him?

He thought back to Dorset and couldn't recall her doing anything that would indicate an investigation. "What did you do to accomplish their request?"

"Very little," she said wryly. "As I said, what did I know about any of that? I looked through your things, I watched your behavior. I found nothing suspicious, of course, and everything you did was above reproach—as far as I could tell."

"I can't believe they would ask that of you."

"Apparently, they believed I would unsettle you, that because you'd never had a partner, you might expose yourself."

"Who told you that?"

"Torrance."

Bloody Kent? Dougal's insides blistered. The man he'd looked up to had doubted him. He stared past Jess for some length of time.

"Dougal?" she whispered, gently touching his forearm. "Are you all right?"

He blinked, then refocused on her. "I feel a bit betrayed, actually. Torrance is Oliver Kent, my superior. I'm hurt that he would question my loyalty."

"I don't think he wanted to. He gave me a cipher to solve, saying it would exonerate you, and he seemed eager for it to do so." Jess slipped from the bed and went to her desk. A moment later, she returned, handing him several pieces of parchment before resettling herself while he read.

He looked over the cipher as well as her notes, smiling slightly at her method. "How long did this take you?"

"Most of yesterday," she said. "I'd only finished it just before you came to see me."

"And you didn't tell me then?" He struggled to draw a breath, feeling betrayed anew. But then, she'd been keeping this from him from the start. Because she'd had to. Of course she wouldn't break the oath she'd taken, especially not to a man she'd been told required investigation.

"I wanted to," she said softly, her cheeks flushing as she looked down at her lap. "I don't blame you for being angry."

He reached over and took her hand. "I'm not. I understand why you didn't tell me, why you couldn't. I'll say it again: you'd make an excellent spy."

She shook her head. "No, thank you."

Returning his attention to the papers, he read the deciphered message. "I'm amazed at how quickly you solved this."

"I was rather motivated when I knew it could prove your loyalty."

He leaned in to kiss her swiftly. "Thank you. And thank you for telling me. I don't think poorly of you at all." He reread part of the message. "I can't believe Giraud was working against us. I've known him nearly four years, and I never had the sense he was disloyal. He had nothing but animosity for his former country and especially for Napoleon."

She looked at him with sympathy. "He was a good actor, I suppose."

"I suppose," Dougal murmured. Again, he thought of the man dead with his throat sliced apart. "He was murdered or perhaps assassinated by someone from the Foreign Office who'd determined his duplicity." Dougal's mind worked. If Kent had wanted Dougal investigated and he'd given this to Jess to decipher, it seemed he wouldn't know what had happened to Giraud. Meaning, if someone from the Foreign Office had discovered him and then killed him, Kent hadn't known about it. The secrets were becoming dangerous. "I think I'm glad I'm finished with spying," he said, setting the papers down. "I take it you haven't given these to Kent yet?"

She shook her head. "I was to put a candle in my window when I finished, but I didn't last night because you arrived. And tonight doesn't seem likely either."

Dougal wondered what would happen after she put the candle in the window. Would Kent or someone else show up to retrieve the information? Or would they wait until tomorrow?

"Let's do it." Dougal wanted to talk to Kent and hoped he *would* show up.

Her eyes widened. "But you aren't supposed to know anything."

She was right, and he didn't want to get her into any trouble. "I doubt they'll come tonight. More likely, you'll receive a message in the morning with instructions to meet somewhere."

"But what if they do?" she asked. "Come tonight, I mean."

"Then I'll hide."

"You could also leave. You can't stay here all night."

"You are unfortunately correct." He exhaled. "Fine, I'll go. But will you send word about what happens?"

"Of course. And if I do have a meeting tomorrow, I'll let you know when and where. You can 'follow' me there."

Dougal grinned. "So clever. Of course I will."

Jess left the bed once more and put a candle onto the windowsill. When she returned, Dougal drew her close and kissed her.

"Did I tell you that my mother is ridiculously happy I'm marrying a *viscount*?" she asked.

"I could see that she was," Dougal said with a chuckle. "And how is your father? I confess I was concerned for you returning home with him tonight. He seemed quite angry."

"Honestly, I've never seen him so furious."

"His ire is perfectly understandable. I behaved horribly with you."

"Please stop. I know what Society would demand of you —of us—and I don't care. I didn't survive unwed to the ripe age of twenty-five so that I could succumb to ruin. We will make our own future."

"How I love that you are unapologetically *you*. I meant what I said in my original, awful proposal. We do make an excellent team. There is no one else I would want at my side."

"I agreed with everything you said. I just wanted to know that you felt something for me."

"I feel everything for you," he said, gathering her close. "Primarily, an all-consuming love, even if I didn't realize it because I was being a blockhead."

She touched his cheek. "I was too. I spent so much time refusing to do my parents' bidding that I failed to see when it coincided with what I wanted. I'm so sorry I refused you."

"You were absolutely right to do so. Having watched my parents in a marriage without love, I understand why it would be of paramount importance to you. It is to me too."

"The Chesmores are an excellent example," Jess said.

"Oh God, the Chesmores." He couldn't help laughing. "The look on poor Mary's face when she finally puzzled it all out."

"And we suspected them of espionage." Jess giggled.

They both dissolved into a fit of laughter, and it was several minutes until they were composed once more. Barely. "They must come to the wedding, or the breakfast, at least," Jess said, wiping her eyes.

"Absolutely. I'll find out from the Ringshalls where they are staying. It sounded as if they are relations of Mary's."

Jess shook her head. "Of all the balls for them to come to. Would we have found our way without them?"

"I know we would have," he said firmly. "I'd already planned to tell you that I love you and to beg you to reconsider."

"I'd planned to do the same. I suppose this way was far more exciting."

He chuckled. "Hopefully only for a short time. We may even wed tomorrow, if I can secure a vicar once we have the special license. But it will more than likely be the day after. Do you want to marry here or at my house?"

"I don't care. I only care that you come back tomorrow night if we aren't wed. I don't want to spend a single night away from you. I know our bed in the Wordsworth room was positively cavernous, but I've missed you since we left."

He wondered how his love for her could continue to increase. But it did, moment by moment. "I have too. I'll see you tomorrow regardless. We'll call once we have the license. Then I thought we might visit the Phoenix Club. My father and Robbie are keen to go, and Tuesday is the best night."

Her brow pleated. "How can I go? I'm not a member. Evie arranged for me to attend before we left for Dorset, when I wanted to surprise you with my disguise."

He recalled that evening and how impressed he was with her. "I almost didn't recognize you. I do believe I might have started falling in love with you that very night."

"I find that hard to believe."

"You're right. I think it was when you touched me that night at Lucien's. Already, you were demonstrating a mastery for performance and subterfuge."

"I'm not sure I believe that either, but I only care that you love me now."

"Always," he corrected.

"Anyway, I can't be a spy, not that I want to be. I shall be too busy being Lady Fallin. I understand we've an estate to explore and manage."

The future had never looked more inviting to Dougal, and he was thrilled that she shared that perspective. "You're certain this life is what you want? It is now my purpose to ensure you are happy."

"I am, and yes, this—you—is definitely what I want. I'm quite keen to travel north, actually."

Dougal was glad to hear it. "I can hardly wait to show you my home. However, my father wants to see London—more accurately, he wants to see what I do here—then we'll return to Scotland. Beyond the Phoenix Club, I'm not sure there's much else to see since most of everything I did was secret."

"I understand you used to be a rake. Perhaps you could take us all on a tour of your youth. I imagine Robbie would enjoy that too." She looked at him with mischievous anticipation.

He let out a sharp laugh. "I'll consider that. I'm not sure which is more terrifying—showing that to you or my father. Or Robbie. He'll almost certainly use it against me at some point. Or try to, anyway."

She rolled him to his back and climbed on top of him. "I think I might like to bed a rake."

Narrowing his eyes up at her, he clasped her waist. "I am, as it happens, a rake, a soldier, *and* a spy."

An eager smile curled her delectable mouth. "Soon you will be mine."

He pulled her down to kiss her. "I already am."

~

*D*ougal and his father secured the special license without trouble, but Dougal was not able to organize the ceremony until the following day. This had slightly disappointed Goodfellow, but he seemed to be in a better mood overall. Jess's mother was ecstatic. She'd already planned a breakfast to follow the ceremony, so they would be wed at the Goodfellows' house.

Unfortunately, procuring the special license meant Dougal hadn't been able to "follow" Jess to her meeting with Kent. So Dougal had sent him a note requesting his presence here tonight. He hadn't received a response and only hoped the man would show up. Dougal hadn't mentioned why he wanted to meet—he wanted to see Kent's reaction when he learned Dougal knew the truth, that he'd employed Jess to investigate him.

The coach stopped in front of the Phoenix Club, and

Dougal climbed down first. His father followed, moving so well that Dougal wondered if the walking stick was more for show. Robbie stepped out last.

"Why are there two doors?" Da asked.

"The one on the right is to the ladies' club. The left is for the gentlemen. On Tuesdays, just about everyone enters on the left."

"London is so stiff," Robbie said, shaking his head. "In Edinburgh, the gents—and the ladies—come over from the New Town, and no one bats an eye."

Dougal's mother had done that, which was how she'd met Dougal's father.

A footman opened the door as they approached, and Dougal gestured for his father to precede him. They stood in the entry hall a moment while Da took in the marble floor and the grand staircase that turned up the far wall. "That's quite a painting," he noted, staring up at the massive bacchanalia.

Dougal pointed himself out and explained how Lucien had included his closest friends in the commission. As if conjured by their conversation, Lucien came down the stairs.

He met them with a wide smile. "Lord Stirling, Robbie, I'm so pleased to welcome you to the Phoenix Club." Lucien knew Robbie from when they'd all served together in the war. "My lord, does this mean you have at last accepted your invitation to join the club?"

They'd invited him when it opened, but Da hadn't ever accepted, likely because he hadn't been to London for several years. "I suppose I must. It seems all the best people do." He clasped Lucien's hand. "It's good to see you, Lucien. What's it been, eight, nine years?"

Lucien nodded. "Something like that. Whenever it was that Dougal dragged me to Scotland."

"Too long," Da said. "I hope you'll come for another visit soon."

Robbie nodded. "Yes. My father still talks about you and Dougal's other friend—Max."

Lucien inclined his head. "How flattering."

"He won't travel that far from his precious club," Dougal said.

"Someday I will," Lucien said with a hint of defensiveness. "It's still new and needs my presence."

Dougal could argue that either Evie or Ada could oversee things just fine, but he did not. He'd already stated that on several occasions.

Lucien frowned slightly toward Robbie. "I apologize that you have not received an invitation to the club. I shall rectify that with due haste."

"That's kind of ye, but I've no idea when I'll be back in London."

"Do we get a tour?" Da asked expectantly.

"Certainly!" Lucien gestured to the left of the entry hall. "Let us start this way with the dining room."

"Dining room?" Da looked to Dougal. "Why didn't we dine here?"

"We can tomorrow, if you like."

"On your wedding day?" Da chuckled. "I don't think your new viscountess will appreciate that."

Lucien snickered. "Even I know not to do that. Where is Miss Goodfellow this evening?"

"Evie is bringing her," Dougal said. "I expect they'll arrive soon."

"Excellent. This way, then." Lucien allowed Dougal's father and Robbie to precede him into the dining room.

Excusing himself, Dougal went upstairs in search of Kent. Hopefully, the man would be here. Indeed, he was seated in the members' den, sipping a glass of port.

Dougal went straight to him. "Come with me to Lucien's office."

Kent stood wordlessly and walked from the members' den toward Lucien's office. Dougal followed him inside and closed the door behind him.

"It's time you explained a few things to me," Dougal said evenly.

Kent sat in one of the chairs and took another sip of his port. He either didn't realize how angry Dougal was, or he didn't care. Or he already knew. "You are no longer associated with the Foreign Office. I don't have to explain anything to you."

Dougal wanted to believe that he and Kent were friends, that their relationship went beyond the Foreign Office. Perhaps foolishly, he'd thought Kent believed that too. "Then why did you come?"

Exhaling, Kent nodded toward the other chair. "Are you going to sit?"

Dougal reluctantly perched on the chair. "You hired Miss Goodfellow to spy on me."

The revelation didn't provoke a reaction, confirming what Dougal suspected—that Kent was already aware Dougal knew the truth. "I understand why you are upset. She is to be your wife. Congratulations, by the way."

Dougal didn't want his good wishes, not until he heard the man's explanation. "Did you really believe I had something to do with that bad message or Giraud's death?"

Kent features creased briefly. "I didn't, no. But others wanted to be sure. You must know that I defended you?"

"I would hope so. I also know you didn't tell me that I was suspected."

One of Kent's brows arched. "You know why I couldn't."

"I know that we bend rules when necessary."

"As Miss Goodfellow did."

That was how he knew. "As you noted, she is to be my wife. We don't keep secrets from each other."

"Of course not," Kent said softly. "Anyway, she told me earlier when I met her to pick up the message she'd deciphered—she's bloody amazing."

Pride and love gathered in Dougal's chest. "I know."

"She said she can't work for the office anymore, that she doesn't want to keep secrets, and that she'd told you she'd been asked to investigate you. Her loyalty is firmly with you."

Dougal knew that, but was glad to hear it nonetheless. "I can't help but feel my work for the Foreign Office is somehow tainted now. I risked myself for four years, and this is how I'm rewarded?"

Kent sat forward. "Not at all. You must understand—two of your missions ended in failure. That had never happened before. You were one of our best operatives." He drew a breath. "Now that Giraud has been found to have been working against us, you remain one of our best operatives. Your record is absolutely untarnished. The office still hopes to contact you in the future."

"I think it's best if they don't." Dougal preferred to put all his energy into his family, which was precisely where it belonged. If he worked in government at all, it would hopefully be in Parliament, where he could work to effect important and necessary change.

Kent frowned. "I'm sorry to hear that. But I do understand. Please know that I never believed you could be guilty of anything nefarious." His gaze was earnest, and Dougal wanted to believe him. He also knew they'd have little interaction going forward so it didn't really matter.

Dougal stood. "I think we're finished."

Kent slowly rose. "It seems so. I wish you and Miss Goodfellow every happiness. Truly."

Dougal watched the man leave the office and eventually

followed him out. However, he didn't return to the members' den. Instead, he went to the library, thinking that was where Lucien would have taken his father and Robbie.

Finding them there, Dougal worked to release the tension from his shoulders. It *was* finished. The double life he'd led was finally behind him.

Feeling much lighter than a short while ago, Dougal made his way to his father and Robbie. Da was seated in a chair with Robbie standing next to him. Lucien was fetching them whisky.

"Ah, here is your bride," Da said, his gaze twinkling as he looked toward the doorway.

Turning, Dougal's breath caught. Jess looked happy and beautiful, her blue eyes more vivid than he could ever recall, especially when they landed on him, and her lips curved into a bewitching smile.

She and Evie came toward them, and Dougal made the necessary introductions.

Evie gave him a scolding look, but Dougal knew she was in jest. "You didn't give us much time to prepare, but I'm pleased to report that Jess will look resplendent in her new gown tomorrow."

She would look resplendent in anything—or nothing. Dougal kept that to himself. Later, when he stole into her father's house for the last time, he would tell Jess.

"Everything is arranged," Da said from the chair. "What a glorious day it will be. And soon I hope there will be even happier news and an heir will be secured." He gave Dougal a sheepish look. "I don't wish to pressure you. That is my fondest hope."

Dougal realized it was his too. He looked at Jess with boundless love and knew that whatever the future held, it would be wonderful.

CHAPTER 23

*T*hey were married.

Jess looked over at her new husband and still couldn't quite believe it. How quickly their lives had changed.

Many of their friends had come for the ceremony and the breakfast Mrs. Goodfellow had planned. Jess and Dougal stood together as they all came to offer their best wishes and love. Jess had been especially happy to introduce her grandfather to Dougal. She noted he was now deep in conversation with Robbie on the other side of the room.

Kat, who wasn't terribly enthusiastic about Jess marrying Dougal, came toward them. "I still can't believe you are wed. We were supposed to be spinsters together."

Jess understood her disappointment. She might have felt the same if their roles had been reversed. "I can't quite believe it either. I certainly never expected it to happen." She glanced over at Dougal, giving him a small smile.

"Well, I'm not falling prey," Kat said firmly.

Jess sobered. "I don't think you will. And our friendship will remain. I promise."

"I'm still happy for you, even if you will be in Scotland and can't be my chaperone."

"We will be back for at least part of the Season," Dougal assured her.

Appearing mollified, Kat looked to Dougal. "Don't disappoint her. She has friends who can make your life miserable." She narrowed her eyes at him before stalking off.

"I've been warned," Dougal said.

"I'd say so. She's a wonderful friend."

"I can see that." Dougal scanned the room.

"Who are you looking for?" Jess asked.

"Your father. I wish to speak with him."

"Do you really need to? He seemed more like himself this morning."

"I do." Dougal kissed her cheek.

"Let me come with you, at least."

"I'd like to do this alone. I promise I'll tell you all about it." He gave her a reassuring smile before crossing the drawing room.

Jess watched them intently, wishing she could hear what Dougal was saying. Her father looked mildly disgruntled at first then...skeptical? When he blinked in surprise, Jess nearly stalked over there to demand what Dougal was saying. Then, shockingly, her father glanced in her direction with a look of...admiration. What on earth had Dougal said?

At last, he returned, and Jess immediately demanded to know what had transpired.

"I merely told him a secret—that our escapade was not to conduct a liaison or anything untoward. I explained that we were working on a sensitive matter for the government. Then I told him he should be proud to know that his daughter is brilliant at solving ciphers."

Jess stared at him. "You didn't."

"I most certainly did. I also I fell in love with you because of your clever mind and sense of adventure. I said we didn't plan for it to happen, but that I am incredibly grateful it did."

"Do you think he believed you?" Jess asked.

"I do. Didn't you see the way he looked at you? I thought for certain you had."

"I did," she said quietly. "Thank you for doing that. You are incredibly wonderful." She kissed his cheek and leaned into him.

He put his arm around her. "It's important to me that your father not think poorly of you. He has absolutely no reason to, and indeed should be exceedingly proud."

Evie joined them, which thankfully prevented Jess from falling deeper into her emotions. "This is the gentleman you spoke to me about?" she asked Jess.

"Yes."

"I feel a bit like a fool when he showed up that day and you didn't seem to know each other." Evie shook her head. "You could have told me the truth. I'm excellent at keeping secrets. Besides, if I'd known it was Dougal, I would have given you different advice."

Dougal looked at Evie in bemusement. "What would you have said?"

"That you are in need of a wife and Jess would be hard-pressed to find someone better."

Dougal smiled. "You are a dear friend."

"How are you two friends anyway?" Jess asked.

"Lucien," they answered in unison, provoking them all to laugh.

"Isn't that how everyone knows each other?" Evie's eyes sparkled with humor. "I am delighted everything has worked out for you both. I so enjoy when my friends fall in love, which seems to be happening often." She glanced around at several couples in the drawing room.

"When will it be your turn, I wonder?" Dougal asked.

She swatted at him. "Never, as you know. I'm going to get champagne. Ask me that again, and I'll dump it over your head." She flashed a wink at him before leaving.

Dougal sidled close to Jess. "You talked to her about me?"

"You know she helped me come up with the Mrs. Smythe disguise. Since she's a widow and I was to portray a married woman, I asked for certain…advice."

He grinned. "Do tell."

Jess rolled her eyes. "It wasn't like that. Though as it turned out, I should have asked for more detailed information. Mostly, she told me how to act so that our marriage would not be questioned. I told her my trip might include an assignation with a gentleman and that we would need to pretend we were wed."

"You fabricated a story?"

She nodded. "That came in handy again later when the Chesmores recognized us at the engagement ball."

"I'll add prescient to your ever-growing list of talents." His gaze moved to the doorway where the couple she'd just mentioned walked in. "You've done it again, for here are the Chesmores."

Gil looked toward them, and he grinned as he escorted Mary in their direction. "Congratulations!"

Mary looked uneasy. "Are you truly Lord and Lady Fallin?"

Jess took her hands and gave them a squeeze. "Yes. Mr. and Mrs. Smythe were our…" She turned her head toward Dougal.

"Aliases. It's imperative you don't share what you know about our…visit with anyone. This isn't typically what happens. We weren't ever supposed to encounter you again."

"You may not have," Gil said. "We rarely come to London. Mary insisted on seeing her cousin's daughter wed to a marquess."

"You're staying until the wedding, then?" Jess asked.

"She talked me into it." Gil sounded beleaguered, but then he flashed a bright smile at Mary. "But then, I would do anything for my duckling."

Jess suppressed a smile, wondering if she would ever grow used to Gil's pet names. "You'll have a splendid time. There is much to do and see here."

"I hope you'll show us some of it," Mary said eagerly.

"For as long as we're in town," Jess agreed. "We'll be leaving for Scotland in a week or so."

Mary shook her head. "I still can't believe you aren't Welsh. You were so convincing." A shadow passed over her features. "And I am *so* very sorry about the ball the other night."

"Please do not give it another thought," Dougal said. "Just promise to keep our secret, and all is well. In truth, we should thank you for ensuring we came together." Dougal slipped his hand around Jess's waist.

"Was there any doubt?" Gil asked. "I could tell you were in love from the moment I met you."

"Could you?" Dougal asked, laughing softly. "Perhaps you should be a matchmaker."

"I'd rather be a spy," Gil whispered jovially.

Jess pressed against Dougal's side. "We can't help you with that. You're speaking to a couple of farmers."

"Farmers who will still visit the sea on occasion, I hope," Mary said.

"I'm sure we will," Dougal replied. Lucien called for everyone's attention so that Dougal's father could make a toast. Footmen delivered champagne throughout the drawing room.

The earl stood in the center of the room, his gaze fixed on Dougal and Jess. "I want to welcome my new daughter-in-law, Jessamine, to our family. This has been a year of incredible sadness, but also overwhelming joy. I know Alistair would have loved you as much as I do already. He's looking down on us today and wishing you all the best. To Jessamine and my son Dougal." He lifted his glass to a resounding chorus of "Huzzah!"

Dougal met his father's eyes and blinked back a tear of love and gratitude. He turned to look at his wife and tapped his glass to hers. "I love you."

"And I love you."

EPILOGUE

Scotland, November

*A*fter hunting with his father and Jessamine that morning, Dougal stole away to visit his brother's grave. His headstone had recently been installed. It was magnificent, just like he had been.

The ground was cold and damp, so Dougal stood and traced his fingers over the letters of his brother's name. He'd been the best of men—kind, generous, humble. Dougal realized those were words his father also used to describe him, but in his mind, he wouldn't surpass Alistair.

And yet here he was, holding his brother's title and living the life that was meant to be his.

"You should be here," Dougal said. "If one of us had to go, it should have been me."

"How about if neither of you died?"

Dougal turned his head to see Jess walking toward him,

the brim of her hat low over her brow since it might yet rain. "Are you following me?"

"*Looking* for you—Robbie just arrived. Though, I suppose I could say I'm honing my espionage skills, which are now entirely moot."

Neither of them regretted turning their backs on the Foreign Office. And thankfully, no one had picked up on Mary's use of the word investigate at the Ringshall Ball—the scandal of Jess and Dougal's escapade followed by their quick marriage had quite overtaken the ton's gossip for several weeks.

She looked to the headstone that was taller than they were. "What a marvelous monument."

"I wish you'd known him."

"I feel as if I do. Between being here where he once lived and the stories you and Da tell, his presence is all around us. Can't you feel that?"

His lips curved up as peace settled inside him. "I can." He turned toward her. "Thanks to you, I feel many things." That included grief. Once they'd arrived in Scotland, he'd finally allowed himself to feel the loss and embrace the sadness. Through that, and with the love and support of his wife and father, he'd actually found solace.

She kissed him gently and snuggled against his side. He put his arm around her, holding her close. "Are you shivering?" he asked. She was wearing a cloak, but it was chilly.

"Perhaps. I still don't understand how you can wear a kilt and not be cold to the bone."

"I thought you liked my kilt." He gave her a randy leer, which prompted her to laugh.

"I adore your kilt, particularly the bits beneath it."

"Bits? Hopefully they're a good deal more than bits." As she shivered again, he said, "Am I going to have to put you in a bath like that first night at Prospero's Retreat?"

Laughing softy, she put her hand on his chest. "I wouldn't complain. But I also don't want to tear you away from Alistair. I didn't mean to intrude. Robbie will keep." She started to pull away, but he held her fast.

"You could never. I am glad to share him—and everything —with you. We should head back anyway. I'm looking forward to seeing Robbie. And my sisters will be here soon. I'm glad you'll finally get to meet them." They were coming for a fortnight, and the castle would be full of children since they each had three. "I hope you're ready to be Auntie Jess," he said, turning with her.

"I am, actually. A more important question is if you're ready to be Da?"

Dougal froze. Then he pivoted to face her, his hands clasping the undersides of her forearms. "Are you with child?"

"I think so. It's probably a wee bit early—your Scottish is wearing off on me—but I felt confident enough to tell you. That, and I am terrible at keeping secrets from you."

"You didn't use to be," Dougal said wryly.

She looked both horrified and amused. "I thought you forgave me for that!"

"Of course I do. It was a poor jest." He looked toward his brother's monument. "Did you hear that, Alistair? You're to be an uncle again, and I'm to be a father. Who would have thought?" For a man who'd long stifled his emotions, the joy streaming through him was almost insufferable.

Sweeping Jess into his arms, he let out a happy cry and kissed her. She held on to him, laughing, until he set her down.

"I should be more careful with you now, I suppose," he said, offering her his arm.

"Not too careful, if you don't mind." She gave him an openly suggestive and seductive look.

"Noted. My father is going to be so pleased." That only compounded Dougal's happiness. His father's health was holding steady, likely due in no small part to Jess's care. When she'd learned he was ill, she'd written to physicians and learned all she could about his condition. Then she'd ensured he followed a specific diet and got just the right amount of exercise. "I can't tell you how happy I am that he will get to meet his next grandchild.

"I know," Jess agreed, beaming. "But I don't want to tell him yet. Soon. When we're absolutely certain."

"It will be difficult to contain, but you're right."

"I often am." She gave him a playful wink.

"I wouldn't have you any other way, my hummingbird."

"How I love you, my stag. Now, kiss me again."

Chuckling, he pulled her into his arms once more, where he planned to keep her forever.

Evangeline Renshaw agrees to tutor the virtuous Lord Gregory Blakemore in bed. But what will he do when he discovers the respectable "widow" was once a successful courtesan? Find out what happens when Evie meets the one man who may finally break down her guard in IMPECCABLE!

Would you like to know when my next book is available and to hear about sales and deals? Sign up for my VIP newsletter, follow me on social media:

Facebook: https://facebook.com/DarcyBurkeFans
Twitter at @darcyburke
Instagram at darcyburkeauthor

Pinterest at darcyburkewrite

And follow me on Bookbub to receive updates on pre-orders, new releases, and deals!

Need more Regency romance? Check out my other historical series:

The Untouchables
Swoon over twelve of Society's most eligible and elusive bachelor peers and the bluestockings, wallflowers, and outcasts who bring them to their knees!

The Untouchables: The Spitfire Society
Meet the smart, independent women who've decided they don't need Society's rules, their families' expectations, or, most importantly, a husband. But just because they don't need a man doesn't mean they might not *want* one...

The Untouchables: The Pretenders
Set in the captivating world of The Untouchables, follow the saga of a trio of siblings who excel at being something they're not. Can a dauntless Bow Street Runner, a devastated viscount, and a disillusioned Society miss unravel their secrets?

The Matchmaking Chronicles
The course of true love never runs smooth. Sometimes a little matchmaking is required. When couples meet at a house party, what could go wrong?

Wicked Dukes Club
Six books written by me and my BFF, NYT Bestselling Author Erica Ridley. Meet the unforgettable men of

London's most notorious tavern, The Wicked Duke. Seductively handsome, with charm and wit to spare, one night with these rakes and rogues will never be enough...

Love is All Around

Heartwarming Regency-set retellings of classic Christmas stories (written after the Regency!) featuring a cozy village, three siblings, and the best gift of all: love.

Secrets and Scandals

Six epic stories set in London's glittering ballrooms and England's lush countryside.

Legendary Rogues

Five intrepid heroines and adventurous heroes embark on exciting quests across the Georgian Highlands and Regency England and Wales!

If you like contemporary romance, I hope you'll check out my **Ribbon Ridge** series available from Avon Impulse, and the continuation of Ribbon Ridge in **So Hot**.

I hope you'll consider leaving a review at your favorite online vendor or networking site!

I appreciate my readers so much. Thank you, thank you, *thank you*.

AUTHOR'S NOTE

The spy plot in *Irresistible* was inspired by the Spy Nozy Affair. In 1797, peculiar tenants moved into Alfoxton House in Somerset. They were interested in nature and in observing and recording everything around them, even going out at night to appreciate the moonlit coast. Their actions, manner, and dress were odd to those in the area—there was a vast difference between country and city folk. This was a time of heightened tension with the French, as there was fear Napoleon would invade.

Concerned that these new tenants could be French, a local doctor wrote to the Home Office. A Bow Street detective was dispatched to investigate. He interrogated a friend of a servant at Alfoxton House who described hearing "seditious talk" at dinner one night. It's true that these supposed spies were a bit radical in their thinking at the time.

They were William Wordsworth and Samuel Taylor Coleridge.

I found this terribly amusing, and the idea to have Jess and Dougal investigate spies who weren't really spies took hold. I went in a bit of a different direction, but I hope you enjoyed it just the same.

For more information, visit:

https://unbound.com/books/dead-writers-in-rehab/
updates/the-name-s-coleridge-samuel-taylor-coleridge

https://suewilkes.blogspot.com/2016/08/the-spy-nozy-affair.html

Coleridge also details the story in 1817 in his *Biographia Literaria*.

ALSO BY DARCY BURKE

Historical Romance

The Phoenix Club

Improper

Impassioned

Intolerable

Indecent

Impossible

Irresistible

Impeccable

Insatiable

The Matchmaking Chronicles

The Rigid Duke

The Bachelor Earl (also prequel to *The Untouchables*)

The Runaway Viscount

The Untouchables

The Bachelor Earl (prequel)

The Forbidden Duke

The Duke of Daring

The Duke of Deception

The Duke of Desire

The Duke of Defiance

The Duke of Danger

The Duke of Ice

The Duke of Ruin

The Duke of Lies

The Duke of Seduction

The Duke of Kisses

The Duke of Distraction

The Untouchables: The Spitfire Society

Never Have I Ever with a Duke

A Duke is Never Enough

A Duke Will Never Do

The Untouchables: The Pretenders

A Secret Surrender

A Scandalous Bargain

A Rogue to Ruin

Love is All Around

(A Regency Holiday Trilogy)

The Red Hot Earl

The Gift of the Marquess

Joy to the Duke

Wicked Dukes Club

One Night for Seduction by Erica Ridley

One Night of Surrender by Darcy Burke

One Night of Passion by Erica Ridley

One Night of Scandal by Darcy Burke

One Night to Remember by Erica Ridley

One Night of Temptation by Darcy Burke

Secrets and Scandals

Her Wicked Ways

His Wicked Heart

To Seduce a Scoundrel

To Love a Thief (a novella)

Never Love a Scoundrel

Scoundrel Ever After

Legendary Rogues

Lady of Desire

Romancing the Earl

Lord of Fortune

Captivating the Scoundrel

Contemporary Romance

Ribbon Ridge

Where the Heart Is (a prequel novella)

Only in My Dreams

Yours to Hold

When Love Happens

The Idea of You

When We Kiss

You're Still the One

Ribbon Ridge: So Hot

So Good

So Right

So Wrong

ABOUT THE AUTHOR

Darcy Burke is the USA Today Bestselling Author of sexy, emotional historical and contemporary romance. Darcy wrote her first book at age 11, a happily ever after about a swan addicted to magic and the female swan who loved him, with exceedingly poor illustrations. Join her Reader Club newsletter for the latest updates from Darcy.

A native Oregonian, Darcy lives on the edge of wine country with her guitar-strumming husband, incredibly talented artist daughter, and imaginative son who will almost certainly out-write her one day (that may be tomorrow). They're a crazy cat family with two Bengal cats, a small, fame-seeking cat named after a fruit, an older rescue Maine Coon with attitude to spare, an adorable former stray who wandered onto their deck and into their hearts, and two bonded boys who used to belong to (separate) neighbors but chose them instead. You can find Darcy at a winery, in her comfy writing chair balancing her laptop and a cat or three, folding laundry (which she loves), or binge-watching TV with the family. Her happy places are Disneyland, Labor Day weekend at the Gorge, Denmark, and anywhere in the UK— so long as her family is there too. Visit Darcy online at www. darcyburke.com and follow her on social media.

facebook.com/DarcyBurkeFans

twitter.com/darcyburke

instagram.com/darcyburkeauthor

pinterest.com/darcyburkewrites

goodreads.com/darcyburke

bookbub.com/authors/darcy-burke

amazon.com/author/darcyburke

Made in the USA
Monee, IL
27 February 2023